By the same author:

SCORPION
DRAGONFIRE
HOUR OF THE ASSASSINS

War of the Raven

ANDREW KAPLAN

SIMON AND SCHUSTER

New York · London · Toronto · Sydney · Tokyo · Singapore

Simon and Schuster
Simon & Schuster Building
Rockefeller Center
1230 Avenue of the Americas
New York, New York 10020

Originally published in Great Britain by Century Hutchinson Ltd.
SIMON AND SCHUSTER and colophon are registered trademarks
of Simon & Schuster Inc.

Designed by Irving Perkins Associates, Inc.
Manufactured in the United States of America

1 2 3 4 5 6 7 8 9 10

Library of Congress Cataloging in Publication Data

Kaplan, Andrew.
War of the raven / Andrew Kaplan.
p.   cm.
"Originally published in Great Britain by Century Hutchinson
Ltd."—T.p. verso.
1.World War,   1939–1945—Fiction.   I.Title.
PS3561.A545W37   1989
813'.54—dc20   89-40454
CIP

ISBN 0-671-70758-2

Extract from "Leda and the Swan" reprinted by permission of A. P. Watt
Ltd on behalf of Michael B. Yeats and Macmillan London Ltd from *The
Collected Poems of W. B. Yeats*
Extracts from *Prologue to Peron: Argentina in Depression and War, 1930–
1943* (edited by Falcoff and Dolkart) reprinted by permission of The University of California Press

ONCE AGAIN FOR ANNE

War
of the
Raven

"A shudder in the loins engenders there
The broken wall, the burning roof and tower
And Agamemnon dead."

WILLIAM BUTLER YEATS

"Over us looms atrocious history."

JORGE LUIS BORGES

PART ONE

Stewart

In 1879, after the War of the Deserts, my father came to inspect the land awarded him by General Roca. He came with eight gauchos, all that were left of those who were with him in the war. They were wild, those men. They would cut a man's throat or take a woman as easily as an animal. Not one of them had ever been inside a house, or eaten anything he hadn't either stolen or killed with his own two hands. They were the last of their kind and I don't know how my father managed to make them obey him, except that perhaps in him there was something more terrible, more to be feared, than the easy savagery that was theirs.

They rode for days on the land that was now my father's. A quarter of a million acres and more. No one could say for certain, for there were no boundaries. Only an endless sea of pampas-grass. The Indians had been eradicated in the war, every last one, and the land was utterly empty. In those days, before the coming of the automobile, a man on a good horse could ride all day and not see another living soul.

Finally, they came upon a towering ombu tree in the middle of the Pampa. It was the only tree, in fact the only thing, that stood above the level of the grass for fifty leagues in any direction. Father ordered one of his gauchos to climb the tree to survey this new domain. Up he went, quick as a monkey, to the very top. There was nothing, he shouted down, not even smoke from a campfire for as far as the eye could see. But he did find something. Caught in a branch near the top of the tree was the rotting carcass of a raven with a dead fieldmouse, clenched in its claw. The raven had been trapped in such a way that if he had let the mouse out of his clutches, he would have been able to free himself. Instead, the bird had chosen to die, rather than release his prey.

This pleased my father immensely. He had the decaying raven nailed to the tree, which he declared would stand in the courtyard of what would be the finest estancia *on the continent. The tree still stands there, even to this day.*

And he gave the estancia *the name "Ravenwood," in memory of the only hate in nature he had ever found to match his own.*

—From the journal of Lucia de Montoya-Gideon

**TOP SECRET.
US Office of Strategic Services. April, 1941.**

1

SEPTEMBER MIDNIGHT in the La Boca district; cobbled streets and a cold fog rising from the river. The man in the gray overcoat waited in a doorway, looking back down the street behind him. Looking for shadows, hidden in the night.

The street was dark and empty, except near the corner of Avenida Pedro de Mendoza, where light from a *confitería* spilled into the darkness. All the man in the overcoat had to do was go in there and give a cigarette to a stranger. A *yanqui*. And leave without anyone noticing. Nothing to it, really. Except that he was afraid of the dark. And someone was trying to kill him.

It had rained earlier that day and the electric signs were reflected in puddles on the sidewalks and the shiny tram tracks. Someone had left their laundry on a line across an alley and the clothes hung wet and limp, like flags of a defeated army. Apartment windows were shuttered and behind one of them a radio was playing, something in Italian. There were a lot of Italian immigrants in this neighborhood, and during the day the streets were alive with workmen and gossiping housewives and the smells of cooking oil and garlic. But at night, La Boca remembered that it belonged to the waterfront, to the bars, tango palaces and narrow alleys where cries for help went unanswered and the police never came till morning.

A lone car approached, the cobblestones wet and glistening in the headlights. The man shrank back in the doorway as the car went by, the headlights sweeping across a vacant wall where an ancient election poster still proclaimed: *"Viva Yrigoyen y la UCR."* Except that the *Radicalistas* had joined the ruling coalition back in '35 and Yrigoyen was long since dead. Across the bottom of the poster a more recent addition: a scrawled swastika and "Death to the Jews." The man waited until the car made the turn, and when it was gone he began to walk toward the corner, his footsteps echoing wetly on the pavement, listening for sounds behind him.

He moved quickly, not running, but faster than ordinary walking, his hands balled in his pockets, like a soldier trying to catch up with the parade. The night was cold. It smelled of the waterfront and more rain. Sodden leaves stripped by the wind from the jacaranda trees along the *avenida* lay on the ground like dead birds. At a *panadería* closed for the night, the bread bins empty and dusty with flour, the man paused to check the reflection of the street behind him in the darkened window. Everything was quiet. There was only the glow of a streetlight in the mist and then he saw it. The red tip of a cigarette in a doorway across the street.

He tried to swallow and couldn't. They were still after him. What was he to do? Amadeo hadn't warned him about anything like this when he had first gotten involved.

"It's a simple thing, truly. A little favor between friends," Amadeo had said in his office above the casino, the desk light gleaming on his brilliantined hair. "Once every few weeks or so, you make a phone call, then a delivery. You leave it in a public place: a loose brick in a wall, under a seat in a cinema. You never have to see anyone."

"What is it? Drugs? Money?"

Amadeo shook his head.

"Something easier to carry, but more valuable. Information," lighting an American cigarette. He smoked it in the French way, inhaling the smoke from his mouth to his nostrils.

"I don't like this," Raoul said.

"No," Amadeo agreed. "But you'll do it."

Raoul got up and went to the mirrored bar Amadeo kept in his office. He poured himself a gin over ice. The ice cubes rattled in the glass and he held it up to show how his hand trembled.

"You see," he said. "I'm no good for this. It's politics, isn't it? This war in Europe." He bit his lip. "Maybe there's something else I could do."

Amadeo looked at him. His eyes were hooded like a reptile's. He had addict's eyes, sleepy and crazy dangerous.

"You owe us money, Raoul. Your fancy friends, the Vargases, the Herrera-Blancas and all these stupid *estancieros*, that's a very expensive crowd you run with," he said, shaking his finger admonishingly. *"Muy costoso,"* his eyes black and glittering like a snake's. Julia said he was spending all his profits on heroin, that he couldn't get enough.

Raoul nervously licked his lips.

"Which side?" he managed to whisper. "At least tell me that. Castillo? Ortiz? The British? The Nazis?"

Amadeo shrugged.

"What difference does it make?" he said.

But that was before tonight, when Amadeo said he was to meet personally with the American. Before the man with the scar on his cheek and the German accent had sat next to Raoul in the streetcar and asked him for a cigarette. That's when he knew he had got in over his head. Because the exchange was supposed to take place in the *confiteria* on Pedro de Mendoza, not on a streetcar, and the man he was to give it to, a *yanqui*, not a German, was supposed to first ask him the time and wait till he offered the cigarette.

"What if I can't make the delivery? What if something happens?" he had asked Amadeo, who had looked at him with those hooded eyes the way Raoul imagined a snake looks at a mouse.

"Then don't come back, Raoul. Let them kill you. You'll be better off," Amadeo had murmured.

Hand trembling, he offered the German an ordinary cigarette, not the marked one, from the pack he had picked up from the drop, a street vendor on Avenida Ninth of July, near the Obelisk. The German noticed his hand shaking and almost smiled.

"Nein, danke. I prefer the whole packet, *bitte."*

Raoul smiled back weakly, his mind racing. The German was a fake. He had to get away from the German, but he had no idea how. The German started to reach for the pack, his other hand holding something in his coat pocket. Raoul began to panic, feeling himself lurching as the streetcar pulled into a stop. It was all happening too fast for him and yet there was a feeling of slow motion. He saw everything as though from outside himself: the lights inside the streetcar and his own reflection in the windows against the darkness of the street outside, the young woman with the bag of groceries and the little girl getting up for her stop and the German smiling, his hand still in his pocket. And then Raoul was up and shouldering the woman aside, the groceries spilling all over, and just as he swung the door open, the sound of shots in quick succession, impossibly loud. He heard people screaming behind him and as he leaped to the ground, managed to turn for a second and see the woman hanging head-down, jammed halfway in the streetcar's door, her long hair dragging on the tram tracks. The little girl was staring saucer-eyed, screaming in a thin high-pitched voice until the German smashed her out of his way as he ripped the door open. He leaped over the woman's body, her dress bunched around her waist, her sprawled legs shockingly white and naked in the glare of the streetcar lights, and into the street. Raoul couldn't see any more because he was running so hard, his breath coming in great heaving gasps. There was another shot just as he turned the corner and down a warren of dark streets and garbage-strewn alleyways, zigzagging around corners and never stopping or looking back for a second until he found the darkness of the doorway near the rendezvous where he could hide and catch his breath.

Oh God, oh God, oh God, he thought. Germans! What had he got himself into? And then he remembered something Arturo had said once: "With the Nazis, killing is a kind of religion. It's their way of dealing with things they don't understand." From Arturo, of course, that was said in admiration, if not envy.

Across the street, he saw a glowing arc as the watcher dropped the cigarette to be crushed out. He couldn't stay by the *panadería* any longer. He began to run.

The sound of his blood pounded so loudly in his ears he couldn't hear if he was being followed. Near the corner he slowed. He walked by the *confitería*, trying to make it look as if he was glancing casually at the misted up windows, the way any passer-by might. At first, he didn't see the *yanqui*. The *confitería* was empty except for a young couple lingering over *mates* and a waiter leaning against the counter, his face buried in the sports section of the *Crítica*. And then he spotted him at a corner table, in a tweed jacket, looking bored. He didn't look particularly *simpático*. And once inside, he'd be trapped, Raoul thought, trying to decide what to do. The *confitería* was too exposed. He needed lights, people. The more the better. And a back way out.

On Avenida Pedro de Mendoza the last streetcar went by, clanging noisily, the windows lit up like a passenger ship in the night. It stopped at the corner and a woman got off. She was an older woman, short and bulky in a heavy coat, carrying a shopping basket. She scurried toward him as the tram started up again, wheels squealing against the tracks as it made the turn. Raoul watched her carefully. No one was to be trusted. What did she have in the basket? He held his hand in his coat pocket as though he were holding a gun, but she never even looked at him as she passed by. He watched her as she walked away, her shoulders slumped as though she had been carrying a heavy burden since birth. Life, they call it, the old priest had said, the night Raoul learned about the woman Lucia's journal. The priest! Was he in on it too?

Madre de Dios, what was happening to him? To suspect everyone like that. He turned away, listening to her footsteps receding, lonely in the night. Then he heard another set of footsteps, more hurried, passing hers and coming toward him. He had to go. Maybe if he just kept moving . . . and above all, he needed a gun. He began walking quickly down the *avenida* in the same direction the streetcar had taken.

There were restaurants across the street and on this side, two *petits hôtels*, right next to each other. A woman standing in the doorway of one smiled at him. He hesitated for a moment and her smile grew wider. Standing against the light like that, he could see that she had nothing on under her dress. Maybe, he thought, risking a glance behind him, and his knees almost gave way.

A man in a raincoat was standing by a newspaper kiosk, shuttered for the night, reading the headlines posted on the side of the kiosk. He was a broad-shouldered man, his face hidden under a fedora, and he was holding something under his raincoat. Whatever he was holding was big and Raoul had to force himself not to just start running and never stop. Think, he told himself. Think. Maybe he's not one of them. Just because he has something under his raincoat. But the man didn't look at him. He seemed engrossed in the news. Warsaw had fallen. A second headline read: *"ATHENIA SURVIVORS OF U-BOAT ATTACK TELL OF ORDEAL."* In Argentina, prices on the *Bolsa* had fallen in heavy trading. But how long did it take to read a headline? The man didn't move.

What's stopping him? Raoul wondered. He was desperate to walk away, but the thought of being shot in the back the minute he turned to go held him frozen. And then it hit him.

The man had seen what he did with his hand in his pocket when the woman walked by. Maybe the man thought Raoul had a gun too! That gave him an idea, and he began to walk down the *avenida* very quickly now. The footsteps resumed behind him.

The Tango Palacio Del Rio was only a block away. It was ablaze with lights and on the sidewalk in front there were people and vendors selling cigarettes and *parrillada* roasted over glowing charcoal braziers. The upstairs windows were open and the street echoed to the sounds of the orchestra. A taxi pulled up outside the entrance and a couple in evening clothes got out and went inside. Raoul could hear the footsteps coming closer and all at once, he broke and raced down the street. He pushed his way through the crowd into the tango palace.

Tino the Dwarf was standing by the door. Raoul slipped him a coin, shaking his head to the cloakroom girl that he would keep his coat. He went up the stairs to the ballroom, the stairway dimly lit and loud with the music and sounds of the crowd. It smelled of cigarette smoke and cheap perfume and sweating bodies; the undefinable musk of urgent sex. The red plush was worn from the stair carpet and the wallpaper showed drawings of dancers in profile, impossibly thin and expressionless. At the top he looked back down the stair. No one had come in yet. For a brief moment, he actually thought he had a chance, until he entered the noisy ballroom and Ceci Braga, looking like a small man in her tuxedo, hair slicked back and short as a boy's, came over and told him someone had been looking for him.

"What have you been up to, Raoul?" Ceci asked, offering him a cigarette from a silver case and when he declined, lighting one for herself.

"Just business, Ceci," Raoul said, looking around.

"Fool's business, you mean."

"Why do you say that?"

She shrugged, looking very much like a woman at that moment, despite her get-up. Because a tango palace was considered no better than a brothel and because of her sexual orientation, her family had ostracized her. Not one of them would so much as talk to her, even though she supported all of them.

"How do you stand it, Ceci?" Raoul had asked her one night after everyone had left, both of them long gone on gin and cocaine and Ceci, her rasping whiskey voice down to a whisper, unable to talk about Julia any more.

"Stand what, *guapo*? Injustice? Bah, women are too wise to believe in heaven on earth," she had said, her eyes so heavily mascara'd they made her face pale as death by comparison.

"The loneliness, Ceci. How do you stand the loneliness?"

"Ah, *guapo*," she had said, putting her hand to his cheek. "I'm in the loneliness business. Didn't you know?"

She put her other hand to his cheek in the same way.

"Because the man who was looking for you spoke in the worst, most thickly German-accented Spanish I've ever heard. You be careful, *guapo*. For the Germans, this war is real, not just business."

Raoul grabbed her arm in a way that made her pull back. "Listen, Ceci. This man. Did he say what he wanted?"

Ceci shrugged and said something, but just then the orchestra struck up the next tango and her answer was lost in the music. The floor became crowded as the couples got up, faces set like statues, already moving to the strains of the violins. The lights dimmed and the mirrored ball revolved over the floor, spinning shining moths of light across the dancers' faces. Raoul watched the dancers, glancing out of the corner of his eye at the entrance. The man from the kiosk still hadn't come in. But he couldn't be sure in all this crowd.

They were mostly locals from La Boca and San Telmo, but there were all types there. Young workmen from the *arrabals* in their best jackets, cigarettes dangling from their lips, dancing with tightly corseted women whose husbands were wise enough to go elsewhere; tough *compadritos* in double-breasted jackets cut tight to show the bulge made by their shoulder-holsters, and their *putas* in low-cut blouses and shiny skirts slit to the hip; and *gente fina*, slumming in black tie and ball gowns, laughing and ordering champagne in silver buckets. As he stood there, he saw Athena de Castro swing by with her new lover, Julio, twenty years her junior and still in high school. Athena wore nothing under a beaded gown so transparent that by the dark smudge between her legs you could see she wasn't a natural blonde, and as she danced by she waved gaily at Raoul, who nodded back, stiff as a soldier. He was running out of time.

Ceci swayed before him, eyes half-closed, moving in time to the music.

"Dance with me, *guapo*. This is a Discepolo tango. You know

I can't help myself when they play one of his," she murmured, pressing her body against his. Raoul held her for a moment, trying to think.

"About this man, Ceci. Is he still here?"

"Dance with me, fool. He's looking right at you," she hissed, pulling him onto the dance floor. They stood face to face, frozen in their poses, waiting for the beat, and when they began they moved, in Julia's phrase, "like angry lovers." As he spun Ceci toward him, the tails of her tuxedo flying, Raoul's eyes searched the crowd. And then he saw him, leaning against the bar. A big man, hair closely cropped, narrowed eyes set in a face that looked as if it had been hammered out of bronze. A brawler's face. The kind you want to sit at the opposite end from in a bar. God, how many of them were there?

The man was looking straight at Raoul, not bothering to hide his interest. They were closing in.

Raoul stumbled, barely able to keep on his feet. Ceci looked up at him sharply. The couples, locked groin to groin, dipped and turned as the *bandoneón* player took the microphone and sang in a nasal, strangely appealing voice:

> *"Tiráte al río! Don't bother me with your conscience.*
> *You're a fool that can't even make me laugh.*
> *Give me bread on the table—you keep your decency,*
> *I want money, money, money. . . ."*

Raoul dipped her down, his cheek pressed to hers.

"Is there a back way out of here?" he murmured.

She whirled up and back to him, leopard spots of light sliding across her face.

"*Oiyée, hombre,*" she said softly. "You really do have trouble, don't you?"

He nodded.

"This way," she said, leading him through the dancers to an unlit alcove covered by a velvet curtain. They slipped behind the curtain to a door that she unlocked with a key from a chain that she kept in her pocket. The door led to a narrow flight of stairs, and when she opened it he could feel a draught of cool air from outside that made the curtain sway. She gestured with her head for him to go.

"You could get in trouble for this, you know," he said.

She shrugged.

"Listen," she said. "I don't like Germans so much. The English are boring, but they have better manners. You go," she indicated the stairs. "I'll send a girl to occupy the German." She started to go.

"Wait," he said. "Have you got a gun?"

Her eyes searched his face.

"*Pobrecito.* That bad is it?"

He didn't say anything. She shook her head.

"I don't. But I'll ask Athena. She usually carries one in her purse. Wait here," she said and was gone.

He stood in the dark alcove, watching the crack of light at the bottom of the curtain, waiting. Almost immediately the old feeling began, as he had known it would. The closed-in feeling. It started with a prickling at the back of his neck and the choked-up feeling in his throat. He began to breathe harder, fumbling to open his collar button, the sweat stinging his eyes.

When he was a child his mother used to lock him in the closet when she went out at night. "Keep you out of mischief," she would say and he would scream, "Please, Momma. I won't touch anything. I promise. I don't like it in the dark. Please!" But she would leave him there all night, crouched among her clothes in the darkness, sometimes until the next day. Once, stirred by something, the smell of her perfume on the clothes, the cool feel of silk, the desire to get back at her, something, he had put on one of her outfits, a short yellow dress, and when she found him wearing it, she almost fell down laughing. "I wanted a daughter! Look what I got!" she shrieked, tears rolling down her cheeks. "A joke! A joke in a yellow dress!"

That was the only time he ever saw his mother laugh.

And she made him wear the dress from then on. Wear it in the street, hem dragging along the ground, and to school until the headmaster sent her a note about it. God, what was keeping Ceci?

He was sweating badly now. Any second he expected to see one of the Germans burst into the alcove. All because of what was in the cigarette. What could it be? he wondered. He started to pull the pack out of his pocket and stopped. He didn't want to know.

The orchestra swung into the finale of the tango, the rhythm faster, more urgent. He could feel the floor vibrating under him and wondered where he could go after here. Home, he thought. He could barricade himself there and call Amadeo. See if he could get these gorillas off his back. Once home . . . he shivered. He couldn't go back to his apartment. They'd be waiting for him there. If they knew about his rendezvous and his coming here to Ceci's, how could they not know where he lived? He tried to think of some place else to go. Maybe his mother's house? Or the casino? Unless it was Amadeo himself who had set him up for this. But why? He looked around, blinking stupidly as a bird, staring at the curtain and the walls. He was trapped. He had nowhere to go.

The curtain moved and he almost jumped out of his skin. But it was only Ceci. She looked at him curiously.

"What's the matter? You look white as a ghost."

"It's nothing. Do you have it?"

"Here," she said, handing him the pistol. It was a .25 caliber automatic, no bigger than his hand, nickel-plated with a pearl handle. A woman's gun, more for cocktail chatter than for real use. But his breathing came a little easier as he hefted it in his hand. At least he had something. He put his hand on her shoulder, thin under the padding of the tuxedo jacket.

"Ceci, thanks."

Her face was in shadow. He could see only her eyes in a slash of light from the edge of the curtain.

"You go, *guapo*. I don't think Lulu is having much luck with the German."

"Tell Athena I'll get it back to her, I swear," he said over his shoulder, starting down the stairway. It was pitch-black and very narrow and the steps creaked under his feet.

"Be careful," she called down. Then, wistfully, "Have you seen Julia?"

Raoul stopped and looked back. He could see only her silhouette, looking very small in the doorway.

"Ah, Ceci," he said, then froze. There was a large shadow looming behind her.

"Run!" she cried and he heard the sounds of a scuffle and then a blow and a cry as he leaped down the stairs in the darkness. He was jumping blindly, heels catching on the stairs, stumbling, and when he hit the landing his leg turned and almost collapsed under him. He caught himself by the banister and ripped open the exit door. Behind him he could hear the sound of a large man hurrying down the stairs. He

ran out into the alley behind the tango palace, leaping over a
fallen garbage bin and back toward the lights of Pedro de
Mendoza, hazy in the mist. He heard a loud curse as the man
behind him fell with a clatter across the overturned bin, just
as Raoul turned the corner and ran out into the middle of the
street.

The fog had become very wet and dense. It had come in
from the river, reducing visibility to only a few yards. The
avenue was deserted, the streetlamps ghostly in the night. He
looked back and thought he saw a figure, dark against the
streetlight glow. Instinctively, he moved away from it.

He ran down narrow sidestreets, dark tunnels in the mist.
The fog seemed to swallow everything, even the sound of his
footsteps. He couldn't hear his pursuer, only the heavy rasp of
his own breathing. He wasn't sure where he was anymore.
Nothing seemed familiar. He began to imagine shadows behind him and whirled, gun in hand, but there was nothing but
the swirling mists. Then, overhead, loomed the shadow of a
giant wooden crane and on the next street, the glow of light
from a *pulpería*. He was near the waterfront. Now he could
smell the mud flats and the sour smell of beer and *aguardiente*
from the *pulpería* and across the street was a woman under a
hallway lamp. She was a peroxide blonde, the roots showing
black in the light. The blonde hair didn't suit her and her nose
was sharp and narrow, a predatory beak, but she was a
woman and he couldn't run anymore. He put the gun in his
pocket, crossed the street and went up to her.

"Isn't it late for a little girl to be out in this *barrio*?" he
asked, looking around.

"If you want me to be a little girl it'll cost you extra," she
said hoarsely, leaning forward and brushing the tips of her
breasts against him. She had been drinking and had dabbed
cheap perfume between her breasts and the smell was over-
powering.

"No, no little girls," he managed nervously, the smell making him nauseous.

She smiled and for a moment, she was almost pretty. It was
a selling smile that showed a lot of teeth, but her eyes were
desperate, not smiling. She had to be desperate to still be
trying to make the price of a room at this hour.

"*Esta bien*. I know how you like it, *querido*," she crooned.
"We go upstairs. We do everything you want. Anything. Only

if you hit, do it with an open hand. No closed fists, *comprende?*" holding out her hand for money. He looked around one last time. Still no one, only the fog. He gave her ten pesos. She didn't move. He added another five and she nodded, raising one of her feet and slipping the money into her shoe.

She led him into a dimly lit lobby, narrow and smelling of insect spray, with a small counter. There was a board with nails on the wall behind the counter, but only one of the nails had a key on it. No one was behind the counter.

"*Hola*, Pepe!" the woman called out. They waited, but no one answered.

"He's drunk, the pig!" she told Raoul. "Pig!" she cried out, spitting the word into the darkness. She went around the counter and got the key. "He is of no value. None," she said, leading him two flights up a rickety stair to a dark corridor so narrow that as they walked down it, his shoulders brushed against both walls at the same time. "He is *nono*, understand?" tapping her finger against her temple. "And a drunkard as well, but his uncle owns this place, so. . . ." unlocking the door to the room and going inside.

She turned on the light, a naked yellow bulb on a wire hanging from the ceiling, and he came in and sat down on the bed, the only furniture in the room apart from an old nightstand with a rusted chamber pot in it. There was a window that looked across an alley to a brick wall. It had finally started to rain, the drops tapping against the window. She stared at the drops sliding down the window, then pulled down the shade. Raoul closed the door and locked it behind him. She watched him do it, but whatever was happening behind her eyes, she didn't show it. She sat down on the bed and started to undress.

"It's all right, *querido*," she said. "There's no one here but Pepe and he's too drunk to hear anything anyway. You can do anything. Even the thing you always wanted to do, but thought was too dirty to ever ask anyone," draping her dress and stockings over the iron railings at the foot of the bed. Naked, she knelt between his legs and started to nuzzle his fly. He pushed her away.

She looked at him. She reached for his erection with her hand and when she couldn't feel it, her eyes narrowed with suspicion. She pulled at him, as at a bell rope. He stayed small, shriveled.

"What's the matter with you? You don't like girls or something?"

He didn't say anything.

Her face changed, softened.

"That's it, isn't it?"

He still didn't say anything. He was listening. He had heard a creaking on the stairs.

"That makes nothing," she said softly, coming closer. "I can be a boy for you."

"Get away!" he said in a strangled voice, taking out the pistol. Her eyes grew very wide. She looked at the gun and then at the door. Someone was coming. She put her finger to her lips for him to be quiet. They waited, then someone knocked loudly on the door.

"Who is it?" she called.

"Towels," came a muffled voice through the door.

"Finally! *Imbécil!*" she shouted.

"Don't open it," Raoul whispered.

"Don't disquiet yourself. It's only the boy," she said, gesturing for Raoul to put the pistol out of sight. He hesitated for a moment, then held it in his jacket pocket, pointed at the door. "It's about time, you pig!" she said, opening the door, and Raoul almost had a heart attack.

It was the German from the streetcar. The one with the scar. He burst into the room, flinging the woman aside and diving on top of Raoul, who just managed to get off one wild shot before the German grabbed his wrist and with almost contemptuous ease, twisted the gun out of his hand. The German pulled a Luger pistol out of his pocket and smashed Raoul across the side of his face, almost taking off his jaw. Raoul fell back stunned, the entire side of his face on fire, as the German whirled and grabbed the woman by her hair as she tried to run out the door. He yanked her almost off her feet, her head twisted back, slinging her naked body across Raoul like a sack of potatoes. By the time she managed to scramble off Raoul and he started to struggle up, the German had closed the door behind him again and was facing them, the Luger pointed between them. In his other hand he held the little .25 automatic. It looked like a toy next to the Luger.

The German smiled. He motioned for the woman to come closer. She came toward him tentatively, trying to smile. The German nodded encouragingly and she began to move more seductively, confident of her body. When she was close enough, the German, smiling broadly, kicked her in the stomach, doubling her over. She fell, retching, to the floor. As she lay there, gagging and bringing up bile, the German took a small roll of wire flex from his pocket and, his eyes never leaving Raoul who was barely able to sit upright, tied her hands behind her. He left her lying on the floor. Then he took off his hat, wet and smelling of the rain, and sat down on the bed next to Raoul, jamming the muzzle of the Luger into Raoul's ear hard enough to make him cry out.

"Now, you will please to give me the cigarettes," the German said in bad Spanish, holding out his hand.

Trembling, Raoul fished the pack out of his pocket and handed it over. The German examined the pack for a moment, then shrugged and put it into his inside pocket. Nervously, Raoul licked his lips. The side of his face ached; the skin felt tight and swollen, like a balloon about to burst. It would be murder to talk, but he had to try. Maybe he could do a deal?

"How'd you find me?" he managed. His mouth felt thick and clumsy. It was like trying to talk under water.

The German smiled. He was pleased with himself.

"You were, as we say, 'in the box,' understand? We had four *Schwanzen*. Watchers, you call them. Two in front, two behind. You were never out of sight. The fog made a difficulty, but not a large difficulty. It was only a question of where to take you. But I have pleasure that you have this little *Spiel* pistol," indicating the .25. "It will make it more simple for the *Polizei*. For the *Polizei* that is the same everywhere. They always like it simple, *nicht wahr?*"

"Please, Señor," the woman whimpered. She was on her knees near the foot of the bed. "I don't know this Señor. Please," her eyes blank with fear like an animal's.

"That makes nothing," the German shrugged and she shuddered. The German turned back to Raoul. "Now you, take off your clothes," he ordered.

"Please. I don't under—" Raoul began.

The German grabbed his hair and banged his head hard against the wall, once more jamming the Luger into Raoul's ear.

"You have not to understand! Only obey," the German shouted. With trembling fingers, Raoul began to undress. When he had stripped down to his undershorts and black socks, he looked up at the German, who gestured with the Luger.

"Leave on the stockings, yes? It makes for the nice touch," the German said. Shamefaced, Raoul removed his under-shorts. The German had him lie face down on the bed and tied Raoul's hands behind him with the flex. Then he tied his feet and had Raoul sit up at the edge of the bed, naked except for his socks, his face dumb with confusion.

"Why?" Raoul whispered. "You have the information. I'm no danger to you and I'll tell you anything. I swear," his eyes glistening, never leaving the Luger.

"I am told you have fear from the dark," the German said, taking a roll of adhesive tape from his coat pocket. "You see, you have nothing to tell. We already know about you. To talk is not your function."

Raoul trembled. He had to urinate desperately and was afraid he might shame himself. None of this was real. This couldn't be happening. Not to him! He was just paying a gambling debt. Amadeo wouldn't do this to him.

"W-w-what is my f-function?" he managed to stammer.

"To serve as 'example.' You have displeased someone very much," the German said, taping over Raoul's mouth and eyes. He couldn't see! My God, he couldn't see! Please don't, he thought. Momma, please don't!

"Come here," he heard the German say, talking to the woman. Raoul sensed her closeness. The German's voice was very near. "Now," the German said. "Take him in your mouth."

"Please, Señor. I know nothing of these things," the woman sobbed. Raoul could feel her tears on his legs.

"Go on! You've had a cock in your mouth before!" the German screamed. There was the sound of a slap and the woman cried out.

Raoul felt himself being taken into her mouth. He felt her tongue and her mouth moving on him, warm and wet, the German's rough hands forcing his thighs apart as much as possible with his feet tied at the ankles.

"All of it," the German ordered. "And you, *maricón*," he hissed in Raoul's ear. "Get hard! Pretend she's a man."

Oh no, oh no, Raoul thought, feeling himself stir in spite of himself. He could feel her sucking hard, taking in all of him, when suddenly he felt the German move and her mouth snapped shut like a trap, her teeth biting into his flesh. Raoul screamed, trying to pull away, feeling her squirming and tearing at him, the pain excruciating beyond belief. Suddenly, there was a shot and the woman was dead weight, pulling him down, but her mouth was still being held closed and he felt his penis being ripped away, the blood gushing like a stream between his legs. He was screaming behind the tape over his mouth, going insane, thinking oh God, oh God, oh God! He was being castrated by a dead woman, the pain appalling, and in the middle of everything there was a knocking at the door.

"Help!" he screamed into the tape. "Help! Help!" He was squirming like a half-crushed insect on the bed, barely conscious, as he heard the German open the door. He was screaming behind the tape. He couldn't stop screaming.

He heard the German say something and then someone else said something. He was screaming and he couldn't hear anything and then suddenly, there were two more shots and the sound of a heavy body hitting the floor. He was still screaming and a hand grabbed his hair and held his head still for a moment and a voice whispered in his ear.

"I came to see, Raoul. I always come. Now do you understand?" the voice said.

Oh God, oh God, Raoul thought at the sound of that voice, still trying to move his head, still screaming inside, because it was impossible. And then, all at once, there was a stillness in the midst of his agony. Because he understood. He finally understood.

"Don't! Please don't!" he screamed into the tape, trying to move his head. Because the truth was worse than anything that had happened before.

"Save me a place in hell," the voice said, putting a gun against the side of Raoul's head and firing.

Death was instantaneous. He never heard the sound of the shot that killed him.

2

October 31, 1939
Lisbon

By MIDMORNING the best seats in the café were already taken.
Those were the tables by the beaded-curtain doorway that
clicked and clacked every time the waiter came through. At
that hour of the morning, the good tables had the shade and
regular patrons would take one of the newspapers that hung
like laundry from bamboo staves and listen to Artie Shaw
beginning the Beguine from the phonograph Senhor Zizi always kept on the counter inside. Patrons at the best tables
were expected to spend more money, and from a doorway
across the plaza he could see Donegan sitting at one of the
outer, less desirable tables, where it was harder to hear the
music and where latecomers and those whose shirt-cuffs were
beginning to fray would sit. Although the war was only a
couple of months old, Lisbon was already a giant outdoor
waiting room, swollen with refugees, and people told jokes
about being able to tell how long someone had been in Portugal by the amount of fraying on their cuffs, or how far away
from the music they sat at Zizi's.
    An outer table was just as well, Charles Stewart thought,
scanning the plaza and the café. It looked all right, but he took
his time, double-checking roofs, cars, pedestrians, windows
shuttered against the sun, the tables near Donegan. Prague
had taught him that. Prague had taught him a lot of things.
    The sun was high and hot over the Plaza Rossio. Flower-
sellers clustered around the tiered fountain in the center of the
plaza. From a nearby *taverna* came the smell of sardines roasting over hot coals, and despite the calendar there was no feel
of summer ending. The heat was tropical, with a suggestion of

Africa in the white buildings, the strangely Moorish facade of the railway station looming over the rooftops and the hot air shimmering over the black and white waves of tiles inlaid in the pavement.

People at the tables near Donegan were reading, or staring glassy-eyed at the plaza. Conversations were desultory, secretive. Some did a little business. Jewelry, papers, sexual favors: the local currencies. Everyone wanted to get to America, but the Lisbon embassy had stopped issuing visas. Each evening, when the nightly clipper flight to New York, via the Azores, took off, there was a silence, a break in the conversation as eyes turned skywards, watching the blinking winglights till they were lost from sight. During the day, most just killed time. They made an art, a ritual, of killing time, turning the pages of the newspaper just so, making every move with slow, deliberate gestures. The men wore suits and ties, despite the heat. Most had sacrificed everything except their self-respect to get to Portugal. If the war lasted long enough, that would go next, Stewart thought, crossing the plaza to Donegan's table and sitting down.

William Donegan was drinking port. He was a big man, in his fifties, with workman's hands, freckled on the backs. He carried his weight in his belly and there were large sweat-stains under his arms. Flies buzzed around his wine glass and he brushed them away, not looking at Stewart. The waiter came over and Stewart ordered a Sagres.

"You're late," Donegan said looking up. His eyes hadn't changed. They were very blue and cold. Cold as the Irish Sea, went the saying in the War Department. Stewart looked around to make sure they weren't overheard. There was a man sitting at the next table reading a week-old *Le Monde*. Stewart looked at Donegan, then at the man. Donegan shook his head imperceptibly, so Stewart knew that either Donegan had vetted him, or he was one of Donegan's.

"There's a war on," Stewart said.

"So I've heard."

"Good. I'm glad it made the papers."

Donegan looked sharply at the younger man. Stewart was in his mid-thirties, with dark hair, the kind of aquiline looks that a woman photographer once said should always be photographed in jodhpurs and a shirt open at the neck, and pale gray eyes that caught the light like silver coins. He had an undergraduate's unconscious grace, even now, as he sagged back tiredly in his chair.

"Rough trip?" Donegan asked, his voice kindly. But his eyes never changed. In Washington it was said that getting sympathy from Donegan was like getting an invitation for tea and cakes from Lucrezia Borgia.

Stewart started to answer, but the waiter came with a sweating glass of beer and a bowl of *tremocos*. Stewart took a handful of the seeds and washed them down with the beer, waiting till the waiter left.

"Travel's a little tricky," Stewart said, wiping the foam from his mouth with his hand. "The Germans are using the trains for all sorts of things these days," remembering not how he had stood sweating, waiting for the train to Pilsen to pull out, while the tall SS officer and his aides worked their way down the platform, checking papers, but being stopped at a siding outside Stuttgart while a freight train clacked slowly by, screams coming from the closed boxcars. He could hear women screaming, the sounds coming from one sealed car after another as they passed, but everyone in his compartment acted as though they hadn't heard a thing. One man, an auto parts salesman from Nuremberg, even offered him a cigarette, raising his voice over the sounds of the screams to ask if *mein Herr* was traveling for the business or the pleasure, and as Stewart lit up, all he could think of was Margarethe and the last look she had given him, as he scrambled out of the attic and onto the roof.

Donegan made a face. He hated extraneous information in a report. He had once fired a hapless aide for not being able to summarize the Tokyo operation in a single page.

"What about the others?" Donegan asked.

Stewart shook his head.

"All of them?" Donegan said, his voice gone very quiet.

Stewart didn't answer. He was thinking about how Donegan had first recruited him. That was in Berlin in '36, during the Olympics. They met in a hotel bar where a woman from Michigan was telling everyone how surprised she was at how charming Hitler was. Afterwards, he had gone for a walk to think it over. He had gotten lost near the Tiergarten, when turning a corner he came upon a gang of Brown Shirts beating an aged Jew to death. Even now, he could hear the smack the old man's head made as it hit the pavement.

But that was before Spain. And Prague, where he had gone to set up a liaison with the fledgling Czech underground. And before Margarethe.

"What went wrong?" Donegan asked in the same quiet tone. He might have been talking about a fumble in last week's football game.

"Same old thing," Stewart shrugged. "Somebody proving how deadly wishful thinking can be."

"No one is blaming you," Donegan said, a bit awkwardly. "There was always the danger of a set-up."

Stewart looked out at the plaza. On the sidewalk, a nicely dressed woman stopped a businessman and spoke to him. The man shook his head and walked away. For a moment, the woman looked after him. She pulled a roll out of her pocket, started to bite into it, then stopped and walked across the street to a bench by the fountain. She sat down and began to crumble the roll to bits, feeing it to the pigeons until it was gone and she just sat there alone, staring at the plaza.

"Who was it?" Donegan asked. "The girl or the old man?"

Stewart looked across the table at the older man. He wasn't surprised that Donegan had figured out it had to have been one of those two. Donegan hadn't gone from a Hell's Kitchen tenement to youngest general in the U.S. Army and a wealthy Wall Street law practice by being stupid.

"The old man. The girl saved me," he said, remembering the terrifying feeling as the gray trucks pulled up outside the shop that was the underground's headquarters, brakes squealing, the sound of smashing glass, the pounding of rifle butts on the door and harsh German voices shouting, *Heraus!* and Margarethe's anguished look at the attic window, as they broke in below and she turned to go back.

"What makes you so sure it was him?"

"He was nervous. Kept glancing at the shop door before they came. I remember noticing it. At the time, I thought it was because of me. And he wore his jacket, like he knew he was going somewhere. Not that it mattered," Stewart shrugged, looking over at the fountain. The woman was still sitting there. Now and then a pigeon would come over, only to flutter away when it realized the crumbs were all gone.

"Why? What happened?"

"After they rounded them all up, they shot him. Just left him lying there in the street. They took the others away."

Donegan took out his handkerchief and mopped his face. He folded the handkerchief neatly into squares before putting it back into his pocket. His wife had died ten years earlier and he had begun to acquire the fussy little rituals of an old bachelor, Stewart noted.

"So they killed their own *agent provocateur*. Why?" Donegan mused aloud.

"They didn't need him any longer. They knew the Underground would never trust him any more. Dead, at least he could serve as a warning."

"I suppose," Donegan murmured. "And what about you? Are you blown?" asked easily enough, as though it was just another question. He didn't look at Stewart, though.

Stewart shook his head.

"No, otherwise they'd have gotten me on the train," remembering the SS officer peering into his eyes, comparing his face to his passport picture and asking questions about what were the capitals of different American states, finally saying, "Neutral, *ja*? *Und* how long will your Jews let you to be neutral?"

"The girl. . . ." Donegan said, uneasily. "She might talk."

"No. She won't."

"They'll make her. . . Well, you know."

"No," thinking of her screaming in agony as they pulled out her fingernails, or whatever they were doing to her right now. Knowing that she would die trying to protect him. He had known that about her ever since that last morning when she had risked going across the Charles Bridge to the Lower Town to make the pick-up without wearing the yellow star required for Jews. "She never knew my real identity. She never really knew me at all," he said, staring at the plaza. The woman on the bench had gone.

"Well," Donegan said, taking a sip of wine. "It's a mess. Still, we anticipated casualties. Early days are like that, don't you think?"

Stewart didn't say anything.

"Charles? I asked you a question."

Stewart looked directly at him.

"I think the Nazis are going to win the war, General. That's what I think," he said.

Donegan nodded, as though what Stewart had said was patently obvious, like two and two makes four.

"Come on," he said, getting up and throwing a bill on the table. "Let's take a walk."

They walked out of the plaza and down the Rua Aurea towards Black Horse Square. The street was hot and bright and the shops were open, colored awnings lowered against the sun. Tile-roofed houses clung to the hillsides, and outside a *mercearia* stout women in head scarves picked over the fruit. It was like a country town, flies buzzing around the stalls, a horse-drawn cart clattering by, and at that moment it was difficult to believe there was a war on.

Stewart glanced back up the street behind him. The man from the café, the *Le Monde* folded under his arm, was following them. Donegan glanced at Stewart, then at the man and with a brief gesture, looked away. One of ours, all right, Stewart thought, letting go the breath he had been holding.

"I've just come from Paris," Donegan said, his face red and sweating in the sun. He had the type of skin that burns, and if he stayed in the sun much longer he'd leave Lisbon with a fiery souvenir. We must all make sacrifices, Stewart imagined him saying, wondering when Donegan was going to set the hook. "The Frogs don't have the belly for this. Instead of attacking, they're hiding behind the Maginot Line, praying Hitler will be satisfied with just Poland. Although why they imagine Belgian neutrality is going to matter any more to our friend Schicklgruber than it did to the Kaiser is beyond me. When the time comes, the Germans'll outflank the Maginot Line and take Paris in a week."

"What about the English?"

Donegan shook his head.

"Even if the British army arrives in time, it's too small and ill-equipped to make a difference. Especially against these new 'blitzkrieg' tactics. No," putting his hands in his pockets, "Poland is only the *hors d'oeuvre*. France and Britain are the main courses. Then it's our turn."

They walked out into the square. Cars and taxis drove past the government buildings that lined the sides of the plaza. In the center was the big statue of King José the First astride his horse and beyond, the waterfront and river, the Tagus gray and glistening in the sunlight. They crossed the traffic and headed past the statue toward the quay along the Avenida Das Naus.

"Our problem is that officially you and I don't exist. America doesn't have a secret service. Someday, that'll change. In the meantime, everything we're doing is illegal. A complete violation of the Neutrality Act. If anyone in the War Department, or the Congress, were to get wind of it, well . . . that would be too bad," Donegan said, mopping his forehead again with the handkerchief. He had taken off his jacket and was carrying it over his arm. "That would be too damned bad."

There was some kind of commotion down by the ferry landing. A small crowd was beginning to gather and they could hear shouts. Without consciously deciding to, they began to head that way.

"Doesn't anybody back in Washington understand what the hell is going on here?"

"They don't even want to know," Donegan went on. "Mind you, I'm not just talking about the German-American Bund, Father Coughlin and that bunch, or the majority of my fellow Irish-Americans, who wouldn't mind in the least seeing the British lion get it in the eye; not to mention Lindbergh and the America-Firsters. Fact is, the American people don't want a damn thing to do with this war."

"But the President . . ."

Donegan shook his head.

"The way public opinion is now, Roosevelt's hands are tied. On the other hand, if we don't do something now, by the time we get into it, it'll be too late."

Stewart impatiently balled his hands in his pockets into fists. When it came to sinking the harpoon, the Old Man usually didn't take so long.

"What do you want, General?" Stewart said. "Because if it's a matter of killing Germans, you don't have to ask me twice."

Donegan looked at him thoughtfully, a network of fine lines working out of the corners of his eyes.

"Can't wait to get into it, can you? All piss and vinegar and save the world for democracy. That's too easy," he said softly, stopping by a parapet where they could look out over the water. "Besides, before this thing ends, you'll get a bellyful, even of killing Nazis."

Stewart had to look up to see Donegan's eyes. He was five-ten, but Donegan was a good three, four inches taller.

"It doesn't matter. I'm fed-up play-acting," Stewart said.

Donegan stood there, his face not showing anything.

"Where will you go?" he asked.

"England, or Canada maybe. Learn to fly. They'll need pilots."

Donegan made a face.

"I know you mean well. Thing is, all being a pilot takes is good reflexes and a bit of nerve. And the nerve'll go, believe me. Maybe it'll go on the first mission, or the fiftieth, but it'll go. Then there's only a desk somewhere. And a wee bit of bullshit at the local gin mill," laying on the Irish brogue. Stewart started to say something, then stopped. Donegan's face was perspiring heavily, but his eyes were calm and clear. During the First World War, Donegan had won every medal awarded by the American government, including the Congressional Medal of Honor. "Besides," Donegan continued, "what I've got is something you're perfect for. The right looks, the right schools, the polo-playing, your fluency in Spanish. For what we have in mind, you are quite," he paused, searching for the right word, "irreplaceable. That is, of course, if you really meant what you said about the Nazis."

Stewart leaned against the parapet and looked out at the river. It was too wide to see across to the other side. Looking at it was like looking out at the sea. Over toward the ferry landing, the crowd had got bigger.

"Never con a con man, General. That whole thing, Andover, Columbia, the polo. That was my father's idea. We weren't rich. He started as an ironworker in Brooklyn. Became a legbreaker for the union. He figured all the fancy stuff would give me a leg up," he smiled. "It didn't work, of course. The other kids always made sure I knew I didn't belong. Always."

"That's why you were meant for this, Charles. You're used to lying," Donegan said, starting to walk again. Suddenly, his face brightened. He had remembered something.

"What is it?"

"Just something my wife used to say," he smiled. "That the most interesting people are the ones who create themselves."

"You're good, General," Stewart grinned. "So good I'm not even going to ask you why you need someone who speaks Spanish."

The two men walked along the quay toward the crowd.

"Argentina," Donegan said.

Stewart stopped. He stood there with his hands in his pockets, looking very American.

"You must be joking. Argentina's not even a sideshow. Maybe not even a sideshow of a sideshow."

"Argentina is very important. It could give the Germans

control of the South Atlantic. They could starve the British out," Donegan said mildly.

"That's real interesting, General. Why don't you do an article on it for the *New York Times*? Impress the hell out of them."

"We could lose the whole South American continent."

"No," Stewart said seriously. "I'm through chasing rainbows. Not after Prague."

"It's not as farfetched as you think," Donegan said, lowering his voice confidentially. "The *Graf Spee*'s been sighted off the Brazilian coast, near Recife."

"Well, and what the fuck am I supposed to do about it? Swim out to a German battleship, cutlass in one hand, American flag in the other, and order them all to surrender?"

"No one expects anything like that," Donegan said quietly, looking back toward the square, his eyes distant as if he were measuring something.

"Good. Because unless you've got something better than that . . ." Stewart stopped. He peered closely at the older man. "That's it, isn't it?" he said, his voice going very soft. "You've got something, haven't you?"

Donegan pulled a pipe from his pocket as a fat man in a *guardia* uniform ran towards them. He took his time lighting the pipe, waiting until the *guardia* was well past them, pushing his way through the crowd.

"We think there's a leak in the German embassy in Buenos Aires," he said.

Stewart went dead still. Shouts came from the direction of the ferry landing, but neither of them spoke.

"Maybe you'd better tell me about it," Stewart said finally.

Donegan nodded, almost imperceptibly, and they both began walking again.

"We were contacted by one Raoul de Almayo. Society type, well connected, apparently. One of these South American playboys," Donegan frowned. A touch of the Puritan there, Stewart thought. "He gave us teasers on the *Graf Spee*. Sailing time from Wilhelmshavn, radio frequencies, that kind of thing. Also information on German contacts with the Ortiz government. Good stuff. The preliminaries all checked out, only . . ."

"Only what?"

"He never made the rendezvous."

"That's it? That's all you've got?" Stewart looked incredulous.

"He didn't make the contact because he was murdered. It was in the papers the next day. Seems he enjoyed a certain local celebrity as a poet."

The two men walked to the edge of the crowd near the parapet. Down below the ferry landing, on a ledge by a bank of wooden pilings, men with long boat-hooks were pulling something from the water.

"All right, General. What do you want? I mean, what do you really want?" Stewart said, staring down at the water. Donegan puffed his pipe, watching the men on the ledge through a fragrant, self-manufactured fog.

"Find the leak. This Raoul's source. Work it. It could be a pipeline right into Berlin. We've, um, even given the supposed source a code name. We're calling him 'Raven.' 'The, um, Raven,' " Donegan said, clearing his throat.

"Funny name."

"It was his idea. Raoul's," Donegan muttered uncomfortably. He looked directly at Stewart. "The President himself wants you on this, Charlie. We need to keep Argentina on the Allied side. Neutral, anyway. Jerry Hartman'll brief you. He's the Consul down there. He'll be your contact."

Stewart looked at him.

"You son of a bitch," he breathed. "You miserable son of a bitch."

Donegan turned the pipe over and over in his hand, working it like a baseball pitcher with a new ball.

"Hartman's all right. He developed the lead."

Stewart just stared at him without a word.

"What happened in Spain is water under the bridge. Forget it, Charlie. Let it go," Donegan said, putting his hand on Stewart's shoulder. Stewart brushed it off.

"Jesus, is that how you do it? Is that how generals sleep at night?"

Donegan pursed his lips. It brought out the lines around his mouth, giving him a whiskey Irish look that made him look older, meaner. He looked at Stewart as if he was seeing him for the first time.

"There isn't an ounce of forgiveness in you, is there? Whoever Jesus died for, it wasn't you, was it? My God, I'd hate to be you when the time comes that you need forgiveness," Donegan said, pulling himself erect. "Here. Go on. Go to Argentina. Save the goddamn world for democracy," he said, shoving his newspaper awkwardly at Stewart. It was heavy, and from the way it felt, Stewart assumed it contained money, papers, the usual. Donegan glanced toward the ferry landing. "You're booked for the flight to New York. There's a boat leaving five days from now for Rio and Buenos Aires. You can just make it."

"What about Hartman?"

"Talk to him. Get a feel for things there. After that, you're on your own. No one else knows about it, not even the ambassador. If it ever got out, it would be—" he paused, "a disaster for President Roosevelt."

"Do you care?"

Donegan looked at Stewart. His eyes were very blue, and Stewart had seen that look only once before, in Spain, over a gunsight, just before a Falangist squeezed the trigger to execute a girl suspected of being a Loyalist courier.

"I'm a lifelong Republican," Donegan said softly. "But now I'm going to tell you something. We're going to get in this war. And the fact that that old cripple in the White House knows it, and is willing to lie through his teeth to the country about it, is the only thing that can keep those Nazi bastards from conquering the world."

There was a shout from workmen on the ledge. They were bringing something in. It was the body of a woman, fully clothed, her long hair trailing in the water like seaweed, her face white as a fish's belly. With a shock like a physical blow, Stewart recognized her. It was the woman from the Plaza Rossio, the one who had fed the pigeons.

Stewart glanced over at Donegan to see his reaction. Donegan just stood there, paying no attention to the scene below, gazing across the wide surface of the river, sunlight shattered on it into a million glittering pieces. At that moment, Stewart hated the older man.

All at once, Donegan spoke.

"We live in a tragic age," he said. "Tragic."

So he knew, Stewart thought. He had recognized the woman too. Down below, they had pulled the body onto the landing. The fat *guardia* was standing beside the body, making notes in a pad. Donegan tapped out his pipe. The ash drifted out over the water.

"The girl in Prague. What was her name?"

"Margarethe."

"Yes, Margarethe," he nodded. "What happened to her?"

Stewart shrugged.

"She was a Jew. That's what happened to her," he said.

December 5, 1939
Buenos Aires

As THE tug nudged the passenger ship toward the breakwater, Buenos Aires filled the horizon, a watery mirage washed of color, like a city risen from the sea. The wind was from the southeast, bringing low clouds and raising whitecaps that turned the normally muddy River Plate the same stony gray as the sky. The weather was cool. Early December was still spring in these southern latitudes, where the seasons are reversed, and although the sun had been out earlier, sparkling on the water, there was a feeling that it couldn't be trusted, that darkness would come early.

Stewart stood at the railing, his coat collar raised against the wind, looking for landmarks. He had been in Buenos Aires once before, in '35 with the American polo team. That was one of the reasons Donegan had wanted him for this. Back then, there hadn't been much of a skyline, and he recognized the Railway Exchange Building and the dome of the Congressional Palace from the last time. But things had changed. They were starting to put up taller buildings. Even from here he could see the Obelisk, that was new, and dominating everything, a tall apartment house with a colonnade on top that someone on the ship had told him was the Kavanaugh. If the war had hurt business, he couldn't see it. The harbor was crowded with ships and there were new structures and docks south toward the Riachuelo. Maybe if they got rich, they wouldn't need a war, he thought.

The waterfront was a sprawl of wharfs, cranes and warehouses that were the city's *raison d'être*. From the water, Buenos Aires looked like what it was: a port city on a shallow, muddy river hundreds of miles wide, whose natives called themselves *porteños*, so no one would mistake what they were about. Stewart lit a cigarette. The wind carried the smoke toward the city. It seemed to stare back at him. Buenos Aires, with its face forever turned toward Europe and its back to South America.

The tug moved them toward a berth next to a German steamer and Stewart felt his stomach tighten at the sight of the swastika flag at the stern. Once again, the Germans were ahead of him. Just like Spain. And Prague.

Hartman was waiting for him outside Customs, with a black Packard with embassy plates illegally parked in front of the terminal building. Stewart took a quick look around at the bustling street, as though he might spot something. Not that it was likely. Terminals and airports were the worst places to spot watchers, because there are always so many people around with nothing to do. They got into the car.

"Good to see you, Charlie. How was your trip?" Hartman asked, lightly punching him on the arm. Same old Hartman.

"Did you bring the gun?" Stewart said, trying to keep the dislike out of his voice. Hartman glanced down at the newspaper on the seat between them. Stewart reached under it and pulled out a US Army issue Colt .45 automatic that Hartman had brought from the embassy. Stewart tucked it into his waistband, buttoning his jacket over the bulge.

"How's Europe?" Hartman wanted to know, pulling out into the street without checking for oncoming traffic.

"There's a war on."

Hartman nodded and kept on nodding to himself, as if he had got exactly the kind of answer he had expected. He drove faster than he needed to along a cobbled street, crowded with trucks and horse-drawn drays and street vendors selling fried *faina* cakes to laborers, then turned onto the Paseo Colon. Here the street was broader and tree-lined, and on either side were cream-colored office buildings and apartment houses with mansard roofs and iron fences. A policeman on an elevated stand directed traffic, and at the corner a man standing in a parked convertible was selling lottery tickets. Stewart looked around, trying to orient himself. He had forgotten the spaciousness of the rounded plazas, the high French windows and Spanish courtyards, the prettiness of the city.

"We've booked you into the Plaza. It's very central, very B.A. Of course, if you want something more, ahem," Hartman cleared his throat, "private, that's no problem."

Stewart looked sharply at him. He didn't want Hartman's help. He didn't want any part of him, or the embassy.

"Plaza's fine, Jerry. This isn't a honeymoon. You don't have to carry me across the threshold."

Hartman reddened, reminding Stewart that they had been friends once; Donegan's other recruit in Berlin. Back then, Hartman was one of the rising stars at the State Department. Good-looking, Brooks Brothers suits and he could say "I love you" and call for a waiter in eight languages. Women loved him, Stewart thought, remembering the night they'd celebrated Jesse Owens's third and fourth golds at that beer-hall on the Ku'damm.

The place had been full of Americans. Eleanor Holm was there and everyone was saying "Screw Brundage," for having kicked her off the team for a lousy glass of champagne when they were all drowning in German beer. What started the row was that woman journalist, what was her name, Helen something. She'd gotten into an argument with one of the Nazi press attachés, Hansie Scholl. She was yelling at him, some damn thing about Spain, and Scholl had turned away, muttering *"Amerikanische Hure,"* when Hartman grabbed him by the lapels, lifting him almost off the floor, and said, "Don't be pissed, Fritz. Just 'cause you got beat by a nigger!"

That was Hartman all over. He had the rare ability to make you both respect and dislike him at one and the same time. But then came Saragossa. And Madrid. Hartman changed then. A lot of things had changed then.

Hartman bumped across the tram tracks, cutting diagonally across the bow of a clanging streetcar toward the far lane. Shops and old brick houses, windows barred with iron railings, lined the boulevard. A billboard on the side of a building showed a man in a tuxedo smoking and proclaimed, *"Fumar Players! El Más A Su Gusto!"* Camped beneath it on the sidewalk was a dark-skinned family, a blanket with stubs of pencils, pins, bent and broken cutlery, spread in front of them. Dirty-faced children sat listlessly beside the blanket, staring at the traffic.

"Looks like somebody still likes the English," Stewart said, indicating the billboard.

"That's an old sign. The Germans have made major inroads here," Hartman said, glancing at Stewart. "Major."

"I thought they liked the Brits down here."

"They used to. You've heard the classic definition of an Argentine, haven't you? An Italian who speaks Spanish and wants to be English. Especially the upper class. They all wear tweeds, snore through Shakespeare at the Cervantes and yell 'Sorry!' in English when they hit a tennis ball out of bounds. All 'veddy veddy,'" Hartman grinned. He was working hard at showing Stewart what a good guy he was. Too hard, Stewart thought.

"So what's the problem?"

"The Limeys blew it. After the Crash in '29, they screwed the Argentines over in the Roca-Runciman treaty. It was the worst time of the Depression and I guess they did it to save their royal behinds, but the Argentines haven't forgotten. They never forgive an injury. With them, it's almost a kind of art form. Maybe they're just getting tired of being an unofficial part of the British Empire," Hartman shrugged. "Especially now that the Germans are the real power in Europe. Mind you, they don't like us *yanquis* at all. We're about as welcome around here as a rent increase. By the way," making the turn into the Plaza de Mayo in a phalanx of cars, buses and *colectivos*, horns blaring, "that's the famous *Casa Rosada*," indicating a big pink wedding cake of a building guarded by armed grenadiers. "Ortiz is supposed to be in there, running the country. Only he isn't, of course," Hartman winked.

"Why not?"

"Who knows? It's a funny country," Hartman said, glancing sideways at Stewart. "Meanwhile, his deadly enemy, *Vicepresidente* Castillo, who's a big fan of our pal Adolf, is in there, spreading his tentacles. Interesting, huh?"

Stewart murmured something. He was watching the street. There were grassy spaces in the center and the sidewalks were dotted with flower stalls and newspaper kiosks. The restaurants and shops were open, white-aproned waiters moving among the tables at the sidewalk cafés, and if it weren't for the signs in Spanish, they might have been in Paris.

"Tell me, are you always so popular?"

A black Hispano-Suiza sedan sat in the side mirror, about three cars back. It had been there since they'd left the terminal building.

"Only recently. Only since this Almayo thing," Hartman said, biting his lip. Stewart reached over and twisted the rearview mirror so he could see without turning around. Inside the Hispano-Suiza were three faces, white and indistinct.

"Who are they? Germans?"

"Maybe. Could be the *Policia seguridad*. These days, it's hard to tell them apart."

Stewart massaged the back of his neck, trying to think. Hartman had come dirty to pick him up, "dirty" the trade term for being followed, so now they would be curious about him too. It was bad, all right. The only question was how bad? He looked at Hartman, wondering if he was unraveling, and if he was, how much was left. The problem was there were no back-ups, no alternative contacts or channels. Hartman was all he had. They were that thin on the ground. He leaned back in his seat and looked out at the boulevard, at the trees along the sidewalks and the old-fashioned buildings decorated with iron gates and filigreed cornices.

"Tell me about Raoul de Almayo."

Hartman took a deep breath, his eyes on the traffic.

"It was good stuff, Charlie. It could've only come from the German embassy," Hartman said, not bothering to hide the bitterness in his voice.

He's touched the Holy Grail, all right, Stewart thought. Was that what was eating him? That he'd had it and let it slip through his fingers?

"You were supposed to meet him the night he got killed?"

Hartman nodded.

"It was his idea. He had something. Said it was *mucho* hot. Besides, I wanted to pin him down. All he was giving us was teasers," Hartman said defensively. "You'd have done the same."

Stewart let that one go by. He was watching the Hispano-Suiza in the mirror, maintaining the same careful distance behind them.

"Why didn't Almayo go to the Limeys?" Stewart wondered aloud. "After all, it's their war. Why come to us?"

Hartman shrugged, grinding the gears as he shifted into

second to get around a horse-drawn wagon standing in his lane.

"I have no idea. Maybe he figured it was too obvious. That the Germans would be watching the British embassy too closely. I guess he thought we'd want to help by passing it along to the Brits."

"Dubious assumption," Stewart said. They both grinned, and for a moment it was almost all right between them. "So he never made the rendezvous?"

Hartman shook his head.

"I waited an hour longer than I was supposed to—I know the goddamn rules," holding his hand up, anticipating Stewart's objection, "but he sounded desperate on the phone. Not that it mattered. He never showed," he said bitterly. "I read about his murder the next day in the *Herald*. That's the local English-language rag."

Stewart took out a cigarette, but instead of lighting it, tapped it thoughtfully on the dashboard.

"So why are they following you, Jer'? What aren't you telling me?"

"What do you mean?" Hartman said, glancing nervously at him.

"I mean the Three Stooges in the Hispano-Suiza. That isn't exactly the most inconspicuous car in the world. I think you know who they are," Stewart said, watching him closely.

All at once Hartman smiled, and for a moment it reminded Stewart of Berlin and the old Hartman and the night the whole crowd had danced up the Unter den Linden at two in the morning all the way to the University Square, where the Nazis used to burn the books, Hartman playfully waving an empty beer bottle like a conductor's baton and singing, "Yes, we have no Gestapo. We have no Gestapo today."

"Same old Stewart. Goddamn bulldog," Hartman said, shaking his head.

"It isn't funny, Jerry. You coming dirty to a rendezvous is how they rolled up the network in Madrid," Stewart said quietly, trying to hold it in. "One by one. Then they stood them up against a wall and shot them." He stared coldly at Hartman. "No more bullshit, Jerry. Who's following us?"

Hartman swallowed, his face suddenly somber.

"Might be some of Colonel Fuentes's people. He wants to meet you," he said quietly.

Stewart sighed disgustedly. He looked out of the window at the boulevard. The sky was low and gloomy; it looked like rain.

"Does he?" he said finally.

"I thought it best," Hartman said. "He was in charge of the investigation into Almayo's murder. Besides," he blurted out, "everyone knows everyone here. There was no way you wouldn't've come to his attention, anyway. Nothing official. We're meeting him for drinks. All very friendly, of course."

"Of course."

Hartman made the turn into San Martin. After a moment, the Hispano-Suiza reappeared in the rear-view mirror. On the right, Stewart could see the National Cathedral, white, massive, and looking enough like the Madeleine in Paris to give him a strange disoriented feeling, as if the city was an illusion, a giant stage set.

"Who's this Colonel Fuentes?" he wondered aloud.

"That's hard to say," Hartman said uneasily. "Fuentes is one of those people you hear about, only nobody ever really knows anything for sure, if you know what I mean. Supposedly, he was one of General Uriburu's officers when he overthrew Yrigoyen, back in 1930. After that, he was one of Justo's people and then switched over to President Ortiz, when Ortiz and Justo came to a parting of the ways. A military career," he smiled to himself, "is a high-wire act in this country. He's been in and out, mostly in. You hear stories, though."

"What kind of stories?"

"Just stories. People disappearing. Torture cells. That kind of thing. There's even one about some poor devil being flayed alive and Fuentes keeping the skin," Hartman shuddered. "It's all a bunch of baloney. People'll say anything. Still, I overheard Fowler, over at the British embassy, hint that Fuentes is head of Military Intelligence. It's possible, I guess," Hartman shrugged.

Stewart didn't say anything. He stared at the broad open area of the Plaza San Martin with its great statue ahead of them. On the *avenida* near the Plaza, the apartment houses were white and gray against the sky and pedestrians in overcoats hurried along the sidewalks as if they were afraid it might rain any minute. *Porteros* stood in front of the more elegant houses and on one corner was a flower stall and next to it, a one-legged man selling balloons and flags; blue and white Argentinian flags and red, white and black flags with the swastika on it. Hartman pulled into the Plaza Hotel driveway. The Hispano-Suiza drove past, ignoring them. They had passed the baton. Someone else would pick up the tail.

"So what does he want, your pal Fuentes?" Stewart said, turning to Hartman as the uniformed *portero* opened the car door. Stewart pointed to the suitcase in the back.

"I'm sure he'll tell you himself. He's not shy," Hartman said primly, as if having done his duty, he wanted as little as possible to do with either of them.

Stewart nodded grimly. He got out of the car, then stuck his head back in. The *portero* was at the curb with the suitcase.

"All right, I'll talk to him. There's just one thing . . ."

"What's that?"

Hartman faltered. Stewart's eyes had narrowed as though over a gunsight. There was a deadly stillness about him and suddenly, Hartman was afraid.

"No more Spains, Jer'. If you ever come to a pick-up dirty again, I'll kill you," Stewart said.

4

THE PROCESSION came down the Avenida de Mayo with the sounds of singing, the voices masculine, harsh, and the tread of jackboots. And then they saw them, crowding out the traffic, the streetcars, *colectivos* and workmen's bicycles that normally filled the *avenida* around dusk. There were hundreds of them in black uniforms, holding torches that sent their shadows dancing on the sides of the buildings. In the front row, one of them carried the Argentine flag and next to him, another held the flag of the Legion, white lettering on black. At a nearby table, someone hurriedly put on his hat and left the café by the inside passageway near the barber shop. A Jew, most likely.

Colonel Fuentes looked at the procession, then at Stewart.

"In Buenos Aires these days," Fuentes shrugged, "everything is imported. Even the politics."

"There's a lot of it going around," Stewart said. At some of the tables people were standing up to give the Fascist salute. Pedestrians began to line the sidewalks to watch and there was scattered applause as the marchers approached.

They were sitting with Hartman at a table outside Tortoni's. They watched the marchers come by like a slow black tide with bobbing white faces, singing of blood and the fatherland. The marchers all had the same face. The Jew probably did the smart thing by leaving, Stewart thought. As they swept by, the streetlights came on and the silver Legion insignias on their epaulettes gleamed in the light. On the corner, a *guardia* in an elevated traffic platform raised his hand in salute when he saw the flags. In the café, everyone went back to their conversations.

"*Bueno*, Señor Stewart. You see how it is with us now, even here on the de Mayo," Fuentes said, finishing his drink and signaling the waiter for another round. He spoke with the *Río Platense* accent they call the "*yeismo*," pronouncing "y" like "j," as in "Majo," instead of "Mayo."

"I'm impressed, *mi Coronel*, at your arranging all this for my benefit," Stewart said, gesturing toward where the procession had passed.

Fuentes chuckled and glanced over at Hartman.

"You might be surprised what can be arranged here," he smiled. "Still, this is nothing. Demonstrations are easy, also meaningless. Struggle is not decided by ballots, or in the streets, Señor. Struggle is decided by this," he said, patting the leather holster on his hip where he carried his revolver.

Stewart looked at him.

"I've seen Brown Shirts before, *Coronel*. Is that what you want in Argentina?"

The waiter brought them fresh glasses, a bottle of Canadian rye and another of Italian vermouth. Hartman drank his rye neat, with a little shudder, as Stewart slowly added vermouth for Fuentes and himself.

"How are you calling this?" Fuentes asked, smacking his lips. He was tall and thin, with olive skin and a strong conquistador's nose perched over a razor-thin mustache. If people were animals, Stewart thought, Fuentes would be a cat. A large self-satisfied tabby in a khaki uniform, leggings tucked into highly polished riding boots. At the moment, Fuentes was licking the liquor from his mustache and studying Stewart the way a cat might dreamily contemplate a particularly interesting mouse.

"It's called a 'Manhattan.' For women, you add a cherry."

"Ah, *si*, the Manhattan. Most good. Always something new from the North Americans," Fuentes grinned, turning to Hartman. "Is this not so, Don Geraldo?"

"You can count on it, *Coronel*," Hartman winked. "A few more of those and you'll be a general."

"Then perhaps we should order a whole case of Manhattan," Fuentes laughed, reaching for the rye to refill his glass. "But to answer your question, Señor Stewart, in this country, many people like the Nazis. Better them than the Bolsheviks, *comprende*? More important, it looks like the Germans are going to win." He leaned back in his chair, a long, elegant Cheshire cat. "Of course, these are political matters, no? For myself, I am merely a sort of military policeman."

"And I'm just a polo player down here to buy a pony or two," Stewart said.

"For a certainty," Fuentes grinned triumphantly. "We are both innocent bystanders, yes? Innocent in a world without innocence," he said, crushing his cigarette out with his fingertips. He did it slowly, almost lovingly, letting his carefully manicured fingers linger on the burning tip as though it gave him pleasure. He showed no sign of pain, glancing up at them to make sure they had seen it. "And what does the United States government think about all this?" Fuentes asked, turning to Hartman.

Hartman shot Stewart a glance before replying.

"Washington has absolutely no idea at all about what's happening here. Not a clue." Hartman smiled, his eyes crinkling at the corners the way they used to long ago when he was about to say something outrageous. "We submit reports marked 'Urgent' and they send us back position papers on beef tariffs and the Good Neighbor Policy."

"You see how it is, *yanqui*. No one is in politics. Not you, not me, not even the politicians," Fuentes said. "We are all neutrals here. Neutrals and sportsmen."

"Then why are you having us tailed?" Stewart asked.

"I'm not. I assure you, *gentlemen*," Fuentes said, using the English word as if it were a slur. "If you are being followed, it is not of my department."

"Ah, but it is of your department, Señor *Coronel*. We weren't followed here from the hotel. That could only have been because whoever was following us already knew where we were going. Namely, here, to meet you," Stewart said.

Fuentes looked at Stewart; his eyelids blinked just once like a camera's shutter. All at once, he smiled broadly, as if auditioning for a part in the Ipana toothpaste ads.

"Come, *yanqui*. Let us be friends, yes? There are things we must, how you say, put on the table from each other."

"You mean like why the Argentine government is so interested in an American polo player?" Stewart said, reaching for his drink.

"I mean, Señor, like a certain *porteño* poet by the name of Raoul de Almayo," Fuentes said.

Stewart put his glass down. He looked at Hartman, who seemed intrigued by the label on the vermouth.

"Never heard of him," Stewart said. "You, Jerry?"

Hartman shook his head, still not looking at them.

"Sorry. Never been much for poetry," Hartman smiled apologetically. "What about him?"

Fuentes put down his glass and looked around. There was a chill in the air and the outside tables were beginning to empty. At the curb, across from the *terraza*, a middle-aged woman was closing up a flower stall. The unsold flowers were beginning to droop. They pointed like fingers at the café.

"He was murdered," Fuentes said. "Ugly business it was. A mutilation, understand? In a hotel room over in La Boca. There were two others: a man and a woman, a *puta* from the district. All of them naked," he shrugged. "I'm surprised you didn't read about it. It was in all the papers, even the *Herald*."

"Now that you mention it, I might've read something about it," Hartman said carefully. He looked at Stewart. "What was it? A *ménage à trois* that got out of hand?"

Fuentes shook his head. He laid his finger alongside his nose, a Latin gesture indicating shrewdness.

"That is what the murderer wanted us to think. That Raoul sought love from the wrong person."

"Doesn't everybody?" Stewart murmured, watching the street. A man, hatless, with dark curly hair walked by. He looked at Fuentes, then away. Stewart watched him continue up the *avenida*, buttoning his coat as he walked.

"No, *yanqui*," Fuentes said, lighting a fresh cigarette from the one still burning. He fitted the new cigarette into his holder. "Raoul was a *maricón*, a butterfly, understand?" twisting his hand back and forth, thumb and little finger extended, to make the sign for a homosexual. "This the newspapers did not say, but everyone knew it. So what was the woman doing there?"

"Maybe she reminded him of his mother," Stewart shrugged.

Fuentes didn't say anything. He watched Stewart through a thin column of smoke rising like an Indian fakir's rope from his cigarette.

"You *yanquis*. Always with the joking. Like in the cinema. Your Laurel and Hardy, yes? In Argentina, we make jokes too," tapping the ash from his cigarette and smiling slyly, a Cheshire Cat with two mice. "I tell you an Argentinian joke, yes?" looking at Hartman and then at Stewart.

"This was years ago, in Entre Rios province," Fuentes began. "Cattle country and still very primitive back then. There was an *estanciero*, a widower named Ramirez, famous for his jokes. He was a fat man, jolly, and he spent much of his time in the *pulpería*, drinking and laughing with his friends. But then he married a poor *colonia* girl many years younger than he. Beautiful, she was. She liked to ride fast, like a man, her dark hair streaming behind her. People in that place called her '*la golondrina*.' The swallow," Fuentes said, smiling reminiscently. Then his expression changed. He looked at them sharply. "But perhaps men of the world, such as yourselves, have no interest in country buffoonery."

Stewart and Hartman exchanged glances.

"On the contrary, we find it most instructive," Stewart said.

"That is good, Señores," Fuentes smiled curiously at them. "But the funny part is still to come. You see, after the marriage, Ramirez changed. He grew sullen, bitter. Now in the *pulpería*, he drank alone. The old story," Fuentes shrugged. "The girl was in love with a boy her own age. Her family had forced her into the marriage, yes? There was much talk, of course. After the wedding, the young lovers had been seen in the fields together and now, when Ramirez came to town, jokesters would laugh and make the sign of the horns behind his back. The two lovers became bolder. They would walk hand in hand in the village plaza, but still Ramirez wouldn't hear a word against her. In this country, we would say such a man lacks *cojones*," he looked at them. "But it wasn't that way at all. It was as I told you, Señores: this Ramirez was a jokester," he said, that curious smile still hovering on his lips.

"Things came to a head on the eve of All Saints' Day. In the villages there are always church processions and fairs, people dress up in costumes and celebrate till very late. That night, the girl and her lover stole away to the stable of a friend. After much wine and making love, they fell asleep in each other's arms. They slept very deeply. Perhaps someone had given them a sleeping draught," Fuentes said, his eyes glittering dangerously. "Because when the girl awoke, her lover's arms were still around her, but stuck atop his neck, instead of his own handsome head, was the bloody head of a goat, its horns encircled with flowers. Ha! ha! Ha! The horns! Wasn't that a good joke, *yanqui*?" Fuentes laughed, slapping Stewart's knee.

The two Americans looked at Fuentes, then at each other. Fuentes wiped his eyes and sighed.

"*Bien*, Señores. In this country, no one will prosecute any man for killing his wife's lover, so Ramirez was soon back drinking and joking in the *pulpería*. Interesting, yes?" Fuentes said.

"Most interesting," Stewart murmured. "Interesting country."

"Ah," Fuentes winked. "But now, Señor, I tell you something you may not find so amusing. The other man. The one we found with Raoul de Almayo and the *puta*. We think from his shoes that he was a foreigner. Maybe English, maybe German."

Hartman steepled his fingers, elbows on the table, as though he were praying. He looked across the table at Fuentes.

"Tell me, *Coronel*. Whose side are you on? Ortiz or Castillo?" he asked softly.

Fuentes's face darkened.

"Argentina's, Señor. First and always, Argentina. But now here is a curious thing. Because there may be a question of military intelligence, I am called into the case. Then, with suddenness, the case is closed. Curious, no?"

"What was the explanation?" Stewart asked.

"It was ruled a murder-suicide. Raoul killed the *puta* and

the man, then shot himself," Fuentes said, folding his hands across his chest like someone asking a question to which he already knows the answer.

"Did they come up with any motive?"

Fuentes shrugged.

"They said it was sexual blackmail. That Raoul killed them both because they were blackmailing him, then shot himself from remorse, or perhaps because he could not face the scandal."

"But you don't buy it?"

"Sexual blackmail for what? Everyone knew he was a *maricón*, so what was his crime? Fucking a woman? Equally, in the crowd Raoul ran with, sexual perversion was merely a tidbit. Pepper on the steak. No, Señores," shaking his head. "All three were murdered by the same person, but it was not Raoul de Almayo."

"Then who was it?"

Fuentes shrugged again. He finished his drink.

"Who can say? In all events, I am no longer on the case."

"Who called you off?" Hartman asked.

"My superiors."

"Superiors in the army?"

"Superiors," Fuentes said, pursing his lips. From his expression, Stewart could tell he wasn't going to give them any more. Fuentes began collecting his things. He picked up his gloves, put on his officer's cap and draped his coat over his shoulders like a cape. "In my business, Señores, people tend to do things for simple motives: sex, money, power, jealousy. Before I was called off the case, I discovered that Raoul had lost much money gambling at the Atlantis Club. Money is an excellent motive," he said, standing up and looking around. "Señor Stewart, a pleasure," nodding his head. At a corner table, a fair-haired man threw a bill on the table and also stood.

"So you think he was a spy, *Coronel*?" Stewart asked.

Fuentes leaned over the table. He was smiling. His teeth gleaming red like a vampire's in the neon light.

"Frankly, Señor, I think everyone at this table is a spy."

From the moment he got out of the hotel elevator and started down the corridor to his room, Stewart knew something was wrong. For one thing, the elevator boy, an elderly "black head," as country peasants who emigrated to Buenos Aires were called, had looked at him a fraction too long, then had turned nervously away, as if suddenly conscious that he had been staring. For another, the floor porter's chair in the alcove by the linen closet was empty. The corridor was still and empty, lit only by the light by the porter's station. As the elevator sank below his floor, Stewart took out the Colt automatic. He removed his shoes and tiptoed down the long narrow carpet to his room.

When he came to the door of his room, he found proof it wasn't his imagination on the carpet next to the door: a tiny strip of Cellophane from a cigarette wrapper, that he had left wedged between the door and the jamb.

Stewart cocked the pistol, checking to make sure the safety was off. He pressed his ear against the door. He stood there for a full minute, holding his breath and listening, but if someone was in there he was either very good, or dead. Unless the door was wired to an explosive. The Germans were getting very good with bombs. They were getting very good with all kinds of killing, if it was the Germans. That was the whole problem, Stewart thought. He had come on the field in the middle of the game, without knowing who the hell the players were, or what the score was.

Stewart's palms were wet with sweat. He started to put the key into the lock, then jumped at the sound of whirring gears from down the corridor. The elevator was coming back up again. Can't stay here all night, he told himself. He eased the key into the lock, keeping his ear pressed against the door. Nothing. He stared at the door handle, taking a deep breath.

In a single motion, he turned the key, flung open the door and somersaulted into the middle of the darkened room. He lay on the floor in the prone firing position, gun ready, but there was nothing there. The empty room mocked at him. Feeling like an idiot, he got to his feet. The curtains were drawn back and through the window, he could see the plaza outside, lit by street lamps. He started toward the curtain and stopped.

Someone had been in the room. He was certain of it. The keys—to locks in apartments he no longer lived in, cars he had sold years ago—left in a carefully arranged pattern on the nightstand, had been moved ever so slightly. He closed the curtains and turned on the light. The hair he had left on his closed suitcase was gone. Everything was still in the suitcase, cover papers, clothes, but the wrinkle patterns were different. He began to search the room. Then he smelled it.

A faint wisp of perfume. A ghostly presence floating in the air. He didn't recognize the scent. It was too faint, and none of the women in his past had ever worn it, and yet there was something about it. What the hell was going on?

It took him twenty minutes to go over the room. He found nothing, no tell-tale scratches around the window locks, no hidden microphones, nothing that shouldn't have been there. He hadn't really expected to find anything, but you never know your luck. Then in an ashtray on a night table, he found it. An empty matchbook cover from the Atlantis Club.

They're doing everything short of shoving me down the chute to that place, Stewart thought, as he changed into formal evening clothes. One thing was damn sure, though. Whoever Fuentes had put him on display for had got the message. They knew who he was and where to find him. He had been marked. As surely as Cain, he thought, tying his bow-tie in the ornate dressing mirror. Still, that's what Donegan obviously wanted. If you're looking for a source, either you find him, or you make it so he can find you.

By the time he was ready, it was almost midnight. As he combed his hair, he remembered Fuentes's story, and Hartman's remark about him flaying someone alive. Jesus, he thought, studying his reflection in the mirror, what have I gotten myself into this time? He felt the way he had when he was first learning to ride, when a horse had broken away under him, heading for a fence he knew he couldn't clear. That same feeling of panic as the fence came closer and the horse galloped toward it, taking him way past anything he knew he could control.

His reflection stared back at him, looking astonishingly normal. Nothing showed. He looked more like the rich polo player he pretended to be, than those who really were. Donegan, at least, would be pleased, he thought, securing the Colt in his waistband at the small of his back. He pulled on his dinner jacket and, resetting his hair and cellophane strip traps, went out the door.

5

THE ATLANTIS CLUB was on Avenida Corrientes, a few blocks
down from the Obelisk: "Argentina's monument to the sup-
pository," Stewart's taxi driver had called it. Stewart stood
across the street from the club entrance, marked by a neon
sign over a black-and-silver sidewalk canopy, watching the
portero in top-hat and knee breeches help guests from their
town cars and taxis. The night was cool and wisps of haze
were tangled around the streetlights.

Stewart leaned against the side of a shuttered newspaper
kiosk, trying to sort it all out. He didn't bother checking for
surveillance. Fuentes's curly-haired tail was still with him,
seated in an old Ford sedan parked near a bus stop. If there
were others, it didn't matter. They were using him for a stalking horse. They wouldn't make a move until he was on to
something.

The key thing was that Raoul de Almayo had been on his
way to meet Hartman the night he was killed. And Fuentes
knew it. He'd done everything but get up on the table and
announce it. So Fuentes had had the embassies covered all
along. The Germans were involved too. Fuentes hadn't even
bothered to conceal that. Christ! With so many agents running around, it was a wonder that they hadn't stumbled all
over each other like Keystone Cops at the rendezvous, Stewart thought grimly. So Raoul had a German source all right.
That's what Fuentes wanted: the source. The Raven. Only
whose side was Fuentes on? Ortiz, who didn't want the Nazis
in Argentina? Or Castillo and the pro-Axis sympathizers in
the Argentine officer corps, and Fuentes's only real interest to
plug the leak?

It was like one of those psychology experiments, Stewart
thought. He was the rat in the maze, everyone watching him

to see which way he would go. They'd let him live until he found the cheese, he thought, crossing the street to the club.

A limousine pulled up outside the entrance and two couples in evening clothes got out. They were talking loudly and one of the men, distinguished-looking with long old-fashioned sideburns, took a long swig from a silver flask before staggering toward the entrance.

"Good evening," Stewart said, going in with them. One of the women, a brunette with short sleek hair, smiled back. The man with her, short, swarthy and middle-aged, squinted sideways at him as if trying to remember his name.

"And to you," the other man said, giving the checkroom girl a pinch on the cheek as he handed her his coat. The short man helped the brunette off with her fur. They were in the entrance hall, an ornate rotunda with tall French windows and frescoes of plump rosy-skinned nudes around the walls. From the open doorway to the salon came the sounds of gambling, the whirr of roulette wheels, the click of chips, the murmur of the betters and under it all, the insinuating rhythm of a tango orchestra. The other woman, a peroxide blonde in an eye-popping silk gown, tossed her white fur cape at the man with the flask as though she wished it were something more lethal. It dropped to the floor and the man almost toppled over trying to bend down for it. Stewart picked it up and handed it to the checkroom girl. The man with the flask just stood there, swaying and grinning wickedly at the blonde. She looked away. The music was loud and the man began to croon the words at the blonde in a nasty off-key voice:

> "This city doesn't exist any more.
> It doesn't have streets for walking.
> It doesn't have homes to share happiness."

The blonde didn't look at him. She turned to Stewart and held up her cigarette for him to light, looking at him for the first time. Her eyes were soft and brown; the touch of her hand as she guided his lighter was cool and light, and it lingered for a moment longer than necessary.

"Listen to him. He thinks he's Gardel," she said, taking a deep puff. Stewart smiled politely, glancing back toward the entrance. A tall fair-haired man in black came in, followed by a second man. The fair-haired man had a scar on his forehead.

Not a brawler's scar, but the kind young students joined fencing clubs in Heidelberg to get. Stewart looked back toward the two couples. The man with the flask was grinning and sweating, working hard at playing the fool; his eyes never left the blonde.

"Well, and if one is not Gardel, should everyone just slit their throats?" he said.

"Not everyone," the blonde said.

"Everyone tries to sound like Gardel these days. It's too much," the man with the flask said, holding himself exaggeratedly erect in the way of drunks and army officers.

"No one sounded like Gardel," the blonde said, turning furiously on him.

"My point exactly."

"You think you can do anything you like. That's your only point."

"Did I say such a thing?" the man with the flask appealed to the world at large. "*Dios mio*, when did I ever say any such thing?"

"You just wish you could sing like Gardel. You just wish."

"Well, and I don't wish I was where he is now," he snapped, and everyone fell silent. The tango singer Carlos Gardel had been killed in a plane crash four years earlier.

"Listen, Ricardo," the short man said, putting his hand on the other man's shoulder.

"Listen, nothing," Ricardo said, flinging off the short man's hand. "This *estanciera* bitch is eating me alive."

"I'm your wife, not your whore," the blonde hissed.

"Worse luck for me," Ricardo retorted, walking toward the *chemin de fer* tables.

They watched him go. No one said anything. They stood in the doorway of the main salon, poised like divers unsure of the water. The salon was a large red plush room with waiters circulating among the gambling tables carrying trays of champagne and *hors d'oeuvres*. Beyond the gambling area were tables for dining and a dance floor, crowded with couples in evening clothes, and on a small stage, the orchestra sliding from one tango to another. An arched doorway on one side led to a small private bar. The blonde threw her hand up like a Roman orator.

"Farewell, Argentina. All these sad-eyed tango dancers. . . ." she declared. The short man glared at her.

"Almayo?" he said. "You quote Almayo?"

Stewart looked sharply at the blonde.

"He was a great poet. People don't know," the blonde said.

"He was a *maricón.*"

"What if he was? Was that any reason to kill him?" the blonde said, her eyes blurring, her mouth trembling.

"It's because of that bitch Julia and these creatures of hers. . . ." the short man started. The brunette silenced him with a look. He stood there, red-faced, chest heaving as though he was finding it hard to breathe. Abruptly, he turned to Stewart and extended his hand.

"A thousand pardons, Señor. Don Jaime Herrera-Blanca, at your service. My wife, Dido and our good friend and neighbor, Dona Athena de Castro," indicating the blonde. "And you are, Señor . . . ?"

"Stewart. Charles Stewart," shaking his hand.

Herrera-Blanca looked at him thoughtfully, his head tilted to one side.

"Not the polo player?"

"The same."

Herrera-Blanca snapped his fingers excitedly.

"Of course! I saw Señor Stewart play in the Olympics in Berlin," he explained to the women. "Come, you must join us for a drink. If you are here to buy a pony, I have the finest string in the Hemisphere," he exclaimed, taking Stewart by the arm. As they headed through the doorway to the bar, Stewart caught a glimpse of the fair-haired man with the scar watching him. "My ponies this year are . . . you will see . . . exceptional!" Herrera-Blanca declared, kissing the tips of his fingers in an extravagant gesture. He had to raise his voice to be heard above the noise. The bar was loud and very crowded. Herrera-Blanca snapped his fingers for the bartender and ordered whiskies for them.

"Oh! And what about Arturo Vargas's ponies?" the brunette said, watching Stewart over the rim of her glass.

"Dogs! All size and looks and no wind."

"You wouldn't say that to his face."

"I'll say that to his mother."

"Well, and here's your chance. *Hola* Arturo!" she called, waving her hand.

A tanned handsome man with an athlete's build nodded and said something to the other men he was with. One was sleek in a tight black tuxedo, with brilliantined hair and sleepy, dangerous-looking eyes; the second, older, wore a white suit, gold-rimmed monocle, and Van Dyke beard and mustache curled up at the ends that made him look like the Devil masquerading as a Hollywood producer; the last was the fair-haired man with the scar, the one that Stewart had already been calling "the German" in his mind. Vargas looked across the room at them, then smiled and made his way through the crowd, followed by the other three.

"Who's the man in white?" Stewart whispered to the woman, Athena, as they approached.

"Casaverde. Minister of Justice. He always frightens me," she whispered back, shuddering.

"And the slick one? The one with the snake eyes?"

"Amadeo Cardenas. He runs this club. Shh, they're coming."

"*Buenas tardes,* Don Jaime. Señoras. Baron von Hulse here was just asking how long President Ortiz is going to continue this farce," Vargas said, gesturing vaguely at the German, who snapped his head toward them in the Prussian manner.

"Which farce is that, darling? We have so many," Dido said, letting her hand fall languidly across her décolletage.

"This farce of Ortiz and his so-called neutrality." Casaverde said disgustedly.

"Ortiz is still the president," Athena said.

"Ortiz is a joke!"

"Neutrality favors the British while Germany starves. For us, this is not neutrality," Baron von Hulse said, his German accent sibilant in Spanish.

"It's not so easy. Ortiz has support among the Unions and the working classes," Herrera-Blanca grumbled.

"It doesn't matter," Casaverde shrugged, screwing his monocle into his eye to peer at Stewart as though he were looking through a microscope. "The people are irrelevant."

"We are hearing Ortiz has diabetes. Perhaps he won't last much longer," von Hulse said, looking at them for confirmation.

"Syphilis, more likely," Casaverde smiled, looking like a gargoyle with a sense of humor. "Castillo will set things right. The only thing that really matters in this country is the Army."

Vargas made a face that distorted his handsome features.

"The Army is worthless. Too many colonels and not enough brains between them to piss and be able to hit the ground."

"What about Peron?" someone said.

"Castillo is smart," Vargas said, taking out a gold cigar case and selecting a long Havana. He amputated the tip with a special gold clipper and lit up. "He got rid of him by sending him to Italy."

"Maybe not so smart. He might learn a few things while he's over there," Herrera-Blanca said, gulping down his whiskey and banging his glass on the bar for a refill.

"Even better. The Fascists have much to teach all of us. Even Army colonels," Vargas said, studying his cigar. "And this is . . ." looking at Stewart.

"Señor Stewart, of the United States," Herrera-Blanca volunteered.

"Ah, yes," Casaverde said, his devil's eyebrows going up. "The polo player."

Fear shot through Stewart. God, they were fast.

"I'm surprised you've heard of me, Señor Minister," he said politely.

"Buenos Aires is a village. Everyone knows everyone else here," Vargas said, his eyes, deep-set, almost black, fastening on Stewart.

"Especially on Florida Street, or the *barrio norte*," Athena de Castro said.

"Where you should spend more of your time. With your friends, my dear," Vargas said, a glint in his eye.

"You should know, Don Arturo," Athena said, reddening. So she was having an affair and they all knew it, Stewart thought. What was surprising in that? "And speaking of friends, where is Julia?"

A kind of shadow came over Vargas's face. It was like watching a field when a cloud passes in front of the sun.

"Indeed," he said, his mouth snapping shut on his cigar. He turned and spat out the cigar end. "With Julia, who can say?"

There was an awkward silence. Von Hulse broke it, peering closely at Stewart, as if he were a new species of man that he had never seen before.

"Tell me, Herr Stewart, are you one of these Americans who appreciate the advantages of neutrality, or are you like your President Roosevelt and his Jew advisers, talking neutrality while you secretly conspire against these 'uncivilized Huns'?"

There was a burst of laughter from nearby and someone called out, "She didn't!" and more laughter. In the group Stewart was in, everyone watched him and the German, like wolves waiting for the first smell of blood.

"You know, Baron, you really shouldn't start believing your own propaganda. That's very dangerous in a war."

Von Hulse's eyes narrowed.

"I am sure our General Staff will be most touched by your concern. No doubt we shall have an opportunity in the future to explore your views. If you will forgive me, Don Arturo. Gentlemen. Señoras," he said, clicking his heels. He turned and walked toward the salon.

Vargas watched him for a moment.

"Interesting," he murmured, turning back to Stewart. "Perhaps we might be able to entice you into a match, Señor. We have one with Tigre coming up at Palermo Park and also something private at our *estancia*."

"I wouldn't mind one against the Germans," Stewart grinned.

"Well, and it must be admitted, their force and their efficiencies are better than their style," Vargas said, puffing his cigar. "In any case, I have a few ponies you might be interested in. That is, after you get your fill of Don Jaime's miniature creatures," blowing on the tip of his cigar, making the tip glow bright red.

"At least mine aren't pouring sweat after half a chukker," Herrera-Blanca growled.

"We shall no doubt see you later, Señor Stewart. I believe Amadeo here has arranged a private entertainment for us, downstairs. And now, with permission, I shall see if we can find Ricardo. He is no doubt at the *chemin de fer*," Vargas said smoothly, looking in turn at Athena, then Cardenas, before touching Casaverde's arm. The two men headed for the tables, Casaverde turning to look back once more at Stewart before leaving the bar.

Amadeo Cardenas took out a silver cigarette case filled with American cigarettes and offered one to Stewart. He flicked his lighter and they both lit up.

"You speak Spanish very well, Señor Stewart," Cardenas said.

"You mean for a North American," Stewart shrugged.

"Yes. Especially for a *yanqui*," Athena said, coming closer.

Her eyes were large and luminous and she looked as if she had something to tell him.

"Have you been to Spain, Señor Stewart?" Cardenas asked politely.

"I'm afraid not."

"A beautiful country," Dido sighed. "It's so sad."

"Well, at least they got rid of the Bolsheviks in Spain. That's one good thing," Herrera-Blanca muttered. "Ought to do it here too. Before Ortiz forces elections in the provinces. Real elections, no less. Can you imagine?"

"In Argentina? There's not much danger of that," Cardenas smiled.

"He must be crazy. In the head, crazy!" Herrera-Blanca said, turning his head from side to side like an angry bull, looking around for someone to disagree with him.

"What about you, Señor Cardenas? What do you think of all this politics?" Stewart asked.

Cardenas's face never changed expression. He looked at Stewart with unblinking eyes, his face so smooth as to be almost featureless.

"Me, I run a gambling club," he shrugged. "Politics mean very little to me. But one thing I have observed, Señor. Regardless of party, whether Radicalist or Conservative, it is always the idealist who causes the most trouble. Never those who are willing to do business. *Salud*," he said, raising his glass to Stewart.

"*Salud*," Stewart echoed, touching glasses and staring into the bronzed mirror behind the bar. The mirror was filled with light and moving shadows so that it was like looking at an aquarium.

"Speaking of idealists, someone mentioned that Raoul de Almayo used to frequent your club, Señor Cardenas," Stewart said casually, still looking at the mirror. Just then someone laughed and a woman's voice rang out. "Clark Gable, *queridos*. About the war between the northern North Americans and the southern North Americans. They're going to have the premiere in one of those horrible Southern states. Impossible place. Nothing but flies, *Negritos* and fornication."

"You mean, Almayo, the poet?" Cardenas inquired politely, his expression frozen. "He may have come in once or twice. I really don't recall."

"Liar!" Athena hissed. Her hands were shaking and her eyes

absorbed the light and gave none of it back. Her eyes were bullet holes in her face.

Cardenas looked at her, then at Herrera-Blanca, who buried his face in his glass.

"Perhaps the Señoras would enjoy trying their luck at the tables, or perhaps a bite of the *parillada*," Cardenas said, making a show of glancing at his watch. "As you know, unfortunately, the entertainment is for the *gentlemen* only. With permission," he bowed, gesturing them toward the salon.

For a moment, no one spoke.

"We'd better find Ricardo before he's too drunk for anything," Dido Herrera-Blanca said, getting up. "Maybe we can even get someone to tango with us," she added, darting a glance at her husband. She took Athena's arm, who looked up at Stewart, a pleading look in her eye. She wanted to tell him something, all right, Stewart thought, watching the two of them leave the bar, not looking back, moving swayingly on their high heels.

"Perhaps the Señor has not heard. I'm afraid the poet Almayo has been murdered," Cardenas said.

"Filthy business," Herrera-Blanca muttered, putting down his drink and getting up.

"So I understand," Stewart said.

"You understand nothing, Señor," Cardenas said, unbuttoning his dinner jacket. From the way he stood, Stewart could see the bulge made by the gun in his shoulder holster.

"And what is it that I should understand, gentlemen?" Stewart said, looking at both of them.

Cardenas shrugged in the manner of a man who knows he's going to collect the house percentage, regardless of the bet.

"This is a gambling club, Señor. Just before we came over, Señor Vargas and Baron von Hulse made a private wager about you?"

"Oh," Stewart said, his eyebrows going up. "What was the wager?"

Cardenas leaned forward, a chilling smile on his face.

"The wager, Señor, was that forty-eight hours from now, you would no longer be alive."

A shadowy tableau in the darkness. They were in a basement room under the main floor of the club. The walls were shrouded with velvet curtains and no sound penetrated ex-

cept for a small phonograph in the corner of the room that
played the scratchy rhythms of tangos with lyrics too sugges-
tive to be heard elsewhere. On a tiny stage, lit only by red
footlights that created an illusion of hellish flames, were three
figures: an exquisite slender young girl, barely in her teens, if
that, wearing the habit of a Catholic novice, a priest in stole
and cassock, almost effeminately handsome, and a huge Negro with a stevedore's build, dressed in the gauzy finery of a
Nubian slave. Behind them was a gold-draped altar and hanging above it, an ornate crucifix which bore not the body of
Christ, but a realistic plaster statue of a grinning naked whore.

Smoke from cigars and marijuana rose around the stage, as
though something was burning underneath. There were about
two dozen men sprawled on couches around the room, facing
the stage. In the darkness, their positions could be determined
only by the glowing tips of their cigars, or the brief flare of a
match. Moving silently as shadows among them were beautiful young women, each prettier than the next. They were
called *"coperas"*, cup-bearers, and there was at least one for
each of the men. The *coperas* were dressed in Merry Widow
corsets, black stockings and high heels. They served the men
whatever they wanted: food, drink, drugs, and as each approached the man she had been assigned to, the man would
reach up and grab or squeeze whatever part of her was most
convenient. Although the *entertainment* had barely started,
already there were the sweaty sounds of several of the men
coupling with their *coperas*.

"Where do you find such beauties?" Stewart whispered to
Cardenas, who was seated on the arm of his couch.

"Flowers from the dungheap," Cardenas said. His hair was
slick and shining like a black helmet. He had disappeared
earlier, and when he came back his eyes were completely dark
and calm. He's on something: heroin, morphine, something,
Stewart thought, looking around for the others. Vargas and
the German were sitting in a corner on a long chaise, sipping
whiskies. A *copera* knelt before the German, her face buried
between his legs, her flaming red hair spread across his parted
thighs like a napkin. Vargas sat next to him, looking vaguely
bored, his *copera* beside him on all fours, like a dog.

"Some dungheap," Stewart murmured, gesturing at the
redhead working on von Hulse.

"Don't underestimate these girls. One day a *copera* is going to sink her claws into the right fellow and become President of the Republic. Now watch," Cardenas whispered. "Casaverde arranged this."

On the stage, the priest was undressing the novice. Under her robes, she wore only a black lace brassière, panties, garterbelt and fishnet stockings. She began to move her hips in a slow tantalizing simulation of coitus, stripping off the brassière and panties, but leaving on the garterbelt and stockings. Her body was slender, smooth as marble, delicately poised between childhood and womanhood, and peeking between her legs, the faintest hint of down.

Now the priest threw off his cassock to reveal himself as a young woman, dark-haired, with up-tilted breasts that she unbound, narrow waist widening to rounded hips and a suppressed wildness in her movements that is the trademark of Spanish women. The woman-priest went to the altar and selected a rubber penis and strapped it on. The novice's eyes grew wide at the sight of it and she feigned pulling away, but the Nubian and the woman-priest spread-eagled her over the altar, securing her hands and feet with leather cuffs, so that her back was arched and her buttocks prominently displayed for the audience, the cunning pucker between her thighs no longer hidden.

The tango music grew louder, more insistent. The woman-priest held out her hand and the Negro licked at her fingers with a long pink tongue. He parted the bound girl's buttocks, exposing her to the woman-priest. A masculine growl came from the audience as the woman-priest began to manipulate the girl, first with her fingers, then her tongue. The girl squirmed at her touch, as though maddened by a terrible itching between her legs. The woman priest began sliding her long tapering fingers in and out of the girl, as the Negro disrobed and stood facing the audience over the girl's body. His naked body was extraordinary, his muscles massive and perfectly sculpted, gleaming purple in the red light, an enormous erection curving up like a scimitar. He leaned across the girl on the altar and pulled the woman-priest to him by her breasts. The woman-priest pushed the rubber penis into the girl, beginning the old rhythm as she bent forward. The Negro kneaded her breasts, thrusting himself at her. The woman-priest hungrily tried to take the Negro in her mouth, barely getting her lips around the massive head of his penis. In the darkness. Stewart could hear the sounds of stirring, *coperas* being pulled down, corsets being unhooked and all around, soft whispers and heavy breathing.

Cardenas leaned closer to Stewart.

"How do you like our little cabaret?"

"In the face of great art, what can one say?" Stewart whispered back.

"This is a Catholic country. Perhaps for us, this has more meaning."

Stewart could hardly keep from laughing in his face.

"You Argentines take everything too seriously. Even fucking."

Cardenas stiffened. He looked curiously at Stewart.

"Pleasure is serious business, Señor. Maybe the most serious."

Stewart looked around the room. The others, the German, Vargas, Herrera-Blanca, de Castro, were watching the stage. Casaverde stood alone, smoking a Havana cigar, his face in shadow. Only Cardenas seemed unmoved by the sex. Things were breaking very fast, Stewart thought. Too fast. He had to find the source before the Germans did. Or Fuentes. Cardenas was the key. He had to be pushed about Almayo.

"No. There's something desperate about it," Stewart shook his head. "As though pleasure was a religion that frowns upon dancing. What was that poet, Almayo's line? Something about tango dancers?"

Cardenas blinked his sleepy eyes, like a snake in the sun.

"Almayo is dead, Señor."

"In this day and age, that is a common affliction."

"Most especially in Buenos Aires, Señor Stewart. You would do well to remember this."

"You might tell your friends the same," Stewart replied, watching him.

On the stage, the woman-priest was undulating her hips, her buttocks tightening as she slid in and out of the girl, who pushed herself back as far as she could to receive her. Suddenly, the woman-priest pulled out and grabbing a silken rope began to play at whipping the girl's quivering buttocks. The girl began to squirm and writhe under the blows of the silken rope, as the Negro stood there, masturbating over her.

Cardenas looked back at Stewart, his tongue flicking nervously between his lips, like a snake tasting the air. In the red

light, with his slick hair and addict's eyes, Cardenas looked
like someone already dead.

"What do you want, *yanqui*?" he whispered.

"You know what I want."

"They'll kill you," Cardenas said, watching Stewart with
his dead eyes.

"Everybody dies," Stewart shrugged. "Ask your friend,
Raoul. The one who only came in here once or twice."

"I can't do it."

"What choice do you have? Your friends are already beginning to worry about you," Stewart said, looking over at Vargas and von Hulse. Cardenas blinked, his eyes darting around
the dark room as though looking for help. When he turned
back to Stewart, there was a trapped, cunning look in them.
Watch it, Stewart thought. He's made up his mind. The only
thing you know for sure is that he'll probably lie.

"Tonight," Cardenas said, weighing every word like a Spanish shopkeeper counting out change. "My office. After hours.
We can . . ." He was about to go on, when a commotion broke
out as Casaverde stormed onto the stage like a madman, holding a riding crop in his hand like a sword.

"This farce isn't what I ordered," he shouted, his face with
its goatish beard demonic in the red glare. "Now I'll show you
what a man requires," ripping the dildo off the woman-priest
and smacking her across the face with it. Stunned, the Negro
only stood there. Casaverde hit her again. He kept hitting her
in the face until, with a muffled cry, the woman-priest
grabbed her robe and fled from the stage. "For pleasure there
are no limits. Otherwise, it isn't pleasure," Casaverde announced to the audience, spittle flying as he spoke.

"Señor. . . ." someone said.

"Don't 'Señor' me! It isn't child's play we've come for,"
Casaverde howled, whirling on the young girl, who began to
struggle desperately against her bonds, unintentionally wig-
gling her buttocks in a way that seemed to excite him even
more. Casaverde made his riding crop whistle in the air once
or twice, before suddenly slashing it across her squirming
behind with a crack like a pistol shot. She screamed, a terrible
high-pitched cry that reminded Stewart of a bird being attacked by a hawk. Her cries only seemed to goad him even
more. He began savagely whipping her all over. Her back,
buttocks, the inside of her thighs; at first, deliberately, but

soon with escalating fury, each blow raising a raw red welt. "Beg for it, you *puta!* Go on! Beg for it!" he screamed, his face red, swinging harder and faster.

"Aieee! Please, Señor! Please! No more, please, Señor! *Madre mia!*" she pleaded.

All around the room, everything stopped. Everyone was riveted to what was happening on the stage. There were streaks of blood on the girl's buttocks and the backs of her thighs. Her skin was criss-crossed with so many red lines that hardly any white could be seen. Still, he kept on whipping her.

The tango record came to an end. The sound of the needle scratching against the center groove became maddening, but no one moved to shut it off. On the stage, the Negro, looking huge, took a step toward Casaverde, who looked up and slashed him across the face with the riding crop. Casaverde and the Negro glared at each other. Everyone could see the Negro's jaw working and waited to see which way it would go. Casaverde motioned and someone stationed near the door stood up. There was the glint of a gun and the Negro looked at it, then back at Casaverde for a long moment, before dropping his eyes. His penis was still curving up erect. Casaverde gave the Negro's penis a contemptuous little flick with his riding crop, staring at him a moment longer before tossing the riding crop away in disgust. The Negro stood there, head down, a look on his massive face that couldn't be read. Casaverde looked around. He crossed to where the dildos were and selected the most massive instrument Stewart had ever seen, a huge leather penis as long and thick around as a man's forearm. Casaverde wiped the dildo on the girl's behind, wetting it with her blood. "There are no limits," he said hoarsely. "No limits, understand?" He spread her cheeks and began to force the dildo into her anus.

"Aiee, *madre! Dios!*" the girl shrieked, flopping on her belly like a fish. Stewart's fists were clenched so tight his nails were digging crescents into his palms. Vargas and the German watched intently. Herrera-Blanca's eyes were closed. De Castro was trembling, a faint smile on his lips. Stewart glanced once at Cardenas's man by the door, then started to move forward, when he felt Cardenas, plucking at his sleeve.

"Do not interfere, Señor," Cardenas whispered urgently. "If you value your life, or what you want later."

The girl on the stage screamed and begged. "Please Señor!

I do anything! No more! Please, no more!" Blood began to drip down the inside of her thighs and there were spots of blood on Casaverde's suit. It's her or the mission, Stewart thought, gritting his teeth, standing there, immobile, watching Casaverde ramming that thing up inside her, again and again. The girl lay twitching and whimpering, the blood running down her legs in a stream.

All at once, there was a motion of someone moving toward the stage. A figure draped in darkness, that at the foot of the stage became a woman in a long fur coat. In the eerie red glow, her eyes were hot coals and her face, seen only in profile, was so compelling that it was impossible to look away.

Later, Stewart would say that she was beautiful. More than that, that in a room of beautiful women she would be the only one you would notice. Clumsy words that could no more describe her than can a butterfly net hold the shape of the wind. Watching her, the most bizarre thought occurred to him. That it was impossible to imagine her as a little girl, playing with dolls. That it was easier by far to imagine her as having sprung full-grown, like some mythical goddess from the forehead of God. That she was, quite simply, like no one else. But Stewart was barely conscious of any of that. All he could do was stand there, dumbfounded, as though a character from a fairy tale had suddenly come to life. Nor was he alone. Vargas too had risen to his feet.

"You bastard! You miserable bastard!" she said, her eyes boring into Casaverde.

He looked down at her from the stage, blood dripping from the hand that still held the dildo.

"You're hardly in a position to make moral judgments, my dear," Casaverde rasped, breathing heavily.

"I am doing it."

"This! This is only a *puta!*" he said, sending drops of blood flying as he gestured at the girl.

"Who isn't?" she said, getting up on the stage.

Stewart had only a momentary glimpse of that extraordinary face, Mongolian cheekbones, silky black hair and the most magnificent Russian sable coat he had ever seen, even as she motioned to the Negro, who helped her untie the girl. She took off her coat and put in on the naked girl, oblivious of the blood. She put her arm around the girl and followed by the Negro, helped her off the stage and down the darkened aisle, pausing in front of Vargas.

"Julia. . . ." Vargas began, his handsome face twisted into a frightening mask that was hard to look at.

"Was it good for you? Did you like it?" her voice a hoarse whisper.

"You don't belong here. This is not your place."

"But *you* do, don't you? All pigs at the same trough."

"You can't talk to me that way. I won't have it."

"Won't you? Won't you, *pues*?"

"You don't understand."

"How could I?" she said, stepping around him. "What can a woman know?"

"I am your husband! You must listen when I speak!" he shouted, but she had already shut the door behind her, leaving him standing there, like the other men in the room, watching after her even after she had gone.

By the time Stewart got back to the Atlantis Club, it was after four in the morning. The neon sign over the entrance was out and the streets were silent and empty. A cat prowled the deserted *avenida*, stopping to look around like a night watchman before going on. Stewart watched it jump onto the curb and disappear into the darkened alley next to the club.

A lone streetlight cast the shadow of a kiosk across the *avenida*. Hidden in the shadow, Stewart waited, watching the alley for tags, in addition to the curly-haired one, Fuentes's man, whom he had spotted in the Ford sedan parked down the block from the club. Although he couldn't see them, they had to be there. Only amateurs covered just the front of a building and it didn't take a college degree to figure that Cardenas's invitation might have been a trap.

Then he heard it. The scuff of a shoe coming from the alley, followed by a cat's yowl and a muffled sound that could have been a curse. Stewart transferred the Colt to his left hand and pulled a leather blackjack from his pocket, moving silently, under cover of the kiosk shadow, around the corner and into the alley next to the club.

The alley was pitch-black. It stank of garbage and stale wine and someone having been sick recently. Stewart could just make out the dark shape of the roofs against the sky. He felt his way cautiously along a brick wall, trying not to make a sound. His foot accidentally bumped against a garbage can, rocking it with a sound that froze his soul.

"Werner! Bist du dort?" came an urgent whisper from the darkness.

Germans! Stewart was positive they hadn't followed him here, so they must've tailed Fuentes's man, or Cardenas had set him up. Either way, it was a trap. Worse, he had lost the element of surprise. He strained his eyes toward where the voice had come from, but he couldn't see a thing. He needed something to throw, anything to mislead them as to where he was. He went down on all fours, feeling around on the ground like a blind man, but there was nothing. He had to move carefully, too. He couldn't afford another sound.

"Wer is das? Werner?"

The voice was closer now. Stewart couldn't wait any longer. He had to have a diversion.

"Halt den Mund, du Scheisskopf!" Stewart hissed back, removing his shoe and tossing it back toward the garbage can. There was a clunk of the shoe just grazing the can. Stewart used the cover of the sound to creep a few feet further away.

"Wo bist du?" the voice said. It was very close, almost close enough to touch. Stewart held his breath. The German was somewhere right in front of him.

Now, Stewart thought. He had the sequence all worked out. The sap to the head, then catch him to let him down quietly. If that missed, he could backhand the sap, kicking the knee to take him down and once on the ground, finish him off.

He heard the German move. Stewart swung, stepping towards the sound. But he must have made some noise, because all at once he saw the whites of the man's eyes turning toward him in the darkness. They were too close, almost on top of one another. The German was a big man, husky, looming over Stewart, who had miscalculated the swing. The sap hit the German too low, glancing off his shoulder. The German cursed. He grabbed Stewart's throat with a massive paw.

Stewart was too close to swing the sap again. He started to
bring the gun up, but the German smashed his fist into Stewart's midsection, slamming him against the brick wall, knocking the breath out of him. Stewart's gun was gone. He tried to
knee the German, but a tremendous punch to the solar plexus
doubled him over. He tried rolling away. The German held
him fast, iron fingers digging into his throat. Stewart swung
the sap against the arm holding his throat. The German
grunted, but held on. He was incredibly strong. Stewart could
feel himself weakening. There were bright spots before his
eyes. He desperately needed air. He tried to swing the sap, but
the German blocked it, pinning his arm. Stewart gasped. He
had only a few seconds of air left, but the man was a brute. He
had pushed his face close to Stewart's and Stewart could
smell his beery breath and the sweaty smell of him. He's taking me down, Stewart thought desperately, as the German
smashed Stewart's head against the brick wall. Stewart felt
wetness on the back of his head and something exploded inside him.

He grabbed one of the German's fingers from around his
throat and bent it back with all his might. The German
screamed, but still wouldn't let go. Going down, Stewart
thought, his mind barely functioning. Down! That's it, suddenly relaxing his legs completely, collapsing to the ground.

The German felt him go and started to follow him down, his
hand still on Stewart's throat. As they hit the ground, Stewart
brought the sap, no longer pinned, around in a vicious arc
that caught the German in the back of the head. The German
sagged, his weight heavy on Stewart, who hit him again and
again in the back of the head till his hand was slippery with
something and the German lay motionless on top of him.

Stewart lay under the German's weight, trying to catch his
breath. It felt like an elephant sitting on his chest. He tried to
push the German off, but the man was immovable. Slowly,
Stewart managed to brace one hand against the brick wall
and with a huge heave, roll the German over and partially off
him. The German's head, lolling loosely on his neck, smacked
against the ground with a sickening thunk. Stewart heaved
again, using his feet, and finally rolled the German off him.

Stewart sat back against the wall, his chest heaving. His
throat was raw and it hurt like hell to swallow. He could
barely move. He felt like he had just gone fifteen rounds with

Joe Louis. Jesus, he said to himself. He tried to stand up. It took him two tries. Can't stay here. Old Werner might be by any time. And he had an appointment with Cardenas, he thought grimly. He felt the back of his head. It was wet all right and there was a painful lump developing that made him wince when he touched it.

He knelt by the German, feeling for a pulse. There wasn't any. Got to get out of here, he thought, searching in the darkness for his gun and shoe. He wondered if he dared risk a match. If anyone was watching the alley, they'd see it a mile away. Too risky, he decided, groping in the dark, almost knocking one of the garbage cans over. His heart leapt into his throat. Jesus! You want to wake the dead? Heart hammering he started again, almost sighing with relief at finding his shoe near the can.

He sat down and pulled it on. Now, the gun. He began to explore the alley inch by inch on his hands and knees. But after what seemed like an eternity, he still hadn't found it. He stood up and brushed himself off. God, what a mess, he thought. He had to find the Colt. It came from the embassy and his fingerprints were all over it, for Chrissake. He couldn't exactly leave it lying somewhere near a dead body. He would have to risk a light.

He was about to flick on his lighter when thinking about the body gave him an idea. He went back and felt all around the body. Then he rolled it over and found the Colt. It had fallen under the dead man whose pockets he began to search. He found only a little money and a Luger pistol in a shoulder holster. There was no I.D. A professional. And a German. Beyond that, who he was didn't really matter. Stewart got up and with his hands outstretched in the darkness, groped his way to the back door of the club.

He leaned against the door, reaching in his pocket for the pick, when with a grating sound, the door swung open. Stewart froze. Cardenas had left it unlocked. It was a set-up.

He wiped the sweat out of his eyes with his sleeve and tried to think. He didn't want to go inside. The club was the eye of the storm. If he went in, the odds were good he would never come out. On the other hand, if he didn't go in, he might as well go to England and try to enlist. There were a lot of ways for Hitler to kill him.

He pushed the door open a little more, the sound grating

loudly in the darkness. Might as well ring the front door bell, he decided. Inside, it was as dark as in the alley. He listened intently, but could hear nothing. He closed the door behind him, the grating sounding even worse than before. He flicked on his lighter as soon as the door clicked shut.

He was in a stairwell. Narrow wooden stairs led up into the gloom. The air smelled stale and sour, as if someone had spilled wine. Stewart thought about Cardenas waiting upstairs for him. He tightened his grip on the Colt. Just you and me, you bastard. He crept slowly up the stairs, one step at a time, his lighter held high and away from him like a character in an old etching, so that if someone shot at the flame, with any luck they might miss him. As he went he kept one eye closed, so he wouldn't lose his night vision.

There was a door at the landing at the top of the stairs. Stewart flicked off his lighter. It'll be open, he thought. It's a set-up. He's waiting for me. His hand hesitated on the knob. They'll wait. They'll want to see my cards. Sure. And what if they're waiting just on the other side of the door? Then what? All right, all right, Cardenas. Just you and me.

Gun in hand, he flung open the door, pushing it against the wall and leaping into an empty corridor. He stood there, holding his breath, listening. He recognized the corridor from earlier that evening. At one end of it was a circular staircase, niches in the walls holding erotic statues, that led down to the basement, where Cardenas put on his "entertainments." The other end led to a small salon for private high-stakes games, off the main salon. There was a light in the main salon and although everything in the small salon was dim and shadowy, he could see.

He went into the small salon, checking behind every door as he went. The key thing was not to be taken by surprise from behind. The chairs were placed around the table and the cards and chips had been left out, as though a game had been set for ghosts. Stewart went through the double doors and into the main salon, filled with the shadowy forms of gambling tables covered with sheets and at the far end, the deserted dance floor and orchestra stand. He moved in a crouch, behind tables, skirting the walls and stopping every few feet to look around and listen.

It was too quiet, he thought, wiping his palm on his pants' leg and getting a firm grip on the Colt. Now he could see the glow coming from the entrance hall rotunda, where the fancy marble staircase was, the nudes on the curving walls looking fleshy and sullenly pornographic in the shadowy light.

Stewart went up the carpeted stairs to the second floor. There was a light at the end of a long dark corridor coming from Cardenas's office. The door was half open. Stewart hesitated, but he couldn't hear anything over the pounding of blood in his temples. The corridor was decorated with rococo moldings and statues on pedestals flanking both sides of the carpet like soldiers. Stewart stepped off the carpet and onto the hardwood floor. If there was an electric alarm, or trip button, it would most likely be hidden under the carpet. He glanced at the statues as he passed them. Their eyes had that empty marble gaze of beings too perfect to feel.

Stewart stood in the shadow, just beyond the spill of light coming from the half-open door. Why doesn't he say something? Or move? He ought to have heard me, Stewart thought, listening to the silence. The air was lifeless and stale, like the air in a tomb. Stewart pushed the door open and stepped inside. The light was coming from a lamp with a green shade on Cardenas's desk. It reflected on the window that looked out at the darkened windows of the building across the street. The room was done in art deco, with smooth strips on the walls and a large desk and sofa that somehow suggested a steamship salon. On a credenza against the far wall was a collection of marble statuettes, each about a foot high. They were imitations of famous Greek figures. There was a running Mercury, a Winged Victory, a couple of nude goddesses and a gap between them where one appeared to be missing. Set into the wall opposite the desk was a lavish bar. The bar was open. The mirrors and glasses glittered in the greenish glow from the desk lamp, and at first, Stewart didn't see Cardenas. He took another step into the room, gun ready, and on the floor behind the sofa a man's hand came into view.

Stewart froze, his eyes darting around. The silence was absolute. He became conscious of a bad smell pervading the room. Someone had been sick in here. He started toward the sofa, his legs heavy, as though he were wading against an undertow.

Cardenas was on his side on the floor, his knees curled up in a fetal position. He was lying in a pool of blood and vomit. His eyes were open and utterly dead. The back of the head had been bashed in and blood and dark matter was still seeping onto the carpet. He had to have been killed only minutes earlier. Maybe even while Stewart was fighting the German in the alley. A few feet from Cardenas's head lay a marble Venus de Milo, the base bloodstained and spotted with lumps of matter. Obviously the statuette missing from the credenza, and just as obviously the murder weapon.

Shit, shit, shit, Stewart kept repeating to himself. Cardenas had been his only lead to Almayo's killer and the German leak. Even worse, unless he could get away without being spotted, the police were almost certain to pin the murder on him. His first impulse was to run. He glanced at the doorway for a second, before he realized how difficult that was going to be.

He went to the window and stood beside it, looking down at the street. The Ford was still there. Further down the street, facing towards the alley beside the club, was a big Mercedes sedan parked in the shadows, just beyond the light thrown by a streetlamp. Sticking out of the window on the driver's side, Stewart could just make out a man's elbow. He was trapped.

His next thought was to call Hartman. There was a phone on Cardenas's desk, next to a microscope, of all things, and he actually lifted the receiver from the hook, before it hit him how absurd that idea was. The embassy wouldn't touch him with a ten-foot pole. He was on his own. Unless Cardenas had left something behind. But he'd have to move quickly. The whole thing was smelling more like a set-up all the time. But whose? The Germans? Fuentes? Vargas and his pals? Donegan and Fuentes were using him as a lightning rod and it was working. It was working too well.

He replaced the receiver, wiping it down with his handkerchief. He pulled on his gloves and going over to the bar, poured himself a Scotch. The whiskey burned going down and after the second sip, he felt a little better.

Holding the handkerchief to his nose against the smell, he forced himself to look down at the body. Cardenas's hands, the fingernails so carefully manicured, were curled into paws. His reptilian eyes stared into his own vomit. Cardenas seemed so helpless now, but alive he'd been anything but helpless. How had he let himself get caught from behind like that? Come to think of it, with a crack on the head like that, death should've been virtually instantaneous. So how could Cardenas possibly have thrown up?

From the position of the body, Cardenas had been heading

toward the bar. Stewart glanced at his own reflection, bruised and shadowy in the bar mirror. If someone were coming up behind him to brain him with a statuette, Cardenas would almost certainly have seen it in the bar mirror. Also, blood would have been splashed all over the bar, but even in this light, Stewart could see that the blood pattern was almost entirely on the carpet and the foot of the bar.

He went over to the statuette and hefted it gingerly. It was real marble all right and heavy, especially around the square base. It wouldn't have been easy to raise it up so high to hit Cardenas in the head.

So Cardenas had to have been already down, maybe on all fours, when he got clobbered. That would explain his position, the blood pattern and why he hadn't seen the murderer behind him in the mirror. But what was he doing on all fours? Stewart wondered, looking down at the body.

Of course! Cardenas was on all fours because he was vomiting. That's when the murderer finished him. When he was down and helpless, maybe crawling toward the bathroom near the bar, its mirrored door open. But what had made him sick? All at once, Stewart raced back to the desk and began running his gloved forefinger along the top of it, like an army officer inspecting for dust.

After a single swipe, there was a white powder line that stood out sharply on the black leather of his gloved finger. Cardenas was a junkie. He had spotted that right from the beginning. Someone had given Cardenas some bad heroin, maybe an overdose, then polished him off with the statuette as he crawled toward the toilet, puking his guts out. Stewart sat in Cardenas's leather chair and lit a cigarette.

The murderer (Stewart thought about him in the singular, but there might have been ten of them) had killed Cardenas and then calmly removed the hypodermic, or other drug paraphernalia. But the murderer hadn't ransacked the place.

Why not?

Assumption: Cardenas was killed because someone knew he was coming here and was afraid of what Cardenas might tell him. That meant that Cardenas probably knew who killed Raoul de Almayo. As a little extra, the murderer would leave the stupid *yanqui* framed for the murder. If he didn't bother to ransack the place, it was because whatever Cardenas had to say, the murderer already knew.

Or because he had heard Stewart come in.

That meant the murderer had calmly walked out the front door. Or else he was still here.

Stewart's scalp crawled. The murderer had to know about the German leak. He was shutting down the network. If Stewart didn't beat the murderer to the Raven, they'd plug that source but good. So, whoever the murderer was, he was working for the Nazis. Only, unless there was something here in Cardenas's office, it wouldn't matter. He'd be at a dead end.

Keeping the Colt in one hand, Stewart went over to the body, almost gagging at the sight of Cardenas's brain through a jagged hole in the back of the skull, a dark serpentine mass, like a pudding of dead worms. The body was still warm and pliable. It turned over with a lifelike thump that made Stewart shudder as he rolled Cardenas onto his back. He went quickly through the pockets, turning them inside out. He found Cardenas's gun, a small Beretta automatic, unfired, an opened paper envelope containing white powder, that he assumed was the heroin that had made Cardenas sick, a silver cigarette case and lighter, Cardenas's wallet and pieces of paper with initials and peso amounts on them that were probably gambling chits.

Stewart glanced around the office. The file cabinets looked interesting. And what the hell was the microscope for? He went over to the cabinets; the drawers were unlocked. They were filled with papers, mostly bookkeeping records. Stewart riffled through a few of them, then stopped. Maybe there was something there that an accountant would find, but even if Stewart knew what he was looking for, it would take him months to sift through it all. It was hopeless.

He turned and looked down at Cardenas's dead staring eyes. Something didn't fit. If Cardenas had been sitting on something hot, something worth killing for, he wouldn't have kept it in an unlocked file. Not Cardenas, who never took sides and only played the house odds.

Stewart smiled to himself. How do you do, Señor Cardenas?

He looked around the office. There were two pictures on the walls. One a nude, the other flowers. The wall safe was behind the flowers. It was a Mofler combination safe, locked, of course. So that was that.

Stewart leaned wearily against the desk. He was through. First Spain, then Prague and now this. No leads, nowhere to

go, and if the Argentine police or Fuentes didn't get him, the
Nazis would. Even if he was very lucky and could somehow
break out of this trap, the best he could hope for would be to
make it across the border and back to Montevideo. Some luck!
he thought, using his handkerchief to wipe down the whiskey
glass and everything else he might have touched. He gave the
place a final once-over. All dead, he thought bitterly. Dead
poet. Dead junkie. Dead end.

Then it hit him. Cardenas was a junkie! A serious one. He
was bound to suffer memory lapses. He wouldn't dare trust
the combination to a memory burned full of holes by heroin.
Stewart went back to the desk and began tearing it apart until
he found the combination taped to the underside of the top-
hand drawer. He left everything strewn all over the place and
went to the safe, twirled the dial and opened it.

The safe was full of money. Stacks of pesos and dollars, a
couple of glass vials of white powder and papers. Gambling
chits, deeds, contracts. Stewart took several stacks of pesos
and one of dollars and put them in his pocket, smiling as he
remembered Donegan's saying, that using your enemy's
money to finance your own operation was like getting a blow
job from a beautiful girl and having her swallow the come.

Stewart examined the papers. Most were contracts with en-
tertainers, government permits and the like, but one caught his
eye. It was the agreement that established the Atlantis Club as
sociedad anónima. Arturo Vargas owned eighty-five per cent of
the stock, with Casaverde owning five per cent and Cardenas,
the remaining ten per cent, with Vargas being deeded his
shares by his wife, Julia, who had inherited ownership from
her grandfather, Juan Gideon. Curiouser and curiouser, Stewart thought, putting the contract aside and feeling for the back
of the safe. His fingers touched a slim metal case. The case was
gray and it had a small lock on it and a diplomatic seal
stamped with a swastika. Stewart used his pocket knife to pry
it open. Inside the case was a single folded sheet of paper. It was
a letter, on German embassy stationery, from Baron von Hulse,
applying for membership in the Atlantis Club.

What the hell? Stewart thought, wiping his mouth on the
back of his glove. Why all the security over a meaningless
letter? It was like building Fort Knox in order to guard a
compost heap. He took the letter over to the desk lamp and
held it up to the light. He flicked on his lighter, heating the
paper in case there was some kind of invisible ink on it, but

there was nothing. He read the letter again. If there was a code, he had no idea what it was. The letter wasn't long enough for an elaborate code. He clenched his fists in frustration. The lead was right in front of his eyes! He knew it was right in front of him and he still didn't see it!

Seeing! Of course!

He placed the letter under the microscope, positioning the desk lamp so he could see, and found what he was looking for in a period at the end of the first sentence. It was incredible! A miniaturized message in German to Arturo Vargas from Admiral Canaris himself, asking Casaverde to convey "our assurances to his Excellency, Herr Castillo, that our ambassador will arrive by December 17, in good time for the planned celebration at your *estancia* for *Herr Präsident* Ortiz."

Stewart's mind reeled. How long had the Germans been using these miniaturized dots? And the message! Canaris was head of the *Abwehr*, German Military Intelligence. He wasn't sure what it meant, but German assurances to Castillo about Ortiz sounded as if they were planning some kind of coup. December 17th was less than two weeks away. If Vargas was luring President Ortiz, who was all that stood between Argentina and the Nazis, to his *estancia* to be kidnapped or killed, Castillo would become president. But why would it make any difference whether the German ambassador was there?

Perhaps if Stewart had not been so engrossed in the letter and its implications, he might have heard the sounds downstairs and had time to make a break for it. As it was, he didn't notice anything till he suddenly heard the creak of footsteps coming up the stairs.

Sweat began to break out all over his body. It might be anybody. The police. The Nazis. Or the murderer coming back. Whoever it was, he only had a few seconds left. He hurriedly stuck the letter into his pocket and started toward the doors, but it was too late. He could hear the swish of footsteps on the carpet coming down the hall. He looked around desperately. The window. The bar. The bathroom. He clicked off the desk lamp and in a few strides he was behind the bathroom door, flattened against the wall, the Colt ready in his hand. The bathroom was dark and he could dimly make out a portion of the office through the crack where the hinges held the door to the jamb.

The footsteps stopped at the office door. Someone pushed it open.

"Amadeo? Are you there?" a voice whispered into the darkness. A shadowy figure entered the room, too dark to make out clearly. "Amadeo?" the voice said, coming nearer. There was the brief flare of a match, hurriedly dropped. "Amadeo!" came a stifled cry, as the figure started to retreat.

Stewart flung the bathroom door open and grabbing the intruder, jammed the Colt into his ear and hauled him across the room. He knocked the intruder down across the desk and clicked on the desk light, only to find himself pointing the Colt into the terrified yet exquisite face of Julia Vargas.

7

IT WAS the way she looked at him. Not her face: the perfectly oval mouth, the high cheekbones, the astonishing features that made her look as if she belonged in a Renaissance painting, the mistress, perhaps, of some infamous *condottiere*. Nor the man's clothing she was wearing: the jacket, tie, pleated trousers, fedora hat. But her eyes, so intensely blue, almost black, he could hardly look at anything else.

"Did you kill him?" she asked, glancing nervously toward the body.

Stewart shook his head. He had let her up and they were facing each other across the desk. He kept the Colt pointed at her.

"What are you going to do with me?" she asked, watching him the way one watches a strange dog.

"I don't know," he said, half-sitting on the edge of the desk. He took out his cigarettes and when she shook her head, lit one up for himself. "It's a funny situation."

"You're the North American, aren't you? The one they call Stewart?"

He grimaced, flicking the ash from his cigarette into the ashtray a little harder than he needed to.

"Maybe I should've taken an ad out in the *Prensa*, just in case there was someone in Argentina who didn't know who I was."

"I don't understand."

"It's a joke. An American joke."

"Can I go now?" she said, eyeing the gun. "I have to go." He shook his head.

"What are you doing here?" he asked.

"I might ask you the same thing."

"You might, but I have the gun."

She looked sharply at him, her eyes blue and full of light, like the sea.

"Tell me, do you think Hitler is the Devil?" she asked.

"I don't know," he said uneasily. He thought she might be a little crazy. "I think he's probably just a son-of-a-bitch."

"Because if he is the Devil come to destroy the world," she continued, as though she hadn't heard him, "maybe it's because we deserve it. But of course, you probably don't believe in such things," she said, coming closer. She was tall for a woman. She could look almost level into his eyes. He found himself wishing she would take off the hat so he could see her without it.

"Why are you wearing men's clothing?" he asked.

"Why? Don't you like? It is the *moda a la* Dietrich," she said, taking off the fedora and shaking out her hair. "Besides, I like men's clothing. There's a feeling of freedom and power for a woman when she puts on a pair of trousers. But you won't believe this for an explanation, will you?" she said, looking at him sideways, out of the corner of her eyes.

Stewart didn't say anything.

"I didn't think so," she said, with a little shrug. "So let us just say, for a disguise. A woman of good family in this country isn't supposed to run around the streets alone."

Stewart shook his head bemusedly.

"Interesting country you have here. Rape and murder are fine, but heaven forbid if one is caught wearing the wrong trousers," he said, watching the rise and fall of her breasts under her jacket as she breathed and wondering how, even in the dark, he could have ever mistaken her for a man. "And you haven't answered my question. What was your connection with Cardenas?"

"I can't tell you."

"Yes, you can," he said, gesturing with the gun to remind her it was there. But her eyes were on him, not the gun.

"Are you sure you didn't kill Cardenas? Because if you did, 'the birds will not weep,' as we say. He had many enemies. Many," she said.

"He was dead when I got here. Why do you keep asking me?"

"With permission," she said, coming close enough to have to look up into his eyes. He could smell her perfume. It troubled him, reminding him of something, although he couldn't say what. "There's blood on your face."

She reached into her pocket, pulled out a handkerchief and began daubing at his face. When she was finished, she showed him the blood on the handkerchief. He took it from her and stuffed it into his jacket pocket.

"It's not Cardenas's blood. There was a German in the alley," he said.

"Did you kill him?" she whispered, her eyes devouring his face.

Stewart didn't answer.

"Good," she said. "I know you won't believe me, but I mean it." She looked around the office, her thumbs looped on her trouser pockets like a man. She had strong hands. They were slim and expressive, the nails blood-red, trimmed short for a woman, for riding he would find out later. Stewart liked the way she used her hands. "Cardenas was blackmailing me. I can't tell you why."

"Why not?"

"Because," she half-smiled, showing a dimple in one cheek, "then perhaps I might simply be trading one blackmailer for another, no?"

She was good, Stewart thought. He might have bought it whole, except that Vargas, her husband, Cardenas and Casaverde had all been partners in the club. He thought about that and her confrontation with Casaverde in the basement, earlier that evening.

"What about Casaverde? What's your relationship with him?" he asked.

"What makes you think there's anything between us?"

"Because of tonight."

She stared at him, her eyes wide with surprise.

"You were there? You saw?"

"You were magnificent," he said sincerely. "The rest of us were just . . . we were pathetic. But you have a hold on Casaverde. What is it? Your husband?"

She shook her head, still staring at him.

"Enrique Casaverde was my first lover," she smiled. It was the kind of sad ironic smile that comes with a memory associated with something you might do differently if you had it to do over again. "When I was twelve. The night the stars fell. That was at Ravenwood. Our *estancia*. Tell me," she said, gesturing vaguely at the mess around the office, "did you find what you were looking for?"

Stewart didn't say anything. She glanced down at the opened letter case on the desk.

"I see that you found something," she said, her voice going very quiet. She looked up at him. "Perhaps we might be able to, how do you North Americans say, '*make the business?*' " she said, using the English phrase.

For a moment, Stewart didn't respond. He thought about using her. That's what Donegan would do. Only he had no way of knowing which side she was on. He wasn't even sure she knew which side she was on.

"Your husband seems to favor the Nazis," he said. She didn't answer. She looked down at Cardenas and shuddered, then held out her hand for a cigarette. Her fingers were backward-curving and tapering, like a Balinese dancer's despite the short nails. He gave her a cigarette and lit it for her.

"Of course he would," she said, coming close. "The Nazis love guns. It's something Argentine males understand."

Stewart studied her closely. Was she telling him that even though her husband was pro-Nazi, she was against them? He glanced anxiously at the window. They couldn't stay any longer. He had to find out which side she was on, one way or another. "By the way, how did you get in here?"

She looked at him uncomprehending. Dammit, what game was she playing? he wondered. The place was covered.

"The front door. First I knocked and when no one answered, I tried the door, found it open and walked in. Why?"

"I'll show you," he said, grabbing her arm and pulling her beside the window. He held her close. The warmth of her against him was electric. Down below, they could see the Ford, still parked in the shadows beyond the street light.

"Who are they?" she whispered, shivering against him.

"I'm not sure. Argentine military intelligence, most likely. There are probably Germans down there, too. All friends of your husband's no doubt."

She turned to look at him. Pinpoints of light from the lamp were shining in the dark centers of her eyes.

"I thought you understood," she said. "My husband is an Argentine male. He keeps his own company."

"Oh? That's interesting."

"You don't believe me, do you?" she said.

Stewart grinned at her.

"No. But it's interesting."

She looked challengingly at him, her breasts rising against the fabric of the jacket.

"What do I have to do to prove it?" she said.

"See if they try to kill you," Stewart said, checking the Colt to make sure the safety was off. "Because we're getting out of here."

She bit her lip as if making up her mind about something.

"If I help you get away, will you let me go, later?" she asked.

"Why should I?"

"Because," she said, edging from the window. "It's our only way out."

"Suppose I said yes and lied?"

She turned and looked into his eyes.

"You're not lying," she said. She walked around the room, picking things up and putting them back.

"Aren't you afraid of fingerprints?" he asked.

"I've been here before. At one time, I even owned this house," she said, picking up the gray metal case from the desk. She held it thoughtfully for a moment, then put it down. "You found what you were looking for, didn't you?"

"Did you?" he said, eyeing her carefully. She came toward him, an enigmatic look on her face, and when she spoke her voice was a soft contralto that sent shivers up his spine.

"With frankness, Señor Stewart, I believe we both came for the same thing," she said.

For a moment, neither of them spoke. He became conscious of an engine starting up somewhere outside. The sky began to lighten to the pale blue that precedes the dawn. They had run out of time.

"What did you mean," he began, "when you said you could help me get away?"

"Come," she said, reaching for his hand. He held back for a moment, glancing down at the street again. The Ford was still there. Further up the street, two shadows detached themselves from a doorway and headed toward the front of the alley. They couldn't stay there any longer. He let her lead him toward the doorway.

"Where are we going?" he asked.

"There's a secret way out, through the wine cellar. I'll show you."

Still he held back.

"How do you know about it?"

She tugged exasperatedly at his hand, like a child.

"My grandfather built this place," she said. "He always made a secret escape for everything. 'Always go in the front door. Never the back way. But always make one and know where it is,' he used to say."

"Some grandfather," Stewart said, letting her pull him down the hallway to the stairs.

"Oh yes. You could say so," she said, as they paused at the top of the stairs to peer down into the entrance hall and listen.

The entrance hall was dim and shadowy, the tall windows just barely beginning to lighten. The faces of the nudes on the walls were hidden in the shadows, the hall silent and empty. They started down the carpeted stairway, moving slowly and silently. They were near the bottom when they heard the scrape of footsteps outside the front door.

Simultaneously, they began to run down the hall and salon toward the kitchen. Behind them, they could hear the front door being opened and the murmur of voices. They ran through the kitchen, pots hanging over the stoves, the air thick with the smell of roast meat that seems to permeate every house in Argentina, then down an old wooden staircase to the wine cellar. As they opened the door to the cellar, they could hear footsteps from upstairs and the dull clang of someone banging into one of the pots. They stepped into the cellar and closed the door. Footsteps pounded down the stairs after them as Julia fumbled with the latch in the dark. They were right outside the door. Stewart was about to push Julia aside and fire through the door, when he heard the sound of a bolt slamming home. The door shook under a barrage of heavy pounding. Julia flicked a switch and a dim yellow bulb lit the shadowy racks of bottles. She was standing in front of the door, breathing heavily, her hand still on the bolt, when all at once the pounding stopped.

Why have they stopped? Stewart wondered, as he tried to catch his breath. Suddenly, his blood froze. He dived headfirst at Julia, knocking her down. As they hit the floor, a volley of gunshots tore through the door. The shots were waist-high, where she had just been standing, and rays of light streamed through the bullet holes as they lay trembling on the floor.

The wine cellar was dark and cool and had a musty grapy odor. Julia flinched at each shot and Stewart suddenly realized that he was growing hard against her. Of all times, he thought, feeling stupid, and yet the urge to crush himself against her was almost overwhelming. He could feel the warmth of her, the rise and fall of her breathing, and then the pounding started again on the door. It sounded as though they were hitting it with their shoulders, and there was a cracking sound. The men redoubled their efforts, slamming again and again against the door. It couldn't hold much longer.

Stewart pulled Julia to her feet and began moving in a crouch, his hand pressing down on her back to keep her low. They weaved among the wine racks, the bottles dusty and gleaming dully in the shadowy light.

"Which way?" he whispered urgently.

"Here," she said, pulling him toward a wall rack. "It's one of these," she muttered, pulling one bottle after another from the bottom of the rack. Then she reached in and with a loud snap, something gave and the rack swung toward them.

"Come on," he shouted, as a volley of shots rang out, followed by the sound of the door splintering and being smashed open.

"No, wait," she said, putting the bottles back into their places. They could hear voices coming around the corner of the rack nearest them. Stewart couldn't wait any longer. He squeezed off a couple of quick shots. A bottle near the corner of the rack exploded, spraying wine and glass all over, and there was a guttural shout and sudden silence. Stewart turned back to Julia. She was gone.

Suddenly, there were shots from the other side of the rack. They were wild, splintering bottles all along the wall rack. Stewart fired back once more, just to keep them busy, then slipped into the darkness behind the open rack and yanked it shut.

He looked around, but it was utterly dark. The air was dank

and moldy and the walls felt close and dirty. It was a tunnel of some kind.

"Julia," he whispered into the darkness. On the other side of the wall rack, he could hear bottles crashing and someone banging on the rack. "Julia," he called again.

"This way," came a whisper and he saw a gleam of flame. She was at the other end of a narrow tunnel, holding up a lighter. He ran down the tunnel toward the light. She was standing by a small iron door set into a brick wall. The door was tiny; it looked as if it had been made for children.

"Can we get through there?" Stewart asked.

"Oh yes, if you can get the key to turn," she said, pointing at the lock. "It's pretty rusty."

He began playing with the lock. The key was a large old-fashioned skeleton key. It was murder to turn. He forced it and felt it give a bit. Just a little more, he thought. It was just a matter of making sure the key didn't break off in the lock.

"Where does it open to?" he asked, as the key suddenly turned with a loud snap. The smashing behind the wall rack at the other end of the tunnel was growing louder. If she hadn't put the bottles back, he realized, their pursuers would have found the latch and trapped them in the tunnel.

"I'm not sure," she said. In the flicker of the lighter flame, her face was a curved surface of dancing shadows and pale marble, like an ancient statue of a youth that has somehow managed to survive the millennia in pristine condition and yet still conveys with striking reality the notion that the sculptor had fallen madly in love with his subject. "I've never used it before."

"Come on," he said, turning the handle and forcing the little door open. It was pitch-dark and smelled of coal dust. The opening was to a coal cellar, next to the door for the chute above the mound of coal. "Looks like we're going to get dirty," Stewart said, getting on his belly and wriggling through the opening. He scrambled over the coal, catching Julia as she came through. He grabbed her hand and they ran up the stairs and down a dim hallway past the concierge's apartment to the front door of the building. The door was frosted glass framed by iron scrollwork and brightly lit from outside by what Stewart took at first to be a streetlight. Then, peering carefully from beside the door, he saw with a sinking heart that it wasn't a streetlight, but headlights from a dark sedan, its engine running, that was lighting the outside of the door.

"What is it? What's the matter?" she whispered.

"We're trapped," Stewart said, slumping back against the wall.

"Are you sure?"

"See for yourself. Only be careful to stay in the shadow."

She went over by the side of the door and peeked out at the street. After a moment, she pulled her head back away from the glare of the frosted glass.

"It's impossible. They don't know we're here. No one knew about this way out," she murmured, almost to herself.

"Don't tell me it's coincidence. I won't believe you," he said, an edge in his voice.

"It's not coincidence. They're covering the front of the alley. It's just bad luck that the passageway led us here."

"I don't believe in bad luck, either."

"Of course you don't. You're not an Argentine," she said, kneeling beside him. She took out a handkerchief and tried to wipe the coal dust off her face. Stewart glanced back down the dark hallway. That wall rack wasn't going to hold forever.

"We can't stay here," he said, moving beside the door to look out again.

"Who are they? Germans?" she asked.

Stewart squinted against the glare of the headlights. He could make out two figures in the sedan's front seat. The rest of the street was still deserted.

"Who knows? Probably," he shrugged. "The car is a Mercedes and they're covering the alley where the other German was." He pulled out the bloodied handkerchief, found a clean corner, spat on it and began to wipe the grime off his own face. He looked over at her. She had taken off her hat. The light falling on her face gave him an idea.

"Do you think you could distract them for a few seconds?"

She turned toward him, a shadowline from the ironwork on the door sliding across the upper part of her face. She wore it like a mask.

"What makes you so sure they won't shoot as soon as they see me?"

"You said yourself, they don't know we're here. You could be anybody walking out the door. Unless you've been lying. This wouldn't be a bad way to find out," he said, taking the Colt out of his pocket and working the slide to cock it. The click as the hammer went back echoed in the hallway.

"They might shoot anyway. It wouldn't prove anything, one

way or another," she said. Her eyes were in shadow. He couldn't see them. But he could feel her watching him.

"They won't shoot you."

"What makes you so sure?"

"They won't."

A strand of hair had fallen down over her eyes. Stewart couldn't help himself. He reached over and brushed it away. She let him do it the way a watchdog lets a stranger pet him, accepting it without giving anything away.

"Take off the hat and jacket," he commanded. "And that tie. Unbutton your shirt halfway. Let them see you're a woman. Make it sexy, like a *puta* who wants to make the price of a room before calling it a night."

"What makes you so sure they won't shoot a woman? For twenty pesos, these types would shoot their own mother!"

"No," he said, shaking his head. "Trust curiosity. And libido. To them you are an unknown and as a woman, little threat. They won't shoot."

"How should I distract them?"

Stewart stood beside the door, his back to the wall, the Colt ready.

"You'll think of something. Just block the car window on this side, where the passenger is sitting. Bend toward them. Give them something to look at. Leave the rest to me."

"How do you know I won't betray you? After all, my husband wants the Nazis to win," she said, unbuttoning her shirt almost to the waist, the swell of her breasts clearly visible in the gap. She saw him watching her and she let him, her hands dropping to her sides.

"Maybe that's why," he said, swaying toward her. They were close enough to kiss and the attraction between them was very strong. He forced himself to hold back. This is war and her attractiveness is a weapon, he told himself. Give her a chance and she'll use it against you. He had to clench his fists to keep himself from grabbing her. The hardest part was knowing that she wouldn't stop him, he was certain of it. He transferred the gun to his other hand and took the blackjack out of his pocket. "Besides, if you betray me, I'll probably be able to get off a few shots. And if I do," he said, roughly pulling her next to him, "the first bullet is for you."

"I won't betray you," she said. "But not for the reasons you think."

"What then?"

"For the same reason you didn't kill me upstairs. Because maybe, just maybe, we're on the same side," she said, opening the door and slipping outside.

He watched her walk toward the Mercedes. At first she moved tentatively, not wanting to attract attention. Then, all at once, she began to move seductively, swinging her hips as she went toward the passenger. Stewart kept his foot in the door so it wouldn't close completely. He saw the window start to come down and a man's face turn toward her. The man had something in his hand that he pointed at her. Stewart had a terrible feeling in the pit of his stomach. He wanted to move, but he needed a few more seconds till she blocked the passenger's view. God, what if he had been wrong about them not shooting? he thought, the burning in his stomach getting worse.

She bent toward the man, leaning her arm on the window. As she bent over, Stewart caught a brief glimpse of a needle-nosed man, smiling at her. Now, Stewart told himself, easing the door open and scrambling out onto the sidewalk on all fours. The only way he would know for sure whether she had blocked their line of sight was if they didn't shoot him.

As he crept behind the car, he could hear the man saying something and Julia laughing. Stewart moved crablike, careful to stay down so he couldn't be seen in the rear-view mirror. The man on the passenger side was talking, but Stewart couldn't make out the words, and as he came around the other side of the sedan the driver said something and the passenger grunted.

Stewart knelt near the driver's door and his heart sank as he looked up. The driver's window was closed. There would be no way to take the driver out with the sap through the window, and if the car door was locked, no way to get at them at all without spraying bullets all over the place. In a shoot-out, he and the girl were as likely to get hurt as the two Germans. There was only one chance left.

Still kneeling, Stewart put his hand on the handle of the rear door on the driver's side. If it wasn't open, it was going to be a mess. He heard Julia cry out in pain. He raised his head slightly. The needle-nosed man had grabbed her wrist and was twisting it. The driver, a big man in a stained hat that had seen one rainstorm too many, was grinning broadly. Stewart eased the door handle down. He felt something give and without waiting any more, he ripped the rear door open and jumped inside, swinging the blackjack across the driver's temple. He felt the sap smack home and the driver tilted sideways, head thunking heavily against the window. Stewart could see the needle-nosed man's eyes wide in the rear-view mirror. The man had let go of Julia and was pulling out his gun as he whipped around. He was faster than Stewart had anticipated. Too fast for Stewart to use the sap on him. The barrel of the gun appeared and Stewart had no time to do anything except watch it come around, like a movie in slow motion. He took it all in, the gun, the needle-nosed man's face, the glare from the streetlight on the windshield, the look of horror on Julia's face.

Stewart shot the man through the back of the car seat. The bullet took him in the abdomen, angling upwards and out the back, punching a hole in the windshield that created an instant spider-web of cracks in the glass. The needle-nosed man was flung back against the dashboard, the gun going wide. But he was still alive. His eyes narrowed with rage as he struggled to aim his gun back at Stewart, who fired again. The second shot shattered the man's jaw, snapping his head back and spraying a big chunk of the back of his skull onto the windshield. Julia screamed as the man collapsed between the seat and the dashboard, blood pouring out of his head like water from a bucket. She stared down at the body and then at Stewart sticking the Colt back in his belt, his hand shaking violently. The windshield was covered with blood and jelly-like lumps of brain tissue and more spider-web cracks radiating from the second bullet hole.

"My God!" Julia breathed, staring at Stewart. "My God!"

"A .45 does a lot of damage," Stewart said, wiping his hands and face with his handkerchief. Julia's chest was heaving and she couldn't take her eyes off him.

"My God, does it not?" she managed.

Stewart looked around. He could see the buildings now and the sky beginning to turn gray. It was almost dawn. Every instinct he had was screaming at him to get the hell out of there. Where was Fuentes's man, the one in the Ford?

"Someone must've heard. We have to go," he said. The Mercedes engine was still running. If they were going to use the Mercedes to get away, he had to get the bodies out now.

Julia nodded. She was holding on to the car window as though she might collapse if she ever let go.

"We have to go," he said urgently. She looked at him strangely, as if in a dream.

"We can take my car."

"Where is it?"

"That way," she said, motioning with her head toward the corner of Esmeralda, near the Methodist Church. Stewart's heart sank when he saw it. It was a "Dusie," a magnificent-looking Dusenberg convertible, the kind of car a blind man couldn't miss if he tried. Stewart got out of the Mercedes. He could see the exhaust coming from the Ford's tailpipe up the street. Then he realized that the Ford was backing towards them. In the apartment house across the street, windows were lighting up. People had heard the shots, all right.

Oh Christ, Stewart thought. He reached across the dead man and grabbed the keys out of the ignition. He helped Julia on with her jacket and hat, and throwing his arm companionably around her neck, began quick-marching her toward the Dusenberg.

"Keep your hat low to cover your face and give me your car keys. Weave a little. Pretend you're drunk. A little sick, even," he said, watching the Ford out of the corner of his eye.

"That won't be hard," she whispered back, staggering slightly as they moved quickly toward the corner. They were almost running and Stewart had to force himself to slow them down. A second-story window in the apartment house opened and a woman in a robe and sleeping cap peered out. She was just above them.

"I see nothing," the woman called to someone behind her in the room. Stewart deliberately exaggerated his stagger, almost pulling Julia down. They looked at each other. He could see the fear in her eyes. He kept his arm firmly around her. They were only a few hundred feet from the Dusenberg.

Second- and third-story windows in the apartment building began to open, spilling light into the street. Still weaving, Stewart risked a glance back up the block. The Ford had stopped next to the Mercedes. The curly-haired man got out and looked inside. He blanched at what he saw and hurriedly got back into the Ford.

"What is it? I heard shots," a man's voice called out.

"There is nothing. Only a pair of drunks!" the woman shouted back.

"What's that?" another voice called out. "Bolsheviks!"

"Jesus Maria! Again with the Bolsheviks!" a neighbor cried out in disgust.

"You wait! Till they stand you up against a wall!"

"*Imbécil!* Go look under your bed for Bolsheviks!" the neighbor shouted, slamming his shutters closed, as Stewart and Julia got into the Dusenberg. They were breathing hard, harder than justified by the walk. She started to get behind the wheel, but he pushed her over. He looked back, thinking about the convertible top, but the Ford was backing toward them again. They'd been spotted!

The Ford was coming fast. Stewart could see the face of the curly-haired man through the car's rear window. Stewart pulled the choke, praying the engine caught right away. So far, no one except Julia could connect him to Cardenas's death. But if he was seen now, Fuentes would be all over him. Not only would he have to forget about the mission, he'd be lucky to get out of Buenos Aires alive. He ducked his head to conceal his face as he hit the starter. It didn't catch. The Ford was almost close enough to block them off. He hit it again.

The engine caught, flooding him with relief. He threw it into gear and floored the pedal, the Dusenberg surging forward with a sudden roar. The Ford slewed around crosswise to block their escape. The curly-haired man reached for something. Stewart didn't plan on hanging around to find out what it was. If he took the sidewalk, there might be just enough room to squeeze by, but they'd have to go across the Ford's line of fire. The tires squealed on the pavement as the Dusenberg skidded toward the narrow gap between the Ford and the sidewalk.

"Down!" Stewart screamed, shoving Julia down. He covered the side of his face with his hand as they came abreast of the Ford. Out of the corner of his eye, Stewart could see the curly-haired man aiming a shotgun out of the window, his eyes narrowed as he sighted across the barrels. All Stewart could do was hope he wouldn't fire. He pointed the Dusenberg at the gap and at the last second ducked down in his seat, crushing Julia beneath him.

Although he was braced for it, the impact was hard and came with a crash of ripping metal. The Dusenberg was wrenched sideways as it leaped onto the sidewalk. Stewart snapped upright, pulling at the wheel with all his might as they slammed across the sidewalk, the front end swinging toward a lamppost, then back like a pendulum, as Stewart turned into the skid. The Dusenberg leaped the curb back into the street, the tires trailing smoke and a smell of burning rubber. Stewart gunned it up Corrientes toward Ninth of July and the Obelisk before he dared a glance in the rear-view mirror. He wished he hadn't.

The Ford, its battered left front fender almost ripped away and hanging by a thread, was already after him. It had hit the fan for sure. And no way of knowing whether or not the curly-haired man had identified him, Stewart thought, as the Obelisk loomed closer, filling the windshield. It wasn't enough that he had to lose the Ford while driving what had to be the most conspicuous car in Buenos Aires. He had to do it and go to ground in a strange city before anyone else could pick up his trail. If he had enough time, the "Dusie" could easily out-run the Ford, he thought. Only there wasn't any time.

"Which way?" he shouted, all four tires squealing as he took the curving circle around the Obelisk.

"Try Recoleta," Julia said, pointing toward one of the boulevards radiating out from the plaza. They skidded across the Diagonal Norte, the Ford falling back but still with them as they turned into Cerrito, past the baroque facade of the Colon Theater, looking more like a museum than a theater. As they raced down Cerrito, Stewart had to swerve around an oncoming car, someone starting his day unusually early, and that gave him an idea.

"Is there a one-way street near here?" he asked, swinging up Cordoba, past the Cervantes, its big cupola distinct against the blue dawn. They were gaining distance on the Ford; the speedometer edging past eighty. They tore past shuttered stores and apartment buildings. Outside a *lecheria*, a man was unloading metal milk cans from a donkey cart.

"A one-way street?"

"For God! There's got to be one!" he snapped.

"Wait! There's one on Calle Paraguay, off Callao. Turn right by the park, after the church," she told him. She had taken off her hat and her hair, unpinned, was streaming behind her in the wind. "Now! Here!" she shouted, as they whipped around a corner and out of sight of the Ford.

He had a few precious seconds, Stewart thought, deliberately turning the corner into Paraguay against the one-way signs. A man on a horse and cart plodding toward them could only stare wide-eyed as they bore down rapidly upon him. The horse, in blinkers, its head down, clip-clopped straight toward them. It was perfect, if he could pull it off, Stewart thought, as at the last second he swung around the horse and cart and down the street, looking desperately for a sidestreet or alley.

He risked a final quick glance in the rear-view mirror. The Ford still hadn't crossed the intersection with Callao. Then he spotted something. A narrow cobbled alley between one of those small neighborhood restaurants *porteños* call a *boliche* and an apartment building. The alley wasn't much wider than the Dusenberg, and almost standing on the brakes, Stewart fish-tailed the car into the alley past the building line and skidded to a stop. Telling Julia to stay in the car, he squeezed out and ran to the corner of the building just in time to see the Ford race by on Callao. As the Ford went by, the horse and cart, partially screening the view, approached the intersection, the driver still staring behind him toward the alley in disbelief.

Stewart felt someone approach and already had the Colt aimed before he realized it was Julia.

"Did you say something before about Argentine women?" he said.

"I had to see," she said, tucking her wind-tossed hair back under her man's hat. The transformation was amazing. When she squared the hat on her head, she was once again a handsome boy. "Is he gone?"

"Unless he doubles back. We'd better wait for a few minutes," he said, reaching for a cigarette. He was about to light it when a sudden loud rattle of metal made him freeze. He peeked cautiously around the corner, but it was only someone raising the iron shutter in front of a neighborhood *almacería*. Stewart slumped back against the brick wall and lit up. That was the best cigarette in the world, he thought, inhaling deeply. Not the one after a meal, or sex, but the one after you kill someone who's tried to kill you. The one that lets you know you're still alive.

"We can't stay here," she said, looking around uneasily at the trashcans against the far side of the building and the laundry hung from lines strung high across the alley. Stewart understood. She wasn't a girl for alleys.

"Where can we go?" he asked.

She frowned. Whether because it was a lover's question, or because it meant he wasn't going to let her go, or maybe it was habitual with her when she thought, he didn't know. There was a lot about her he didn't know.

"Don't you have someplace?"

"No. We need someplace private. Someplace no one who knows either of us would know about. Just for a little while," he said, peering around the building at the street. Things were quiet. If the Ford had backtracked, he hadn't spotted it.

"What about a hotel?" she asked.

"Two men. No luggage. They would think we were *maricons.*"

"And if they did?" she shrugged, as if the idea didn't entirely displease her.

"Perhaps," he said, weighing the idea. He knew the Plaza was out. Whoever was after him would be all over the place there. What he needed was something temporary, where they could both go to ground till he could figure out what to do. "Trouble is, there are always too many people hanging around who can spot you at a hotel. Also, if you get a nosy reception clerk, there's the question of your *cedula*, your identity card. No," he said, putting his hand on her shoulder. "The best would be a private apartment somewhere. Something discreet."

Then it hit him. She was the one who had suggested they head toward the Recoleta district. She must have had a reason.

"What's in Recoleta?" he asked quietly.

She colored. It gave him a funny feeling. Not because he had found her out, but because suddenly something was unfolding in front of him. A chasm that he sensed, once entered, would allow no going back. You either jumped off the cliff, or you didn't. "There's something there, isn't there?"

She nodded, looking down at the ground.

"Athena de Castro keeps an apartment there. She uses it for trysts with that schoolboy of hers." She gazed up at the narrow strip of sky between the buildings, the laundry swaying stiffly as wooden signs from the clotheslines.

"What about the keys?"

She didn't answer. He started to touch her, then stopped himself. She looked defiantly at him her eyes filling.

"Well, damn you! I never said I was an innocent."

Stewart didn't say anything.

"Don't you dare judge me, *gringo!* Not any of us! In this

country, we do what we have to do. Whatever piece of life we can grab is something else. Believe me, not all the *putas* in Buenos Aires are on the Avenida Veinticinco de Mayo!" she declared, her firm little chin thrust toward him like a weapon.

Stewart heard something. He shoved her back against the wall. She started to say something and he shook his head.

"Be still," he mouthed, crouching beside the wall and easing back the hammer on the Colt. He motioned her behind him and getting down on his knees, peeked around the corner of the building. He ducked back immediately. The Ford was stopped at the intersection. The curly-haired man sat in the car, anxiously scanning the street. Stewart motioned with his hand to let Julia know what was happening.

"Did he see you?" she whispered into his ear.

"I don't think so."

"God, he came back," she said, unable to suppress a smile.

"What's so funny?"

"Oh," she laughed to herself. "We would have to be followed by the only efficient police agent in Argentina."

He put his finger to his lips for her to be quiet. Someone was approaching the alley, the footsteps heavy and slow. An elderly woman wearing a kerchief on her head and carrying a basket of clothes glanced sideways as she walked by. For a moment, everything was frozen, the three of them all staring at each other in surprise. Suddenly, Julia bent forward and buried her face in Stewart's crotch. He responded instantly to the feel of her mouth, soft and warm, as her fingers fumbled with the buttons on his fly.

"Filthy *maricóns!*" the old woman said, spitting disgustedly into the gutter. "There's no hope for this country," she muttered, shaking her head as she walked on. As soon as she passed, Julia pulled away and stood up. She smoothed her clothes and straightened her tie, her eyes darting from Stewart's face down to his crotch and back up again. They heard the sound of a car moving and he peered around the building again.

"He's gone," he announced, trying to sound normal. The way he had reacted to her was incredible.

Julia fell back against the brick wall, letting out a long sigh. Stewart eased the hammer down, put the Colt back in his belt and buttoned his jacket over it.

"Do we take the car?" she asked.

He shook his head.

"Too obvious. We'd be spotted again in five minutes. Is there a bus we can take?"

"There's a *colectivo* stop by the *almacería*. They usually start around this time of the morning," she said, consulting her watch. "Just give me time to change."

She went back to the Dusenberg and opened the trunk. She took out a bag and unbuckling it, pulled out a brightly patterned dress, high-heeled shoes, a handbag and a small beret-like hat.

"Turn around," she ordered, and he heard the whisper of silk behind him as she changed. What the hell had he gotten himself into? he wondered. Everything was breaking incredibly fast. The Germans were about to send some kind of balloon up. They had killed Cardenas to try and prevent him from finding out about it. And now, this incredible woman. Up to her neck in it, but who could say how or why? She confused him. In some ways she didn't seem to belong to any of this. Yet in other ways she was almost a professional, like the way she had pretended to give him a blow-job to fool the old woman, feeling himself stir at the memory of her mouth on him.

"Come on," she said, coming up behind him and taking his arm. "We don't want to miss the *colectivo*."

She was transformed. Instead of a young man, she was now an attractive young wife, hanging on her husband's arm. No one looking for two men would recognize her in a million years. After checking the street, they walked out of the alley and down the block as though they had been doing it every day for years. Stewart glanced around, but everything was quiet. Two men in straw hats and a woman were waiting by the curb for the *colectivo*. One of the men was writing in pencil on a copy of the morning *Crítica*. When Stewart peered over his shoulder, he saw that the man was circling the names of horses that were running at the Hipodromo.

The *colectivo*, a dilapidated miniature bus with colorful *fileteado* designs painted on the outside and both sides of the hood raised like a gull's wings, pulled up in a foul cloud of diesel *hollín* and everyone got in. Stewart and Julia sat side by side, thighs rubbing against each other, as the *colectivo* rattled over pot-holes, gradually moving toward Recoleta. Stewart kept his eyes on the street, but he didn't see the Ford again.

The sun peeked over the tops of the houses. The streets began to come alive. People were walking to work, or to cafés just opening with a slamming up of iron shutters for a morning coffee. They passed a corner park with trees and benches and grass, where people were lining up for the bus to Retiro. The sun was shining on the *colectivo*'s windows, and as they approached Recoleta the buildings were white and very Spanish. The morning was already warm and there was a feeling that it would get hot later on. As the *colectivo* turned into the Plaza Franzia, Stewart felt Julia take his hand, her fingers intertwining with his the way children's do, and they got off. They walked toward the Cemetery on Calle Junin, Stewart checking around as the *colectivo* pulled away, trailing black fumes. It seemed almost incredible to Stewart, but no one was following them.

They came to a gray three-story apartment house. The *Río Parana* according to the brass plate next to the front door. Julia took a key-ring out of her purse and unlocked the door. The top part of the concierge's Dutch door was open and the hallway was thick with the smell of grilled *chorizos*, but the concierge, a tiny woman with hair so red and stiffly curled that it had to be a wig, barely glanced once at them.

Athena's apartment was on the third floor. The high windows overlooked a wide expanse of green and white, and it wasn't until later that Stewart was to realize that it was the Cemetery. As soon as they were inside, Julia locked the door with the bolt and threw herself into his arms. Holding her hand against the back of his head, she kissed him hungrily, desperately, lips pressing his, her tongue probing, searching, thrusting into every corner of his mouth. Her body moved against him with sudden urgency, molding herself tightly to him. All at once, she pulled her head back. Her lipstick was smeared, her eyes so blurred he wondered if she could even see him.

"God, *yanqui*," she said breathlessly. "I've been wanting to do that all night."

THAT MORNING, the summer came. The sky was hazy blue, and by midmorning Stewart could already feel the heat. After Julia left the apartment, he walked down the Calle Junin toward Palermo Park. He went past the Cemetery, its statues and marble mausoleums gleaming among the cypresses and crowding close upon each other, a miniature Rome of the dead. The cemetery workers in their gray suits and straw hats, were raking the paths and arranging flowers in concrete urns with studied slowness. The workers didn't hurry; like gods their perspective had expanded to include eternity.

Stewart walked until he found the *tintorería* Julia had mentioned. The tailor, he was a Jap, all the *tintorerías* were, clucked over the sad state of his suit—"for mohair of such quality one must pay attention, Señor"—and fitted him with an off-the-rack summer suit and a Borsalino hat. Stewart felt nervous having the Jap touch him. Ever since the Japs had sunk the American gunboat, *Panay*, in the Yangtse River, no American felt that comfortable around them. Still, Stewart figured his accent was good enough that to the Jap he was just another foreign-born Argentine. He left his other suit to be cleaned and stopped at a *confitería* across from the park for coffee and a *pastel*.

The jacaranda trees along the street and in the park were in purple bloom and the flower stalls were bright with color. It was getting close to Christmas and the flower-sellers were featuring poinsettias, that people called *estrellas federales* because red was the color associated with the tyrant Rosas, still hated after nearly a century. It seemed strange to Stewart for anyone to be thinking about Christmas when it was so hot, but then, Argentina was a strange country.

Stewart read the *Herald* with his coffee. The story about

Cardenas hadn't made the papers yet. He would have to check the afternoon editions. The war news was all bad. A German U-boat had somehow managed to sneak into the British naval base at Scapa Flow and sink the battleship *Royal Oak* as it lay at anchor. Somebody had screwed up, Stewart thought grimly. An American merchant ship, the *City of Flint*, had been captured by the Germans, and in the South Atlantic the German battleship *Graf Spee* was on a rampage, sinking two ships, the *Doric Star* and the *Tairoa*, within a day of each other. Stewart put the paper down. The war, that had seemed so close when he had been in Europe, seemed very far away when you read about it in the papers. It was a little like following baseball, the casualties only numbers, like a box score.

Stewart finished his coffee and lit a cigarette. The *avenida* was alive with trams and motor cars. There was a summery feel in the air; people moved differently. Women were wearing their summer dresses and virtually overnight, as though someone had given a signal, the peanut vendors, with their roasters shaped like locomotives and their eternal cry of "*Mani*," had been replaced by uniformed ice-cream vendors selling "*Smak*" pops from bright red carts. There was a prewar feel to the scene. It was like watching a movie, he thought. These people no longer existed in the same way; they just didn't know it.

Stewart watched the street and tried to sort it all out. Whoever had killed Almayo had most likely also killed Cardenas. Probably for the same reason: the letter he had found in Cardenas's safe. The whole thing had German footprints all over it. Von Hulse must have found out that there was a leak somewhere and was trying to plug it, starting with Almayo and Cardenas. But the Nazis wanted more than to find a double agent. They wanted Argentina.

Which brought him to the German connection to Vargas. And through him to Casaverde and Vice-President Castillo and whatever the hell was supposed to happen on December 17th.

And to Julia.

What had she been doing in Cardenas's office? That fairy tale of hers about blackmail sounded about as real as a Hollywood starlet's biography. How could you blackmail someone who admitted to her indiscretions, whose husband couldn't control her and who was fabulously wealthy in a country where a twenty-peso *coima*, as bribes were called here, was enough to buy off a police captain? Which brought him to Colonel Fuentes. What was he after? Not Almayo's killer. He already knew that was political dynamite. Whose side was Fuentes on? Stewart stubbed his cigarette out in frustration. There was something else going on, he thought. Something he wouldn't know until he found whoever had murdered Almayo and Cardenas. Hopefully, before they found him.

In any case, he had to alert Donegan about the coup.

He went over to the public telephone by the counter where the sandwiches and *pasteles* were displayed, put a ten-centavo coin on the counter and dialed.

He tried the embassy first, but Hartman wasn't there. Then he tried Hartman's home number. No answer. He let the phone ring for a long time. There's something wrong, he told himself. Hartman was his only link to Donegan.

He lit another cigarette and tried to think. The man behind the counter looked curiously at him and Stewart smiled back, his mind racing furiously. In two weeks the Nazis might own Argentina. There wasn't time for channels. But the only way he could think of was to break one of the cardinal rules of the trade about never mixing Services, or operations. He put another coin on the counter and dialed.

The phone was answered on the second ring.

"Major Portsmouth, please. Tell him Mister Cornwall is calling," Stewart said in English.

"I beg your pardon?"

"Major Portsmouth. From Mister Cornwall."

There was a hesitation. The man at the other end cleared his throat before he spoke.

"One moment please," the man said. Stewart could hear the nervousness in his voice. He waited while the man consulted his code-book. Then he heard a series of dialing clicks and another voice came on the line.

"This is the trade attaché's office. May I inquire who is calling please?"

"I'm trying to reach Major Portsmouth. Of the Second Irish Guards," Stewart said.

There was a sudden intake of air.

"You must be mistaken, sir. There's no one here by that name."

"Sorry. I thought I saw him in Palermo Park, by George. I must have the wrong number."

"Indeed, you must," said the voice at the other end, frostily. As Stewart hung up, he couldn't help smiling to himself. They must've wet their pants at the emergency code intro he had used: Portsmouth and Cornwall were reserved for White House to Downing Street communications only. He dropped a bill on the table and caught a taxi to the Retiro subway station.

The subway was crowded with people going home for lunch. Stewart waited near the foot of the escalator, under an arch painted with a rural village scene. A group of children in school uniforms led by a nun gathered on the platform for the Plaza Italia train. The children were shoving each other and laughing until silenced by a savage look from the nun. The moment her back was turned, they were at it again, but silently this time. For some reason, it made Stewart happy to see them making silly faces at each other. It was as if humanity still mattered. Everything wasn't lost yet.

The station was hot and sticky and most men took off their jackets and hats and rolled up their shirtsleeves. The train roared into the station with a metallic screech of brakes. The platform filled with people getting off the train, then began to empty. Stewart waited till the train pulled out, then crossed to that side of the platform, as though he had just missed the train. He leaned against a pillar and opened his paper, but all the while he was watching the people coming down the escalator and thinking about Julia.

He thought about her long slim legs entangled with his, the arch of her spine in the ornate mirror on the wall opposite the bed, the little cry she gave when he first entered her and afterwards, the wetness on his shoulder where her face was. At first he thought it was saliva, until he looked at her.

"What is it?" he asked. "What's wrong?"

"Don't you know?" she said, her eyes brimming.

"No. Tell me."

"God!" she exclaimed. "When it comes to love men are such amateurs."

It made him feel funny when she said that. Of course he wasn't in love with her. He wasn't sure how he felt about her, but he knew it wasn't love. In fact, in the quiet moments when he was honest with himself, he wasn't sure he ever had been in love. Not the kind of mad all-consuming passion, the "love" that rhymed with "stars above," that all the songs were about. He didn't even know whether it really existed, or whether it was something people just talked themselves into because they thought it was something they were supposed to feel.

But that didn't explain what happened when later, her slender body nestled closely to his, she told him, "I have two children. Boys." Without knowing why, her words were like an ice-pick probing toward his heart. He got up on one elbow to look at her.

"Why are you telling me this?"

She looked at him, her eyes dark, unreadable.

"So there are no mistakes," she whispered, suddenly diving headfirst at him, nibbling and kissing her way down his body with rose-petal lips and sharp little teeth until she had him in her mouth and they couldn't get enough of each other and the rest had to wait till they were finished again.

Afterwards, they shared a cigarette. Stewart lay with his head back on his arm, watching the smoke rise and lose itself against the curlicued moldings of the ceiling; the two bodies, his hard, dark from the sun; hers white, and except for her fine breasts and womanly hips, slender as a boy's, reflected in the mirror. There was a distortion in the glass, so that in the mirror they looked like a single two-headed creature.

"Back there, at the Atlantis Club. Why did you decide to trust me?" he asked.

"What makes you think I trust you?" she said, stealing a puff from his cigarette before giving it back.

"For all you knew, I was the one who killed Cardenas. Doesn't that bother you?"

"Not really," she shrugged, getting up and pulling on a sheer silk robe. She sat on a chair and began to pull on her stockings, smoothing them up her legs with her fingers as though she were molding a vase on a potter's wheel. She looked even sexier with the stockings on than she did naked, uncrossing her legs so he would be sure to see the white skin between the garter snaps contrasted against the dark triangle between them.

"That's pretty cold," he said, watching her.

"Do you want me to lie? To say I was sorry to see Cardenas dead? God! People are such hypocrites." She came over and sat next to him on the bed. "The truth is that nothing quite matches the perverse pleasure we take in the misfortunes of people we don't like."

Stewart sat up. She reached over and plucking the cigarette from between his lips, took a drag.

"It's true, isn't it?" she said, looking at him from under those incredibly long eyelashes of hers. Stewart sat up in bed, crossing his arms over his chest.

"That explains Cardenas. What about you and Casaverde?"

Her face darkened and she looked away.

"I told you. We were lovers."

"When you were twelve, you said."

She nodded, still not looking at him. Stewart winced inwardly. The thought of her with someone like Casaverde was obscene enough. But at twelve! He took her hand.

"What happened? Did he force you?"

She looked at him strangely.

"No," she said softly. "It was a warm night. There was a meteor shower and I went down to the stables and took off my clothes. I stood naked in the moonlight, watching the stars fall. Casaverde had followed me there from the main *hacienda* and when he stepped out of the shadows, I could see him sticking out like a tent pole against the fabric of his trousers. I mounted my stallion, Chaco, and rode him without a saddle. We galloped across the Pampa like an arrow aimed at the moon, my hair flowing behind me in the wind, Chaco's warm sweaty horseflesh sliding between my naked thighs. I knew Casaverde was behind me on another horse and when we stopped, finally, I sat on Chaco, feeling him tremble as the stars fell, one after another, as though it was the last night of the world. Then Enrique grabbed me and pulled me down on the grass and got on top of me, there under the horses. There was no forcing," she said, looking at Stewart. "Why should there be? It was what I wanted."

"What about your parents? Did they know what was going on?"

She smiled again. That sad, ironic smile.

"My mother died when I was born. As for my father. . . ." she shrugged, as though anything she might say about him was of no importance. "I was raised by my grandfather."

"Well, surely he wouldn't have approved."

"On the contrary. He wanted me to seduce Enrique. It was his way of making sure that Casaverde was under his thumb," she said, freeing her hand from his and getting up. "Now, are you satisfied?"

Jesus! he thought. The water was getting deeper and murkier by the second. Something told him to get out while he still could. But watching that lovely troubled face, he knew he wouldn't.

"For now," he said.

"Well, and you should be," she laughed, suddenly flirtatious again, looking down at him, still naked.

He got up, pulled on his trousers and went to the window. He looked out at the Cemetery, at the imposing statues, the classic Greek mausoleums. The lavishness of the tombs was beyond any love or mourning, he thought. It was a kind of necrophilia. There was the rustle of silk as Julia came up behind him.

"Ahhh, the Recoleta," she murmured. "Our well-documented fascination with death." She rested her head on his shoulder. "It's the most expensive property in the country. We *porteños* have a saying: 'It is cheaper to live your whole life extravagantly than to be buried in the Recoleta.' "

"Do you have family buried there?"

"Of course. Correct social form is always a necessity. Even for the dead," she said, suddenly shuddering.

Stewart put his arms around her and held her.

"Why were you crying before?" he asked.

"Not love," she said fiercely, shaking her head. "We Argentines know how to love our country, but not each other."

The train came pushing a warm rush of wind ahead of it. The platform was crowded once more, but for Stewart there were only two men of interest. One was a thin man with fly-away straw-colored hair, a tweed jacket much too heavy for the climate, fawn-colored gloves and a polka-dot bow-tie in place of an old school tie. The second was a stocky man in a workman's cap and shirtsleeves, who carried a copy of *Das Innere Reich* folded under his arm. The straw-haired man looked neither right nor left as people surged onto the train. He marched in with the crowd and stood holding a strap, followed by the workman. If he had noticed either Stewart or the workman, he gave no sign. The doors began to close.

At the last moment, Stewart looked up guiltily, as if he had just realized that he was about to miss his train. He sprinted toward the doors, leaping at the opening. A seated woman with a deathgrip on a string bag full of vegetables and an Italian peasant's face, looked disgustedly at Stewart as he just managed to squeeze aboard. Stewart grabbed for a pole as the train lurched forward, smiling apologetically at the Italian woman for whatever his transgression had been. He glanced around quickly. The workman had found a seat. He had buried his face in his German paper, seemingly having no interest in anyone.

Stewart positioned himself so that he wasn't looking at either the straw-haired man or the workman, but could see their reflections in the windows against the darkness of the tunnel racing by. The passengers were rocked back and forth by the motion, like Jews praying, as the train rocketed on, electric bulbs on the tunnel walls shooting past the windows like flares. Stewart was worried about the workman, but the straw-haired man only stood there, ramrod-straight, refusing to acknowledge the existence of the crowd pressing around him. God bless the English, Stewart thought. In a way, they were like God. If they didn't exist, you would have to invent them.

At the stop before Palermo Park, the workman got off. The workman didn't look at anyone and Stewart breathed a little easier, until he noticed the Italian peasant woman staring at the straw-haired man. Oh shit, Stewart thought, already starting to choreograph what he would have to do in his mind. It would have to be fast, he decided, letting the deceleration pull him forward as the train slowed for the station. The doors opened and the straw-haired man surged out with the crowd. The Italian woman got up to follow. As she passed him, Stewart tripped her with his foot, sending her sprawling. As she fell, he grabbed at the string bag, which burst open, spilling the vegetables all over the floor of the car. Stewart knelt with his back to the open door, blocking her way out as he pretended to help her sit up.

"With permission. Let me help you, Señora," he said, as he tried to stuff the vegetables back into the bag, awkwardly dropping as many vegetables on the floor as he put back. She tried to shake him off.

"Let me up, *bruto!* What a barbarity!" she muttered, glaring up at him as she tried to get up.

"But gently, Señora. You've had a bad fall," Stewart said, smiling up at the people gathering around them. At the same

time, under the guise of helping her up, Stewart grabbed her
shoulder, holding her down as she tried to get to her feet.

"Take your hand off me, *cabrón! Asesino!* Leave me alone!
All of you!" she shouted, glaring around her.

There was a hiss of air. The doors were about to close.

"She's had a shock," Stewart explained, standing up. He
snapped his fingers as if he had just remembered something.
"I'll get help!" he declared, suddenly whirling and stepping
off the train. The Italian woman muttered something and
struggled to get up, but the doors were already closing. Stewart watched her shaking her fist at him through the window
as the train began to move. Stewart turned and walked to the
Salida and up the staircase to the street.

The straw-haired man was well ahead of him. In a way, that
was an advantage, because it gave Stewart the chance to do a
quick street sweep and check for tails without worrying that
someone might connect him with the straw-haired man. For
the moment, things looked all right. There was no guarantee
of that, of course. The Germans could have switched off, as
they did on the train, or they might be trying something so-
phisticated, like an eight-box, that would have been almost
impossible to spot, but nobody had unlimited resources and
even the Germans couldn't completely cover everyone who
worked at the British embassy. Still, they didn't have a huge
amount of time. The Italian woman would get off at the next
stop and get to a phone faster than you could say, "Jack Rob-
inson," Stewart thought, as he followed the straw-haired man
past the massive Spanish monument and into the park.

The paths in the park were wide and sunny. They led past
leafy glades and palm groves and miniature lakes, where fat
complacent ducks paddled around waiting for breadcrumbs.
In front of a small lake, there was an ice-cream vendor standing beside a statue of George Washington, of all people. The
sun was bright on the water and Stewart had to squint to look
toward the lake. George Washington didn't seem to mind,
though. Neither did the ice-cream vendor, who wore a
military-style cap like a Prussian general and stood with his
red cart in the sun, although there was a shaded bench near
by. The straw-haired man stopped and bought an Eskimo pie
from the vendor, who nodded toward a bower of white and
pink roses, not far from the statue. The bower was partially
surrounded by a high green hedge that screened it from the
path around the lake. Stewart walked around the bower from

the other side. The straw-haired man was sitting with his legs stiffly crossed, like someone at a party he didn't want to attend, on a wooden bench concealed in the bower. Stewart sat at the opposite end of the bench, as far away from the man as he could get.

"Pardon me," said the straw-haired man in English-accented Spanish. "What hour it is?"

"I'm afraid I left my watch at home," Stewart answered him in English.

"One is apt to do that when one is in a hurry," said the straw-haired man, following him into English.

"Unless the alarm clock rings twice."

The straw-haired man heaved a sigh.

"I hate all this cloak-and-dagger mumbo-jumbo. Bloody nuisance, if you ask me. Always makes me feel like a character in one of your American flicks. George Raft, perhaps. Or Humphrey Bogart. Only I could never manage all those 'dese,' 'dems' and 'doses,'" the straw-haired man said, squashing his nose to one side with his finger to exemplify his version of an American tough guy.

"That's funny," Stewart smiled. "I always thought of myself as more the Ronald Colman type."

"Too noble. That sort of thing went out with spats and salutes from chaps in open cockpit airplanes. By the way, I'm Fowler, if you need to put a name on me," the Englishman said, opening his newspaper, in case anyone were to look in.

"I'm Stewart."

Fowler nodded stiffly, pursing his lips. He moved carefully, like a man in a cast. His bottom barely rested on the bench. Stewart wondered privately how he ever took a crap.

"Indeed," Fowler said frostily. "Everyone is talking about you, Mister Stewart. Whether you know it or not, you're quite the *nouvelle sensation* here in B.A."

"So I understand," Stewart growled. "It's a little hard not to be, what with all the coverage on you embassy types."

"If you mean that Jerry on the 'Chapodyf,'" Fowler said, using the local term for the subway, "you needn't have worried. I had him spotted." He allowed himself a little inward smile. No doubt putting the bloody Colonials in their place, Stewart thought irritably.

"What about the Italian woman? Did you have her covered too?"

Fowler paled.

"What makes you think she. . . ." he sputtered.

Stewart grinned widely.

"I wasn't sure until just now. But you saw her even before you went down to the 'Chapodyf,' didn't you, pal?"

"Quite," Fowler muttered uncomfortably, looking around as though he expected to find the bushes populated with German spies. "Now that we both understand how difficult this is, perhaps you can tell me what we can do for you?"

Stewart shook his head.

"Not what you can do for me, Major, or Colonel, or whatever the hell your rank is. What I can do for you."

"I see," Fowler muttered, fishing in his pocket for a pack of Players. He offered one to Stewart, jerking his gloved hand quickly away to avoid touching him. They both lit up. "And why should we be the object of your largesse, if I may be so frank, Mister Stewart?"

"Be as frank as you like," Stewart grinned. "I like honesty. It saves time. Not much, but some. And like the girl under the streetlamp says, I didn't say I was giving it away."

Fowler looked at him as only an Englishman can, as though he had just swallowed something that he was going to have a hard time keeping down.

"What do you want, Stewart?"

He'd been demoted from "Mister," Stewart noticed. He held up his hand as if in surrender.

"Not money," he said. "A *quid pro quo*. Besides, for the time being, it's your war, not ours. It's the kind of thing that you need and, frankly, right now we can't touch."

Fowler looked at him as if trying to decide whether or not to take a chance. Stewart tried to look trustworthy.

"Before I look at the *quo*, Mister Stewart. What's the *quid*, as it were?"

Stewart raised his eyebrows. He'd been promoted again.

"The same thing you're getting from me. Information. Communications."

Fowler nodded thoughtfully.

"And I suppose the fact that the Huns are all over your Mister Hartman has nothing to do with any of this?"

"*Touché*," Stewart said, throwing up his hands in surrender. "Of course, if you're not interested. . . ."

"Now, now. Of course, we're interested," Fowler said, sighting along his cigarette before tapping the ash off with precision, as though he was practicing using a bomb-sight. "The code introduction you used threw poor Dickson in an absolute bloody panic. H.E. was all up in arms, too. We're suddenly discovering we need all the friends we can get, and no one wants to get on the wrong side of your Mister Donegan. And by the way, it's Commander, not Colonel," he confided.

"All right, Commander," Stewart said, beckoning the Englishman closer. "The fact is, if I went through channels I'm not sure whether the powers that be would let you have what I've got or not. Thing is, you guys are the ones fighting the krauts right now. Even if they wanted you to have it, I have a hunch that by the time you got it, it might be too late. As you already indicated, our own communications are less than wonderful. Besides, this is hot."

Fowler nodded, as if he were carefully filing away Stewart's reply for future reference. But he didn't lean closer. It was starting to get to Stewart. Then all at once, he understood.

"Tell me something, Fowler. How many times a day do you wash your hands?"

Fowler looked at him, horrified. A sickly grin broke across his face.

"Several times," he murmured.

"Yeah, I'll bet. All those nasty little germs, just waiting to get you."

Fowler looked green. He shrank away from Stewart.

"Don't talk about that. It's disgusting. This is a filthy place. You have no idea. Sometimes when the wind comes up it blows the water away from the beach and all you see are these disgusting mud flats. The whole bloody city stinks of it and people come and get their drinking water from the public fountains. You should see them. It's ghastly!" he shuddered.

"Germany's a clean country. Very neat and orderly," Stewart said carefully.

"A façade! Inside they're festering, simply festering," Fowler said, dismissing them with a gesture of his gloved hand. He leaned forward, confidingly for the first time. "Frankly, I think the Germans are bacteria invading the body of Europe. Think about it. Millions of faceless gray creatures. All identical, unthinking, pitiless. Some idiot yells "*Sieg heil!*" and their right hands shoot up as one, like robots. You can't talk about good or evil. Bacteria have no morality, no thought. Only this huge destructive mass moving from organ to organ.

The Rhineland, Austria, the Sudetenland, now Poland. Europe is old and diseased, dying really. We're witnessing its death-knell. It's the end of the world," he finished, his face white as a corpse's.

Stewart looked at him curiously.

"You've heard something, from the war. Something the papers don't know. What is it?"

Fowler looked startled. He started to pull back.

"Don't play games, Fowler. We're on the same side, even if we are just bloody Colonials!" Stewart growled belligerently.

At that, Fowler almost smiled. He nodded, almost unconsciously.

"Things are bloody awful. Argentina is hanging by a thread. We're denying it publicly, but the U-boats have already sunk over 150 of our naval and merchant ships. The Admiralty had assured the government that their Asdic system would deal with the U-boats, but no one's talking about how bloody Asdic is going to save us any more. The *Graf Spee* has virtually shut down shipping in the South Atlantic and the only hope we've got left is the French Army. Imagine! And there isn't anyone who believes they can last a fortnight against the Germans. At home, we have barely three weeks' supply of food. Less than that of iron ore," he concluded glumly.

For a moment, both men were silent.

"Now I understand something I didn't," Stewart said, shaking his head.

"Which is?"

"Why you risked meeting me even though my cover's been blown."

"And why is that, pray tell?"

"Because you're desperate. Grasping at straws, like the rest of us. And something else," Stewart smiled.

"Go on," Fowler said, looking like a superstitious man who is about to have his fortune told.

"Oh, just that there's a career to be made for someone who pulls something off in times like these. *Sir* Fowler," Stewart grinned suddenly.

Fowler smiled back, a conspirator's smile.

"You're an interesting man, Mister Stewart. And the name's Ian, actually," he said, leaning forward, although still careful not to get too close. He looked around anxiously. The park was quiet. They could hear the faint drone of bees in the rose trellis. "What have you got?"

"A message. No bigger than a pinhead. Looks like an ordinary 'period' at the end of a sentence. You'll need a microscope to read it."

"You're joking."

"Am I? In fact, it was the microscope on Cardenas's desk that first tipped me off."

Fowler peered at him, paling visibly.

"You're bloody serious, aren't you?"

"It's a message from Admiral Canaris to Arturo Vargas," Stewart said, pulling the letter out of his pocket.

"Canaris!" Fowler exclaimed. "And we know Vargas has sympathies. Where does he fit in?"

"Vargas is a conduit. The message is for Castillo. It says the German ambassador will be arriving December 17th for some kind of shindig for President Ortiz planned at Vargas's *estancia*. As you can see, the note was from Baron von Hulse on German embassy stationery," Stewart said, pointing out the dot as he handed it over.

"Is that it?" Fowler asked, holding the letter up to the light and squinting at the dot as if he could read it with the naked eye.

"That's it."

"Astonishing. Such a busy people, the Germans. Always so busy," Fowler said, shaking his head. "We'll have to analyze it, of course. What makes you think it's not a plant?"

"Uh-uh," Stewart said, shaking his head. "I got it out of Amadeo Cardenas's safe at the Atlantis Club. Someone killed him to get it. And the place was crawling with krauts. That's your knighthood you're holding."

Fowler looked at Stewart, his eyes alive with curiosity.

"For a newcomer, you do get around, Mister Stewart. And was it you who, um, shall we say, dealt with this Cardenas person?"

"No. I got rid of a few krauts who got in the way, but Cardenas was already dead when I got there," Stewart said. He didn't say anything about Julia. He wasn't sure why, but he felt almost proprietary about her. "Now it's your turn. What do you think?" he asked, indicating the letter.

"Sounds like Jerry might be planning a bit of a coup. Von Hulse, eh?" Fowler said, flicking his finger at the signature.

"Do you know him?"

"Mmm. He's Abwehr. One of Canaris's lot. A real bastard, though. Nasty piece of goods, even for a Nazi. It's the part

about the German ambassador arriving on the seventeenth
that I find so puzzling."

"Why is that?"

"Because, dear fellow," Fowler said, putting the letter down
for a second. "The German ambassador is already here. And
quite well established, I might add. He was at a dinner party
at the Casa Rosada hosted by Vice-President Castillo just the
other day. We stayed away, of course," he explained. "Naturally, we don't want to make things difficult for our hosts.
Fortunately, there are still a few beef barons who want to
maintain their British markets, otherwise we could've kissed
this continent goodbye already."

"Maybe Berlin is thinking of replacing the ambassador. Get
somebody more enthusiastic for the New Order?"

"Not bloody likely. Von Thermann has supported Hitler
since the beer hall days in Munich. Besides, if someone were
coming out to replace him, we'd have heard something. No,"
Fowler said, tapping the letter. "This is something else."

"An assassination?"

Fowler looked sharply at Stewart.

"Get rid of President Ortiz? There's a certain direct kind of
logic in that, I suppose. He is the major force in the government who supports us. Still. . . ." Fowler said doubtfully.

"What's the problem? Not quite cricket?"

Fowler reddened. His skin was very fair and it showed in
bright red spots on his cheeks like a Hals painting.

"That isn't what I meant. But you're right, it's not the kind
of thing we would do. Tell me," Fowler said, studying Stewart
carefully, "if you had the chance, would you assassinate Hitler? It would probably cost you your own life, of course."

"Sure. Why not?"

"Why? What's your reason?"

"I don't like his mustache."

"Jolly good," Fowler said, smiling in spite of himself, and
Stewart could see he was filing the response away to use on
someone else. "Mind you, it could backfire on them. Might
make Ortiz a martyr. Might not be the worst thing that could
happen," Fowler said, looking strangely at Stewart.

"Uh-uh," Stewart said, shaking his head. "They'd find a fall
guy to blame it on. They'd have to. Probably a Brit."

"Or an American."

"Or an American," Stewart agreed. "So who's Canaris sending to the party? This 'ambassador' in the message?"

"An assassin, perhaps? Or should I say a 'gunsel,' as you Yanks so colorfully put it?"

"Why bother?" Stewart shrugged. "There's got to be a million people in Argentina who wouldn't mind seeing Ortiz dead. Why not use local talent?"

"Why not, indeed?" Fowler muttered thoughtfully. "Well, we'll keep a watch out. Let you know what we come up with. We'll set up a dead drop," he said, getting up. He looked around to make sure he hadn't forgotten anything.

"Where?"

"Here should do nicely. Under this stone," Fowler said, poking a flat stone that formed a part of the border for the roses with the tip of his shoe. "By the way," Fowler said awkwardly. He stood there, rigid as ever, hands clasped in front of him as if he had been called into the headmaster's office. "It has nothing to do with anything really, but, well . . . Why are you still here, if you don't mind my asking? You've been blown since you got here. If we know you, you can bet the bloody Huns do too, so why risk it? I mean, they've shown they don't mind getting rid of anyone who's in their way."

Fowler stood there, hatless, head tilted slightly to one side, the perfect civil servant for whom germs and foreigners were equally abhorrent, waiting for an answer. Maybe that's why he had come, Stewart thought. Because that's what he really wanted to know. Maybe he believed that if he could understand why Stewart was there, he would find a reason for himself too.

"I had to. There was no one else," Stewart said. Fowler nodded and turned to go. "One more thing. Did you know Raoul de Almayo? The one who was murdered?"

Fowler turned back. He hesitated for a moment before answering. His face was red, perspiring. With his fair skin and heavy tweed jacket, he looked like a candidate for heat stroke.

"Only vaguely. He ran in some very *distinguado* company. The de Castros, the Herrera-Blancas, the Vargases. The wives, especially. He was, you know, what they call a 'butterfly' down here?"

"The husbands didn't mind?"

"Actually, having a house queer around can be awfully useful in certain social situations. Especially with a husband too busy or indifferent," he said with a certain satisfaction. "Try Athena de Castro. Or, if you can get to her, Julia Vargas. The notorious Julia!" he grinned.

Stewart froze, but Fowler didn't seem to notice. Suddenly his expression changed, softened. "One odd thing about her, though."

"What's that?"

"Well, as you may know, her husband is said to be rabidly pro-Axis, but she herself is English. Or at least her grandfather was. Chap by the name of John Gideon, I believe."

"What about him?"

"Don't know that much, really. Just that he was English. Still," Fowler shrugged. "He's long dead, so I don't suppose that matters any more. If we find out any more about who the Germans are bringing in on December 17th, we'll let you know. Check the drop. In the meantime, I'd bloody watch my back if I were you. Argentina can be a very dangerous place," a shudder crossing his features. "One mustn't confuse hospitality with friendship."

"Are you trying to tell me to watch out for my own embassy. For Hartman? Is that it?" Stewart asked sharply.

"I'm not implying anything at all, dear fellow. But you've done us a good turn," Fowler said, flicking invisible specks of dust off his gloves. "I'd like to reciprocate." He looked around nervously. Stewart stepped a little closer. Fowler covered his mouth and nose with his gloved hand, but let Stewart come nearer. "I have to confess. We'd already heard—never mind how, although you can guess that we pay a fair amount of *coima* to more than one Argentine official—that Cardenas was dead. For some reason, that's got the Jerries stirred up like a hornet's nest. Now I think I know why," he added, tapping his jacket pocket where he'd put the letter. "Just be careful. Very careful."

"You haven't answered me about Hartman. Do you think he's keeping something back?"

"I don't know," Fowler shrugged. "I suppose. Everyone does, don't they? You might say it's the nature of our peculiar craft. No, it's just . . ." he hesitated.

"Look, Commander. Let's forget all the 'jolly good show' crap. If you've got a bitch, let's have it. I've got my own opinions about Hartman. But he's no goddamn traitor."

"No, of course not. It's just . . . He's worse than a traitor!" Fowler burst out. His expression was venomous, and Stewart had the feeling he was glimpsing the real man for the first time. "He's a rank bloody amateur! The Germans are all over him. Everyone knows about his connection to Fuentes. You put a hobble on him or he'll get us all bloody killed!"

Stewart crushed out the cigarette on the bench and field-stripped it. He took his time, waiting until he had finished before he spoke.

"Sounds like you think it's more than incompetence," Stewart began mildly. "Almost as if he's being used for a stooge. . . ."

"Or, how did you put it before? A 'fall guy?' "

The two men stared at each other.

"Shit," Stewart breathed. "If an American embassy official gets blamed for Ortiz's assassination . . . I've got to get him out of Argentina. Now!"

Stewart stood up, feeling for the Colt under his jacket. He started to leave.

"Wait! Please!" Fowler called after him.

"What is it?" Stewart said, turning back for a second.

"Maybe it isn't Hartman who's being set up. Maybe it's someone else."

"Have you got a better candidate?"

Fowler stepped forward. His face was slick with sweat, but his eyes were blue and clear.

"Frankly, Mister Stewart, it could be you."

SHE WAS waiting for him on the Costanera Drive near the amusement park. The sun was low over the city and the air smelled of grilled meat from the little carts, called *carritos*, on the promenade along the river. The electric lights outlining the power plant twinkled like Christmas lights; the offshore breeze was warm and mild. The amusement park hadn't opened yet for the evening and the Ferris wheel loomed finely traced and shadowy, an angular spider's web against a tangerine sky. The sounds of radio music came from a *whiskería* across from the promenade. Through the open door, Stewart could see workmen from the power plant crowded around the bar, their faces dark and grimy with coal dust, their eyes outlined white from where they had worn goggles, like minstrels in blackface.

A fence around a construction site was plastered with posters from the CGT. Someone, using a crude brush, had painted red hammers and sickles across all of the posters and if you didn't already know it was a working-class neighborhood, the posters would have told you, Stewart thought, crossing the street.

She didn't see him until he was almost upon her. She looked older than she had the previous night at the Atlantis Club. She had crows'-feet around her eyes under the heavy make-up and in them the fear that she was starting to lose the war every woman fights against time. Her blonde hair shone like a helmet in the setting sun and like last night, she was dressed too young for her age in a tight flowered dress with a plunging neckline. Her body was still good, though. Damned good, Stewart thought. He wondered what her husband's problem was.

"I'm glad you called," Athena de Castro said, taking his arm. The way she did it wasn't sexual. They weren't a couple; it was just for walking.

They strolled along the promenade overlooking the river. Traffic was heavy on the Costanera, headlights coming on as the home-bound rush began. Along the river, barges piled high with coal were moored near the powerplant and out toward the horizon they could see the lights of a freighter, anchored against the tide.

"How about a drink?" Stewart suggested.

"God, yes! But it has to be someplace where no one will see us."

"What about over there?" he said, indicating a *cantina* across the way. It was a shabby-looking place with a couple of empty wooden tables outside, next to a small marketplace. The market stalls were already lit with kerosene lanterns and shoppers were silhouettes against the light as they made last-minute purchases before heading home.

"All right," she said, looking around nervously. They crossed the street and went inside. They sat down at a corner table. A fat man came out from behind the bar, wiping his hands on an apron stretched tight over his belly. The apron was badly stained; it smelled like it had been washed in beer.

"The Señor wishes?" the man asked.

Stewart gestured toward Athena, fishing in her purse for a cigarette.

"I'll have a *clarito*," she said, leaning forward for Stewart to light her cigarette.

"We don't have the 'cocktails' here, Señora," the man said, looking down at Athena. He took his time in doing it, and Stewart wondered if coming here hadn't been a mistake.

The *cantina* was small and dimly lit. About half the tables were occupied; dock workers, mostly, Stewart guessed. Bulky, close-faced men who wore their caps indoors and who knew how to size up strangers without being too obvious about it. One thing at least, Stewart thought. They wouldn't run into anyone she knew down here.

"What do you have?" Stewart asked the man.

"*Cana.*"

"All right. Two *canas*."

The man brought two glasses of clear liquor brimming to the rim and set them on the table without spilling a drop. At the other tables, the dock workers had gone back to their conversations. Now and again, one or another of them would glance over at Stewart's table, but that was all. One of the workers, a man with a red bandana around his neck, said something about the FORJA party and another shushed him, glaring around suspiciously. More politics, Stewart thought to himself. This country is a lunatic asylum of politics. They like it better even than sex or football.

"*Salud*," Athena said, raising her glass. She drank as if she needed it, shuddering as she swallowed. Stewart raised his glass back at her and drank, feeling it burn all the way down. The liquor couldn't, he decided, have been more than a couple of days old. Even as he swallowed, he could feel it already working on the lining of his stomach.

"About last night. I wanted to apologize. Ricardo shouldn't drink," she said, making a face.

"What's his problem? Another woman?"

"Not at all," she said, coloring slightly. "It's just that he drinks too much and then he gambles. Sometimes more than we can afford. I try to stop him, so naturally I'm the villain."

"I thought you all had plenty of money."

"Not everyone," she said, shaking her head. "The de Castros have more name than money. Not like the Herrera-Blancas, or the Vargases. Did you know Julia is a Montoya, as well as being John Gideon's only grandchild? You don't know what this means in Argentina."

"Sounds like she has a few pesos," Stewart said slowly.

"Beyond imagining," she said, her eyes gleaming.

Was that her Jerusalem? Stewart wondered, remembering that same gleam in his father's eyes when he had once introduced him to one of the Rockefeller boys.

"Is that why you let her use your apartment in the Recoleta? Think maybe some of it'll rub off?"

There was a sudden intake of air. She sat rigidly in her chair, her cheeks bright red.

"I thought you were a 'gentleman.' Julia said. . . ." she started, then changed her mind. "I thought you wanted the truth."

"Whose truth? Which side are you on?"

"I don't know what you mean," she said, fumbling with her cigarette.

"Yes. You do."

She didn't say anything. She nervously tapped her cigarette in the ashtray as though she were sending a message in Morse.

"Why did you agree to see me?" he said finally.

"To explain about Ricardo, about last night."

"*Eso es?*" he shrugged. "Just for that? Just to tell me you keep an apartment for *cinq à septs* because your husband has bad manners when he drinks?"

She looked around at the *cantina*, slightly dazed, as if wondering how she had got here. Her hands dropped to the table and as she did so, the small gold cross around her neck slid deeper into the valley between her breasts. When she looked up, her eyes were bleak with suffering, an aging Catholic princess who had lost her way.

"My God, you *yanquis* are quick to judge, aren't you? What do you know about us?"

"Only what you tell me."

"There are things. . . ." she began. "Ricardo is not a bad man; it's only. . . ."

He watched her grope toward telling him, hesitating midway like a tightrope-walker balanced over an abyss.

"I know. Sometimes it's families that marry, not people," he said, covering her hand with his. She let him, and he knew that he could sleep with her if he wanted.

"You should have seen Ricardo when we got married. He was so handsome," she said, her voice warm with the memory.

"He was handsome last night. You were both handsome. This is a handsome country."

"That is our charm, no? To be handsome liars. Do you know the saying, 'Better a good lie than a bad truth?' That is a saying we have," she said, a sad smile on her face.

"*Digame,*" he said, patting her hand. "Why was your husband so angry with you last night? I saw it when we met. Anyone could see it. Why? Because of your lover, your 'schoolboy?' "

"I don't know," she said, shaking her head. "Truly. There's no reason. Maybe he hates women. Sometimes I think you men all hate women. Why? What terrible thing have we ever done to you? What?" she beseeched him, looking at him as though he could really tell her.

"Maybe he's old-fashioned when it comes to adultery."

"What? Ricardo?" she said, almost triumphantly. "You don't know him. That means nothing. Nothing!"

She picked up her drink, the surface of the liquor trembling in her hand. When she saw where he was looking, she put the glass back down on the table.

"This is an interesting *cantina,*" she said, glancing around. "I've never been in a place like this. Have you ever been here before?"

Stewart reached into his pocket. He pulled out a crumpled Chesterfield. He smoothed the cigarette out and lit it.

"Why does your husband hate you, Dona Athena? What have you done?" he asked softly.

"He blames me for Raoul's death," she blurted out suddenly. "Because I gave him the pistol!"

She looked better after she finished her drink and repaired her make-up. The barman brought another round and they took their time with this one. The sun was going down, and through the open doorway they could see the sky over the river streaked with red. Lights were going on along the promenade where they were setting up for outdoor dancing.

"That's why I wanted to see you," she told him. "Not just because of the apartment, or the way Ricardo behaved last night. Cardenas lied to you. Raoul de Almayo had been to the Atlantis many times. With us and also with Julia. Raoul was foolish with his gambling. He owed Cardenas money."

"You think Cardenas had something to do with his death?"

She nodded emphatically.

"Why else would he lie?"

"What makes you so sure?"

"It's not just the lies," she said. "Or that Raoul owed Cardenas money. There's something else. Arturo Vargas owns the Atlantis. It came to him from Julia when they married."

"*Qué va?* Of what importance is that?"

"It is of much importance," she said. "Most especially to the Fascists. As you saw last night, Arturo is very close to Minister Casaverde. Also to that German, von Hulse."

"What about von Hulse?"

"The night he died, Raoul was running away from the Germans. I was with Julio," she colored slightly. "We were at the Del Rio. A tango palace in the Boca," she shivered suddenly. "Raoul was terrified. He didn't have a gun, so I lent him mine. Why was that so terrible? Why?" she appealed to him, her lower lip trembling like a child's.

Stewart felt something like a cold wind on his spine.

"You saw him? You spoke to him that night?"

She shook her head.

"Only for a moment. Ceci Braga spoke to him. She's the *propietaria*. She came and asked to borrow my gun. Much good it did him," she said, finishing her drink and picking up her handbag as a sign she wanted to leave. She wet her lips nervously. "I have to go," she said getting up.

"I appreciate your coming," Stewart said, looking around carefully. The barman was behind the bar by the radio, listening to the *futbol* scores.

"For nothing," she shrugged, starting to go, then stopped. "Listen. If you want to know about Raoul that night, talk to Ceci."

Stewart nodded that he would, but she had already turned to go. He watched her walk out of the *cantina*, her silhouette framed in the doorway against the purple sky. For an instant, he caught a glimpse of what she must have been like once, young and slender and he watched her disappear from view with a curious sense of loss. He turned and motioned to the barman for another drink.

Hartman was missing. The panic in the official's voice when Stewart had tried to phone him at the American embassy had been unmistakable. They were spooked, all right. So unless this Ceci Braga that Athena had mentioned, had a lead, it was already too late, Stewart thought in the taxi over to La Boca.

He had the driver drop him off at the corner of Avenida Pedro de Mendoza and walked the rest of the way. It was an Italian neighborhood. The signs on the shops were all in Italian and the windows of the *tiendas* were strung with sausages and strands of garlic. The night was warm and neighborhood toughs stood outside a *bodega*, talking louder than they had to and forcing people to step off the sidewalk to get around them. As Stewart walked, he had the feeling of being watched, but it didn't mean anything. It was the kind of neighborhood where outsiders were always watched.

When he came to the Palacio del Rio, the door was locked. He looked up at the second floor, but the windows were dark. A vendor with a *carrita*, smoke rising from the coals, watched him silently from the gutter. Stewart knocked on the door. There was no answer. He knocked again, harder.

"Too early! Come back in the *tarde!*" a voice shouted from behind the door. *Tarde* was afternoon, which in Buenos Aires meant not merely after lunch, or after dark, but any time up to midnight. Stewart kept pounding on the door with the side of his fist.

"*Caramba!* Do you want to destroy the world?" the voice grumbled, opening the door a crack. It was dark behind the door and Stewart could see only an eye peering out, somewhere around the level of his belt. He passed it a ten-peso bill and the crack widened. "*Lo siento*, Señor. We are closed until ten. Better for you to come back then. Better tangos. Many pretty ladies," said the *portero*, a dwarf with flat Indian features, a misshapen nose and a pronounced hump that thrust his head forward like a battering ram. Stewart was surprised. Argentina was a white country; traces of Indian blood were rare.

"I'm searching for the Señorita Braga. I'm told she is the *proprietaria,*" Stewart said.

The dwarf squinted suspiciously up at him.

"The Señorita Braga never comes here. What do you want with her?"

"To talk only. I'm a friend of Dona Athena de Castro. I approach the Señorita Braga only at her suggestion."

The dwarf looked at Stewart curiously, his head tilted to one side at an odd angle to accommodate the hump.

"Hey, pal, you an American?" he asked in English.

"Sure," Stewart replied in English, sensing the way in.

"That's what I thought. On account of the accent," the dwarf said happily. "I been all over America."

"No kidding."

"Oh yeah. You name it, I been there. Santa Anita. Saratoga. Hialeah. Churchill Downs, even. The whole friggin' country. I'm a jock," he explained. Then his face changed. "Well, I used to be."

He looked at Stewart as if making up his mind about something. Stewart stood there, trying to look like an American flag.

"Hey, you want a drink? I got some of the real stuff upstairs. Jack Daniels, straight from Kentucky."

"Why not?" Stewart said.

He followed the little man up a dim carpeted stairway to a narrow door off a huge darkened ballroom.

"It's like I said. The place don't even open till around ten, ten-thirty, and nobody will show till after eleven," the dwarf explained, opening the door with a key. Inside was a tiny windowless room, barely large enough for a small cot and night table. The cot was unmade; the room smelled of unwashed laundry. Stewart sat on the cot while the dwarf poured the bourbon into two grimy glasses. The walls were covered with nude pin-ups cut from Spanish magazines and yellowing newspaper photos of horses and jockeys and owners smiling in the winner's circle. The dwarf noticed him looking around at the pictures.

"My art collection," the dwarf grinned. "That was me," he added, thumbing at the racing photos. "I'm Tino Valtoreno. They used to call me 'Valentino,' on account of I'm so good-looking," he winked, mugging broadly so Stewart would know he was kidding. "Maybe you heard of me?"

"Sorry," Stewart said.

The dwarf's face fell momentarily, but he recovered quickly.

"Yeah, well. If you followed the ponies back in the twenties, you'd've heard of me," the little man shrugged. "Hey, remember Texas Guinan? 'Hello, suckers!' Jeez, she was a hell of a dame, wasn't she?" he toasted and drank.

"Happy days," Stewart toasted back.

"I'm surprised you never heard of me," Tino said, making an odd, futile gesture at the photos on the wall. "I was pretty big there for a while. In only my rookie year, I came in second in the Preakness and it took a horse by the name of Man O' War and a jock named Clarence Kummer to do it! Those were the days, huh?" he said heartily, slapping Stewart's knee.

Stewart took another sip. It was strange sitting there in that tiny room pretending it was the Biltmore bar. The dwarf drank his drink like water and poured himself a refill.

"Yeah, I knew them all. Kummer, Eddie Ambrose, Georgie Wolff, Earl Sande," Tino reminisced. "You know what was the best part?"

"No, what?"

"The early morning workouts. Most jocks used to hate it. Having to get up so early, when it's still dark. Hung over, most of 'em. Some dumb bimbo in the trailer and freezing your ass off outside. But I'm from down south, see? Around Patagonia. So the cold never bothered me much. It was kind of nice, you know? Dew all white on the grass, the horses snorting and smoke coming out of their nostrils on account of the cold and everything real quiet, except for somebody cracking wise, a dirty joke maybe, or the sound of the horses' hooves galloping on the damp turf. It's funny. You'd think it'd be the winner's circle you'd miss, wouldn't you?"

"I guess."

"Sure. You know how it is. Everybody applauding, champagne flowing and the dames all around. Well, I guess it don't make no difference how many times you win, huh?"

"What do you mean?"

"In the end, everybody loses, don't they? The Yanks got rid of Babe Ruth, even," the little man said, drinking.

"How come you quit?"

"They got my hands," Tino said, holding them up like a surgeon. His hands were appalling, the fingers all twisted and bent at odd angles like twigs on a branch. Stewart tried to look away, but there was nowhere else to look.

"Who did it?"

"Some guys," Tino shrugged. "I was supposed to lose a

race, but the horse didn't know that. Goddamn horse," he said, almost smiling. "A filly. I couldn't hold her back, she was that good. I tried, but in the stretch, the crowd screaming their heads off and everything and her damn near pulling my arms out of their sockets and I thought, 'What the hell?' I wasn't too worried. There's always guys like that around a track. I figured I could square it. But they told me it was a matter of 'principle.' Then they busted every bone in my hands. Every one. That's a helluva thing, that 'principle,'" the little man said.

"Why'd you come back to Argentina?"

"Had to," he shrugged. "They came to see me in the hospital. Same guys. They had a big bunch of lilies they dumped on my bed. Said if they ever saw me again, the next bunch was for my funeral. Only this country's no good," he said, making a face.

"How come?"

"Nothing works! The electricity doesn't work. The money's no good. Even the fucking toilets don't work! You can't mail a lousy letter without you got to bribe the *cabrón* mailman and if they ever had an honest election the whole country'd drop dead from the shock! But talking to these people," he said, shaking his head. "They don't know nothing about America, about how things are supposed to be. Am I right, or am I right?"

"Sure," Stewart nodded, watching him. "When did you leave?"

"Back in '29. It's been ten years. Even my English is getting rusty."

"The Depression changed things, you know?"

"Yeah, I heard," Tino frowned, obviously unconvinced, his eyes still shining with the vision of an America of gleaming plumbing, flappers doing the Black Bottom and the steaming breath of horses on cold mornings. "If you ask me, the whole goddamn world's going down the toilet." He picked up the bottle and topped off their glasses. "Listen," he confided, leaning forward. His words were beginning to slur from the bourbon. "What do you want with Ceci?" he asked, pronouncing it "Sheshi." "I mean, just cause you and me are both *gringos*, like, don't mean shinola. I don't want nobody fucking with her. She gave me a place when nobody would give me pennies for my eyes."

"I just want to ask her a couple of questions."

"What about?" Tino responded, belligerence starting to come back into his voice.

"Raoul de Almayo. I understand she saw him the night he died."

"She had nothing to do with that! *Nada*, understand?"

"I never said she did. I was just hoping she could help me," Stewart said carefully.

"You cops," Tino said in an aggrieved tone, not stopping to reason that even if Stewart had been a cop, he couldn't possibly have any jurisdiction in Argentina. "Just cause Ceci's that way, you know," tilting his hand up and down like a seabird in flight, "you think she's got the scam on every fag and Lesbo in Latin America."

"Does she?"

"Well, what if she is a dyke? So what?" the dwarf demanded truculently. "I've know guys'd screw their own grandmothers."

"I'm trying to help. The Nazis killed Raoul. They might be after Ceci too."

Tino looked up at Stewart. He held his glass between his misshapen hands as though it was something priceless and very fragile.

"Nazis, huh? That's just another kind of gangster, ain't they?"

Stewart didn't say anything. He let the little man work it out on his own.

"Listen. About Ceci," Tino went on. "Is this the straight skinny? 'Cause if it ain't. . . ." he muttered darkly.

"Where is she?"

The dwarf's shoulders suddenly sagged.

"Well, you'd find out anyway. It's no secret. She's got a place just off the Caminito, not far from here." He told Stewart the address.

"Is she there now?"

"Probably," Tino shrugged. He got up and walked Stewart to the door. "Listen. Ceci's okay, you know? Don't hurt her."

"I mean her no harm, I swear," Stewart said.

"That's the trouble. It's always the ones who don't mean it personal, who do us the worst," the little man said, opening the door.

*   *   *

"Of course the Germans killed Raoul," Ceci Braga said, letting the smoke from her long-stemmed hashish pipe seep from between her lips like steam rising from a pot lid. She had a whiskey voice. Low and hoarse, and in an oddly appealing way it suited her. "I told the police that weeks ago. But then one of them, a curly-haired man, told me no. That it was something else. That Raoul owed money to the Jews. Some such imbecility," she shrugged.

She was reclining on a divan in her living room. She had Oriental tastes. Persian rugs, a brass-topped table on which she had set out sherry for them both, Chinoiserie on an ivory-inlaid sideboard. Moorish drapes and arches framed the doorways and windows and embroidered Moroccan cushions were scattered around the apartment. The curtains were open, revealing the lights of the tenement building across the street. There was dirt on the windows. They looked as though they hadn't been opened in years. There was a hot-house quality to the room, perfumed with incense and the smell of hashish. Ceci was small, petite even, and yet, despite her mannish garb—she wore suspenders over a starched white shirt and dark pleated trousers—and short, slicked-back hair, there was still something feminine about her, Stewart thought.

"Athena told me that her husband blames her for Raoul's death," Stewart said.

"Why? Because of the pistol. *Qué estupidez!*" she said, waving the idea away like smoke from her pipe. "Why not blame the Germans? Or the Jews like the idiot police? Or me? I gave Raoul the gun, poor fool. Although at least I understand why Don Ricardo blames Athena and not me."

"Why is that?"

"Because," she pronounced, as though she was chiseling the words into the air, "what man would choose to blame something on a stranger when he's got a wife?"

She said it for effect, her hands held just so. Stewart watched the way she held her hands, the nails clipped short and like a man, but with an unconscious grace that didn't belong to a man. She's trapped, Stewart thought. Lost in a sexual no-man's-land, somewhere between the male and female front lines.

"Is that pure cynicism, or do you really mean it?" he asked.

She paused, putting her pipe down for a moment.

"Do you know? I'm not really sure myself," she said, and

they both laughed. Stewart leaned back, smiling, watching the blue haze of the hashish smoke forming around the lamp.

"So you think Don Ricardo was looking for an excuse to hurt Athena?" he asked. "Why? Because of her lovers?"

Ceci half-smiled. She took another puff from her pipe.

"Athena didn't know how lucky she was," she said. "She had a lover too young to make demands, a *mari complaisant* and a *distinguido* address in San Isidro. What more could any woman want? Naturally, she was miserable."

"Why miserable?"

"Ah, Señor, you don't know women. You can love a woman, or hate a woman, but God help you if you ignore her."

"You mean the way you are ignoring my question, Señorita Braga," Stewart smiled. "It seems silly. Why would Ricardo de Castro be so *perturbado* over Raoul's death?"

"*Quien sabe?*" she shrugged. "The human heart is a foreign country; its laws are different from ours."

"I don't understand."

"Listen, *hombre*, do you see that apartment? That one over there?" she said seriously, pointing with the long stem of the hashish pipe at a lighted third-floor window across the street. "A shoemaker and his family lived there. He was a quiet man, never bothered anyone. He had three children, all girls. I remember his wife used to make the sign of the evil eye at me," she said, showing him the two-fingered sign, pinkie and index fingers extended like horns. "You see, there is a pecking order in everything, even perversity," she said enigmatically. "One day, this shoemaker, a quiet man who had never even raised his voice to anyone, came home and without a word began tossing his children out that very window to their deaths, one by one. I remember the last one, she was the oldest, a shy, awkward girl with big eyes—they said she wanted to become a nun—clinging desperately to the balcony railing. I watched her from here. It all happened so fast, there was nothing anyone could do. She was screaming 'Papa, papa,' while he went back for his cobbler's hammer. 'Papa! Papa!' as he hammered her fingers till she let go. Afterwards, the only thing he said was, 'Crocodile shoes.'

"You see," she explained, tracing a thin line of smoke in the air with her pipe, "there was a fashion then for women's crocodile shoes. It seems this shoemaker hated the smell of the *cocodrilo* skin on his hands. In short, Señor I do not know why

Don Ricardo de Castro is so disturbed over Raoul's death."

For a long moment, neither of them spoke. Somewhere in the apartment a clock chimed the hour. Ten o'clock, Stewart thought. Dinner time in Buenos Aires. Outside, there was a sudden roar from a motorcycle accelerating down the street.

"That's very convincing, Señorita Braga," Stewart said, pulling his cigarettes from a pocket and lighting one up. "Why don't I believe you?"

She darted a glance at the foyer. Stewart caught it. He had seen a copy of the *Prensa* folded on a marble-topped console table when he had first come in. So she knew about Cardenas's death. When she looked back at him, she licked her lips. The way she did it, if he hadn't known about her, he might have thought it was sexual.

"You know, Señor Stewart, you are a most handsome man. Those gray eyes, I think, especially. If I were not otherwise inclined. . . ." she smiled. "But then, I think you have had many women, yes?"

Stewart smoked his cigarette. Jesus, he thought. She was flirting with him!

"I'm not a virgin, if that's what you mean," he shrugged.

"Don't be absurd!" she said, eyes flashing. They were enlarged by the hashish, dark and translucent. "Sex is easy. The difficult decision for a woman is not whether to have sex, but whether a man is worth her passion. Whether, in fact, he is fooling her, or himself, when he talks about love." She drew herself up, the hashish pipe in her hand like a dagger. "And before I answer any more questions, Señor, I wish to know why you have such interest in what happened to Raoul?"

Stewart leaned forward, his forearms on his knees. It was time to drop his trousers ("*die Hosen herunterlassen*," the Germans called this moment in the espionage business) and show what he had. It was a bad moment, because apart from his gut feelings about her, he had no way of knowing if she wouldn't take everything he said right back to the Nazis. He reached for the sherry and took a polite, guarded sip.

"*Muy bien*," he said slowly. "All right. Raoul was a courier. That's why the Nazis killed him. The information he was carrying came from Amadeo Cardenas. The Germans got Raoul, and now Cardenas, too. It's in the paper," he said nodding toward the foyer. "What I don't know is who Cardenas's source was. And I've got to find him before the Nazis do, or they'll kill him too. And maybe take Argentina with him, if anybody cares."

"Everyone cares," she said softly.

"It nags at me, like a pebble in a shoe," he said. "Why does Ricardo de Castro take the death of Raoul so hard? Was he the source? Is that what Athena was hiding?" His eyes burned into her. "You know. I can see you know. It wasn't her affairs. Ricardo didn't care—what was it you said? A *mari complisant?* So what does Ricardo care about? Why is he so angry?" he demanded.

"Because," she said, biting her lip. "Athena didn't love Raoul. Ricardo did!"

They sat across from each other; she on the divan, Stewart back in his chair. She had laid the pipe on the table and they sipped their sherries in silence.

"Quite a little social circle, this *haut monde Argentine,*" Stewart murmured. He looked over at her. "You're sure about Ricardo and Raoul?"

She nodded once. No hesitation, he noticed. A soldier of the heart.

"Once I went over to see Athena at their villa in San Isidro. She wasn't home and I was about to leave when I heard a noise from the study. I assumed it was her and opened the door. Raoul was bent over the sofa, his trousers and shorts down around his ankles. Ricardo was behind him. He was plunging into Raoul, his face red as a beet, grunting and sweating like a pig. I closed the door and left. I don't think they saw me."

"Now I understand about the schoolboy. Poor Athena," Stewart muttered. He looked at her. "What do you think? Could Ricardo be the source?"

"That's absurd!"

"Is it? Two *maricons* together. One day one of them says something. . . ."

"Sweet Jesus God, I'm glad I am not a *yanqui!*" she snapped, her face darkening. "You know everything and understand nothing! This is a man's country, *comprende?* Have you ever heard of *machismo?* Of what it means to be a man here? It is difficult enough for *me* here, but for a man in Ricardo de Castro's position. . . ." She stared at him. "Don't you understand, *hombre*, that there are deeper secrets in this world than those sought out by spies?"

"All right," Stewart said. "All right." He stared through the window to the balcony railing across the way from which the girl had hung while her father hammered her fingers. She had wanted to be a nun, he thought. She'd had two fathers, one in heaven, one on earth, and they'd both betrayed her. And the Nazis were winning the war. You better not push that kind of thinking too far, he told himself.

He looked across the table at Ceci. She was the epitome of not-belonging: an attractive almost-boy with breasts. He passed her a cigarette, lighting it from his. She puffed at it expertly, holding it between her fingers like a man.

"Besides," she said finally, "Ricardo has no connection to the Germans, except maybe through the Vargases. And even if he did," she paused to pick a shred of tobacco from her lip, "Ricardo works as a manager for the Great Southern Railway. It's an English company," she shrugged. "Why would he need Raoul as a courier to pass information to the *Ingleses?* He could do it at work."

"You're good," Stewart said, grinning suddenly. "Maybe you should be doing this instead of me."

"No," she said, shuddering. She put down her drink. The glass was crystal and it tinkled like a bell as it grazed the edge of the cut-glass ashtray. "That one night with the Germans and Raoul was enough for me." She looked at him thoughtfully. "What will you do now?"

"Don't know. It's a dead end."

She looked at her watch and stood up.

"I have to get dressed," she said. "We open in an hour. The tango never ends," she said, walking around the room, straightening up. She moved with a kind of elfin grace, and there was something heartbreaking to him about the idea that she would never share that grace with a man. All at once she stopped and looked straight at him.

"You said Raoul worked for Cardenas and that the Germans got him too. Is that right?"

"More or less," he said.

"So is that where the path, how do you say, comes to the *callejon* without exit?"

"Almost," he nodded. "There is one more person. The most incredible woman I've—" He stopped suddenly.

Her face had gone white. She could have been a corpse, except for her eyes, dark and full of pain.

"Julia!" she gasped. "It's Julia!"

He got up and grabbed her by the shoulders.

"What about Julia?" he demanded.

A cry broke from her; an animal sound. She collapsed back on the divan, doubled over as if in pain, her arms across her stomach. He tried to get her to look at him, but she turned her face away.

"What do you know about Julia?" he shouted, shaking her. She grabbed the lapels of his jacket as though she were drowning.

"Have you seen her?" she asked in a small voice. He knelt beside her, his hand on her arm.

"Tell me about Julia, Ceci."

She looked at him, defeat in her eyes like a drooping banner.

"Have you made love to her yet?" she whispered.

Yet, he thought. The word was sharp as a knife.

"I don't understand," he said softly. "You and Julia . . . the two of you. . . ." In his mind he was seeing the two of them in Athena's apartment, the sun streaming through the window on two naked bodies intertwined on the bed, moving and murmuring, nipple touching nipple, one woman short-haired, sleek as an otter, the other with long raven-dark hair spread on the pillow. But he couldn't picture Julia's face in the scene. He just couldn't. "How long have you two. . . ." he said, then stopped.

"It doesn't matter," she whispered, wincing as though she was physically tearing the words out of her heart. "Buenos Aires is littered with the bodies of Julia's former lovers. All of us left lying there, gasping like fish flung on a dock."

"It's not possible," Stewart said, then remembered Julia and Casaverde in that dark room in the Atlantis Club, Casaverde saying to her, "You're hardly in a position to make moral judgments, my dear." Stewart looked at Ceci and knew that it was true.

"You don't know her. Not really," she said, a note of pride in her voice. That's her triumph, he told himself. Her consolation. But what about Julia? Did anyone know her, really? Maybe there was nothing to know. Maybe Julia was a mirror in which everyone saw only what they wanted to see, he thought, and suddenly the pieces fell into place.

"Vargas's wife. The source?" he wondered aloud.

"No," Ceci shook her head. "Not Vargas's wife. Gideon's granddaughter."

He grabbed her arm again.

"What are you talking about?"

"About her grandfather, John Gideon."

"What about him? I thought he was dead."

"And what difference does that make?" she said fiercely, wrenching her arm away. "She's Gideon's granddaughter! That's who she is! That's what Argentina is!"

"This is crazy," Stewart said, standing up. The lamp cast his shadow across the room. Ceci sat in his shadow. "You're saying all of this has something to do with someone who's been dead for God knows how many years?"

"You're not an Argentine. You don't understand." Ceci's voice was hollow and full of truth, the way a woman's voice gets sometimes after sex. "You think the past is something dead and finished with. Something you read about in a book. But it isn't. The past is everywhere, lying about in bits and pieces, like snares in the forest. You don't see the pieces, but sooner or later, you step on one and it's got you."

Stewart looked strangely at her. A bizarre idea had occurred to him.

"Tell me, Ceci. At the Vargas's *estancia* there's a party scheduled. Does the date, December 17th, mean anything to you?"

She picked up the hashish pipe, an enigmatic smile on her face.

"Many people in Buenos Aires know this, Señor Stewart. There has always been a celebration at the *estancia*. December 17th is John Gideon's birthday."

She started to light her pipe, then changed her mind.

"I have to get ready now. Truly." She got up and walked him to the door. With the candles and incense burning in the foyer and the Buddha in a small niche, he might have been in an Oriental temple. She handed him his hat and he put it on.

"I'll tell Julia I saw you," he said.

"No, don't!" she said, looking startled. "Don't. You are very *simpatico* for a *gringo*, but as we say in Buenos Aires, 'Silence is better than money, sometimes.'"

"Silence, then," he said, offering his hand. She shook it once, firmly, like a man.

"If you want to talk again, Señor, you must be very careful.

The *guardia* keep an eye on my tango palace now, ever since this business with Raoul. The Germans, also," she said, glancing over at the newspaper on the console.

"With thanks, then," he said, starting to go. Then stopped. "About Julia," he began awkwardly. "I know it sounds strange, but I get the feeling that there's more to this than sex, or politics, that it's almost . . ."

"Yes. Say it," she murmured, her mascara'd eyes oddly seductive. "It's not a dirty word, a *porqueria*."

"It feels a little like love," he said, almost blushing.

"Of course!" she declared triumphantly. "It feels like love because it is love. That's Julia's great talent: she loves! She is a *lover, una enamorada*, in the truest sense of the word!"

"Then what's the problem?"

"*Ay, gringos*," she sighed, shaking her head. She thought for a moment. "In this country, Señor, we grow up with the custom of the *coima*, understand? As a child, if you want a better grade from your teacher, you give him something," she said, rubbing her thumb against her fingers in the universal sign for money. "You want medicine that won't kill you, the electrician to come today instead of *mañana*, the postal clerk to stamp your receipt, always there is the *gratificación*. Everyone understands this, yes?"

"Yes, but what does that have to do with Julia?"

"Don't you see?" she said. "In Argentina, even love is a bribe."

10

THEY HAD planned to meet at the Alvear Palace Hotel, under the clock that had the letters "ALVEAR PALACE" on its face instead of numbers. The clock hung from the high ceiling of a lobby that with its potted palms and archways was reminiscent of a Spanish courtyard. Part of the lobby had been set aside for dancing and the floor was crowded with couples already dressed for the evening. A jazz band was spread along the far wall, near the bar. They were playing "Jeepers Creepers," and if it wasn't Louis Armstrong, it wasn't a tango either, Stewart thought, as he walked in under the arches.

He spotted Julia right away. He had expected her to be alone, but she was standing near the bar in a circle of people: Casaverde, Herrera-Blanca, Vargas, and several women too young to be wives. Stewart started to leave, but Arturo Vargas saw him and waved him over.

"*Hola!* Señor Stewart!" Vargas called. "It's Don Carlos Stewart, isn't it? Vargas was slim and elegant in a fawn-colored afternoon suit and he had exquisite manners. The kind of man, Stewart thought, that was difficult to dislike and almost irresistible not to take his wife from.

"Don Carlos," Julia said, extending her hand to be kissed, her eyes alive with the memory of their lovemaking that morning. The way she did it made Stewart wonder how much she'd been drinking.

"Don Carlos is a famous polo player. We're hoping to have him play for us soon," Vargas explained to the young women.

"I love polo. All those men in tight jodhpurs," one of the women, a bleached blonde, exclaimed.

"A pity to waste it on the horses," Julia laughed, and the others laughed too. All except for the youngest woman, an intense brunette, thin-faced, very pretty, with dark intelligent eyes.

"And what about you? Don't you like polo, too?" Stewart asked the brunette, conscious of Julia's eyes on him.

"I like many things," the brunette said. Her voice was surprisingly deep for such a thin little thing.

"Eva is an actress," Julia explained. "On the radio."

"A would-be actress. I'm still auditioning for parts," she said.

"I'm an actress, too. We're doing 'Ten Pretty Girls' at the *Actual.* You'll have to come and see me," the polo-loving blonde said breathily to Stewart.

"That's right. All actresses," Casaverde said, chucking her under the chin, making her giggle.

Julia laughed again.

"Aren't we, though? It's just that some of us don't get paid for it." She looked at Stewart in a way that made it impossible for her husband not to notice. Her color was high and she

wore a black silk cocktail dress that showed plenty of neckline. Stewart thought she was the most beautiful woman he
had ever seen. "*Salud* everyone!" she toasted, plucking a Martini from a passing waiter and downing it. "There," she declared. "Isn't that good acting? Aren't we good at pretending
to be happy?"

She said it to all of them, but she was talking to Vargas, who
stood there, slim and elegant as ever, and in spite of his politics, Stewart almost felt sorry for him.

"Julia's upset," Vargas said. "Because of Cardenas's death.
We weren't that close to Amadeo personally, but the Club
used to belong to Julia's grandfather, so naturally . . ." he
finished awkwardly, looking at Casaverde.

"Had you heard about it, Don Carlos? It happened last night
after closing," Casaverde said, screwing in his monocle to
peer at Stewart. He was wearing a white suit again. According to Julia, he owned dozens of them, all identical. Her first
lover. And always around, watching.

"I saw something in the newspaper," Stewart said, unable
to resist glancing at Julia. A waiter with a tray had come by
and she had exchanged her empty glass for another Martini.
The young woman, Eva, was also watching her. With a start,
Stewart realized that the way Eva was standing mirrored
Julia's posture exactly. She was imitating her.

"Tragic. Very tragic. It's these son-of-a-bitch *compadritos*.
Filthy foreigners," Herrera-Blanca mumbled, motioning to
the waiter for another round.

"It seems there were things taken from the safe in his office,"
Casaverde said, watching Stewart with professional interest.

"Were there? Then it must have been thieves," Stewart said.

"Not ordinary thieves," Casaverde said. The light glinted
on his monocle. "They left money behind. Much money. Curious, no?"

"This is so fascinating!" the blonde said, shivering her
shoulders as if to prove how thrilled she was to be part of such
a conversation. "What do you suppose they were after?"

"Papers," Casaverde said, still looking at Stewart. "Business papers. But the murderer made a mistake."

"Which was?" Stewart asked.

"For one thing, he left behind a letter case the papers were
taken from, so we have some idea of what is missing," Casaverde said.

"Caramba, that's so clever! That murderer doesn't stand a chance, does he?" the blonde exclaimed, pressing up against Casaverde. She seemed enthusiastic enough over his investigative abilities to want to rip off his pants right then and there.

"Oh, we'll catch him all right," Casaverde smiled. "Argentine justice always has the final word. Don't you agree, Señor Stewart?"

"Argentine justice, or German?" Stewart parried.

Vargas and Casaverde exchanged glances.

"Perhaps the two are not so very different," Vargas ventured. "Perhaps we've been an unofficial colony of the English long enough."

"They should make a demonstration, the Nazis! Blow up a few English ships in the Rio Plata! At the very least, it would send up the price of beef," Herrera-Blanca thundered, blowing out his cheeks like a chipmunk. "That would teach the English!" he thundered, pounding his fist on the table. "Them and their *cabrón* Roca-Runciman treaty! The 'Treaty of Shame' we call it."

Vargas and Casaverde looked at him, alarmed. Vargas came over and put his hand on Herrera-Blanca's shoulder.

"Don Jaime is our resident *Fascista,*" Vargas said, smiling, but his fingers were white where they pressed into Herrera-Blanca's shoulder. "But I suspect the Germans have more important things to do these days."

"Don Jaime drinks too much. It's our Argentine blood," Casaverde said, staring at Stewart. "We drink hard, we fight hard, we—" here he said a vicious word that shocked even the polo-loving blonde hanging on his arm, "hard."

The blonde disengaged her arm. Her cheeks were splotched bright red.

"I am not used to such conversation from *caballeros,*" she declared.

"No? Go home, then," Casaverde said nastily.

She didn't say anything. She stood there, her body trembling.

"Go on!" Casaverde snapped. "This city is full of *actresses.* Go on! Tomorrow I'll tell that toad Suarez to change the play to 'Nine Pretty Girls.' "

The blonde stood there, chest heaving, not moving. The little one, Eva, reached for her, but the blonde shook her off.

"Well, go on! *Vaya!* Get out!" Casaverde shouted.

"They were traitors, signing that treaty. *Hijos de puta,*" Herrera-Blanca muttered, his voice filling the sudden silence.

"*Qué va?* Are you still here?" Casaverde said to the blonde. She stood there, her face a violent red, not saying anything.

Casaverde looked around at all of them.

"*Bueno,*" he said slowly. He looked at the blonde. "If you want to stay, you have to kiss my hand," he told her.

The blonde remained motionless, her hands at her sides. She looked at Casaverde, her eyes stunned, helpless. Moving like a sleepwalker, she raised his hand to her lips and pressed them against the back of his hand.

"You see how it is," Casaverde sighed. "I'm too soft. A real man wouldn't be so forgiving." He rubbed his hand over her bodice. She let him do it, hands at her sides, a terrible smile on her face. A smile like death, when the rictus draws the mouth back and wide and there is nothing human left in it.

Everyone stood there watching. No one said a word. The little brunette's face was all eyes as Casaverde pinched the blonde's nipples till she winced, closing her eyes against the pain, but otherwise not moving. The orchestra began to play a Lambeth Walk and Julia walked across the circle to Stewart.

"Dance with me, *yanqui,*" she said, taking his hand.

"What about Don Arturo?"

Vargas stood there in his elegant fawn suit, almost unnaturally still.

"Arturo likes only tangos. It's so boring. '*Da da dee da, da da dum, you'll find they're all, doing the Lambeth Walk, 'oy!'* " she sang in English, moving her hips in time to the music.

"Tangos, yes. Why not? I am an Argentine," Vargas said gravely, watching Stewart and his wife together. He was smiling at them, but there was a sickness in his eyes that made Stewart want to look away.

"With permission, Don Arturo?" Stewart asked, feeling Julia's pressure on his arm.

Vargas waved them away, turning toward the bar so they couldn't see his face. Stewart was conscious of Casaverde's eyes following him as they weaved through the tables to the dance floor. Everyone was dancing around them, stepping smoothly to the sprightly beat, but with faces set and serious, as though it were a tango.

"We have to talk," Julia whispered in his ear as they danced. "I've thought of nothing but you all day."

Her perfume disturbed him. It reminded him of something, but he still couldn't put his finger on it. It was something by Guerlain, he thought and then he had it. It popped into his mind, just like that.

"I thought you would be alone," he told her.

"Arturo insisted on coming. And Enrique was planning to meet his *putitas* anyway. What difference? I had to see you." She leaned against him for a second. "Oh God, *yanqui*. Things are such a mess!"

"I know," he said, watching Casaverde and Herrera-Blanca head toward the dance floor with two of the women. The one called Eva stayed with Arturo, who was standing by their table, staring at them over his drink. "Where can we go?"

She thought for a moment. "There's the boathouse, in Tigre. We could . . ."

Before she could finish, there was a disturbance by the entrance, underneath the arches. A man ran in, his jacket torn, his face bleeding. He was shouting something. At first the band played on and everyone continued to dance, but then he looked behind him and screamed out *"Ayuda!"* Help! and everyone stopped. The man stumbled over a chair and someone screamed. Suddenly two *guardia* stormed in and grabbed the man, who cried out in fear. They started to drag him away.

"What's going on?" the *maître d'* demanded, coming forward. A crowd began to gather.

"This man resisted arrest. We're taking him in," said one of the *guardia*, a big man with a bushy mustache.

"Please! I have done nothing! I was on my way home from the work," the man cried out. His Spanish was mangled, foreign. There were purplish bruises all over his head and his mouth was bleeding from where his front teeth had been knocked out.

"Pay no attention," the *guardia* with the mustache said, twisting the man's arm behind him, forcing him to his knees. "He's a Jew! They're all liars."

Craning his neck to see, Stewart noticed that both of the *guardia* were wearing the silver collar insignias of the Civic Legion.

"One moment, Señor. This is Argentina, not Germany," the *maître d'* declared. Just as he said that, Stewart felt a tug at

his jacket pocket. He reached down and felt a folded piece of
paper that someone had just put into his pocket. Then a hand
squeezing his. He looked around. Julia.

The others were all around them. Vargas, Casaverde,
Herrera-Blanca, the young women. Vargas was watching him
and Julia, his face a pale mask.

"You are not to interfere, or these *distinguido* people will
see a little something they're not used to," the *guardia* growled
at the *maître d'*. He started to pull at the Jew, who looked
around desperately.

The *maître d'* was a short man. He wore a tuxedo, his belly
swelling against his cummerbund, and when he looked
around for his waiters they had all mysteriously disappeared.
The *maître d'* took a deep breath, rocking slightly on the balls
of his feet to make himself seem bigger. One of the band members started to play a note and somebody shushed him.

"All the same, I must insist. This is private property," the
maître d' said.

The *guardia's* hand went to the holster on his hip. Stewart
eased his hand around in back under his jacket to where his
gun was. The crowd was utterly still.

Suddenly, there was a stir as someone made his way
through the crowd. It was Arturo Vargas, cigarette in hand,
coming up to stand next to the *maître d'*.

"You've done your duty, *Subteniente*," Vargas said, glancing at the *guardia's* epaulettes for his rank. "But you must
leave. This hotel is, as the Señor says, private property."

"Even an *hidalgo* may not interfere with justice," the
guardia began.

"*Subteniente!*" Vargas's voice rang out. He looked impossibly handsome and elegant standing there. "I am sure you
know your duty," he said, eyes narrowed.

The *guardia* looked at Vargas, who unobtrusively tapped his
pocket. A slow nasty smile spread over the *guardia's* face.

"Go on, then! Keep your Jews, if you like them so much,"
the *guardia* said, shoving the man at Vargas. The *maître d'*
caught the man in his arms. As the *guardia* turned to go,
Vargas caught his sleeve. Stewart thought he saw Vargas slip
money to the *guardia* as the orchestra started up again. They
played "Deep Purple," the song you couldn't go anywhere
that year without hearing, and the crowd began to break up.
The *maître d'* led the Jew away. He was holding a handker-

chief to his mouth and people were patting him on the back, congratulating him on his lucky escape. Julia and Stewart resumed dancing.

"Your husband surprises me. I thought he liked the Nazis," Stewart said.

"It isn't that," she shrugged. "With Arturo, class always supersedes politics. But you're right. He has his moments," she smiled. It was an odd secret smile, the kind shared between husbands and wives and only sometimes, lovers. Stewart felt a pang of jealousy at that smile. They swayed together, not touching, yet so close a knife edge couldn't have slipped between them. He could feel the heat of her body and knew that if he gave in to it, there would be no stopping this side of love. But he couldn't, he told himself. There was too much at stake. And also that paper, like a time bomb ticking in his pocket.

"Why don't you stay with him? He's pretty impressive," Stewart asked.

Julia leaned back in his arms to look at him.

"He's very good, you know. In his own way, he loves me. It makes me feel like a *putita* to hurt him. But God, *yanqui!* If ever a man cried out for horns. He suffers so! That pathetic look of humiliation in his eyes sometimes makes me want to tear off my clothes and fuck every man in the world right in front of him!"

Stewart held her close in his arms. He was conscious of Vargas watching him in the whirl of dancers.

"It was you that night in my hotel room, wasn't it? I recognized the perfume," he said.

She didn't answer, but only clung to him like someone drowning. The bandleader was crooning of when "deep shadows fall over sleepy garden walls," and Casaverde glided by, laughing loudly with the blonde. She had a doll-like smile painted on her face.

"What do you know, *yanqui?*" Julia whispered back.

"It's been you all along, hasn't it? You're Raoul's source," he said, letting go of her to applaud as the music ended.

The band had swung into a lengthy version of a new hit song, something about going "over the rainbow," from some movie for children that had just come to Buenos Aires and was playing to big crowds lined up outside the Cine Andaluz. Julia had gone to the *sala de damas* and Stewart was alone at the bar with Vargas. They were drinking Martinis and Vargas speared his olive with a toothpick and chewed it thoughtfully.

"I could have you killed you know, like that, *como eso*," Vargas said, snapping his fingers.

"Seems to me like you already tried," Stewart said.

Vargas's eyebrows went up, but otherwise his face showed no emotion.

"Do you want another?" he asked. "Alfredo makes the best *claritos* in Buenos Aires, which is to say, the world."

"Why not?" Stewart said. "A condemned man deserves the best."

Vargas motioned to the bartender, who brought them fresh drinks and a bowl of olives.

"Cardenas," Stewart said, picking up a handful of olives as though they were peanuts and popping one into his mouth.

"What about him?"

"Did you kill him, *como eso?*" Stewart asked, snapping his fingers as Vargas had done.

"No," Vargas shrugged. It was a Latin shrug, part indolence, part indifference. "Did you, *pues?*"

"No."

"What a pity we can't believe each other, Señor Stewart. Just think how much time and trouble it would save us," Vargas laughed. He looked very handsome, and Stewart was surprised to find himself liking him. That was the thing about war, he thought. Hating your enemy was easy. But killing somebody you liked, whose wife you liked, that was hard. He raised his glass to Vargas and drank.

"We're having a polo match at the *estancia* on December 17th," Vargas said, a gleam in his eye. "I hope you'll play for us. With permission, I'll arrange a pony for you."

"Is that the big fiesta President Ortiz is supposed to attend?"

Vargas looked annoyed. He had the same unnatural stillness about him as when he faced the *guardia*.

"So you know about that. What else do you know, Señor Stewart?"

Stewart didn't answer. He spat an olive pit into his hand and put it on the plate with the others.

"I think you should leave Argentina, Señor Stewart. I think you should go very soon," Vargas said quietly. "*Y pues*, I think you should stay away from my wife."

Stewart looked up at him. That awful expression was shin-

ing in his eyes again. What is it about her that does that to
him? Stewart wondered. He put down his drink.

"What about Julia?"

"Yes. What about me?" Julia said, coming up. She had
taken her pearl necklace and somehow arranged it in her hair
like a tiara. On anyone else it would have been absurd, but on
her, with her sleek raven-black hair, it was stunning. It made
her look more than ever like a Renaissance princess, at once
virginal and yet utterly desirable. She put her hand posses-
sively on Stewart's arm, where Vargas couldn't miss it.

"I think you should stay here. With me," Vargas muttered,
his voice barely audible.

"Don't be boring, Arturo. Don Carlos is our guest," she said.

"You bitch!" he hissed. "You think I'll put up with anything."

"But you will, *querido*. That's just what you'll do."

"Bitch! *Puta de putitas!*" he said. His face was frightening,
as though he had broken apart inside and was trying not to let
it show.

"My man! My *macho* man!" Julia said. She turned to Stewart. "Please, Don Carlos. I want to leave."

Stewart got off his stool. Vargas looked like a man in a
dream. Stewart wasn't sure which was worse, to stay or to go.
Julia took his arm and they started toward the arches. Casaverde and Herrera-Blanca had disappeared with two of the
actresses. The third one, Eva, stood alone near the band. She
was looking uncertainly toward them, as if wondering
whether or not to come over.

"Julia!" Vargas whispered after them. "You're my wife!"

Julia turned back to him.

"That Eva is all alone, Arturo. She's young, pretty. She'll
think you're wonderful," she said softly.

"I'll never give you a divorce, understand? Never!"

"I know, *querido*," she said. "We have to stay married. It's
our punishment."

"And love, Julia. Don't forget love," he said.

"How can I forget love?" she said. "The worst punishment
of all."

She looked at Vargas a moment longer, then she and Stewart turned and walked out of the hotel together.

*   *   *

For a time, riding in the Dusenberg, they didn't say much. They drove with the top down, a warm night breeze whipping around the corners of the windshield. It was fast going on the new *carretera federal* to Tigre, but the highway hadn't been completed yet and before they got to the Avenida General Paz, the traditional boundary of the city, the construction ended and they were on a narrow two-lane road that ran past the football stadium and on through San Isidro, parallel to the river.

The countryside was flat and dark and they could smell the river from across the railroad tracks. The land reminded Stewart of the Veneto and that area around Venice where, no matter where you are, there is always the feeling of water around you. The road wasn't lit, but there were plenty of shanty towns, *villas miserias*, they were called, stretching for miles along the flats. The huts were made of tin cans and tar paper. They were lit by innumerable cooking fires, like a vast army encampment. Peasants from the countryside, who had come to Buenos Aires looking for work, gathered around the fires, their faces shining in the flames. As they drove, Stewart could smell meat roasting and he remembered something Hartman had said, about how for the poor in Argentina, there was always plenty of beef and not much else. A drunk stood beside the road, shouting and waving a bottle at them as though it were a club. Stewart flicked the headlights at him and when that didn't work, swerved around him as Julia leaned forward and turned on the radio.

She found a station playing *"La Cumparsita,"* but the music was just ending. Suddenly, with a flourish of martial music, the announcer came on with a news bulletin. The Russian attack on Finland was encountering fierce resistance from the outnumbered Finns. Despite this, armored units of the Soviet Army were continuing to advance on the Karelian Isthmus amid reports of heavy fighting in bitter cold and snow. They listened in silence to the broadcast and when the music started again, Stewart flicked it off.

"By the time this thing is over, there won't be much left of Europe," he said.

"No," Julia said softly. "This is no time for small countries."

Stewart glanced at the rear-view mirror. The headlights he had spotted earlier were still with them. He eased back on the speed to see if they got any closer. Julia was curled into a corner of her seat. Her cigarette was glowing and blowing sparks and her hair was stirring in the breeze. She looked so beautiful that it hurt to look at her.

"We have to talk," he said.

"About Arturo?" she asked.

"About Arturo. About everything."

"Everything is a lot," she said, exhaling a stream of smoke that was whipped away by the wind.

"You were Raoul's source, weren't you? You had him set up the rendezvous with Hartman. Only it went wrong and the krauts got to him first. Who tipped them off?"

"Cardenas!" she said. "It had to be Cardenas! No one else knew."

"Okay, Cardenas," he nodded. "So where were you getting the information from? Who's the German leak?"

"There is no leak," she smiled. "I got the information from the same place you did."

"Cardenas's safe?"

She nodded excitedly, as if relieved to finally be able to tell someone.

"It all belonged to my grandfather. I knew the combination and I could always slip away during an evening at the Club by pretending to go to the *sala de damas*."

"All right," Stewart nodded. "So Cardenas was part of the pipeline between the Germans and your husband, is that it? Arturo would pass it to his *amigo*, Casaverde, and he would give it to—"

"Vice-President Castillo," she said.

"Sure. The pro-Axis faction in the Argentine government. Only you decided to siphon off some of it and until Cardenas spotted it, they wouldn't have even known it was happening. Fair enough," he said, studying her carefully. "But I'm curious. Why give it to us *yanquis* instead of the Brits? They're the ones who really need it."

"Too obvious," she said, shaking her head. "Buenos Aires is a madhouse of spies these days. Everyone's chasing everyone else. The Germans are all over the English, as is our own Argentine intelligence. A direct approach to the English would have been crazy. So instead, I thought about the Americans and using Raoul. Poor Raoul," she nodded. "Only Cardenas found out."

"How?" he looked at her. "Who tipped him?"

"I don't know," she said. "When they killed Raoul I was frantic. I thought they might come for me next. And I was desperate to open another channel. You found the letter in Cardenas's safe, didn't you?"

"Uh-huh," he nodded.

"So you know about the coup planned for December 17th?"

"What about it?"

"I think they're going to kill Ortiz and replace him with Castillo. I had to stop it. I had to find a way," she declared, her fingers gripping his arm. "That's why I went to your hotel room and left you that matchbook, so you would come to the Club. It's almost funny," she smiled. "I had to bribe the *portero*. I'm sure he thought I was your mistress!" Her expression changed. "And now I am," she said, stretching toward him.

She leaned over and kissed him on the cheek. He didn't respond. She felt it instantly and pulled away.

"Have I made a mistake?" she asked quietly.

"Several," he said, not looking at her.

"What is it?" she asked, her voice barely audible.

"I'm getting tired of listening to you lie."

"*Por Dios*, Carlos, what lies?"

"It's boring, Julia. All these lies. Don't you understand?" he snapped. "We're running out of time!"

"What are you talking about?"

"About the Nazi agents who've been sitting on our tail since we left the Alvear, for one thing."

She started to turn around to look, when he grabbed her shoulder and shoved her back.

"Don't turn around!" he snarled. "I don't want them to know they've been spotted. Besides, we've got a lot more ground to cover. Like why you want to help the English, when your husband favors the Germans." He glanced at her out of the corner of his eye for a second. "Do you really hate him that much?"

She slumped back in her seat, her limbs suddenly disconnected, like a doll's. When she spoke she wouldn't look at him.

"When Arturo and I got married, we had no choice," she said, her voice hoarse and low. "Our families were to be united. No one even asked us. He isn't bad," she shrugged. "It's just that we never really belonged together. Besides, Arturo is an Argentine male. There is a law in this country. It's

called the *patria potestas*. It gives a husband absolute ownership over his wife and children, as much as over his cattle and
horses. Only nobody owns me!" she said, eyes flashing. "Nobody!"

All at once, Stewart grinned sideways at her.

"You know, you did tell the truth one time tonight," he
said. "To Casaverde, when you said you were an actress. Especially all that Latin fire when you talk about the indignities
of Argentine law. Too bad we don't have more time for it."

"What don't you believe?" she asked, her face illuminated
like an icon by the dashboard light.

"That you're prepared to betray your country and your class
because your husband is a typical Argentine male," he told
her. "What's the matter? Are you that in favor of the Roca-
Runciman treaty, or is it that you think Hitler just looks a
little too much like Charlie Chaplin for your tastes?"

"Neither," she said quietly, looking down. "Not everyone
considers fighting the Fascists a betrayal. And also," she
paused, "my grandfather was English."

"John Gideon?" he asked.

She looked up sharply, her eyes intense.

"You've heard of him then?"

"Seems like everybody has," he said slowly, remembering
something Ceci Braga had said. That Julia wasn't Vargas's
wife; she was Gideon's granddaughter. "Was he that important to you?"

"You can't imagine." She stared at the windshield as
though she could see her grandfather in it, plain before her.

"God, that's great! You're going to save the bloody British
Empire because of dear old Grandad! And I'm supposed to
believe that?"

"But I've told you the truth," she pleaded, her eyes filling.
"What more can I do?" she whispered, thrusting her body
toward him as though presenting him with her breasts.

Stewart laughed abruptly. It was a harsh bitter laugh.

"It's no good, Julia. This is a sucker's game. Only I'm not
your husband. I won't play. In fact, that's the whole problem
in a nutshell."

"I don't understand."

"Cardenas's safe was supposed to be your source. So
where'd the message tonight come from? Cardenas is dead."

She wouldn't look at him. Stewart wiped his mouth with
the back of his hand.

"That's all right," he said. "You don't have to answer. I know where you got it."

She tapped her cigarette into the ashtray. Her hand was shaking.

"And where's that?" she said.

"From the only place it could have come," he told her. "Your husband."

"Well," she said brightly, her eyes blurred. "You've got it all figured out, haven't you? So what's the problem?"

"Stop it!" he said angrily. "Stop lying to me. If you were stealing the information from Arturo, the last thing in the world you'd want to do would be to alienate him. That wouldn't be killing the goose that lays the golden eggs, that'd be blowing it to pieces and burying it! Except you're not only confronting him, you're shoving his nose in it. Why? I don't get it."

She covered her face with her hand and looked away.

"I can't tell you," she said, her voice muffled behind the hand.

"You've got to tell me—and fast!" he demanded. "We're running out of time! Look!" he pointed at the rear-view mirror, filling with light from the headlights of the car behind them. A cry escaped her.

"Please, Stewart, I'm afraid," she whispered. "Truly."

"Just tell me why?" he insisted. "Why does everyone in Argentina have to know that we're lovers, especially Arturo?"

"Because he wants me to," she blurted out, her lips trembling.

He looked at her as if she had lost her mind.

"Are you crazy? What are you talking about? Why would he want you to do that?"

"Can't you guess?" she said, challenging him. Her voice was suddenly firm and under control. "Even now, can't you?"

Stewart sat there, staring at her for so long he had to jerk his eyes away and swerve the car to keep it on the road.

"Jesus Christ," he said, as much to himself as to her. "It's an act. The pair of you. It's almost funny," he said, shaking his head. "The goddamn Latin Laurel and Hardy. But why?" He turned to her. "Why?"

"To protect me. It's what we decided."

"I don't understand. Decided what?"

"*Dios mio!*" she said, exasperated. "Don't you see? It isn't me. I'm just a go-between. Arturo was Raoul's real source."

*   *   *

They were nearing San Fernando, the flatlands of the Delta dark and silent around them. The sky seemed to surround them, black and full of stars. The sedan tailing them had fallen back about a quarter of a mile and Stewart drove easily, his mind racing.

Julia was leaning back in her seat, smoking a cigarette, at once impossibly beautiful and distant. What she had told him had the ring of truth, Stewart thought. It all fitted. The only reason she had lied was to protect Arturo, who was not only her husband, but her source. He remembered how they were all standing when the message had been passed to him, just before Arturo had confronted the *guardia*. At the time he had assumed it was Julia who had done it, but it could have just as easily been Vargas himself. It even explained why Vargas had stood up for the Jew. Something that all his malarkey about *noblesse oblige* hadn't really done. It was, he had to admit, an incredible scheme. He and Vargas had the ideal connection through Julia. He could meet Julia whenever he wanted to. They could be as public as they liked. Everyone would assume it was because they were having an affair. The sheer perfection, the symmetry of it was breathtaking. He glanced over at her.

"About us," he began hesitantly. "Was any of it true?"

She looked solemnly at him, her face shining in the moonlight.

"That's the incredible part, don't you see? I didn't expect to like you and instead. . . ." She turned away. "It's killing Arturo. But I don't care. I don't care anymore," turning back to him, her eyes blazing. "It's true, *yanqui*. I'm alive!"

For a time, neither of them spoke. They sped through the night, the lights of the dashboard gleaming in the darkness.

"This boathouse of yours, is it far?" he asked finally.

"Not far," she said. "There's a turn-off just past the casino. You'll see it."

"Because we'll have to get away from whoever is tailing us," he said, indicating the rear-view mirror.

"If you can get enough of a lead, they'll think we're either on the road, or that we'll have turned off to the casino. We have a boat. Once we're on the Delta, they'll never find us among all the islands and channels."

Stewart nodded, checking the mirror again. The tail had

fallen back, their headlights like two distant moons on the dark horizon.

"It's just that the land is so flat here. They could give us a three days' start and still see us," he grimaced.

"There's a slight rise in the road just before San Fernando. The only one for a thousand kilometers," she offered.

"It'll have to do," he nodded, closing one eye and narrowing the other to try and get some night vision. He would need any edge he could get. He looked around. "Get rid of that cigarette," he ordered.

She let the cigarette go. It shot back in the stream of air, spraying sparks like a miniature rocket. He checked the dashboard. The Dusie was a marvel. Its speed was the best thing he had going for him. The fuel gauge showed a third full, which gave him some lightness, but all the gas he needed. It was as good as it was going to get. He checked the rear-view mirror one last time. The headlights were slightly bigger. They were starting to close up. Ahead, Stewart could see a few lights and the silhouettes of buildings in the darkness.

San Fernando.

It was now or never. They exchanged one last glance. Looking at her sent shivers through him in a way that he couldn't explain to himself. It was a way he had never expected to feel. Somehow it was all tied up with the night and the war and somehow he knew, absolutely knew, that nothing would ever be this way again.

"Hang on," he yelled, simultaneously killing the Dusie's lights and shifting gears as he floored the accelerator.

The Dusenberg seemed to hesitate for an instant, then suddenly took off, the impact of their acceleration forcing them back in their seats. The road had disappeared. They were in darkness. He was driving virtually blind. The wind was deafening; it was like being in an open cockpit plane, he thought, risking a quick glance in the rear-view mirror.

The other car had been taken by surprise. The headlights were pin-points of light, like stars, in the mirror. But that wouldn't last long, Stewart thought.

He could see the town now. Outlines of low buildings, a church, a single street lamp in the plaza. It was coming up fast. There were trees in the plaza and young people clustered around a *carrito* lit by a kerosene lantern. The people in the plaza froze, wide-eyed, as the Dusie roared into town, hitting the rise and sailing airborne into the plaza, scattering chickens and a terrified goat, setting a dozen dogs to barking, then disappearing in a cloud of dust down the narrow street.

Like a sudden visitation of the gods, Stewart thought, holding tight as the Dusie skittered over the cobbles, then skidded onto a gravel road outside town, churning up a hailstorm of pebbles. Stewart stomped on the accelerator as if he wanted to put his foot through the floorboard. The engine howled so loudly he could hear it over the roar of the wind and he was glad he couldn't see the tachometer. He had to be doing over a hundred miles per hour almost blind. Ahead, all he could see was darkness and stars, and if they hit a mudhole, or a fence post, or an animal, they were as good as dead.

He tried the rear-view mirror again. He couldn't see the other car's lights. Jesus, had they done it? Or were the other car's lights out too? he wondered. There was no way to know. He hunched over the wheel, trying to get everything the Dusie had, straining to see. Then he felt a tug on his sleeve.

"See there," Julia said, pointing.

The casino, a fairyland of lights off to the right down a drive of eucalyptus trees, loomed in the darkness like an apparition. "Slow down!" she shouted, her voice barely audible in the wind. "The turn-off is less than a kilometer."

Stewart touched the brakes, fighting the slew of the Dusie as it fishtailed. They were past the long drive to the casino. Ahead was only darkness and the turn-off coming up any second. As he slowed, he looked back for a second. Far behind, he could see the lights of the other car, coming on fast. She tugged at him again and he saw it, an opening between two fence posts, barbed wire extending on either side. About a hundred yards down the lane, he could just make out the shadows of outbuildings of some kind. Suddenly, it was coming faster than he anticipated. It was going to be very close.

He slammed on the brakes, turning right and putting the Dusie into a bad skid. The front of the car spun right and it was almost out of control, the fence post on the left coming up hard. Stewart spun the wheel back to the left, fighting for control, then right again, the tires squealing, as they just squeezed through the fence posts, grazing the left one with the bumper, and onto the dirt road. Stewart sped up, bouncing down the badly rutted lane. He pulled in behind the first outbuilding, killed the engine and leaped out, the Colt in his

hand. Julia started to follow and he motioned her back. He
peeked around the corner of the building, waiting.

The night was still and dark and he could see across the
open fields to the road and the brightly lit casino. Stewart
tried to listen for the sound of the other car, but his ears were
still filled with the roaring of the wind. It was as if his ears
were covered with seashells and he shook his head to try and
clear them. He saw the headlights of the other car coming
fast, carving twin cones of light in the darkness. The lights
turned into the avenue of trees that led to the casino. He
watched the car drive up to the casino and park in front. Four
figures got out and went inside. He'd have to move quickly
now, while they were inside, Stewart thought, turning back
toward the car, just as Julia flung herself into his arms.

"Oh God, that was incredible!" she breathed, her eyes shining. Her mouth was all over him, kissing his face, his lips, her
tongue invading his mouth. She put his hand on her breast
and he felt it rise, the nipple hardening, and he could feel her
other hand, touching and squeezing him through his trousers.

"I love you, Stewart. I swear I love you. Please," she whispered, gathering her dress up around her hips. "I want you.
Now. Here, feel me. Feel how wet I am," guiding his hand
between her legs. She was kissing him, squirming against
him, trying to pull him down. "Do it," she begged. "Do it here,
in the dirt," fumbling with the buttons on his fly. She sank to
her knees, her breath warm on his crotch. He felt himself
sway, experiencing the male discomfort of making love standing up and suddenly conscious of the powerful smell of the
earth and manure and the chorus of the frogs from the rushes
along the river bank.

"We can't stay here," he whispered, pulling her up by her
arms. "They'll be by any second."

"Oh God," she said, falling against him. "I don't want to
wait any more."

"Where can we go?"

"The house. The boat. Anywhere. I don't care. My God, don't
you understand? I don't care," she said, snuggling against
him, her lips pressed to his neck. "That ride, in the darkness,
like flying. Did you feel it?" she whispered, her hand squirming in his lap like a little animal.

"Yes. My God! Wait a minute! Please wait!"

"I know. But hurry. There's so little time."

He put the Dusie into gear and drove in darkness to the hulking shadow of the house. "A boathouse," she had called it. More like a kind of colonial Versailles, Stewart thought. It was a massive white house with classical pillars and a circular fountain in front and garages off to the side. As they drove up, a man came out of the house, holding a lantern, and guided them into one of the garages. The man was short and swarthy. He wore old-fashioned loose trousers and a red handkerchief around his neck. His face was old and well creased and he acknowledged Stewart with a nod.

"*Bienvenidos*, Dona Julia. Will you be wanting the *coche* later?" the man asked.

"I don't know, Manolo. Close the garage door and keep it ready. If anyone asks, we are not here," Julia said, getting out and the man bowed in a formal, old country way. She didn't bother introducing Stewart. "Is the boat ready?"

"*Si, mi niña*. The boat is ready and also the *lancha* has *gasolina*."

"Thank you, Manolo. Stay here and I want the lights out," Julia said, leading Stewart to a side door and into an interior courtyard. The courtyard was cobblestoned and bordered with colonnaded arches and flowerbeds, and along one wall were carved hitching rails for horses. Julia led him across the courtyard and through a carved wooden door into a darkened salon, filled with heavy Victorian furniture, shrouded with sheets. The room was dark and still, the silence almost a presence. No one had been here for a very long time. The walls were lined with books, smelling of dust and mildew. Through the windows running across the enormous length of the room, they could see the river, silvery and secret in the moonlight.

"I thought you said this was just a boathouse," Stewart said, his voice sounding strange to him in the stillness.

"It is," she said, taking his hand and holding it tight. "I haven't been here in a long time."

"And yet the boats are fueled and ready."

"Gideon's orders," she smiled.

"I thought he was dead."

"He is," she said, leading him down a long hall, wood-panelled and hung with old portraits. "He died in 1926."

"And his orders are still followed?" he asked, not bothering to disguise the disbelief in his voice.

She looked at him, hesitating at a heavy wooden door.

"You didn't know him," she said softly. "Otherwise, you wouldn't even ask."

"*Ya lo creo*, I believe it," he said, looking wonderingly around, as she led him into the boat shed.

The shed was dark and cavernous, with high arched openings to the water. There were three boats, each secured to its own dock. An enormous white yacht that must have dated from the turn of the century, a thirty-odd-foot sailboat and a gleaming wooden motorboat. The walls of the shed were wet, the sounds of dripping magnified in the huge enclosed space. Julia led him along the slippery wooden dock and onto the big yacht. They went into the main salon. She lit an oil lamp, the light shining on her face like a painting. He pulled her close and kissed her, holding the length of her body against him.

"What about the message, in your pocket?" she murmured, pressing tight against him.

"I know."

They kissed again, their hands exploring under each other's clothes and just when he thought he would go crazy, they separated.

"Maybe we better have a drink first," she said, swallowing.

"Maybe we better."

She went to the bar and took out a bottle of Scotch, a siphon and two glasses.

"Whiskey-soda?" she asked.

"All right," Stewart said, sinking down onto a large sofa. She brought over the drinks and sat beside him as he took the crumpled paper from his jacket pocket and held it to the light.

It was a typed note from Baron von Hulse to Arturo Vargas, thanking him for his graciousness and accepting his invitation to join him for the *fiesta* at his *estancia* on December 17th.

"You wouldn't happen to have a microscope handy, by any chance?"

She smiled wryly. "What would I ..." she began, then looked at him curiously. "Would a magnifying glass do? My grandfather used to keep one around here for charts and things," she said, getting up and rummaging in a closet. "Here!" she exclaimed, handing it over as he held the note up to the light.

He found it in the dot over the second "i." Two words that froze his blood. He tried to swallow and couldn't. He was holding the war in his hands.

"What is it?" she asked.

"Never mind," he said, slipping the note back into his pocket. He got up and walked to the bar. He needed to think.

"What's happened?" she asked.

"We have to leave. Arturo has outdone himself." He shook his head in admiration.

"I don't understand."

"Good," he smiled grimly. "But I've got to get this to where it can do some good," he said, the image of those two words burned into his mind as onto a screen.

Graf Spee.

That was the German "ambassador" due on December 17th! With her armor plating and her 11-inch guns, she could wreck a good chunk of the British merchant fleet, who thought they were safe in neutral waters, and no one could do a damn thing about it. She would dominate Buenos Aires, invincible, invulnerable. If there were any elements of the Argentine military who wanted to remain loyal to Ortiz, they wouldn't dare stand up to her. Even if they did, it wouldn't matter. Not against 11-inch guns, it wouldn't.

The Germans were taking no chances. With the *Graf Spee* in Buenos Aires harbor, the Nazi coup couldn't fail. Argentina was theirs.

Stewart swallowed his drink, his hands trembling. He couldn't believe what he had been walking around with. No wonder they were after him. He could change history. He could help determine who would win the war.

Now he understood why Casaverde and Vargas had been so upset when Herrera-Blanca had started to shoot his mouth off about Germans in the River Plate.

Jesus! he had to get this to Fowler at once. If the British fleet could catch the *Graf Spee* in the shallow waters of the Plate, they could neutralize her gun-size advantage. The German battleship's range wouldn't count for as much and she wouldn't be able to maneuver the way she could in the open sea. They could bottle her up like a cork in a bottle!

"We have to go. Right away," he said, finishing his drink.

"What about you and . . ." she started to say.

Suddenly, they heard a noise. Someone had boarded the yacht. Stewart's hand went to the Colt. There was a knock on the salon door. Stewart tiptoed behind the door, motioning to Julia to open it. From the voice and the way she stood when she opened the door, Stewart could tell that it was the servant, Manolo.

"A thousand pardons, Dona Julia. There is a *coche* coming," he said.

"Get rid of them. Don't let them in," she told him, as Stewart came out from behind the door.

"I hear. Will you take the *yate?*"

"Is it ready?" she asked.

"The *lancha* would be better. Faster. More quiet," he said, looking at Stewart's gun.

"All right," Julia said, touching the servant's arm for a moment. "But hurry."

"*Me voy.*" I go, the servant said, turning and leaping stiffly from the deck down to the dock with a kind of grave agility. He turned out the lights as he left, plunging the boat shed into darkness.

"One moment," Julia said, as Stewart started out onto the deck. She went back and hid the whiskey and glasses behind the bar and blew out the lamp. With Julia leading, they groped their way down to the dock and around to the small motorboat.

The boat shed was dank and gloomy, the only light coming from the reflection of the moon on the river. The water made no sound. It was flat and still as a pool of oil. Stewart felt the sudden tension from her hand as she jumped into the motorboat. It bobbed slightly because of the weight and there was a faint slapping of waves against the piles. They could hear noises coming from the house, but because of the way sound echoed in the shed, Stewart couldn't tell just what they were or how close. He cast off the line and jumped in, feeling the boat move under him as he pushed off. She was sitting behind the wheel and he sat next to her, as the boat floated slowly toward the opening.

The sounds from the house were louder. They could hear voices now. The boat's movement seemed as slow as eternity. Someone was at the door to the shed. He reached for the starter and she stopped his hand, putting her fingers to his lips. He nodded, waiting breathlessly, as they drifted through the opening.

The boat was barely through the opening when all the lights in the shed came on. Stewart could see Manolo squirming in someone's grasp and a number of men, he couldn't tell how many, running on the docks.

"Now!" Stewart yelled, whipping around in his seat and snapping into a shooting position as Julia hit the starter. The starter whined as the engine coughed and died.

Someone shouted something and then started firing at them. One of the shots sent a piece of the gunwale flying a few inches from Stewart's hand. Stewart fired three shots in quick succession and there was more firing. Someone in the shed was screaming hysterically.

The starter whined again, Julia playing with the choke, as they floated in the light from the shed, an easy target. He could hear the terrifying plunk of bullets hitting the sides of the boat. Come on, come on, he thought, squeezing off another shot. A man with a rifle was running to the front of the yacht. They had only seconds before he was in position.

Suddenly, the engine caught. With a cry of triumph, Julia gave it full throttle. The boat took off, cutting a swath of muddy water as it raced headlong into the darkness. Someone fired one last shot at them, but it no longer mattered. They held on tight as the boat raced out into the river, the wind in their faces, water churning behind, before she turned parallel to the shore, heading toward the casino.

When they had enough distance, Julia eased up on the throttle till the engine was a soft comfortable throb that would have been hard for anyone to hear any distance over water. They glided easily on the river, the boathouse a distant shadow against the starry sky. The shore was dark and tree-lined and on the other side were low wooded islands. Between the islands were silent channels overhung with branches, black as unlit tunnels. As they neared the casino, they could see the lights on the water and a small forest of sailboat masts and along the shore were rowboats tied to stakes, or turned upside-down on the flats. The sound of the orchestra playing "Deep Purple" floated across the water. There was something haunting about it, something that had to do with Julia and Argentina and the beginning of the war.

Stewart and Julia looked at each other, not saying anything. She turned into one of the channels, winding around islands and through the darkness until they had lost sense of which way they had come and anyone hunting them would need a miracle to find them. As they went, Stewart tore up von Hulse's note, rolling the pieces into tiny balls and dropping them one by one into the water.

Julia turned off the engine. They floated on a narrow channel, invisible between the darkness of the water and the sky, shrouded by bushes on either side. There was a half-moon that gave a silvery sheen to the river and just enough light for them to see each other. In the distance, they could barely hear "Deep Purple" above the insect whine.

"We'd better wait here for a while," she said. She had a look in her eyes that he couldn't describe. Although it wasn't cold, she was shivering in her dress. He put his arms around her. The touch of her skin made him tremble. All at once, she shuddered and pulled his face to hers. They kissed and he could taste the salty taste of something, tears or blood, on her lips, and then they were lying down in the well of the boat, their mouths all over each other, hungry and eager as though for the first time ever.

"Hurry, *yanqui*. We don't know how long we'll have each other," she whispered, unbuttoning his shirt.

"I know," he said, the silk cloth of her dress bunched in his fingers.

"We have to. You know we have to," she whispered, her mouth all over him. Now on his neck, his chest, pausing at his nipples till they hardened like a woman's, then opening his belt and fly, going at him right through his undershorts, wetting them with her saliva until she had him out and hard as a rock. She took him into her mouth, wet and sliding and hot as an oven.

He peeled off her dress, up over her head and undid her stockings. The feel of her skin was softer and smoother than the silk and he ran his mouth down the length of her, till his lips were kissing her lower lips, tasting the salt-sour taste of her even as she took him deep into her mouth. They moved against each other, squirming and sliding, the feeling building up and then the rhythm, her legs parted to receive him, his tongue flicking at her lips, probing deep inside her. She moved her hips against his face, her fingers clutching at his buttocks as he thrust himself into her mouth, harder and faster.

"Please *yanqui*! Please!" she moaned, breaking away for a second. Her body was moving faster and faster, almost out of control as he whirled around, sinking himself up to the hilt inside her.

And now it began, the two of them, moving as one in a single accelerating rhythm. The boat moving too, beneath them, in the same movement, as if they were without weight, floating beyond gravity, beyond the earth itself, and nothing around them but stars. The feeling was almost intolerable, building in wave after wave. They kissed and suddenly he was feeling her, feeling as she felt, no longer sure what was him and what was her. Every exquisite sensation and more, he felt her inside him too. And then it came, building from beneath his scrotum, an incredible growing surge. With a savage cry, her nails tore at his hips, pulling him into her as far as she could, even as she let go, riding the invisible rollercoaster as though it would never stop. Wave after wave, as he exploded into her, filling her with fire, thrusting over and over like a machine that is broken and cannot stop.

Afterwards, they lay in each other's arms legs entwined, still floating between the river and the sky.

"It's never been like that for me," he said finally, looking up at the stars. He didn't recognize any of them. It was a southern hemisphere sky, alien to him, for all its beauty. She turned his face and he felt the warmth of her lips on his.

"Nor I," she said hoarsely. "Not ever!"

He looked at her. In the moonlight her face was white as marble and unbelievably beautiful. Just looking at her made something tighten inside him and he thought, now I know. All this time, I thought it was only words, but if I die, at least I won't die not knowing.

"We'll have to go soon," he said softly.

"I know," she said, sitting up.

He stroked her back. The smooth white skin, the ridge of her vertebrae down to the cleft of her buttocks, there was something so sweet about all of it. Then he thought about Arturo and the thought was like a knife.

"About Arturo. . . ." he began.

"Please don't, *yanqui*," she said, her mouth twisting in a funny way. "Don't make it harder."

"I want you. I never knew till now how much. How much it matters."

"Stop," she whispered. "Please."

He looked at her, at the nakedness of her body, at all of her. He looked at her for a long time.

"I'm sorry. I should know better," he said.

She put her arms around him and pressed her forehead against his. Her breasts brushed against his chest.

"There are all kinds of wars, *yanqui*," she said hoarsely. "Love is only one."

She kissed him one last time and began to pull on her

clothes. He watched her for a moment more, then began to get dressed himself. When they were ready, she started the engine and they began winding back through the channels. As they approached the shore, the music became more distinct. The orchestra had switched to tangos, the guitars throbbing over the sound of the engine.

The casino was still lit up, its reflection shimmering in the water, so that it was hard to tell where the real shore ended and the reflection began.

"Buenos Aires," Julia said, gesturing at the lights. "City of water and illusion."

"Why illusion?" he asked.

"What else?" she shrugged. "In this land named for silver in which no silver was ever found."

Something about the way she said it struck him. She's quoting somebody, he thought.

"Who said that? All that about 'water and illusion?' " he asked.

She smiled warmly at him. Somehow, recognizing that she was quoting had made her happy.

"My grandfather," she said.

"John Gideon?"

"Yes," she nodded.

"He seems to come up a lot. What's he got to do with you and Arturo?"

"Arturo . . ." she made a face, "was my grandfather's disciple. In a way, it's why we married. It's why everything," she said softly. Then her expression changed. "But that was all a long time ago. Besides, we're here," gesturing at the shore.

She guided the boat to the shore and ran it aground. Stewart had his gun out, but the shore was deserted. He grabbed the line and jumped onto the muddy bank. He tied the boat up and was just holding out his hand for Julia when he heard footsteps behind him. He whirled, reaching for the Colt, but they were all around, flashlights blinding him.

"Put up your hands!" a voice ordered loudly.

Stewart raised his arms high. Rough hands grabbed him and stripped away the Colt. Someone yanked his hands behind him and cuffed them. Someone else, a big man smelling of garlic, grabbed his jacket and kneed him in the balls. Stewart fell to the ground, doubled over. The pain was incredible.

"*Hijo de puta!*" the man growled, kicking Stewart in the face. His cheek felt as if it had exploded as the man hauled him to his feet. The man pulled his massive fist back, cocked to hit him again, when another voice rang out.

"*Bastante!*" Enough! the voice said, coming into the circle of light. "You are under arrest, Señor Stewart," the voice said, and this time Stewart recognized it.

Stewart spat out a gob of blood. He turned toward the voice, blinking blindly into the lights. He was dimly aware of a crowd of faces, watching down from the casino balcony.

"What for? What's the charge?" Stewart mumbled. He could barely stand and the whole side of his face felt numb, as though it had been set in concrete.

"For the murder of Don Amadeo Cardenas," Colonel Fuentes said. He motioned to the big man to lead Stewart away. Stewart twisted to try and see Julia, but Fuentes's men were all around her. He could see her face for only an instant, looking despairingly at him. Fuentes put his arm familiarly around Stewart's shoulders. "Come, my friend. We have much to talk about. And I am sure you will tell me everything. Everything," he repeated, in a way that gave Stewart the creeps.

They brought him up to Fuentes's car and leaned him against the door. Before they put him inside, they shackled his hands and feet and slipped a leather collar with a kind of loop in it around his neck. Stewart looked around desperately. He had to find some way out of this. And to get the information about the *Graf Spee* to Fowler.

"Listen, Señor *Coronel*," Stewart began, talking with great difficulty, as though it was an art form he had yet to master. "What has all this to do with John Gideon?"

Fuentes looked at him as if he were raving.

"What are you talking about, *gringo?*"

"John Gideon. Don't tell me you never heard of him," Stewart snapped.

Fuentes's face darkened. He nodded to the big man, who slipped a short stick into the loop around Stewart's neck and began to turn it. The collar tightened, and all at once he couldn't breathe. He twisted and flopped around desperately, but it was useless. He felt his eyes bugging out. God, they were killing him! He couldn't stand it! He couldn't!

Suddenly, even while he was choking, Fuentes grabbed a handful of his hair and twisted his face close.

"Do not mock me, *gringo*," Fuentes snarled. "Every schoolboy knows of John Gideon. *Qué va?* What of it? Gideon is dead."

PART TWO

Gideon

No story begins in the present; we walk on bones.

And yet my father rarely spoke of his past, of anything that might help us understand who he was. What he was, *my mother would say, as if he were not a man, but an evil presence with whom we were condemned to share eternity.* El maldito, *she called him. The evil one.*

That was a secret between my mother and me. One of many. Ours was a house of secrets. My father, sealed in hate, never revealed himself.

Except once. The night the girl, Luz, gave birth.

That night—who could forget that night?—was one of those breathless sultry evenings that come in midsummer, so hot they make your skin crawl. All the windows in the ha-cienda had been thrown open, but no hint of breeze stirred in the gauze curtains. The air was full of static electricity and I remember jumping every time I touched anything. Dry thunder rumbled in the distance and there was the feeling of a storm coming. A terrible night for birthing. And then the gypsy, Joaquin, came and told my father the child had come.

Grabbing his silver-handled riding whip, my father stalked out of the house without a word, but with that look in his eye that we had all learned to fear.

He rode across the Pampa in a straight line, across planted fields as though they didn't exist. The moon was full and waxy; it cast the shadow of my father and his horse as sharply on the ground as if it were the sun. The night was still, too hot even for dogs to bark. The only sound was the heavy breathing of the horse and the pounding of hoofs on the soft ploughed earth. My father galloped hard and fast and the horse was lathered by the time he arrived at the hut. Inside, the girl, Luz, lay on a straw pallet, soaked with sweat. With her was the midwife, Antonia. She had swaddled the infant in a ragged cloth and was cradling it in her arms. The old man, Esteban, who had been with my father at Rio Negro, was also there and he rose and removed his hat when my father came in.

The room was like an oven, lit by candles that only added to the heat. Like the wind that cannot be stopped except by a wall, my father strode across the dirt floor of the hut to the stone fireplace, before stopping and turning to the midwife. Luz watched him from the pallet, her legs still splayed apart and bloody.

"Well, and what is it? Bull or cow?" my father demanded.

"A boy, praise God. A healthy one," Antonia said, jiggling the infant in her arms, her old face wrinkled with pleasure.

"Worse luck. More's the pity. Let me see it," my father said, holding out his hands for the child.

On the pallet, Luz whimpered like an animal. Her eyes were flat with fear, like a rabbit's caught by the light. Antonia handed the infant to my father, who stripped away the cloth and looked at it, naked. The infant began to cry. Without a word, my father dangled the infant by one of its legs and with a sudden swing, smashed its skull against the hearth with a soft, sickening thud.

The girl, Luz, screamed once. A terrible cry, torn from her very bowels. My father whirled on her.

"I warned you not to have this child, didn't I? Well, didn't I?" he shouted, his face red and twisted with rage. He flung the limp tiny body from him as though it was a piece of garbage and left. He was soon back at the hacienda.

My mother was waiting for him when he came in. How she knew what he had done, I don't know. But she knew. I could see it from the way she held herself. She was standing near the foot of the stairs and I could see it all from behind the banister near the top, where I was hiding.

"Cabrón! Maldito! What have you done? Is there anything you won't do?" she demanded, her fists tiny and white, clenched impotently at her sides.

"Is it the child's death? Is that it?" he said, lighting a cigar, the smoke twisting in the light from the chandelier. "Well, don't let it bother you. I've seen children die before. Even my own."

That was the first time I ever became aware that he'd had a family before us. Long ago, in England.

—From the journal of Lucia de Montoya-Gideon

11

December, 1864
Manchester, England

THE GASLIGHT sputtered and hummed, stirring shadows to life on the walls. The room was icy cold, as cold as outside, where they could hear the sleet rattling on the oilcloth window pane. The old woman, Deathwatch Mary everyone called her, raised her head from the child's chest.

"Yer coulda' saved yersels th' trouble. 'Tis the Cholera, sure. She'll not see Chrismuss," Deathwatch said, getting up.

"Be still, you old crone. She can 'ear you," Gideon hissed, grabbing the old woman by the wrist.

"An' if she do?" Deathwatch said, wrenching her hand away indignantly. "Let 'er make peace with 'er Lord and Saviour an' done wi'it. Sich goin's-on over a child. A female yet, poor soul. H'aint natcherel-like, an' ye take my meanin'," she muttered darkly, rubbing her wrist. She gathered up her spoons and bottles. "There's tuppence due. One fer th' Godfrey's Elixir an' one fer me service," holding out her hand and not handing over the bottle.

"An' I'll give ye tuppence," Gideon growled, raising his hand as if to backhand her. He was a tall young man, his arms powerful and muscular, and he towered over her as over a child. But the old woman stood her ground, glaring up at him until the woman, Lucy, barely more than a girl herself, got between them.

"We'll pay thee, Mary. When we get our jobs back at the mill. I swear 't," Lucy said.

The old woman looked at her suspiciously, her eyes almost disappearing in a network of wrinkles. Her hair was wispy and wild and she wore layers upon layers of ragged clothes, stolen it was whispered, from the corpses of her patients as they breathed their last. If she had ever been a girl, it had been so long ago that even she couldn't remember it.

"No yer won't. They'll be no cotton fer work till this American War be done, an' not then fer yer man. 'Tis said 'e's a bleeding Chartist."

"The Chartists're long gone, woman. There ain't no more. Nor nothing else for working men," Gideon muttered.

"Th' bloody workin' man, is 't? Ain't we th' bleedin' Methodist Revival, tho'? An' nary a lump o' coal, or even crust o' bread for Chrismuss. An' ye'll be needin' a shillin' an' more fer th' burial," the old woman said, glancing at the little girl.

"Shut your beak, ye hag! You're scaring 'er," Gideon said.

"Listen to 'im," Deathwatch said, cocking her head and making a mock curtsy. "Th' bloody Marster o' the 'ouse! An' where's me money, m'Lord?" holding out her hand again.

Gideon's eyes flashed. As he reached for the old woman, the child cried out, "Papa!" from her pallet. Gideon stood there for a moment, his fists balled, then turned with a snarl of frustration and rushed over to the pallet.

The little girl lay in a pool of light from the gas jet. At the wispy ends, her hair was long and blonde like her mother's, but now most of it was dark and matted with sweat. Her eyes were glassy from the fever. When she breathed, her puny chest barely raised the ragged coverlet that she clutched with tiny white hands, white as if carved from ivory. Even sick, she was extraordinarily pretty, like a fairy child misplaced in this world, and Gideon remembered how in earlier days, when they would walk in the street, people would stop what they were doing and stare after her, as if they had seen something they couldn't explain.

"It hurts, Papa! Make it go away," she said.

"Shhh," he whispered, picking her up and rocking her in his arms. "Papa'll fix it. Papa'll fix everything." He turned to the old woman. "Leave the treacle. Ye'll get your money 'fore Christmas Day. By Almighty God, I swear 't."

The old woman pulled a long face.

"First th' tuppence. Then the Elixir, if you please," she clucked, wrapping her shawl around her as she scurried out the door.

On the pallet, Gideon cradled the little girl to him. She was limp as a rag doll in his arms. Her eyes were blue and strange, as if she were dreaming wide awake.

"Is 't Christmas yet?" she asked. She had a bad wheeze. It whistled through her words like wind.

"Not yet," he said, holding her tight. The child weighed hardly anything. He might have been holding air.

"Papa," she whispered, her eyes shiny. "For Christmas Day, c'n we go to the Magic Place?"

"Wot Magic Place?" Gideon said, looking not at the child, but at Lucy, standing in the middle of the room, hugging herself to keep warm.

"You know. Where you wuz a soljer."

"Ah, the Crimea."

"Yes. An' we're goin' there for Christmas, amn't we, Papa?"

"Well, mebbe. Soon's you're better."

"What's it like there, Papa?"

"Wot, again?"

"Tell me," she ordered, in the peremptory way children have. "You h'an't telled me in a long time."

"Well," Gideon sighed, remembering Inkerman and the frozen hills and the bodies that filled the ravine near the Sandbag Battery. Mostly, he remembered the harbor at Balaclava. There was nothing in all the world like that harbor. Thick as soup with things floating in the water: rotting stores, amputated limbs, dead horses, bloated corpses. And on the decks of the ships crammed side-by-side into the narrow bay, half the army dying of exposure and the cholera. "Th' Crimea is a magic land, with mosques an' minarets, like castles in a fairy tale. Th' grass is green an' 'edged with flowers. It's always warm and sunny an' summer never ends. An' children laugh an' play an' eat warm bread an' honey. An' they's all kinds o' fantastical people. Rooshians with beards so long they touch the floor an' Turks flying by, riding carpets as if they was clouds. An' there's 'orses an' railway trains for all th' children to ride an' ever'one wears clothes o' silk, that shimmer with color like butterfly wings. An' good children wot goes to bed when their papa tells 'em," he said, kissing her and putting her down. As he tucked her in, she motioned him close.

"Papa," she whispered.

"Aye, Princess."

"That woman," she said, screwing up her face. "Is she a witch?"

"No, why?"

"She scares me," she confided. "She smells terrible bad."

" 'At's nothing. You won't be seeing her no more."

"Promise?"

"Aye, I promise," he said, kissing her forehead. It felt hot enough to cook an egg on. He stood up and grabbed his scarf and cap.

"Where're thee going now, Johnny?" Lucy asked him, her eyes dark and full of fear.

"Look arter Judith. Don't be leaving 'er," he said, opening the door. The stair below was black and cold.

"Thee be going to Quayle, ain't thee?"

"I'm going to get money," he said. "I ain't letting her go for want o' it."

"I'm not trusting him," she shuddered. "The way he looks at me. It's like his hands are on me."

"Well, an' let 'im want," Gideon said, thrusting his chin out. " 'E touches you 'n I'll kill 'im."

She looked at him strangely then, her eyes the same pale blue as the child's.

"Thee's a fool, John. A most partickler fool."

"Aye, mebbe," he said, stepping into the stairwell. "But at least I'm a man."

"Aye, and where's the difference?" she said softly, closing the door behind him.

It was sleeting hard and the wind was blowing as he made his way down the street and along the canal. At night, the dark water couldn't be seen, but he could hear it lapping against the embankment like the sea. There were few street-lamps in this part of town, and doors and windows were closed and shuttered. Despite the cold, there were families huddled in doorways and under arches over by the market. The workhouses were full up and people slept where they could, bare feet sticking out from under burlap sacking. Gideon hurried along, head bent into the wind, his hands balled in his pockets to keep them warm. The image of the little girl burned in his mind. The thought of her dying was like a knife, and beyond it, nothing. There was nothing beyond it.

Around the corner, the gin shop was an oasis of warmth and light. The windows were steamed up and he could hear the noise and smell the tobacco smoke even from outside, and it occurred to him that once he went through the door there would be no turning back. What Lucy had said about Quayle bothered him. Maybe she was right. He thought about that and about the money. He went inside. Quayle was waiting for him.

"I thought mayhap you mightn't be coming," Quayle said, as Gideon sat down.

"I'm 'ere," Gideon growled. "That's all as matters, ain't it?"

"Indeed, sir," Quayle said, whipping out an extravagantly

colored handkerchief to wipe his forehead, "there is much in our business that matters. But will you join me for a drop of the Blue Ruin?" he said, motioning to the waitress. "Two of the best, Maggie. Cream of the Valley, if you please," he called out. The waitress brought two tall glasses filled with gin and placed them on the table.

"And now to business, sir," Quayle said in a quiet tone that could not be heard over the shouted conversations all around them.

"Aye, business," Gideon said, taking a long swallow of the gin.

"Two thousand pounds of business, if you please, Mister Gideon. Cash money. And one hundred and fifty golden guineas. All in the box. Just waiting for Christmas Day for Mister Davenport, Esquire, to deliver to his Lordship at Prestwich, lest any doubt his God-fearing charity, or his secure place in the very front-est pew of Heaven. Him what sacked you and a thousand and four hundred others for to save thruppence on the week, that ever kindly soul of philan-trophy," Quayle smirked, smacking his lips with mock piety. He was a plump jowly man, with coarse features and cunning eyes that gave him the look of a butcher in a poor neighborhood, the kind with a quick wink for the wives and an even quicker thumb for the scale.

"Two thousand," Gideon breathed. Just saying such an amount was like a prayer.

"And one hundred and fifty golden guineas," Quayle intoned, leaning still closer. Gideon could just see the stacks of gold coins sitting in the box. "It's all supposed to go to his Lordship and any he deems deserving, to be sure. It's only a question of which deserving it's going to," Quayle winked, producing a key from his waistcoat and passing it under the table to Gideon.

"Wot about th' beak?"

"No Peelers. The porochial never shows on nights as these. Only the beadle at eleven o'clock, if he isn't ploughed under at the Boar and Chain," Quayle laughed.

"At's all, then? Easy as 'at?"

Quayle nodded. He looked around, motioning Gideon closer.

"There's an iron bar in the coal scuttle. Knock things 'round a bit," he whispered. "Make it look like Rogue Riders, or some such desperate villains. I'll meet you at one by the Victoria and we'll split then and Devil's the wiser."

"No tricks, Mister Quayle," Gideon said quietly, turning his sleeve so Quayle could see the edge of a knife blade glinting in the smoky light. "You be alone, come one, or you'll rot in your grave this night."

"My dear *contraire*, you cut me to the quick," Quayle declared, laying his pudgy fingers on his chest. "'Pon my soul, sir. 'Tis I who must trust you. Or have you forgotten? You'll be the one holding the ah, exchequer, so to speak. It is I who lack assuages, not you."

Gideon eyed him suspiciously. Over by the board there was raucous laughter. They were giving a toddler gin and he was sucking it straight from the bottle as though it was milk.

"I know you, Quayle. Let's not be playacting wi' each other."

Quayle colored. He fumbled for his clay pipe and tobacco.

"I don't take your meaning, Mister Gideon. What do you take me for?"

"Davenport's dog, Mister Quayle. That's wot I take ye for. I know you. I know wot ye are an' that you've an itch for my missus. Don't scratch that itch, Mister Quayle," Gideon said, finishing his gin and getting up. Quayle's ebony walking stick was leaning against the chair. Gideon picked it up and with a single movement, broke it across his knee and threw the pieces down. "Wood c'n break, Mister Quayle. An' men too."

"Now, now, dear fellow," Quayle paled. "No need for such burletta. Not at all. 'Tis the gloomy season," he laughed loudly, looking around in case anyone was watching. But everyone was busy with their gin and talk. "It's bloody weather. Affects the spirit. In October, the Englishman shoots pheasant. In December, he shoots himself, ha, ha."

"Aye, December. I'll remember that about shooting, Mister Quayle."

"Indeed, sir. Caution is never amiss," Quayle muttered, not looking at Gideon.

"All right, then. One o'clock," Gideon said. He turned and headed for the door.

"One," Quayle said, raising his glass to his lips.

The mill was near the river, over toward Blackfriars. The building was brick, two blocks long, and smelled of coal dust and smoke, even at night, with the fires of the Watt engines banked. There were families camped in front of the main gate, shivering in the wet snow, though everyone knew there was no work. A "dosser" slept across the step of the side door, his face blue as ink, snoring and stinking of gin. Gideon stepped carefully over him and let himself in with the key.

The mill was dark and empty, the only light filtering in from the streetlamp through the high dingy windows. The spinning-jennies and looms were still. They stood in rack after rack, an orchard of machines. Silent now, the air still filled with that fine lint and dust that the "devils," as the young boys were called, would run through with the shuttle, so you could see their passage through the dust in the air like a ship's wake. The machines were coated white with it, like hoarfrost, or spider-webs, and Gideon saw the place where his Lucy used to stand, her face still pink from the country then. He came to the end by the stair and the Wadding Hole, where the cotton scraps and damaged strips were salvaged by little ones like his Judith, their bodies bent like corkscrews to get under the machines, so that after fourteen hours in a day down there, they couldn't straighten till morning, if then. She'd only been down there four months, not only for the monthly twelve pence she earned, but the thruppence a week they saved from giving her over to the old woman who kept the little ones on laudanum and treacle all day to keep them still, so she was a ragdoll when they came for her each night. And now, only four months in the Wadding Hole and she was dying, the rage rising in him as he mounted the stair to Davenport's office.

Sounds of scuttling in the office; sweat prickled all over his body. Be easy, he told himself. It's only rats. He opened the door. The room was cold and still, the shadow from the window forming a cross on the polished floor. Gideon went to the coal scuttle and found the iron bar, just where Quayle had said it would be. Hefting it gave him a feeling of confidence. He crossed to Mister Davenport's desk. It was locked, but with the iron bar he had the drawers open in a second. He began to go through the drawers, looking for the box. His fingers were itching for it. The money was practically in his hands. But he couldn't find it.

He began to get angry. Quayle had said it was in the desk. The last drawer was locked. The wood splintered and cracked as he pried it open. The box was in the drawer. It was wood, gleaming in the light from the window. There was a padlock on it that he snapped easily with the iron bar. He ripped it open and reached for the money.

It was empty. Only papers. No two thousand pounds. No one hundred and fifty golden guineas. Nothing. He threw the box down and looked around wildly. He tried Quayle's desk. But there were only more papers. He started to tear the place apart and then he heard a noise downstairs.

Gideon froze.

Someone was down there. Jesu, the beadle, he thought, a terrible chill creeping up his spine. But Quayle said he only came by once, at eleven, if at all. And it was after midnight now. The footsteps were coming up the stairs. They were slow and cautious. Not like someone making ordinary rounds, but like someone expecting to find something.

And then he understood.

Quayle and Davenport had Judas'd him. They'd taken the money for themselves—Quayle had been free-spending lately, he remembered noticing—and they needed a scapegoat. Someone to blame for the missing money. Lucy had been right. And he, desperate because of Judith, had been fool enough not to see it.

His only chance was to get away. Then, his thoughts simmered darkly, then he'd settle with Quayle and Mister-bloody-Davenport. He headed for the door, so full of his thoughts that he wasn't paying attention. He opened the door. The beadle was standing in front of him.

The beadle looked thunderstruck. He had a lantern in one hand and a staff in the other, that he raised, as if to ward off a blow. But he was too late. Gideon punched him in the face with a savage blow and was halfway down the stairs before the beadle hit the floor. Gideon raced across the mill to the side door and tore it open.

The constable was there, waiting. He was a big dog-faced man in belted coat and top hat, glowering at Gideon, irons ready in his hand. Men with torches were already beginning to gather, "dossers" and workmen from a nearby public house, and the constable rattled the irons triumphantly, as Gideon stepped into the light from the streetlamp.

"Come 'ere, you," the constable ordered loudly. He reached for Gideon, who hesitated for a second, then smashed away the constable's hand with the iron bar that he still held. The constable shrieked. He dropped the irons and as the men came toward him, Gideon raised the iron bar menacingly, backing them off. He turned and ran.

"Stop! In the Queen's Name!" the constable shouted, and with an animal howl the men were after Gideon.

"Ten shillings for 'im as brings 'im in!" someone shouted, and as if by magic the crowd began to swell. Suddenly, pursuers emerged from shadows and doorways, some in nightclothes, some wearing everything they owned. It was as if they had all been in hiding, waiting for a signal.

Gideon ran desperately, heading for the Shambles. The streets were a warren of narrow unpaved alleys, muddy and rutted, with snow-covered mounds of garbage where squatters lived and dark frozen puddles of filth from the privies. They were bordered by tiny cottages, most no bigger than dog kennels, with patched-over fronts sagging over the mud, and now, out of them, came sleepy men pulling on their hats and scarfs to join the hue and cry. In the darkness and the flickering torchlight, they looked like a subterranean race coming out of their dens to hunt. They were coming fast behind Gideon. The sleet and ice made it slippery going, and turning a corner into a narrow court, he slipped and fell on a patch of ice. A howl went up from the mob.

Gideon staggered to his feet. He looked around wildly, his breath coming in gasps. He was in an open space behind a block of dilapidated terrace houses, some practically falling down. The mob was at the corner. They were shouting, and in the midst of it all a woman was screaming. Somewhere, improbably, he could hear the bell of the Cathedral in the distance, tolling one o'clock. Quayle, Gideon thought in a rage. He'd never intended to meet him under the arches at Victoria Station. He was probably still at the gin shop, smoking his pipe and relishing what he had done.

The crowd was getting louder by the second. Their blood was up. If they got hold of him in this mood, they would tear him to pieces, Gideon thought, looking around desperately.

There were three mews leading out from the court into darkness. Gideon hesitated. He'd never been in this court before. The torches were close behind him.

"Ere 'e is!" someone cried out. A roar rose from the crowd.

Gideon plunged headlong into one of the mews. The nearest and darkest. He ran like a wild man, knocking over a barrow to slow them for a second. There was no light. The passage smelled utterly foul, as if something dead had been left there to rot. He glanced behind him. He had gained a few yards. He might even have a chance, he thought. He looked ahead and felt as if he had stepped into an abyss.

He had chosen wrong. A blank brick wall was at the end of the mews.

In desperation, he sprinted at the wall. At the last second, he leaped as hard as he could, clawing for the top. It was too high. For an impossible second, he hung by his fingernails from the brick, then toppled in a heap at the foot of the wall. When he got up, the crowd had gathered around him in a semicircle. They were silent. The steam from their breath formed a cloud that hung like fog over the mews.

Gideon looked at them, his eyes like nothing any of them had ever seen. All at once, he dropped his hands to his sides and they were on him, screaming and beating at him savagely, as though he had been the cause of everything that had ever gone wrong in their lives.

At the Assizes, he was sentenced to life at hard labor. What the judge found particularly reprehensible was that Gideon showed no remorse, nor would he name his confederates, to whom he had undoubtedly passed the stolen money during his flight from justice. For this, the judge intoned, Gideon was to be taken down to Newgate. And from thence to ship, to the penal facility at Perth in the Australia Colony, "as far from this land's blessed shores as possible, and still to be in this world."

As Gideon was led from the court, Lucy begged leave of the baliff to speak to him for a moment. Quayle was with her. He lounged against the far wall watching them, a nasty smile on his face. For the first time, he let his hate shine through in his eyes.

"Judith's dead. I thought thee ought to know," Lucy said.

Gideon looked down at her. He was like a man who had just been shot. The same surprised terrible look. Lucy stared back at him, horrified. She stared as though she had never seen him before. His face was changing. The bones seemed to rearrange themselves under his skin, right in front of her. He looked at her as though from a great distance. When he spoke, his voice was different too. Everything about him was different.

"Did she know—about this?" he asked, rattling his irons faintly.

Lucy nodded, still staring at his face.

"'Twas Deathwatch Mary. She came again for her money. She told her, tho' she were nearly gone. She looked to me, the little 'un, but she were too weak to say she didn't believe. But it were in her eyes, John," she said, her voice breaking.

"I wish I could believe 't."

"Here's tuppence," she whispered, slipping two pennies into his pocket. "I put 'em on her eyes, but she were only in a sheet, not a coffin, an' they kept falling off. I thought thee'd want them."

"Where'd ye get the money?"

"Borrowed," she said, not looking at him.

He looked at Quayle, then back at Lucy. Her cheeks and lips were rouged, he noticed, and she had on a new hat tied with a pink ribbon and she smelled of scent.

"You're with 'im, then?" he said, his voice showing no emotion. It was like a statue talking.

Her eyes filled and she shook her head to clear them.

"I needed money for the burying. I couldn't just leave her there. Oh, I begged thee not to go! I told thee he were wanting me."

"An' so ye went," he said, in the same emotionless voice. "An' arter it'll be the night-house. An' then skirts up for 'tuppence ha'penny behind the shed."

"And if I do," she snapped, eyes flashing suddenly. "It's food, ain't it?"

"Aye. It's food."

"Better 'n thee, with thy book-reading. To get on, thee said. They were laughing over thee, Quayle told me. It's why they chose thee. Him and Mister Davenport. 'Cause thee were uppity, John. Thee needed taking down, he said."

"I never said ary a word."

"Nay, Johnny. But it were in thy eyes. It were always in thy eyes," she said, bursting into tears as Quayle came up and grinning broadly at Gideon, put his arm around her waist, with a familiar pinch for her backside, and led her away.

Gravesend. The prison ship *Eurydice* stirred with a faint clanking sound against her anchor chain, waiting for the turn of the tide. The night was icy cold and the prisoners, chained in rows on long wooden shelves, shivered restlessly in their sleep. The nightwatch had sounded two bells, and through the barred porthole Gideon could just make out the lights twinkling in the darkness. But from the angle he was at, he could see so little there was no way of knowing whether they were stars, or other ships, or lights from Tilbury and along the shore. On Gideon's plank, only Gideon and the prisoner next to him, a skin-and-bones cut-purse named Coffey, were still awake. Gideon was working furiously at his ankle shackle with a nail he had pried from the plank. His fingers were torn and bloody and the skin on his ankle and the back of his heel had been rubbed raw. He had managed to bend back the cross-piece of the shackle pin about a quarter of an inch. Coffey watched him work.

Gideon grabbed the shackle with his hands and heaved, trying to spread it apart. His back muscles bunched, his shirt splitting with the effort as he pulled till his arms couldn't take it and blood seeped from beneath his fingernails. He let go, panting. It was hopeless, he thought. Hopeless. Like Judith. The image of her on that pallet was before him. It was branded on his soul. He drew an angry breath and then he was at it again, pulling till he thought his fingers would shatter and he felt the pin give slightly. He spread the shackle as wide as he could. Pointing his toe like a ballerina, he pushed at the anklet with all his might. The edge of the iron on the raw flesh of his heel was utter agony and still he pushed harder, clenching his teeth to keep from crying out.

Suddenly, it was off. Gideon got on his hands and knees, wincing at the pain. Coffey watched him through half-closed eyes and didn't say anything. Gideon looked at Coffey, then turned and crept over the other prisoners sleeping on the plank. He crawled on all fours to the porthole, leaving bloody prints wherever his hands and foot touched the plank.

Through the bars he could see the Thames. There were lights from other boats and barges at anchor and in the distance, only the darkness of the estuary towards Southend and that invisible place where the river becomes the sea.

He tried both bars over the porthole. One was solid, the other turned slightly in the wood. That was the one he attacked with the nail. He stabbed the nail into the wood at the base of the bar, wedging it and prying, trying to widen the hole. Again and again. He used the nail like a dagger. With each stroke, he imagined it was Quayle's head. And Davenport's, who had sacked him from the mill; Quayle's partner in all of this. And Squire Cobbett's, who enclosured him and Lucy off the land. And the bailiff, Swithey, who threatened to have him flogged if he didn't leave that same day.

They had taken everything from him. Except for Lucinda. And Judith, that tiny spark of sunshine that had somehow come to earth. Just that would have been enough for him, but they had to have that too. They had to have it all. He was to have nothing. He was nothing; an obnoxious insect. He deserved to have nothing. Except hate. It was a good thing he had so much of it, he thought grimly. He would need a lot of it to make it go around.

The wood began to splinter and he grabbed the iron bar. He planted both feet against the side of the ship and straightened, pulling the bar with every ounce of strength in his body. With a sudden crack, the bar came partly out of the wood.

Gideon stopped. He looked around the plank and down below. No one moved. No one seemed to have heard. Then Coffey sat up and smiled at him.

"Take me wi' ye," Coffey whispered.

Gideon shook his head. It would take too long to free Coffey's shackle. It was a miracle he hadn't been found out already. Besides, he didn't trust the little man.

"Lookee. Ye takes me wi' ye, or I sounds th' alarum an' be damned," Coffey hissed, his eyes narrowed to tiny holes.

Gideon held up his hand in surrender and made his way back to Coffey, smiling grimly.

"Tha's more like," Coffey murmured, extending his foot for Gideon to work on. But his foot never made it. Gideon grabbed Coffey around the neck and with the heel of his hand on Coffey's jaw, pushed sideways with a vicious twist. There was a terrible crack as Coffey's neck broke before he could make a sound.

Gideon let Coffey's head down gently on the plank. Coffey's eyes were bulging wide. Gideon closed the lids and crept back to the porthole. As quietly as he could, with excruciating slowness, he bent the loosened bar to the side and squeezed headfirst through the porthole. The fit was too tight. He wasn't going to make it. Like a bloody cork in a bottle, he thought, wriggling and squeezing desperately. He scraped the skin on his sides and chest and with a final savage thrust was through and falling with a splash into the river.

The water was dark and unbelievably cold. It knocked the

breath out of him. He felt himself blacking out and tried to fight it. He was under the water, completely blind, with no idea which way to swim or even, he suddenly realized with terror, which way the surface was. His hands and ankle were stinging badly and he was striking out, swimming one way, then another, but it was no good. He was almost out of air, barely conscious.

Something stirred inside him. Something that wouldn't die. It stirred like some loathsome creature in the mud. I won't die, he told himself, watching the bubbles rise from his lips. They were silvery in the darkness, rising slowly as if time didn't matter, and all at once he knew which way was up. He followed the bubbles to the surface and broke through. When he looked around, he saw that he was midway between the *Eurydice* and the dark outline of another ship, a big sailing vessel also riding at anchor, waiting for the tide. Shivering violently from the cold, Gideon turned and swam toward the other ship's anchor chain.

The chain was cold and slippery. He clung to it like a monkey, pulling himself up hand over hand. Halfway to the top, he slipped and slid back down into the water. He was shivering very badly now. If he didn't get out of his wet clothes and into something warm soon, the cold would kill him. As it was, he was losing strength very quickly. He looked up at the anchor chain to the deck. He regretted it instantly. It seemed impossibly high. And he was getting colder and weaker by the second.

Last time, he vowed, pulling himself slowly out of the water. His hands were shaking badly and losing sensation. With each handhold he had to look to see whether he had a grip on the chain or not. His fingers were too numb to feel it. He pulled himself up, concentrating on each handhold. The climb took forever. Near the top, he began to slip again. The image of Judith flashed before his eyes. He struck desperately up for another handhold. His fingers hit something. He grabbed at it, hanging by his fingertips, kicking and heaving himself up and onto the deck.

There was no one on deck. It was piled high with boxes and bales of implements. Iron goods, mostly, it seemed. Good for hiding, he thought. He lay trembling, barely able to move, but he couldn't stay there. He had to get under cover, he thought, getting up. He was on the forward deck. Sternward was the ship's housing and there was a cabin and hold forward. Both were too risky, he thought, looking at a skiff covered with canvas, lashed to the deck. It would have to do as a hiding place, until he was rested enough to try for shore. Then, Quayle and the others, he thought grimly.

He crept to the side of the skiff and untied the lashing. He looked around before ducking under the canvas. Everything was in shadow. The ship's crane rose from the deck and the masts, sails furled, towered like giant crucifixes against the starry sky. Only a hundred yards or so away, the *Eurydice* lay silent. His escape hadn't been discovered yet. The Thames was dark and still as a pond. He started to crawl into the skiff when the sound of a pistol cocking sent a tremor down his spine.

"Du calme, monsieur. Du calme," a voice behind him said.

Gideon started to turn around.

"Do not move! Or I will 'ave to shoot you," the voice said. Gideon felt a hand patting him down for weapons. *"Eh bien,* turn around," the voice said.

It belonged to a medium-sized man, bareheaded, his hair worn long and over his forehead in a style that was out of date. He wore a heavy seaman's coat and his eyes were dark and, except for the pistol, might have seemed amused. He had the look of a man for whom life, except for its pleasures, was something of a joke. A Frenchman, of course, Gideon thought.

"And what are you? Thief? Or stowaway?" the Frenchman asked.

"A stowaway," Gideon said, looking at the pistol. The Frenchman saw it and backed away another step. Too far away to jump.

"I think not. You're from that prison-ship, yes?" the French-man said, moving his head in the direction of the *Eurydice.* "I saw you swim over. What was your crime?"

"Poverty."

"Oof! The most serious crime of all," the Frenchman said gravely, with complete seriousness. There was something about the way he said it. Suddenly, an idea struck Gideon with absolutely certainty, like a revelation.

"Wot was yours?"

The Frenchman looked at him sharply. He raised the pistol. Gideon was sure he had blundered. But then the Frenchman gave an odd Gallic shrug.

"Politics," he said. "I was a *'Socialiste.'* In Paris at the barricades in '48. That is also a crime. Especially if one is on the losing side," he said, studying Gideon. He lowered the pistol. "Come with me," he said, turning and walking back to his cabin. Gideon hesitated, wondering whether to trust him. After a moment, he followed.

The cabin was cramped and tiny. The Frenchman lit a lantern. He looked at Gideon, then rummaged in a trunk and took out a bottle and poured two glasses.

"Calvados," the Frenchman commented, handing Gideon a glass. "The *capitaine* is a Normand. Go on. You look like you need it."

Gideon drank. The Calvados warmed his body like fire. It was delicious and for the first moment since he had left Judith and Lucy in that garret, he felt alive.

"Eh bien," the Frenchman said, draining his glass. All at once, he pulled back his long hair to reveal the letter "P" branded on his forehead. "You see, *mon ami*, I was also a *prisonnier*. At the Conciergerie. How fitting that in our Age of Iron, Marie-Antoinette's last *palais* should have been turned into a prison. Well," he shrugged, sitting down. "That was a long time ago. *Ecoutez*, my friend, what was your plan?"

"Get to shore. Escape."

The Frenchman only smiled. He refilled their glasses.

"With those eyes?" the Frenchman said, gesturing at Gideon with his glass. "No, *monsieur*. You were thinking not of escape, but of revenge."

Gideon stood up and put down his glass.

"I ain't going back. If you're turning me in, shoot me now and be done."

The Frenchman looked up at him, his expression unchanged.

"It was a bad plan. Without clothes, money, how far do you get, *hein?* They would raise the 'hue' and the 'cry' for you and it is *fini. Ecoutez*," he said, leaning forward. "I am badly, 'ow you say, short of the hands. You look plenty strong to me and for myself, it is better to 'ave as little to do with the *fonctionnaires* as possible. As for the *capitaine*, so long as he 'as 'is Calvados, he will do as I say. Also, he is no lover of the English. Besides, *mon ami*, it is not you who is leaving the England. It is England which has already leaved you," he said, gesturing with his glass in the direction of the *Eurydice*.

"You've a point," Gideon said, sitting down and finishing his glass. "Where're you bound?"

The Frenchman leaned forward. In the yellowish cabin light, the "P" on his forehead looked like a sign from some strange religious sect. Gideon could smell the liquor on his breath.

"To the Argentine. The *République* of Buenos Aires."

"Where's 'at?"

"At the end of the world. For you, perfect. As far from England as one can be and still see the Atlantique."

Gideon looked at him suspiciously. He was beginning to feel the Calvados.

"Wot's it like, this 'ere Argentine?"

"*Alors*, you will like it, *mon ami*. It is a land of cut-throats. When they find the biggest cut-throat of all, they make him President," the Frenchman grinned.

12

December 8, 1939
Buenos Aires

A POOL of light in a darkened cellar; in the center, a wooden chair bolted to the floor, heavy leather straps around the prisoner's wrists, ankles, chest and neck. Colonel Fuentes was in darkness. Only his hands, fingers drumming on the table, could be seen at the rim of the circle of light. Next to him, the sound of a pen scratching, taking down every word.

Stewart slumped in the chair. One of Fuentes's gorillas, an ugly brute with ape-like arms and a gold front tooth, had been going at him with a rubber hose, and his sides and stomach ached viciously at every breath. One of his eyes was blackened and his lip swollen, but so far it had been pretty crude stuff. Now Fuentes himself had come in and Stewart couldn't help shuddering. Not only because of Fuentes, and the stories about skin-flaying and all, but because of the pair of enormous long-armed pliers Fuentes had placed on the table, near the edge where Stewart could see it.

Silence. Everyone waited, the only sound the creak of a chair and Stewart's heavy breathing. Earlier, when they'd kept Stewart in a dark featureless cell, he'd heard screams coming from this room. Terrible screams. The worst sounds in the world. Despite the stone walls, sound escaped from this room. They must want it that way, Stewart thought. So that you were half disarmed by fear even before you entered here. That's what the room smelled like. Fear and urine and the unwashed stench of bodies destroyed before they were dead.

Stewart heard a sigh from the darkness of the table beyond the rim of light, then Fuentes's voice, calm, detached, indifferent.

"*Pues*, why did you kill Cardenas?" Fuentes asked.

Stewart made a face into the darkness.

"Don't be stupid. Why would I kill Cardenas?"

A huge fist came out of the glare like an express train. It smashed into the side of his injured jaw. Everything exploded inside his head and then he was back, his jaw feeling like it had been busted and his mouth full of blood.

"*Perro!* To talk thus to the Señor *Coronel!*" Gold Tooth growled. "Let me deal with him, *mi Coronel*," Gold Tooth appealed to the darkness.

Stewart saw a dismissing flick of Fuentes's fingers. Forget Gold Tooth, Stewart told himself. There's only Fuentes. Every interrogation is a duel of two wills. Never more. He remembered the Fascist captain at that café in Saragossa who told him that. The one who, when Stewart asked about the missing Americans, had said, "We have no American prisoners, Señor. In this country, we have only Spaniards. Spaniards," the Fascist turned and spat on the ground, "—and lice."

"*Pues*, why did you kill Cardenas?" Fuentes asked again in the same tone of voice. It implied infinite patience, that Fuentes was prepared to sit there forever asking the same question, till he got what he wanted. What every interrogator wanted, Stewart thought. Not merely the truth, but his victim's soul.

"Cardenas was killed to prevent him from talking to me. I'm the last person in the world who would want him dead,"

Stewart said, squinting into the lamp glare as if trying to see Fuentes's face. "You ought to know, *Coronel*. You sent me there."

"You were seen leaving his club only minutes after he was killed," Fuentes said.

"Of course I was seen. It was a trap! Or didn't your curly-haired friend mention the Germans crawling all over the place?" Stewart said nastily, steeling himself for another punch from Gold Tooth. Instead, the chilling scrape of the pliers being picked up from the table. Gold Tooth reentered the circle of light, hefting the heavy pliers in his hand as though it was a toothpick.

"The problem here, *yanqui*, is that you lack anticipation. The rubber hose for a man of your background, lacks refinement. It was simply to get your attention while we attended to more important business," Fuentes said, snapping his fingers for Gold Tooth to proceed.

Gold Tooth took out a rusty pocket knife and jabbed it viciously under the nail of Stewart's little finger. Stewart closed his eyes against the pain. Gold Tooth pressed open the tip of the pliers against the little finger, pushing the skin back from the nail.

"*Coronel*...." Stewart began desperately. Gold Tooth closed the pliers, twisted and bent back and Stewart almost leaped out of the chair, the straps digging deep into his flesh. His little nail was bent up at an impossible angle, the appaling pain shooting all the way up his arm to the shoulder. Gold Tooth let go for a second, repositioning the pliers to get a better grip. He began to pull the nail out by the roots, millimeter by millimeter, with excruciating slowness, bending it back till it was curving up like a bow. Stewart gritted his teeth, sweat pouring from every pore of his body. The nail came free, dripping blood, and Gold Tooth held it up for a second like a trophy, then tossed it away. Gold Tooth flicked with his finger at the raw exposed flesh where the nail had been and Stewart jumped.

"Anticipation," Fuentes repeated. "Now, have you my meaning, *gringo?* We begin with what you need least, the little finger of your left hand, yes? But you have many more fingers and toes and then, *pues*, we go on to things which are truly painful, yes? Things which make you a man. Have you clarity now?"

"Clear," Stewart gasped, his head dropping to his chest. His chest was heaving and slick with sweat and it took him a great effort to raise his head again. He licked his lips. They tasted of blood and salt. "Only we both know I wasn't even in Argentina when Almayo was killed. And whoever killed him, also killed Cardenas. So why don't you just ask me what you really want to know and we can get this over with?"

"Such insolence," Gold Tooth said, starting forward again. Stewart groaned when he saw him.

"Wait," Fuentes said softly. "You intrigue me, *gringo*. Who do you say killed Cardenas?"

"The Germans. Probably the same ones outside the Atlantis Club that night."

"And then no doubt they committed suicide? One in the alley, the other in the Mercedes where we found him."

"No," Stewart admitted. "I did that. They were trying to kill me."

"Clearly. How terrible to be a *yanqui!* So unpopular," Fuentes sighed theatrically, and whoever was writing with the pen chuckled. "And as long as we are pursuing this North American fantasy, why would the Germans want to kill Almayo and then Cardenas?"

Stewart hesitated. His thoughts kept banging into each other like bumper cars. It was a delicate balance. He had to give Fuentes enough or they would torture him to death. But if he gave him too much, it would mean the end of everything. Fuentes might kill him anyway, if he thought he knew too much. And all the while, the clock on the *Graf Spee* was ticking.

"Come, *gringo*. It shouldn't take so long to think of a good lie," Fuentes laughed.

"There was a leak. Someone in the German or Argentine government was passing information to us. The Germans found out and were trying to close the pipeline down."

Stewart sensed Fuentes's sudden tenseness, but Fuentes's voice was still soft, mocking.

"Who, *gringo*? Who in the Argentine government?"

"I don't know," Stewart shouted, trying to make his anger sound real. "You picked me up too fucking soon!"

"Not too soon for you to 'pluck the hen' with Señora Vargas," Fuentes said viciously.

Watch it, Stewart cautioned himself. There's something

there. Something sexual, Argentine male pride—they don't like foreigners—something.

"I was after information."

"Is that what you *gringos* call it!" Fuentes laughed harshly and the others joined in. "Tell me, *yanqui.* What else besides killing and fucking do you do for your country?"

"What do you do for yours?"

A growl came from Gold Tooth. He advanced into the light. He was leaning forward and with his massive chest and arms, he looked like a lower order of human being; one who had only recently learned to walk upright. His mouth was open, hungry for violence.

"I would like to kill you," Gold Tooth told Stewart. "I would like to kill you now," he said, looking down at his hands, the thick fingers curled into claws, as if they didn't belong to him.

"Clearly. Only the *patron* wouldn't like it. Would he?" Stewart said through battered lips. Gold Tooth raised his fist. A word from Fuentes stopped him.

"So, *gringo,* this of the Señora Vargas is more an 'affair of the state' for our two countries than an 'affair of the heart.' Maybe we should let you go, so you can fuck the *concha* of the Señora Vargas for our benefit!" Fuentes said and the man writing laughed again.

"The sooner the better."

"With the Order of San Martin for valor in the pursuit of, how you *yanquis* say, 'pussy,' perhaps?"

"You think I'm lying?"

"Why not? You are in the 'business' for it," Fuentes said, using the English word.

"We're all in it, Colonel. And I'm not lying."

"Oh, but you are, *gringo.* You are a most terrible liar," Fuentes laughed, motioning to Gold Tooth, who picked up the pliers and began pulling out the nail from Stewart's ring finger. Stewart gasped in pain. His body snapped and jerked uncontrollably against the straps, the flesh bulging around the leather till it looked as though either the leather or the skin would break. The room filled with the metallic smell of sweat and fear.

"Of course you are lying, *gringo.* That is to be expected. But that you expect us poor Latins to be so *estupidos* as to not see through such clumsy lies shows a want of respect." Fuentes nodded to Gold Tooth, who tapped Stewart's raw fingertips with the pliers. Stewart groaned. It was while he was groaning that he realized that Fuentes had switched from the formal *usted* to the more familiar *vos*. The interrogation was entering a new, more intimate stage.

"Now," Fuentes said softly. "Enough lies, *yanqui*. Why don't you tell me what was in the letter case? The one you got from Cardena's safe."

Stewart's fingers were throbbing badly. Sooner or later he would break down. He could feel it, like a wall giving way inside him. And with it, maybe the war. In the twentieth century, this is how wars were lost. In cellars to men whose faces you couldn't see.

"Answer well, *gringo*. Much depends on it. Including that trivial little thing, your life."

Stewart licked his lips. He was breathing hard. He wasn't sure how much more he could take. He squinted into the glare in the direction of Fuentes' voice.

"Which side are you on, Colonel? Ortiz or Castillo?"

"That is none of your concern! You have only to answer. Nothing else! Understand?" Fuentes shouted, banging his fist on the table.

Gold Tooth grabbed the pliers and the pain shot through Stewart like an electric bolt. It seemed to go on and on and finally through a haze, Stewart seemed to be looking down and it was with a kind of amazement that he realized that his fingers were still attached to his hand. But now three of his nails had been ripped away.

"What was in the metal case?" Fuentes repeated.

Stewart shook his head.

"I can't," he whispered. "I can't tell you."

"In that, you are much mistaken, *gringo*. You will certainly tell us," Fuentes sighed. "Or else we shall have to stop being so gentle. I shall not ask again, *gringo*. What was in the letter case?"

Stewart had come to a dead end. He had to give Fuentes something. Only he couldn't. Even if Fuentes did support Ortiz, which wasn't likely, telling him might still alert Castillo, since anyone in the room might be one of Castillo's agents, whether Fuentes knew it or not. Or Fuentes might sell Ortiz out for a pay-off from Castillo. And if Fuentes did support Castillo, telling him about the *Graf Spee* would ensure Castillo's success, as well as his own death. He'd have lost the war right here. He tried to look up. The lamplight blinded him. It was like looking at the sun.

"The case was empty," he croaked, his voice ragged, dry. "Whoever killed Cardenas beat me to it."

He heard a strange sound in the darkness. His heart sank when he recognized what it was. Fuentes laughing.

"*Ay, gringo, gringo.* You *yanquis* are so amusing, yes? Such stories," Fuentes laughed. "*Hombre,* this is better than your Edgar Bergen and your Charlie MacCarthy." His laughter went on, then subsided. "Now, *gringo.* Now you will tell us everything," the finger motioned to Gold Tooth.

Gold Tooth was coming closer. Stewart could smell him. He smelled foul, like an animal that lived on carrion. "Listen, *Coronel,* maybe we could make a good *trato.* You and me," Stewart said. And all the while, in the back of his head the clock on the *Graf Spee* was still ticking. If he didn't get the information to the English soon, it wouldn't matter what he told Fuentes.

"You want to *make the business,*" Fuentes said, using the English phrase. "Here, there is only one kind of *business, yanqui.* I ask the questions, you answer. If I am satisfied, maybe I let you live. Maybe." He leaned forward so that part of his head could be seen in the light. His teeth were white and even under his razor-thin moustache.

"I thought you wanted a 'stalking horse,' *Coronel.* I thought you wanted me to find Almayo's killer."

"That was several days ago, *gringo.* Now I need to present my superiors with Cardenas' murderer. That was very bad, *gringo.* A prominent man like that, with, how you Americans say, 'the fingers in many cakes,' foreign nationals murdered on Avenida Corrientes, newspapers," he sighed. "This is Buenos Aires, not Chicago." Fuentes lit a cigarette. Stewart could smell the smoke. "I need to give them someone."

"Try the Nazis. After all, they're the one who really did it."

Fuentes shrugged as if he had already considered the idea and rejected it.

"I don't need the real killer. Just a believable one."

"Why not the Nazis? They like to kill. They like it better than the *futbol.*"

"That means nothing. To me, nothing. To my superiors, less than nothing."

"What does?"

"Politics. In this country we have a saying: 'When the *pampero* blows, even the earth moves north.' Unfortunately for you, these days, the wind is blowing from Germany."

In that moment, Stewart understood that they would never let him leave here alive. He had already shown them that he knew too much. If they got anything out about the *Graf Spee* or the plot against Ortiz out of him, that would only ensure its success, because such knowledge was too dangerous for someone at Fuentes' level. Fuentes would have to use it to ingratiate himself with Castillo. How else had Fuentes survived the ins and outs of Argentine politics since Uriburu's coup had overthrown Yrigoyen back in 1930?

But how could he stand up to the torture? That he didn't know. He remembered Margarethe and the way she had looked at him when he had climbed out that attic window. She had put a lifetime into that look. The longing, the regrets and the foreknowledge that she was going to her death. How had she done that?

"Unfortunately, Señor *Coronel*, the case was empty," Stewart said, steeling himself.

"*Qué va?* And our discussion was progressing so nicely, *pues,*" Fuentes sighed, signaling to Gold Tooth, who grabbed Stewart's mangled little finger and began sawing at the tip with his pocket knife. The pain was appalling. The knife was dull and rusty and it went on and on and suddenly, through a haze, Stewart saw Gold Tooth brandish the tiny piece of flesh, then shove it, warm and bloody, into Stewart's mouth.

"Eat, *gringo!* Eat!"

Gold Tooth was holding Stewart's mouth and nose closed so he couldn't breathe or spit out. Stewart could feel the finger, like a lump in his throat, his gorge rising up and then the body took over and he was swallowing it all: the bile and blood and the fingertip. Gold Tooth let go and Stewart gasped for air, feeling sick to his stomach.

"What do you think, *gringo?* Taste good?" Gold Tooth asked. Stewart didn't answer, trying not to open his mouth in order to keep from throwing up. God, I don't want to die this way, he thought, dimly aware of whispers in the background between Fuentes and someone else. While Gold Tooth had been cutting off his fingertip, another officer had entered the room. Even more astonishing, someone, the man with the pen, Stewart guessed, was putting a tourniquet and bandage on his finger to stop the bleeding.

"This is most interesting, *gringo*. I have orders to release you at once," Fuentes said, coming around the table. Gold Tooth loosened the straps on Stewart's hands and Fuentes offered him a cigarette. Stewart took it with his right hand, the one that was still good. His fingers trembled as he held it. Fuentes spotted that as he lit Stewart's cigarette, but didn't say anything. "You have powerful friends, *gringo*. This," Fuentes flicked a paper in his hand, "is signed by both Minister Casaverde and Vice-President Castillo himself. Interesting, no?"

"Very," Stewart said, looking down at his injured hand. It was as if he were seeing it from a great height. The bandage was completely red, but the blood flow was starting to slow down.

"You're a lucky man, *gringo*," Fuentes said, clapping him enthusiastically on the shoulder.

"Lucky," Stewart laughed harshly.

"Oh yes, you have much luck, *tiene mucho suerte*," Fuentes smiled. "You don't know how lucky. Another hour and Garcia here would have left you not much more than your mouth, ha, ha, ha." Fuentes laughed loudly and Gold Tooth joined in, grinning broadly. *"Ay, gringo, gringo,"* Fuentes said, wiping his eyes. "Destiny is such a whore. With luck like yours, I would be at the Hipodromo every day. Tell me, who is going to win the war?"

"Not the Germans."

Fuentes looked surprised.

"No? Why not? Everyone thinks the Germans."

"Everyone is wrong. That's very common," Stewart said, taking another drag on his cigarette. Fuentes was right. He was lucky. The bleeding had stopped.

"But the Germans are invincible. They are always winning."

"That's the trouble with being invincible, *Coronel*. You only have to lose once for everyone to see it isn't true."

Gold Tooth had removed the straps and Fuentes helped Stewart to his feet. He had to help to support Stewart toward the door. Stewart felt nauseous again. He could feel his fingertip in his esophagus. Everything was backing up and he fought it down. He wasn't going to give the bastards the satisfaction, he told himself, pulling away from Fuentes to walk on his own.

"Whoever wins, Argentina must be on that side," Fuentes

muttered. They were in a long dark corridor, with metal cell doors on each side. The cells were utterly silent. Prisoners were not allowed to talk. The punishment for talking was to be beaten to death. They came to a barred door. Fuentes pounded on it and a guard came and hurriedly unlocked it. "So, *gringo*, what do you do next?" Fuentes asked, as they climbed up a stairway. Stewart cradled his injured hand, cigarette dangling from his mouth. Gold Tooth brought up the rear, blinking in the light as they walked toward the main office, like a troll emerging from the depths.

"The same as before, *Coronel*. Find out what happened to Raoul."

"No, *gringo*. I mean your *friend*," giving the word *amiga* a savage twist.

"What friend?"

"The Señora Vargas, of course. She is waiting in the office. No doubt it is she who arranged your release," Fuentes winked. "Perhaps it isn't only luck, perhaps it's also the talent," Fuentes grinned, making a circle of his thumb and forefinger and sticking his other forefinger through it to make the sign for intercourse. Stewart looked at him.

"You have a dirty mind, *Coronel*."

"As I said before, *yanqui*. We are in a dirty business."

They came to another door. Another guard unlocked it and Fuentes gestured Stewart through. Behind a glass door at the far end of the office, Stewart could see Julia waiting in the anteroom. She looked pale, worried. "Go, *yanqui*. Go to your *amiga*. But remember, I will be watching. And waiting for us to continue where we left off."

Stewart started forward, then stopped.

"About John Gideon, *Coronel*. . . ."

Fuentes frowned.

"What about him? Gideon died long ago. And he was a very old man when he died, Señor. Why is he of such interest to you?"

"Because he seems of such interest to everyone else in this affair," Stewart said, glancing toward the glass door. Fuentes followed his glance without responding. "I was told he was an Englishman."

"Yes, what of it?"

"So how'd he become so important in Argentina? How did he get so rich?"

Fuentes looked at him curiously, as if he wasn't sure whether to take Stewart seriously or not.

"I believe he became a soldier in the war with Paraguay. In those days, a military career offered certain rather, how shall I say, *unique* opportunities."

Cordoba Province, 1868

AHEAD, IN the distance, death was waiting. It could be seen by the presence of the *chimangos*, carrion hawks, circling in the blue sky. Earlier, one of the *gauchos*, Gaspar, had hamstrung a cow and killed it so that they could use its horns for tethering the horses. They cut loin steaks from it, that they barbecued over a fire of grass stalks and cattle chips. They sat around the fire, eating and washing down the meat with *mate*. There was no hurry about going on. The dead would wait.

A strong wind was blowing. It came from the north, from the Chaco lands, and the horses stirred uneasily at their tethers. Bernardo, Gideon's *rastreador*, looked up, his nostrils widening as he sniffed the wind.

"After this comes the *pampero*," he said, naming the terrible wind that swept up the Pampa from Tierro del Fuego and the bottom of the world.

"Of a certainty?" Gideon asked.

"After such a north wind, always," Bernardo said, watching the horses. *"Norte duro, pampero seguro."*

"What of the Captain Montoya? Will he be able to meet us as agreed?"

"Easily," the *gaucho* shrugged. "He is only two leagues behind us, maybe less. Look!" he said, pointing. "You can see the smoke from his fire, as he no doubt sees ours. This *pampero* will not come till sunset. You can still see the birds." He

gestured toward the *chimangos,* a column of black shapes
swirling over the *quinta.* When Gideon looked that way he
could see the distant plantation as a blue-green island of trees
in an otherwise featureless sea of pampas-grass. Waves of
grass made by the wind raced endlessly to the horizon. Gideon
watched the waves as a sailor does the sea and thought about
what they would find when they got to the *quinta.* Not much,
he thought. The Indians wouldn't leave much.

After three years of war he had learned that. What else had
he learned, he wondered, glancing around their encampment.
He had less than twenty men left, all *gauchos* except for the
Negro, Joao, he had purchased from that Brazilian sergeant.
Some had stretched out on the ground for a siesta, their faces
turned up to the sky like dead men; the rest were still eating.

He had learned that a man faced more danger from his own
side than from the enemy. That was always true, but in this
land there was nothing more true. The worst were the Paraguayans. He had learned that after the Argentines had captured Humaita. Not even in the Crimea had he ever seen
anything like it.

The fortress at Humaita was made of mud and stone and
wood and the square inside the walls was carpeted with bodies. And on the ground north of the fortress were more bodies,
most of them headless. From the parapets they could see the
Paraguayan machete squads still working, cutting down their
own Indian troops, their punishment for having lost the battle. In the midst of the retreat, a group of Indian slaves carried
a giant red plush four-poster bed, rising and falling over the
uneven ground like a raft on the sea from some bizarre children's tale. Seated on the bed, resplendent in a gold uniform
and waving a sword like a conductor's baton, was Lopez, the
corpulent Paraguayan dictator himself, and next to him, her
hair red as fire, the notorious Señora Lynch, the English
whore he had made Chief Justice of his Military Tribunal.
They were eating and drinking champagne and every now
and then Lopez would wave his sword and another dozen or
so heads would come off.

After Humaita, the Paraguayans fell back to Angostura for a
last stand. The Argentine and Brazilian armies pursued them
into a land of swamp and jungle. There were no men in that
land. Only women. So many, the soldiers got tired of raping
and would sometimes shoot them so as not to have the bother

of feeding them. Everyone was dying there anyway and Captains Gideon and Montoya had been relieved when Colonel Roca had sent them south to fight the bandit chieftains rampaging the pampas, while he took the rest of the Army north, after the retreating Paraguayans.

The *rastreador*, Bernardo, got up suddenly and moved away from the fire. He climbed up on the dead cow, his hand over the brim of his hat to shade his eyes against the sun's glare. He stood there, absolutely still, staring into the distance. One or two of the other *gauchos* watched him, but didn't get up. Only Gaspar stopped eating. He let his steak drop from his knife onto the ground, wiping the grease from the blade on his sleeve.

"Men coming. A whole troop," Bernardo said finally, turning to Gideon.

Gideon climbed up on the cow's side, next to him. He looked out across the plain, squinting against the glare. The pampasgrass was a golden green all the way to the horizon.

"There," Bernardo said, plucking at his sleeve and pointing. Gideon strained his eyes. He had perfect vision, but still there was nothing. Then he saw it, a tiny black dot, like an insect, moving in on the distant plain.

"Can you see anything?"

Bernardo looked again, his face set like stone. Like most *gauchos* he was olive-skinned and bearded and his eyes were dark and deep-set, as though they needed the protection of the skull.

"There are at least forty of them," he said. "All well armed. The one in front is on a brown bay with silver on the reins," the *gaucho* said. Gideon looked again in the same direction, but still he could make out no more than a moving black dot. Bernardo jumped down off the carcass and grabbed his rifle. "I think it is maybe the Ricardo Lopez Dias, *jefe*," he said, crossing himself. "I think maybe that is who it is."

"How long till they reach the *quinta*?"

"Two hours. Maybe more," Bernardo shrugged. "They are not riding so hard."

"Then we go. *Vamonos*," Gideon said, jumping down and crossing to his horse. "I want to be waiting at the *quinta* when they come."

"They will see us. Also, there are the birds," Bernardo said, gesturing with his rifle.

"Good," Gideon said, checking the girth on his horse. "I want them to see us. You, Gaspar!" he shouted, getting up on the horse and pulling on the reins to turn it around.

"*Si, jefe.*"

"You ride hard to Captain Montoya. Tell him the Ricardo will attack us at the *quinta* within the two hours. Tell him to come fast with the main body and he can take the Ricardo from the rear. Tell him we will finish the *culo* here."

Gideon wheeled his horse around. "To the *quinta!*" he shouted. *"Adelante!"*

The *gauchos* sprang onto their horses, kicking awake those still sleeping. Ahead of them, they drove a herd of mares. The mares provided fresh mounts and flesh to eat if ever there were no cattle around, and with them the troop could cover a hundred miles a day and never need provisions.

They trotted easily toward the green line of trees that marked the boundary of the *quinta*, the cylindrical white *mirador* grain tower typical of rural plantations already in sight. Suddenly, Bernardo stiffened, standing up on his toes in the stirrups. All at once he veered off in a mad gallop away from the *quinta*. Gideon straightened in his saddle to see what it was. By the time he saw it, more than half the *gauchos* were tearing off after Bernardo in a small storm of dust.

They had put up a rhea, a kind of small ostrich. Bernardo raced after it, leaning forward over his horse's neck as he untied his *boleadores* from around his waist. The rhea was dashing madly across the pampas. The *gauchos* rode after it, crying out in excitement. Next to this, the impending battle was nothing to them. Bernardo was in the lead, ahead of the pack and it was something to see as, galloping hard, he held the *boleadores* high, holding it by one lead ball and whipping the other two balls attached by the leather thongs in a circle over his head, whirling them around and around until they were a blur. The rhea was running straight and incredibly fast across the pampas, Bernardo's horse galloping fast and smooth, and Gideon felt something inside him that was like sex, only cleaner, stronger.

"Why doesn't he release the *bolas?*" Gideon asked Honorio, a stolid flat-faced man, who favored *botas de potro*, untanned leather leggings, and iron spurs on bare feet, riding beside him.

"Wait," Honorio said. "He's waiting for it to break. *Mira!*"

The rhea turned suddenly, almost at a right angle to the

left, then after a zigzag dash made a complete 180-degree turn back toward the right, diagonally across Bernardo's oncoming rush.

"The *avestruz* is the most *gaucho* of the animals," Honorio said, just as Bernardo let the *boleadores* go. They flew in a swirling arc far across the plain, the balls whipping around as if pulling each other across the blue sky, and suddenly a roar of excitement went up from the *gauchos* as the *boleadores* entangled the stilt-like legs and the rhea went down in an explosion of dust.

By the time Gideon rode up, Bernardo had dismounted and was unwrapping the leather thongs from around the rhea's legs. But instead of looking happy, Bernardo's expression was bitter. He wouldn't look at any of them.

"What passes?" Gideon asked him. He remembered how Bernardo had crossed himself when he had first seen the Ricardo.

"It's dead. *Esta muerte*," Bernardo said, picking the bird up by its long neck. The head flopped over, as though he was holding a length of rope. "Broken neck," he added, not looking at Gideon.

"An evil omen," one of the other *gauchos*, Diego, said, turning and spitting.

"Better to cut the throat," said a third.

Bernardo looked up. His eyes were strange.

"I wanted to cut the throat, *jefe*. Always it is better to cut the throat," he said.

"Take it anyway. We'll have it for dinner," Gideon said.

"I take it, but it makes no difference," Bernardo said, tying it by the neck to his saddle. "I will not live to eat it."

"What kind of talk is this?" Gideon said, looking around at the others. "This is woman's talk."

"It's true, *jefe*," one of the other *gauchos*, Guillermo, a sad-eyed man with long drooping moustaches, said. "At noon, I saw three owls. They were on the ground."

"*Qué va?* There is a *pampero* coming. The animals sense this."

"It's a bad sign, *jefe*. A sign of death. *Un agüero de la muerte!*" the man insisted.

"Yes. An omen of the death of the Ricardo," Gideon snapped, drawing his revolver. "I say it is his death. Does any dispute this?"

No one answered. Bernardo finished tying the rhea and remounted. Guillermo looked down at the ground. "Then the Ricardo should have seen it," he muttered stubbornly under his breath.

Gideon shot him. Guillermo looked at Gideon for a long moment, his eyes seeming not so much angered or astonished, as disappointed. He leaned sideways on his horse as if reaching for something, but instead of straightening, he kept leaning further and further until he toppled over. He was dead when he hit the ground.

"It was his own death he saw," Gideon declared harshly. The *gauchos* only looked at him, their faces blank.

"Clearly," one of them said.

"Clearly," another echoed.

"He had sad eyes. Always he looked sad."

"Then perhaps he did foresee his fate," the second one shrugged.

"It wasn't his eyes that killed him, but his mouth," Bernardo snapped.

"Clearly," the first man said.

Gideon let them talk. He gazed off at the distant line of trees.

"*Vamanos*. We need to be in position at the *quinta* before the Ricardo comes," he said finally.

Without another word, he turned and began to ride toward the trees. The *gauchos* looked at each other and after a moment, one by one, they followed.

They approached the *quinta* from the south, facing into the sun that sent the long shadows of the *alamos*, as poplar trees were called, stretching toward them. An avenue of trees made a lane to the *hacienda*. The trees swayed and whispered in the wind, and as soon as Gideon rode into the shadow made by the trees, he saw the first of them.

It was bad. He had known it was going to be bad, but it was bad all the same. The first was the body of a small boy, perhaps seven or eight years old. He had been pinned to the ground by a long Indian lance, his hands still clutching at the spear as if it was a pole he was trying to climb. The *chimangos* had been working on his mouth and eyes and there was a bird on him as they rode up. One of the *gauchos* snarled a curse, cracking his *revenque* at the ugly brown bird, who flapped easily out of range of the whip, a piece of something red dangling from its beak, while overhead more *chimangos* wheeled and screamed, their cries piercing and terrible in the wind.

As Bernardo rode past the boy, he grabbed at the spear to check the markings, but he didn't bother saying anything. It was clearly Araucanio. They had known even before they had come, that it had been the Araucanios. A large war party had been reported in this district.

Further down the avenue of trees was the body of an old man, the boy's uncle or grandfather, perhaps. They had forced a war-lance down his throat till the point stuck out his back. There was a large pool of blood around him, the surface black and moving with insects. In all, they found five bodies, two inside the low mud *hacienda* and one in the *mirador*. All male, of course. The Indians would have carried off the women.

Gideon set up his defensive line along the avenue of trees. He put two of his best sharpshooters in the *mirador*. The rest were in the *hacienda*. There was a small garden in back and they carried the bodies back there for burial in the soft soil, later, when there would be time. He sent two men away, behind the *mirador*, with the horses. Then they made a fire to brew *mate*. And to wait for the Ricardo.

"Why did you cross yourself before? And all this talk of dying—it is woman's talk," Gideon said to Bernardo.

At first Bernardo didn't answer. He rolled himself a cigarette, then lit it with a hot coal he lifted from the fire on the tip of his knife blade.

"I know it, *jefe*," he shrugged. "Didn't you ever know such a thing?"

"No man knows such things," Gideon said.

Bernardo blew out a cloud of smoke. They could smell the strong green smell of the tobacco.

"You are not of this country, *jefe*. Here a man may know such things."

"*Si*, remember the *curandero* in La Rioja," Honorio said. "He could see such things in pools of water and entrails of beasts. He told my brother once to beware of black colts. And it was a black horse that threw him, breaking his neck."

"It was his bad riding that killed him," Diego said.

"It was foreseen by the *curandero*. Everyone in La Rioja knew of him," Honorio insisted.

"Then why was your brother fool enough to ride a black colt?"

"You could tell him nothing," Honorio said. "If you told

him not to do a thing, then that became the very thing he had
to do. After that, he sought out every black horse in the province, if only to knock everyone on their ass, *para caerse de
culo."*

"Entonces," Diego said, slapping his forehead with exasper-
ation. "If your brother only rode black horses, one of them
was bound to kill him."

"It was foretold," Honorio said stubbornly, readying his
mate gourd. "That *curandero* was a famous man."

Bernardo didn't say anything. He only stared moodily into
the fire. After a moment, Gideon spoke to him.

"You are no *curandero*. How could you know such things,
pues?"

Bernardo shifted uneasily. He puffed at his cigarette with
great intensity, as though he knew he would never have another.

"You remember yesterday," he began, "when we camped
by the two *ombu* trees for the afternoon siesta? While I slept,
that Oraldo Martinez, the deserter whose throat I cut, remember, came for me. I could see him clear as day. As clear as I see
you all now. His brown puppy eyes, his chin with the dimple
in it and lips like a girl's, and his throat, still slashed open and
bleeding from my knife. "I will see you tomorrow, Bernardo,"
he told me. *'Hasta mañana,'* he told me, the slash in his throat
leering at me like a smile. When I awoke, I was sweating like
a pig. Worse yet, I was lying in the shadow of the *ombus*. And
that brings no luck, *jefe*. Everyone knows that brings no luck,"
Bernardo said, looking around the fire. Several of the other
gauchos sitting there nodded.

"Es verdad, it's true," Diego said. "What that one says about
the *curandero*, who can say? But this about the *ombu*, is
truth."

"So that's why you wanted to kill the rhea with your knife,"
Gideon murmured.

"Clearly," Bernardo nodded. "But it was for nothing. God
holds us in his palm like an insect. When he lacks amusement,
he squeezes. And all our squirming and struggling goes for
nothing, either."

For a moment there was silence. Then they all heard it: the
sound of horses' hoofs.

"They're coming. Make ready," Gideon said, grabbing his
revolver. The *gauchos* ran to their places. They were still run-

ning when they heard the first shots. Bernardo and Gideon looked at each other.

"*Adios, jefe,*" Bernardo said, his face pale and twisted.

"Shut your *hijo-de-puta* mouth about dying, or I'll shoot you myself," Gideon snarled, turning toward the direction of the attack.

A ragged volley was fired from trees where Gideon's men were. Several of the Ricardo's *gauchos* went down, but Gideon could see no one on a bay horse matching Bernardo's description. Too soon, Gideon thought disgustedly. They always fire too soon.

The shooting intensified. Three horsemen came clattering down the lane of poplars, firing wildly. One of Gideon's *gauchos* crumpled. Bernardo stepped out into the lane as though he were immune to bullets. He levelled his pistol, firing calmly as the horsemen came on. Shots tore leaves from the trees. They fluttered down as the firing became very heavy. One of Bernardo's shots caught the second horseman, who fell over, his foot caught in the toe stirrup. The horse dragged the dead man, the head bouncing along the ground like a ball, as the horses closed on Bernardo. Suddenly, Gideon fired, taking down the lead horseman as shots rang out from the window at the top of the *mirador*, knocking down the third. Bernardo turned and waved, then headed for the tree line. The main charge still hadn't come. The Ricardo could be seen now, lining his horsemen up to charge the trees with a single rush. Shots popped from both sides and if Montoya came now, the Ricardo was finished, Gideon thought.

The thought sent a sudden chill through his bowels. Where was Montoya? He should have been here by now. Even without Gaspar's message, he should have been here. Gideon turned. He wanted to signal the men in the *mirador*, to ask them if they saw Montoya coming, but it was too late. Ricardo's *gauchos* had begun their charge.

For an instant, for Gideon, everything seemed frozen in time. Ricardo's men came on like a wave racing toward the trees. They were screaming their war-cries, leaning forward over their horses' necks, charging and firing. There is nothing like it, Gideon thought, his mouth dry, his heart pounding as he levelled his revolver. To see men coming at you to kill you. At first only a wave and then individual men and then finally, the one or two or three who have set their sights on you. And then it becomes utterly intimate and personal, just him and you and only one of you can live. Gideon fired again and again. He had one shot left. One of the horsemen, a *gaucho* with narrowed eyes, dressed in red country shirt and *bombachos,* closed in on him. A bullet hummed close by Gideon's ear. He could feel the air tremble on the side of his face and then he could see the man's eyes and the black hairs coming out of his nostrils, the horse almost upon him, and he fired. A piece of the *gaucho*'s head flew off, like a pebble ricocheting off a rock. The *gaucho* fell from the horse as it shied wild-eyed away from Gideon and the noise of his gun.

There were screams and shouting coming from the trees. A whole troop of the Ricardo's horsemen charged down the avenue. Where the hell was Montoya? Gideon thought furiously, whirling and running for the *mirador*. Honorio was squatting by the wooden door, his face gray, and he had his rifle across his knees as though he was on guard duty at some quiet post where the enemy never came. Gideon grabbed his arm, but Honorio didn't move. He just stared ahead at the oncoming horsemen. Pulling at him was like pulling at a sack of grain.

"Get inside," Gideon ordered.

Honorio didn't move. His eyes didn't move. Gideon wasn't even sure he had heard him. He started to put his revolver to Honorio's head, then remembered that he hadn't reloaded. He pulled out his knife and put it to Honorio's throat. The point made a dimple in the skin.

"Get inside or I'll kill you," Gideon said. Honorio turned slowly to look at Gideon. He looked at him as though he were in a dream.

"Now!" Gideon shouted, the point of his knife drawing blood.

Honorio got up and stumbled inside the door. Just as Gideon began to swing the door shut behind him, he saw Bernardo running down the avenue of trees, just ahead of the Ricardo himself. Bernardo's face was set and grim. He was running hard, his knife in his hand, but the big bay horse gained rapidly on him. At the last second, Bernardo turned, raising his knife, to defend himself. The Ricardo straightened in his saddle, his sword glittering in the sun for an instant as he struck down with a sweep, taking off both Bernardo's hand and his head in a single blow. The hand flew somewhere, but the head rolled toward the *mirador* and as he slammed the door shut, Gideon saw Bernardo's eyes, wide open and on his lips, a horrible self-mocking half-smile that had something triumphant in it. A kind of final "I told you so," Gideon thought, as he barred the door and shoved Honorio ahead of him, up the ladder to the top platform.

They were firing from the platform and from outside, from the direction of the *hacienda*, they could hear the screams of the dying. When they got to the top of the ladder, Honorio collapsed against the round white wall. Of the two men Gideon had sent up here, only one was still firing. The other, gut-shot, was writhing and moaning on the floor by the far wall.

"Kill me," the wounded man begged. "For the love of God, Faustino. Don't let them take me alive."

"Shut up! *Tapa la boca, culo!*" Faustino shouted, glaring over at the wounded man before turning back to the window and firing. "Ha! Ha!" he cried out. "You like that, *cabrón?*"

"For the love of the mother who gave you life, *hermano*. For the sake of the milk from the breasts you suckled, shoot me now! Let me die a man," the wounded man pleaded.

Suddenly, a mocking falsetto voice came from below.

"Shoot me, *por favor*, Don Faustino. Don't let the Ricardo take me, *hermano mio!*"

"You shut up too!" Faustino shouted, sticking his head into the open window space and firing. A fusillade of shots peppered the window and walls as he quickly jerked his head back. As the shots died away, Gideon took advantage of the moment to peek out the window. Below him the *quinta* and the Pampa stretched flat and empty all the way to the horizon, and moving across it all alone, like an ant on a blank page, Gaspar's horse, galloping riderless across the plain.

Montoya was nowhere to be seen. Even the smoke from his campfire was no longer to be seen. Except for the bodies and the Ricardo's men, their guns poking out from behind trees and horse carcasses, there was nothing anywhere but sky and pampas grass. They were trapped, Gideon thought.

"Faustino!" the mocking voice called out from below. "Please shoot me, Faustino! I'm just a girl and too *delicado* to be fucked by a real man!"

The wounded man, curled into a fetal position on the floor, groaned loudly.

"Faustino! You promised!" he cried. His wound was making him sound peevish and the voice from below picked up on it immediately.

"Faustino, you naughty *muchacho!* If you don't cut off my *cojones* right this minute, why I'll just have to get those nasty *gauchos* of Ricardo's to do it," the voice mocked.

Faustino looked over at Gideon, his face flushed and beaded with sweat, his fingers white around the rifle.

"What do we do now, *jefe?*" he whispered.

"Wait," Gideon said, trying to think. "We have to wait until the Captain Montoya comes." But he's not coming, he thought.

"Faustino! Oh, Faustino!" came the voice from below. "We found your Negrito. Come see what we have waiting for you, Faustino. Come and see."

A terrible scream came from outside. It was like nothing human. Faustino and Gideon peeked out the window. There was no way not to look. They had staked out the Negro, Joao. He was spread-eagled, naked, face-down on the ground. They could see him squirming, jerking his limbs at leather thongs that bound his hands and feet to pegs in the ground like a fly in a spider's web. He was screaming non-stop, unbelievably, and at first Gideon didn't understand why, and then he saw it. They had positioned him over the fire so that his privates were dangling down into the red-hot coals.

"*Dios mio*," Faustino said, crossing himself.

Joao was screaming. It didn't sound like words, only sounds. And then Gideon realized that he was screaming, "Shoot me, Captain!" in his mangled Spanish. "Shoot me!"

"*Hijo de puta*," Faustino growled, starting to aim his rifle.

"No, wait," Gideon said, plucking at his sleeve. He held out his hand for the rifle and stood by the wall beside the window, waiting.

"Shoot!" Joao screamed. Inside the *mirador*, the wounded man was sobbing. Honorio only sat there, staring blankly.

"Maybe it's too much fire, even for a Negrito. *Hola*, Faustino!" the voice called. "Want to see me put out the fire?"

All at once, the screaming intensified. "Captain!" Joao called, "Captain!"

Suddenly, Gideon moved. He could see a burly *gaucho* in a red poncho and *chiripa*. He was standing over the Negro, a revolver in one hand, his penis in the other as he urinated onto the Negro's head.

Gideon fired. Plaster exploded next to his face, fragments stinging his cheek as he jumped back.

"One less," he announced, smiling grimly. He handed the rifle back to Faustino, who started to take his place again, then stopped. He sniffed the air like a dog. Gideon looked at him for a moment, then he smelled it too.

Smoke.

They peeked out the window. Dark clouds of smoke rose from dry grass piled by the base of the *mirador*. The smoke grew dense very quickly. Gideon got down on all fours and crawled over to the wounded man.

"They've set the *mirador* on fire," Gideon told him, looking around.

The man held himself with his hands. His lips trembled as he struggled to form the words.

"Do it, *jefe*," he managed.

Gideon took out his knife. Something came into the wounded man's eyes. Gideon wondered if seeing the knife had made him change his mind. The wounded man's mouth moved. He was trying to say something.

"My hat. My hat," the man murmured, reaching feebly for his flat-brimmed hat, his hand opening and closing spasmodically like a mindless claw. Gideon picked up the hat and set it on the man's head.

"Better, *pues?*" Gideon asked.

"Like a *gaucho*," the man smiled weakly. "Many thanks, *jefe*."

"For nothing," Gideon said and slit the man's throat. He went over to Honorio. The smoke was thicker and there was heavy firing around the window. The walls of the *mirador* were made of adobe and the sound of the bullets hitting them was like the sound of an axe striking soft wood.

"We're going," he told Honorio. "Better to die from a bullet than the fire." Honorio looked at him, but didn't move. There was no expression on his face. It was as if he was dead already.

Gideon shrugged. "Stay here and burn if you like."

"You should have listened about the owls. Guillermo was right. Bernardo also," Honorio said. His voice was toneless. He spoke as an animated dead man might speak. Gideon grabbed him by the throat.

"Enough! *Bastante!* Enough stupidity!"

"You should have listened, *jefe*."

Gideon spat in his face. Spittle dribbled down from Honorio's eyebrow onto his cheek. He looked at Gideon unmoved, his voice unchanged. The smoke was getting very thick now and Gideon could feel the heat from under the platform.

"It was an error, *jefe*. This of the owls and the rhea was a grave matter," Honorio said calmly, like a bureaucrat explaining the denial of an application.

Gideon reloaded his revolver and put it to Honorio's head.

"Are you coming or not?"

"These are matters of weight, *de peso*," Honorio said, blinking monotonously every few seconds, like a bird. "Such matters must not be taken lightly."

Gideon fired.

"Stay then," he growled, as Honorio's body slumped over. He motioned to Faustino as he headed for the ladder.

"With permission, *jefe*," Faustino said, ducking beside the window opening, "I'm staying."

"You'll die."

"So will you. But at least this way, I'll take one or two of them with me when they come to get you," Faustino said, patting the side of his rifle.

"Are you certain?"

"It's better here. With all this smoke, once they see you, they won't look up."

"Go with God then," Gideon said. *"Vaya con Dios."*

"Better the Devil," Faustino grinned. "What would God have to do with such a world?"

Gideon went down the ladder. The ground level of the *mirador* was black with smoke. Flames shot up the walls where upcurrents of air were. The bar he had thrown across the door was burning. Gideon wrapped his handkerchief around his hand and grabbed the bar. He lifted it up and threw it aside. In the few seconds it took, smoke had already started to come from the handkerchief. He stripped it off and took out his revolver. Flames licked around the edges of the door. There were only seconds left. He cocked the revolver, flung open the door and ran outside.

A smattering of shots greeted him. A *gaucho* aimed his rifle from behind a dead horse. Gideon shot him. Another leaned out from behind a tree. Gideon fired as he ran, missing. So did the *gaucho*. A gun boomed from the *mirador* window above and the *gaucho* fell. Gideon leaped over the body of the Negro, still wailing and thrashing mindlessly over the fire.

Gideon headed around toward the back of the *mirador* where the horses were. Heavy firing erupted from around the *mirador* on that side. He was trapped. He hit the ground, near the Negro, jerking with his whole body at the leather thongs.

The Negro's eyes rolled white in their sockets. Gideon didn't know if the Negro saw him or not. The Negro screamed. Gideon had never heard a scream like that. It seemed to go on forever. Gideon shot him in the head. The Negro stopped screaming, but the scream still hung in the air like smoke.

Faustino's gun boomed again and there was a heavy fusillade from the trees and the *hacienda*. There was no answering shot from the *mirador*. When Gideon looked up, the top of the *mirador* was engulfed in a wall of flame. All around him, men were coming out. Gideon stood up and aimed at the nearest one. A shot sounded and something hit his shoulder like a club. It sent his revolver flying. He stood in the middle of a contracting circle, holding his shoulder where he had been shot.

The Ricardo stepped out from behind a tree. He was a big man, full-bearded, with small sharp black eyes that were very pleased with themselves. His poncho, *chiripa* and baggy *bombachos* were all red. He wore a silver gunbelt and carried a silver-handled whip. He had a swagger to him. He was, Gideon thought, the kind of man who swaggers even when he's asleep.

"So," the Ricardo grinned. "An officer. A *Capitano*, no less. This is much better than a Negrito," he said, nudging the Negro's body with his boot. "But I am curious. Why did you stay and fight? For what?"

Montoya, Gideon thought. He didn't answer.

"Truly," Ricardo said. "A matter of curiosity. You must have known there was nothing worth taking here. After the Araucanios, there could be nothing. Why fight over nothing? Why did you not run?"

"I hadn't finished my *mate* yet," Gideon shrugged.

The Ricardo stared at him. All at once, he began to laugh. The men around him began to laugh too. One of them slapped his knee. They were a jolly group, all right, Gideon thought. His shoulder was hurting. He wished they would get it over with.

"Very good. *Muy bien, Capitano.* Your men fought well. You killed fourteen of mine. They died well. For you, though, it is not so good," Ricardo sighed. He turned to his men. "Tie him to the ground," he ordered.

Three of them jumped forward. One of them knocked Gideon down with the butt on his rifle. The others jumped on him and began cutting off his clothes with their *facóns*.

"Of course, we expect better of you than a Negrito," Ricardo said, kicking the Negro's body. He turned back to Gideon, now naked. He was struggling against two of them, holding him down, while the third staked him out, face up, with leather thongs attaching his wrists and ankles to pegs hammered deep into the ground. "Steel yourself," Ricardo said. "It is a matter of honor. You against a mere Negrito."

Gideon ignored him. He looked up at the blue sky. It was an intenser blue than he had ever seen before. Something was different about it. A ripple seemed to pass through the air, like the surface of a pond when a stone is thrown in. All at once the air was full of white thistles, floating all around them like filaments of cotton from a mill. The *gauchos'* horses began to whinny and paw restlessly at the ground. Gideon raised his head. The *gauchos* were all looking nervously toward the southwest.

"*Mira!* Look!" one of them pointed.

"The *pampero*," another of them said, leaping onto his horse and wheeling it around. In the far distance, Gideon saw a solid blue line on the horizon. Ahead of it, the air was black with birds heading towards them and on the ground, something else.

"Jesu Christo!" one of the *gauchos* whispered, crossing himself. "It's the Araucanios. The *pampero* has brought them back. They're coming back!" he cried, springing onto his horse and galloping away at breakneck speed. The others began to race for their horses.

Ricardo looked down at Gideon, hesitating. He pulled out his revolver. He put the muzzle to Gideon's head, cocked it and started to squeeze the trigger. Then he stopped, let the hammer down and stuck it back in his belt.

"Shooting you is too generous, *Capitano*. Such generosity is not in my nature. We will leave you to the Indians. When they come, you will wish very much that it had fallen to us to kill you. They are not nearly so merciful as Christian men, such as we," he said, smiling broadly, and was gone. Within seconds, the *quinta* was deserted.

Gideon lay on his back, staring up at the sky. It was filled with thistles from the pampas-grasses sent flying by the first puffs of wind. He could hear the rumble of the approaching wind. Birds began to fly by, fast as bullets, it seemed. First one or two and then the sky was darkened with millions of them. The poplars began to bend and whisper and the leathered thongs holding him quivered like plucked guitar strings.

What had happened to Montoya? Gideon wondered, as he heard the first sounds of horses' hoofs. The ground began to tremble. He craned his neck and saw what looked like a thousand Indians galloping toward him, their hair blowing in the wind, their faces daubed with mud, a moving forest of long war lances gleaming in the strange blue light. If only Montoya had . . . the thought began and all at once, he understood.

Gideon began to laugh. He laughed loudly, savagely, wildly as the storm itself. He was still laughing when the first Indian came up to him, his hair wild as an animal's mane, and peered curiously down at him. The Indian began laughing too. He was laughing hard as he raised his spear high and plunged it down into Gideon's belly with all his might.

14

JULIA WAS waiting in the outer office. A soldier was behind the desk, writing, and Stewart had to wait till he was finished. The soldier gave Stewart a form to sign, looking not at Stewart but at Julia, impossibly beautiful in tennis whites, standing in the sunlight coming through a window. Stewart, still cradling his injured hand, went over to her. She bit her lip when she saw his face.

"God, *yanqui*. What have they done to you?" Her face was white and scared and her eyes were the darkest blue he had ever seen them. "What happened to your hand?" she whispered.

"I'm all right. Let's get out of here." From behind the glass panel of the inner door, he saw the blur of a face watching them. Fuentes.

It was a beautiful day. The trees were green, the girls were in their summer dresses and on the corner a man was selling brightly colored parakeets in cages from a lavishly decorated cart. It was another world. The room where they had cut off the tip of his finger might never have existed.

A silver Rolls-Royce limousine was waiting at the curb. Stewart bumped his injured hand getting in and almost passed out from the pain. His gorge rose again. He could feel the tip of his finger sticking in his gullet and he had to swallow hard to keep from vomiting. He sank back into the leather seat as Julia rapped on the partition. The uniformed chauffeur adjusted his mirror, started the Rolls and pulled out into traffic.

"Where do you want to go? You need a doctor," she said, looking at him and then at the chauffeur. The way she did it should have alerted him, but his hands were throbbing too badly to notice anything else.

"Palermo. The Plaza Italia," Stewart said through gritted teeth. "Got to get the . . ." he started to say and she kicked him. He glanced at her. She was smiling, her mouth a red lipstick oval, but her eyes weren't smiling. She opened the bar compartment and poured them both whisky from a Waterford decanter.

"I'm sorry," she said, looking again at the chauffeur. "It took time to arrange your release. I came as soon as I could."

What was she trying to tell him? Stewart wondered. And the limo? Arturo's car, probably. What happened to the Dusenberg? They were driving down the Avenida Belgrano. It was broad and tree-lined and people were getting ready for lunch, the linen white and the glassware shining in the sunlight at the restaurants and sidewalk cafés, but all Stewart could think about was the *Graf Spee*. He had to call Fowler right away. Even a public phone would do. Anything. He clinked Julia's glass and they drank.

What is it? Stewart mouthed to her over his drink. She shook her head. She was afraid to talk because of the chauffeur. Why? Because he was Arturo's man? He didn't get it. He saw a Union Telefonica sign outside a shop.

"Tell him to stop there," Stewart said. She picked up the phone and almost immediately, the chauffeur slowed and brought the limousine sedately to the curb. Stewart started to get out.

"Wait. I'll be back in a minute," he said.

"Yes. Of course," she said.

A sedan pulled alongside, blocking Stewart from opening the door. The door on Julia's side flew open and two men jumped in. They both had guns. One of them moved across and sat next to Stewart, pinning him in, an automatic jammed into his side. It all happened so quickly and professionally that Stewart wasn't sure, even if he had been uninjured, whether he would have been able to do something. He looked desperately at the chauffeur. He was their only chance.

But instead of jumping out, or driving, the chauffeur turned slowly around in his seat. He tilted his cap back on his head to reveal gleaming golden hair, and in his hand was a Luger pistol pointed at Stewart's chest.

"So, Herr Stewart. We are going to have our little talk after all," Baron von Hulse said.

They drove south across the city, out of the center with its wide boulevards and plane trees and over to Barracas, a bleak industrial sector of factories and trucks and cobbled streets reeking of the smell from the tanneries. When they reached the Riachuelo, they turned and went along the river, where the big meat packing plants were. No one spoke in the limousine. Julia sat white-faced, staring straight ahead. Stewart nursed his injured hand, trapped between the two Germans. Once he shifted position slightly and one of the Germans, a thin-faced man in a snap-brim hat, jammed his pistol hard into Stewart's ribs, causing him to grunt out loud. Von Hulse, driving, looked up for a second in the rear-view mirror, but that was the only sound until they pulled up outside a long concrete building. The *Frigorifico Stollner*, according to a sign on the roof of the building.

They were on a narrow cobbled street deep in shadow between two big factory buildings. Stewart tried to think of a way out, but there wasn't anything. The street was empty; it looked as if no one had been here in a long time. Even before they got out of the limo, Stewart could smell meat and somewhere nearby, the river. It was the kind of place where you could scream forever and no one would ever hear you. It was bad all right, he thought. They'd been brought there to die. The thin-faced German who had jabbed the pistol into his ribs before did it again, even harder.

"Aussteigen!"

Stewart got out carefully, favoring his bad hand. They stood in the empty street while von Hulse went to a side door of the *frigorifico*, unlocked it and motioned them inside with his Luger. Julia stood there uncertainly, watching Stewart. If there was a time to make a break for it, it was now, he thought, glancing back down the long narrow street toward the intersection.

Stewart stumbled as the thin-faced German shoved him roughly towards the door.

"Gehen Sie herein! Schnell!"

Stewart faked falling, going down on one knee, hoping the thin-faced German would come close. But the German spotted it. He stood back, almost smiling, his pistol trained on Stewart, who got up, brushed himself off awkwardly and walked toward the door. Julia followed.

Inside the *frigorifico* was a cavernous and gloomy space, a good football field in length. The light was gray. It came from a row of windows high on the wall on the river side of the plant. Overhead, long rails suspended from the ceiling ran the length of the plant. Hanging from the rails were hundreds of steel hooks that could be slid along the rails. There were long metal counters for cutting meat and along one wall were three giant refrigeration tanks, each the size of a railroad box-car. On the river side were giant metal doors, bolted shut. Probably used for loading the frozen meat onto ships, Stewart realized. It was an ugly utilitarian place, dark and smelling of dead meat. A rotten place to die, he thought, as von Hulse led them to an office off the main plant floor.

Von Hulse sat down behind an old desk without a second glance, as though it belonged to him. He steepled his hands, tapping his forefingers together as though he was sending a message in Morse to the gods in Berlin. The other two Germans closed the door and stood beside it, guns ready, in case anyone was fool enough to make a break for it.

The air in the office was stale and full of dust. Stewart could see the dust suspended in the light from a barred window. No one said anything, and after a moment Stewart and Julia sat down uneasily in two creaky wooden chairs in front of the desk. Her eyes were brimming, but she didn't say anything. In her tennis whites, she looked as if she'd come to sign something drawn up by a lawyer and go back to her game. She sat, legs pressed tightly together, like a schoolgirl called into the principal's office, her legs seeming tanned and very naked in her short white skirt.

"It appears our Argentine friends have already begun to question you, Herr Stewart. You were fortunate we arrived when we did," von Hulse said. He had taken off the chauffeur's cap and unbuttoned the top button of his tunic. His blond hair was the brightest thing in the room. Except for his Heidelberg scar, he was a handsome man, with a wide cruel mouth and eyes so pale it was hard to tell what color they were. He leaned far back in his chair, very much at ease.

"Yeah, you were swell," Stewart said. "All over Europe everybody's saying how swell you Germans are."

Von Hulse's eyes gleamed. He smiled appreciatively, revealing even perfect teeth. He really was a very handsome man, in a movie matinee sort of way. The sort who plays the second lead, the one the girl is engaged to before she runs away to marry the leading man in the end.

"That's very good, Herr Stewart. I knew you would be the kind of man who would appreciate our efforts," von Hulse said, leaning across the desk. "I am hoping you will appreciate everything we are doing."

Stewart felt a sudden surge of anger. They were certainly going to kill him. So what was the point of all this cat and mouse?

"Look, Herr Baron, or whatever the hell your real name is, I don't like you either. So why don't you just get out your rubber hoses and get on with it?"

Von Hulse laughed softly. He held up his hands imploringly.

"But I assure you, Herr Stewart, we intend nothing of the kind. And if we did," he frowned, "it would be nothing so crude as what the Argentines do. Would it, Schmidt?" he said, looking over Stewart's head. The thin-faced German stood there, saying nothing. He had pushed his hat back, showing a bad bruise on the side of his head, purplish and angry-looking. Von Hulse waited for a reply and when it didn't come, he sighed, turning back to Stewart. "I am afraid Herr Schmidt doesn't approve. He would prefer to simply wring whatever information you have out of you and then kill you," von Hulse confided. "You see, you've met Herr Schmidt before. In the *Wagen* outside the Atlantis Club, where you killed two of my men. Herr Schmidt was the one you hit in the head. I regret but Herr Schmidt is most displeased about what you did. Most displeased. He wants very much to kill you, Herr Stewart. You see," von Hulse smiled slightly, "our colleague, Schmidt, is from the Gestapo and that is the way they tend to approach things. A crude approach, I grant you, though in general, surprisingly effective. Unfortunately, it doesn't always work. Does it, Schmidt?" von Hulse said, his voice hardening.

"Der Mann war schwachlich!" Schmidt protested angrily.

"Genug!" von Hulse's voice cracked like a whip. "We want no more such miscalculations! Herr Stewart has been injured by these stupid Argentines. See to it!" he snapped. Then, more calmly, to Stewart, "things will go better once we take control of this country. Unfortunately, subtlety is not one of Herr Schmidt's strong points," von Hulse said, a wry expression on his face, very much a man put upon by incompetent subordinates. He reached into his pocket and offered them cigarettes from his morocco-bound case. Stewart hesitated, then took one. Von Hulse smiled. Score one for you, you bastard, Stewart thought. But he figured he might as well. They were going to kill him anyway.

Julia took one also and the other German, not Schmidt, leaped to light it for her, clicking his heels and bowing as he did. It was all so comic opera-ish, Stewart thought. That was the thing about the Germans, he remembered Hartman saying once, back when they were in Berlin. They acted like characters in a comic opera, only they saw it as high tragedy. They were bound and determined to make people take them seriously, even if they had to kill them to do it. Hartman had been at his best then. He wondered where Hartman was now.

Schmidt went to a shelf and got down a box and opened it. He took out bandages and a bottle of antiseptic. Jesus, Stewart thought. They're all ready. They've used this place before. Schmidt came over and ripped the bandage away from Stewart's finger. Stewart almost passed out from the pain. Schmidt just grinned.

"Haben Sie hier Schmerzen?" Schmidt flicked his finger right where the fingertip had been cut off.

"Jesus! Aaagh!" Stewart shouted, jerking his hand away.

Schmidt roughly grabbed Stewart's hand again and peered at it for a moment. He opened the bottle of antiseptic and poured it over the red raw end of Stewart's finger. Stewart gasped, rising almost vertically out of his chair. He had to clench his teeth to keep from crying out. Tears started out of the corners of his eyes. There was nothing he could do to stop it. He couldn't help himself.

"Es ist nicht infiziert. Sie brauchen sich keine Sorgen zu machen."

"I'm glad to hear it. Especially coming from you," Stewart gasped, closing his eyes against the pain. When he opened them, von Hulse was staring at him, amused.

"You must forgive me, Herr Stewart. It's just so odd to see Schmidt—of course that isn't his real name, you know—doing anything other than giving pain. That's his specialty. Herr Schmidt was trained for it. We have places now in Germany where such arts can be perfected. Alas for Herr Schmidt, this is an Abwehr operation. But then, you knew that, didn't you, Herr Stewart?"

The thin-faced German stopped working on Stewart's hand and looked over at von Hulse.

"Du hast den grossen Mund, Herr Baron," Schmidt said venomously. Stewart's heart sank. He'd known all along that they were going to kill him, but hearing the words said, somehow made it official. He knew that von Hulse never would have admitted to being a member of the Abwehr if they'd meant to let him live.

"Nonsense. Herr Stewart is a professional. He understands these things," von Hulse said, airily waving his hand. "Besides, we're not telling Herr Stewart anything he doesn't already know, are we?"

Stewart didn't answer. He was more concerned with Julia, sitting on the edge of her chair, staring at all of them as if she had wandered into the wrong room by mistake. Schmidt finished bandaging Stewart's hand. He straightened and went back to the door. Stewart crossed his legs and rested the bandaged hand on his knee, the pain subsiding to merely awful.

"Why are you fixing me up?" Stewart asked von Hulse.

"Because of a previous error in judgment," von Hulse said, glowering at Schmidt. "So. We have need of you in as undamaged a form as possible. However, we have several days yet, so you should be just fine when needed," von Hulse smiled.

"What about Señora Vargas?" Stewart said, indicating Julia. "How'd you get her to help you? Or was she in on it all along?" he said, turning suddenly on her.

"Carlos, no!" she cried out, the words torn out of her. "You don't understand!"

"Sure, I understand," Stewart said bitterly. "I just don't know what you're getting out of it."

"Please listen," she begged him. "You have to listen. They threatened my children! My babies! And you were in prison anyway. They knew I would try to get you out. They were waiting. What could I do? You have to understand. You have to," she finished, her voice a whisper.

Stewart looked at her. At her eyes, her jet-black hair and the way it fell over the collar of her white shirt and the slim perfect body.

"*Esta bien.* It's all right," Stewart said, finally. "It's all right."

"*In der Tat*, in the act, the Señora was most helpful. We have found mother-love extremely effective in getting cooperation. More than anything else. Even with the lower races, one finds such strong feelings. Like animals in nature, one supposes," von Hulse said, tapping the ash from his cigarette onto the desk. He looked at Schmidt and then back at Stewart with his cold colorless eyes. "And now perhaps we could have our little discussion, Herr Stewart."

"Sure. Why not?" Stewart shrugged. He knew they were going to kill him as soon as they finished talking. All he could do was try to think of a way to spike the German's plans before they finished him off.

"Good," von Hulse beamed, glancing over at the thin-faced German. "You see, Schmidt. Herr Stewart is perfectly willing to cooperate. We have him, also the woman. He understands the situation perfectly. Now, Herr Stewart," the smile disappearing from von Hulse's face. "Tell me about the letter."

"What letter?"

"Don't be tiresome, Herr Stewart. You know what I am talking about. The letter from Cardenas's safe. The one you took."

"Oh, *that* letter."

"Please, Herr Stewart. Spare us your Anglo-Saxon witticisms. We can still make it very painful for you, I assure you. Or perhaps you would prefer that we apply our methods of persuasion on Frau Vargas? It would be a pity. A woman's beauty is such a fragile thing, Herr Stewart. Our friend Schmidt could turn her into an old woman in a matter of hours."

Stewart nodded, glancing at Julia for a moment.

"First let her go," he said. "She doesn't know anything about this."

Von Hulse chuckled for a moment. His amusement seemed quite genuine.

"I'm inclined to doubt that, Herr Stewart. I'm inclined to doubt that very much. Let us get back to the letter, shall we?"

"What about it?"

"You had it, of course?"

"Of course."

"And did you discover its significance?"

"You mean you didn't really want to join the Atlantis Club?" Stewart said, wide-eyed.

"Do not make the joking with us, *Amerikanischer Schwein!* It is not appreciated!" von Hulse shouted, pounding the desk with his fist.

"And if I said no, I didn't, would you believe me?"

Von Hulse's anger subsided as suddenly as it had begun. He looked curiously at Stewart.

"I am a professional, Herr Stewart. I do not think I would believe you." Von Hulse's voice sharpened. "Now, *bitte*. What was in the letter?"

"You mean about the coup scheduled for December 17th and the planned assassination of President Ortiz?"

Von Hulse smiled broadly.

"Very good, Herr Stewart. You accomplished a great deal in so short a time in Buenos Aires. It's almost a pity to have to put an end to so promising a talent. And did you also manage to discover who 'The Ambassador' in the message referred to?"

Stewart grinned impudently at him.

"Oh that? We figured that out to be the *Graf Spee* in a minute."

Stewart heard a sudden intake of air behind him. Von Hulse looked sharply at Schmidt, then back at Stewart, his eyes suddenly narrowed.

"You have done very well *in der Tat,* Herr Stewart. We underestimated you Americans."

"People do that all the time, Baron. But then, you Germans have a genius for underestimating everyone except yourselves."

"Oh yes, *in der Tat.* You are a most dangerous man, Herr Stewart. We did well to capture you when we did." Von Hulse began to pick at his fingernails, not looking at Stewart. "And tell me. Have you passed this information about the *Graf Spee* back to your superiors in Washington yet?"

"Of course. The jig's up, Herr Baron. You better find someplace else to send your battleship."

Von Hulse continued to pick at his fingernails.

"And just how did you pass this information? Who was your contact?"

"Come on, Baron. I thought you said we were professionals. Don't you know?"

"You are referring to your embassy man? Herr Hartman?"

A shiver rippled through Stewart. If he confirmed it, he was signing Hartman's death warrant. Except no one knew where Hartman was. If he could make them believe he had passed the information on, they might have to abort the coup. Compared to that, Hartman was expendable. They all were.

"Sure, Hartman," Stewart said. "He was my contact. You knew that."

All at once, von Hulse leaned back in his chair. He was smiling broadly. If he was acting, Stewart thought, he was doing a hell of a job.

"No, Herr Stewart. I am afraid I don't believe you. We have been watching your embassy around the clock. Hartman hasn't been there in days. And why use an embassy contact, unless the plan was to send sensitive material by radio transmission, or by diplomatic pouch? No, Herr Stewart. The information never left your embassy. As for Hartman, even if you knew where he was hiding, I do not believe your War Department ever got the message."

A sudden chill went up Stewart's spine. When he was a child, people said when you got that feeling, someone had just stepped on your grave. How could von Hulse know all that about Hartman?

"It doesn't matter," Stewart said, exhaling a pale stream of cigarette smoke with elaborate casualness in von Hulse's direction. "There was a back-up channel. The British."

"*Ach so*, the British," von Hulse said, still smiling. That bothered Stewart. Why was he still smiling? What did he know?

"I sent them a message too. We used a dead drop."

"So! And where was this drop?"

"A shop, a *tintoreria*, in Recoleta. If you don't believe me, suit yourself," Stewart shrugged.

"*Ach*, Herr Stewart, this is *wunderbar!*" von Hulse said, laughing. "Look! Even Herr Schmidt appreciates your performance too."

Stewart turned around in his chair. Schmidt was grinning from ear to ear.

"We have had the British under constant surveillance. Especially since yesterday. Not one of them has gone anywhere near the Recoleta. Not that it matters," von Hulse said, standing up suddenly. "I do not believe you had time to pass the information before the Argentines arrested you, Herr Stewart. That is most unlikely. And you would not have told anything to Colonel Fuentes, either. Firstly, because he might be working for Castillo, or even us, possibly. And secondly, I must tell you our Argentine sources are very good. We would have heard. So, I think we now have everything from you we need," von Hulse smiled. It was a nasty smile. The smile of someone who as a kid liked to pull the wings off of insects. "Under normal circumstances, I would now turn you over to Herr Schmidt. However, we still require you to perform one final service for us, Herr Stewart. So we must keep you alive and intact, but immobilized for a few days. 'On the ice,' as I believe you *Amerikaners* say. And what better place for that than a refrigeration plant, *nicht wahr?*" Von Hulse gestured vaguely at the walls around them. "And now, we shall say *auf Wiedersehen*, Herr Stewart. I will see you again, one more time. But you will not, I am afraid, know it. You will be dead."

Von Hulse flicked at the lapels of his jacket with his driving gloves. "So dusty in here," he remarked, coming towards Julia. "Señora Vargas," he said, clicking his heels. He turned and barked an order to the other Germans.

Schmidt grabbed Stewart by the collar, yanking him out of the chair. He brutally jammed the pistol into Stewart's kidney and marched him out the door. The other German followed with Julia. The last Stewart saw of von Hulse, he was lighting a fresh cigarette from the still burning butt, looking absurdly pleased with himself.

The Germans marched them across the plant floor. Stewart tried to look at Julia, but a sharp pain from another poke to the kidney brought him up short. Schmidt grunted with satisfaction. At the big double doors of one of the refrigeration tanks, Schmidt motioned to the other German, who took a key out of his pocket and unlocked a padlock on a long sliding bar. The bar secured the heavy iron doors from the outside. The

German slid back the bar and with a loud sound of grating metal, swung the heavy doors open.

A whiff of foul air came out. It was dark inside the tank. The German reached in and clicked on the light. Julia and Stewart looked at each other. He thought for an instant about trying something, but another sharp jab in the kidney got him stumbling forward into the tank. Julia was just behind him, reaching for him. He heard her gasp before he saw it. All at once, he understood why they were keeping them alive.

At the far end of the tank, dangling naked from a meat hook, was Hartman. They had used piano wire around his neck and the head had flopped far over. With a snarled curse and a final punch to the kidney, Schmidt sent Stewart flying to the metal floor of the tank. Before he could get up, Schmidt and the other German had stepped back outside and slammed the iron door shut. The sound wave of the banging door rumbled inside the tank like thunder, setting Hartman's body to swaying. Julia and Stewart stared at it and then at each other, as they listened to the sound of the outside bar sliding home, followed by the faint metal click of the padlock snapping shut.

"THEY'RE GOING to kill us, aren't they?" Julia said. In the confined space, her voice had an echo to it. She squatted on the metal floor of the refrigeration tank the way a young girl does, her hands around her knees. Without the refrigeration motor on, the tank was hot and humid, the air increasingly foul.

"Yes," Stewart said.

She looked at the body, hanging from a hook near the other end of the tank, its naked toes pointed downwards like a ballerina. The piano wire was embedded so deep into the flesh of the neck it couldn't be seen. All at once, she shuddered.

"Do you know him?"

"Yes. It is . . . It was Hartman. He was from the embassy. I tried to get in touch with him all day yesterday. No one had seen him. Now I know why."

Stewart got up and started toward Hartman's body, then stopped. He didn't have to get any closer to see that Hartman had been tortured before he died. There were dozens of ugly purplish burn spots all over his body, a large cluster of them around his stomach and genitals. Stewart turned away.

"Was he a good man?" she asked.

"I don't know," he said, sitting down beside her. "I don't think so. He tried to be once," he said, remembering Berlin and Hartman's lighthearted grace as he skipped under the trees on the Unter den Linden. Now the handsome head hung sideways at an impossible angle like one of those goose-neck lamps. "Maybe at the end, he tried again."

She grabbed his arm. Her eyes searched his face, the fear in them expanding like a blot in water.

"When I was a girl," she began, "I used to think, what if we are just a dream of God's? Something He won't even remember when He awakes. What if that's all we are? Characters in a dream. And everything destined to disappear in a split-second. That's what happens when we die anyway, isn't it?" she said, her fingers digging into his arm.

"I don't know what happens when we die. It's a little too early to be talking about dying."

"Is it? Is it?" she beseeched him, her eyes an unbelievable blue. He put his arms around her.

"No. It isn't."

She gestured wearily at the hanging body.

"Why'd they do it? What were they after?"

"What? Hartman? They probably wanted to find out what he knew. Whether he knew about the coup and the *Graf Spee*. And who the Raven was. Poor Hartman," he said, shaking his head.

"Did he? Know any of it, I mean?"

"What? No. That's the hell of it. He never knew a thing." Stewart got up. He had just noticed something. A tag, a piece of paper, something, tied by a string to Hartman's penis. He went up to the body. It was a single word on a piece of paper and it sent Stewart staggering backwards, his mind reeling.

Verrater. Traitor.

"What is it?" she asked. "What passes?"

It isn't possible, Stewart thought. He never liked Hartman, but he was an American. It couldn't be. It made no sense. But the hell of it was that it made a great deal of sense.

"What is it?" she asked again.

"Traitor," Stewart managed, breathing hard. "They called him a traitor."

"Qué va? He was a spy, wasn't he? They knew that. So?"

"No!" he said, grabbing her by the shoulders. "Not spy! They didn't call him 'spy.' They called him 'traitor!' Traitor to them! Hartman was working for the Nazis!"

Suddenly, it all made sense. The network destroyed by the Fascists in Madrid. And how the Germans knew about Raoul. And Hartman coming dirty with tags to the boat when he arrived in Buenos Aires. And why the Germans always seemed to be one step ahead of them. Like how the Germans knew to wait for him that night at the Atlantis Club. And how they knew to get to Cardenas before he did. The only reason the Nazis hadn't already eliminated the Raven was because Stewart hadn't told Hartman who it was. It was Hartman all along. But why? Why?

"Why?" he shouted in English. "Why'd you do it, you son-of-a-bitch? Why? Why?" He punched the body savagely with his good hand. It smacked against the ribs, sending the body dancing leadenly in the air. He punched it again and again till it was swinging like a pendulum, banging against the metal sides of the tank. "You bastard!" Stewart shouted, watching it swing. "You fucking Nazi bastard!" He started forward again, to do God-knows-what, when Julia grabbed him. She wrapped her arms around him. Her face was horror-stricken.

"Stop it, *yanqui!* Stop it! It's crazy. He's dead. Stop. Please, stop!" she cried.

Stewart stopped. He looked at her, panting.

"Why?" he asked her. "Why did he do it?"

It was an impossible question, but she blinked as though she took it quite seriously.

"What was his name? What you said before?"

"His name was Hartman. Why?"

"No sé," she shrugged. "It's only that it sounds like a German name."

Stewart looked at her. It couldn't be that simple. The State Department only took native-born Americans, Ivy League types. They were all like that. He started to shake his head and then he remembered something Hartman had said at their first rendezvous in Madrid when they were trying to set up the network.

There was heavy fighting then, at Jarama outside Madrid, he remembered. The Loyalists were trying to keep the Valencia road open, the city not completely cut off yet, and in Madrid they had hung red flags from the windows in the Plaza Mayor that said: *"No pasaran!"* They shall not pass! The shelling had begun, day after day, and in the cafés you would see men in berets stopping off for a glass of *fino* on their way to the front, their rifles leaning against their chairs. Hartman had said something about Berlin, about his parents having relatives in the Hansa Viertel, and how when he had gone to look them up, they were all gone, moved. "It was weird, Charlie," he remembered Hartman saying. "None of the neighbors knew anything. No one wanted to talk. They'd been living there for a half-century and nobody knew a goddamn thing. I mean," he'd said, exasperated, "it's not like they were Jews, for Chrissakes!" And at the time, Stewart had been so annoyed about what he'd said about the Jews, he'd paid no attention to the other part, about the relatives. It hadn't seemed like anything. All kinds of funny things were going on in Germany in those days.

A sudden thought stopped him cold. Hartman had been clean at that first Madrid meeting. He'd done everything right; it was all fine. It was only later, when Hartman had gone to Vienna to set up the initial contact with the Czech underground, that everything began to go bad.

The Underground. Prague.

And Margarethe.

That's when they turned him. Vienna. That's when he had changed.

Stewart looked up at Hartman's face, the eyes open, staring. They'd been blackmailing him, Stewart thought. His relatives in a concentration camp. Something like that. The oldest goddamn ploy in the world.

"You dumb bastard," Stewart said to the dead man. "You stupid stupid man." He turned to Julia. "How did you know, *guapa?* In America we're so used to everyone's ancestors coming from somewhere else, we don't pay attention. He was born in the States. The family information was only background. History."

She came up to him. He could smell her perfume over the odor of dead meat that permeated the tank.

"Family is everything. Don't you understand?" she said.

"I'm beginning to."

"*Entonces*, he was of them? Of the Nazis all along?"

"For a long time," he nodded. "Too long."

"But there is no consistency in this. If he was working for them, why kill him? And in such a way?" she said, shuddering.

"For the same reason they bandaged my hand. Once I was on the scene and it was clear I didn't trust him—he would have told them that himself—his value was diminished. Also, they needed to close down any possible link to the Raven. They couldn't afford to rely on blackmailing him forever. Besides, they had a better use for him."

"For what?"

"To take the fall for Ortiz's assassination. An American diplomat. The final nail in the coffin for Argentine public opinion after Castillo's coup. Only our *compadre*, Schmidt, probably got a little too zealous trying to persuade Hartman about what a privilege it is to die for the Fatherland. That's why they need me. Alive."

"Why?"

"To take his place," Stewart said, grimacing. "They'll make sure my body is found near Ortiz's, probably with the gun used to kill him in my hand. The *Prensa* will be outraged. More *gringo* interference in Latin America. It's quite clever in a heavy-handed Teutonic way."

"Except that you know what they are preparing for," she said. "You are smarter than them."

"Oh, for *cierto*. I'm a genius after the fact, when it's too late. That's the only reason we're still alive," he said bitterly, glancing at the metal walls. "*Tu sabes*, picking a refrigerator to hold us is almost poetic in its symbolism. Because that's all we are to them now. Fresh meat. Something to be kept alive so our flesh is in the correct condition when we're found dead."

Julia stared at him. "We have to do something," she said.

"Like what?"

"I don't know," she snapped. "You're a man. Be a man! Do something!"

Although Stewart didn't think they had a prayer, he began to walk around the tank, if only to have something to do. He searched the walls and ceiling, the seams and along the sides, looking for a crack, a handhold, ventilation holes, anything. Apart from a row of hooks on a ceiling rail, like the one Hartman was dangling from, there was nothing. They were locked inside a big iron box. The heavy door barred from the outside was the only way in or out. Houdini couldn't get out of here, he thought miserably. Apart from the body and the overhead hooks, there was nothing else in the tank. Nothing they could use. Even the body was naked, he thought.

The body!

That and the fact that they wanted them alive till the last minute.

Stewart began to study the body, walking around it. Julia watched him as though he were performing a ritual of some kind. He got up on his toes, reaching as high as he could to where the piano wire was tied to the hook. He was about a foot too short.

"Come here," he said, motioning her over.

"What is it?"

"Get on all fours. Make yourself as compact as possible. We need to get the body down," he said, pointing up.

"Why bother?"

"Because," he said fiercely, grabbing her arms. "We're getting out of here. Alive."

She looked at the body, at the ghastly face and the wire attached to the hook. She looked at Stewart questioningly, but he only stood there, waiting. After a moment, she got down on her hands and knees. He pushed her down, forearms braced flat on the ground and got up on her back, teetering to keep his balance. He reached up and grabbed Hartman's body around the middle with his bad hand, wincing as he raised it up to take the weight off the wire. He worked feverishly with his right hand, trying to loosen the wire from the hook. She shifted under him. He almost lost his balance and had to grab onto the hook to hang on.

"Hurry, I can't hold it," she gasped. "My back is breaking."

"You've got to. Hold on! Another second!" he shouted, struggling with the wire. It was cutting deep into the ball of his hand. He could feel her going. He inched the loop of wire over the tip of the hook as she shifted suddenly. They collapsed in a heap on the floor, Hartman's body sprawled stiffly on top of them.

Stewart rolled the body off and pulled Julia to her feet. Her face was pale. She was breathing hard and wearing a moustache of perspiration on her upper lip, and at that moment no one had ever looked more beautiful. He put his arms around her and kissed her.

"What passes, *yanqui?* What?" she said, trying to catch her breath.

"We're going to do it," he said. "We're going to do it, or die."

He knelt by the body and began unwrapping the wire from around its neck. He had to tug hard to get it out from where it was embedded between rolls of hardening flesh. When he freed the wire, he took off his belt and looped it back around Hartman's neck.

"What are you going to do?" she asked.

"Hang him back up. Alive he wasn't worth spit, but dead, he may have value for us."

"And then?"

"They want us alive. They'll be back, Schmidt and the other one, to check on us, feed us, something. When they come back, I need to get one of them to step inside for a few seconds. That's all."

"Why bother to put this one back?" she said, looking disgustedly at the body.

"They left a naked body hanging. They'll expect to see one."

"But won't they notice that he's hanging from the belt instead of the wire?"

"No," Stewart shook his head. "The body'll just be a general impression. They won't be looking at it. They'll be looking at you."

"At me? Why? What will I be doing?"

Stewart smiled grimly.

"Fucking."

"*Qué va?*" she snorted. "And if we give them a show, what does that serve?"

"You won't be fucking me," he said, shaking his head.

"If not you, who *pues?*"

"An illusion," he said, taking off his trousers and shoes. Her eyes grew wide with understanding. "Have you anything in your pockets? Anything at all?"

She looked and pulled a small gold cylinder from her pocket.

"Only a lipstick."

"Good. Give it to me," he said, holding out his hand. She gave it to him and he tied one end of the piano wire to it to make a handle, grimly pulling it tight.

"And where will you be, while I make the performance?" she asked.

"Up there," he said, pointing at the ceiling over the door. "Those hooks were used for beef carcasses. They move."

She held his face between her hands, like a priest raising an ikon.

"Listen, *yanqui*. This thing we do. Can it be done?"

He touched her hair, then let his hand drop.

"Truly?"

"Yes, truly."

"No. I don't think so," he said. "It would take a miracle. And the Germans have outlawed miracles."

"Then we're going to die?"

"Yes. Very soon."

"Then make love to me," she whispered, pulling him down to the floor. "Make love to me now—in truth, not for illusion."

"In front of *that*?" he said, jerking his head toward the body.

"Yes," she said urgently, "especially in front of that. He tried to kill us, but we're still alive. Here, feel me alive," she said, guiding his hand to her breast.

He could feel the soft warmth of it, the nipple popping erect and beneath it, the beating of her heart. They kissed long and passionately, lips into lips, breathing each other's breath, her hand sliding down his chest and belly into his undershorts, clasping and then freeing him.

His mouth worked its way down her neck, found her breasts and tasted them, first one, then the other. And on down her rib cage and the swell of her belly until they were tasting each other, the warm salty taste of life, now burning hot. The imminence of death was like a goad to his desire. She was there, moving underneath him, the most beautiful woman in the world, wanting him, desperate for him, her knees parted wide to receive him, her hips thrusting up towards him, again and again, surging like the sea. And it had built up inside him like nothing he had ever felt. He was going to die and this was going to be the last time. He had to have her. He was insane for her. If she suddenly were to change her mind, he would rape her, he realized, putting his hand down and guiding himself into her. Inside, she was as hot as a furnace. He could feel the heat of her engulfing him as he plunged deeper and deeper, the two of them going at each other like crazed souls, kissing and biting and pulling each other tighter and tighter together until they were part of each other. And then the tempo, faster and faster and she screamed, her mouth wide like an animal's, and he couldn't hold back any more. He erupted and it came and came until they were drained and left clinging to each other, castaways on each other's shore.

Afterwards, after they rested, after they hung the body back up and he moved two of the hooks to a position over the doorway, after they set up his shoes and trousers on the floor at the back of the tank, stuffing the trouser legs with her clothes to give them shape, and readied the piano wire, they sat against the metal wall, naked as Adam and Eve, his arms around her.

"What happens to us? If we were ever to get out of here?" he asked.

"We could meet," she said shyly. "There's a hotel in San Telmo, the Siracusa, where Ceci and I . . ." she stopped, reddening.

"No, afterwards. What about us?"

She turned, covering his lips with her fingers.

"You mustn't," she said. "There is no us. Please, *yanqui*."

"But why?" he said earnestly. "Don't you want to?"

"My God, don't you think I want to? You know I want to. I would do anything to be with you. Be anything. I would be your whore if you wanted me for that only. My God, don't say that to me!"

"But I love you," he said stubbornly, suddenly blurting it out. He hadn't meant to say it, but now that it was out, he realized it was true. She closed her eyes when he said it.

"Yes. I knew it. I knew it!" she said fiercely.

"Then leave him. You don't love Arturo. You know you don't."

"And my children. What of them?"

"Take them! We'll leave together. I'll love them. If they're yours, I'll love them. I will!"

"Oh God, *yanqui*. It is like a knife turning inside me when you say that. Don't you think I wish I could? But Arturo would have my children. I would never see them again."

"But you're the mother," he said lamely.

"*Aiee, caramba, yanqui!* This is Argentina, not Nuevo York! Arturo owns the children, not I."

"But you hate him. Even with the play-acting. I've seen it."

"Yes!" she hissed, her eyes blazing. "Of course! What better reason for marriage? Why else would a Gideon ever marry?"

He pulled back from her. "I don't understand," he said. "Is that why you married Vargas? Out of hate?"

"Of course," she shrugged. "Arturo is a Montoya. A distant cousin, really. We were born to be married."

"But I thought that the Gideons and the Montoyas were friends. Allies," he said, remembering something Athena de Castro had said. About how Julia was not only a Gideon, but also a Montoya, and that he didn't know what this meant in Argentina.

Julia looked at him strangely.

"Where did you find such an idea? The Gideons and the Montoyas have always hated each other. Our marriage," she said, her mouth screwed up in a sad ironic smile, "was inevitable."

"But didn't Montoya save your grandfather from the Indians, or something?"

She shook her head.

"Montoya betrayed him. For greed, so there would be one less to share the land with. Gideon told me that himself. He was an old man by then, but you should have seen his eyes when he spoke of it. It was as if he were seeing it happen again. You don't know how he was," she said, looking at Stewart. "Only those who knew him knew what eyes can be, what can be inside a man and yet for him not to die."

"Then how did he manage to escape from the Indians?"

"I don't know. No one knows."

Stewart made a face of disbelief.

"But it's true," she said. "He was staked out to die, only he didn't die. No one knows how he survived. The only time he ever talked about it was when I was a little girl. He showed me the scar on his belly. That was a scar, *yanqui*. And then all he said was, 'They left me to die. Only I didn't. I couldn't, could I?' "

"*No entiendo*. What did he mean he couldn't?"

"You didn't know him," she said passionately. "If you knew him, you would understand."

"Then help me. Help me understand. What did he mean?"

"Because he couldn't die!" she exclaimed. "He had a plan. Some great design. That's why he needed power and money and land, and a wife of the Montoyas and all of it. Even the

Indians, primitive beasts though they were, must have sensed it. You couldn't be around him and not know it. How could the Indians compete? They knew about bravery and cruelty, but he was something else. Trying to subdue Gideon, to kill him, would be like trying to subdue the tide." She stopped. She stared at the iron wall, then back at him. "What's the point, *yanqui?*" she went on, quietly. "You didn't know him. You don't know our world. The world of the Pampas, with its vast empty sky, like the eye of God, from which there is no hiding."

"Then why didn't he kill Montoya?"

She looked at him derisively, her eyes flashing.

"That's what any man might do. What you or I might do. But that made nothing for my grandfather. *Nada.* My grandfather's hate was like God's love. Infinite. Eternal. He married for hate. Everything he did was out of hate. He was a saint of hate. Its apostle."

"Is that why you married Arturo? For Gideon?"

She pulled him close. She took his hand and guided it down and inside her, still warm and dripping wet.

"Feel me, *yanqui,*" she said, pressing her face into his neck. "Feel my heart. Feel it beat in my womb. Now, I will tell you only truth. Arturo and I cared for each other in the beginning. We were like two enemy soldiers trapped between the trench lines who find they have much in common. When I married Arturo, it was to betray Gideon. But isn't that what we all do? Betray our parents. Isn't that the only way to survive?"

That stopped him. He thought about his father. About his workman's hands, the grime embedded under the nails no matter how much he washed, and how they were always covered with cuts and bruises after a day's work. He thought about his shabby clothes and gray Brooklyn streets and how he had lied to his friends in college about his father. "Who? My dad? Oh, he's in construction. You know, the big skyscrapers in New York."

From outside the tank came the sound of approaching footsteps and the faint snap of a padlock being opened.

Buenos Aires, 1880

THAT NIGHT there were parties and bonfires in the northern
suburbs to celebrate General Roca's election victory. In the
city itself, Nationalist soldiers patrolled the streets, although
the rumor was that Carlos Tejedor, the opposition candidate
who had led the rebellion, had already fled to Montevideo.

The best parties were in Belgrano. The most lavish was at
the Villa Gideon, the immense Mediterranean mansion that
had served as President Avellaneda's temporary headquarters
until the Army had crushed the rebellion. Now the estate was
lit up like a Christmas tree for the inaugural ball. The long
curving drive to the house was crowded with horse-drawn
conveyances and sedan chairs. Liveried servants scurried to
help the elegantly dressed guests alight from their carriages.

Inside the mansion, the rooms were brilliant with the newly
installed gaslights. In the dining hall, a whole barbecued cow
was turned on a spit. Servants wandered among the guests
with trays of *hors d'oeuvres* and drinks.

In the main ballroom, a full orchestra, complete with grand
piano, played Viennese waltzes. The air was alive with chatter and laughter, *distinguido* guests from both camps, *porteño*
and Nationalist, mingling in the salons.

Also there, though not by choice was the *porteño* wheat
broker, Estanislao Casaverde, and his young daughter, Alejandra. They had been summoned.

Casaverde was a stout, middle-aged man with gray mutton-
chops and a look of permanently offended dignity. His daughter was small, raven-haired, exceptionally pretty. She had
dark intelligent eyes, sparkling with the secret of a fifteen-
year-old girl who knows she is becoming a woman. The mo-

ment they stepped into the columned entrance hall, someone handed them both glasses of champagne. Two young women in bell-shaped dresses, one white, the other rose, that made them look like floating tulips, walked by.

"*Hola!*" one of them said. "Have you seen the horse?"

"In the main ballroom," the other giggled.

"A white stallion. They said he paid twelve thousand pesos for it," the first one said, rolling her eyes.

"For twelve thousand pesos, he could ride more than horses," the second one said, covering her mouth with a gloved hand, as they both sniggered happily. Casaverde started to respond, but they had already moved on.

Casaverde peered after them disapprovingly for a moment. He and Alejandra made their way through the crowd into the main ballroom. People were everywhere, eating, drinking, waltzing to the orchestra. A circle had gathered around the horse, a magnificent white creature with a blue ribbon around his neck. Alejandra didn't know where to look first, as a woman in a gaudy purple gown stopped them, waving excitedly as she exchanged her empty champagne glass for a full one from a passing tray.

"But it's Don Estanislao!" she cried delightedly. "And little Alejandra. *Qué bonita!*" she said, extending her hand for him to kiss. "But of course, she doesn't remember me," she pouted briefly. "And how is Dona Carlota and the little boy, Enrique? Such a *niño!*"

"All well, thanks to God."

"Of course. Isn't this something? Everyone is here. Even the great man himself, President Roca."

"Where?" Alejandra said excitedly, swiveling her head despite her father's frown. Even though her father, as a loyal *porteño*, had supported Governor Tejedor, ever since his conquest of the Indians the previous year, Roca had been the name on everyone's lips. Idealized pictures of him in uniform, gazing off into the distance of the Pampa, had been sold on every street corner and in the *cantinas* there were songs about his bravery and "piercing eyes of blue."

"Oh, somewhere," the woman said airily, moving on.

"Who was that, Papa?" Alejandra asked.

"Dona Elena Morena Ruiz. A friend of your mother's," he said, turning and bowing to a tall mustachioed man balanced uncertainly at the edge of a divan, staring at an almost empty glass of whiskey in his hand as if he didn't know what to do with it. *"Buenos tardes*, Don Felipe. How are you?"

"Don't talk to me in Spanish," Don Felipe pronounced with drunken solemnity. "Spanish is dead. Nobody in Buenos Aires speaks Spanish anymore. Only English. And *Italiano. Momentito*, you!" he said, grabbing a passing waiter by the arm.

"Si, Señor?"

"Spanish. Do you speak Spanish? *Habla usted español?"*

"Claro qué si, Señor."

"You see," Don Felipe announced drunkenly, releasing the waiter. "He's lying. Must be a wop," he whispered loudly. "They're all like that. Liars, every last one of them. The English are even worse. Do you know why the *Ingleses* all have long noses? So they can look down them at everyone else," Don Felipe said, holding his nose up in the air in a pinched imitation of aristocratic superciliousness. "Look at them! Always together, conspiring," he said, waving his hands disgustedly at a group of Englishmen talking earnestly to each other. "Argentina is doomed," Don Felipe went on. "We've got to learn English."

"Some of us are doing well enough," Casaverde muttered, looking around the ornate hall.

"Ah, Gideon," Don Felipe pronounced heavily. "There's an *oficial* who understands *Inglés*. Speaks it like a native, they say. English to the bankers, *Italiano* to the *peóns*. There's a future in it," he declared grandly, pointing his finger in the air.

"But how did he get so rich?" Alejandra asked.

"Stole it, of course," Don Felipe announced blithely. "Only way to get really rich. He was a 'Mitrista.' One of Mitre's 'Army of Purveyors,' during the War of the Triple Alliance. Of course the only thing they purveyed was land for themselves. And everything else they could steal," he grinned, breathing into their faces. His breath was so laced with alcohol, she thought one could set a match to it. "One interesting thing, though," he winked broadly. "How everywhere he and his gang acquired land was exactly, to the very foot of the letter, where the English just happened to build their railroads. *Qué coincidencia!"*

Alejandra stared at him, fascinated.

"That's enough," Casaverde muttered.

"For you or me, clearly," Don Felipe said. "But for Don Juan Gideon it was only the beginning. After the railroads came, the value of his *latifundias* in Cordoba and Rosario increased a hundredfold. Then he bought land outside Buenos Aires. In the Retiro, Palermo, Barrio Norte, where in those days you could not give it away. A common speculator, but with an Army commission. And a troop of *gauchos* to cut any reluctant throats," he said, drawing his fingers across his neck.

"Any fool can make money. Keeping it is another matter," Casaverde remarked.

"He has the Devil's own luck," Don Felipe said thickly. "His real killing came in the Crash of '72, when all the rest of us . . ." his voice trailed off.

"What happened?" Alejandra asked.

"He kept all his land debts in paper, but he himself held gold, that Devil. After the Crash, one gold peso was worth a hundred on paper. But how did he know there would be a Crash, *pues?*" he demanded drunkenly. "That's the question! Of course, being one of Roca's closest allies hasn't hurt him either," Don Felipe said, gesturing off-handedly at the giant portrait of Roca gazing off into the Pampa, the oil original of the street-corner ones, dominating one wall of the ballroom, over a buffet table.

"Be still, fool," hissed Casaverde, looking around anxiously. "Are you mad?"

"Have no fear, Don Estanislao. They don't speak Spanish here, only English," he confided in a stage whisper loud enough to be heard halfway across the room.

Alejandra looked around at the glittering ball like a girl in a fairy tale.

"But surely you are not serious, Don Felipe," she said earnestly. "No one could steal all this."

Don Felipe smiled indulgently. He patted her on the head, as though she were a much younger child.

"Listen, *mi niña*. That man lived many years with the *gauchos*. When a man is used to killing," he shrugged, "what does a little thievery matter?"

Casaverde looked at him severely. It was a Spanish severity, without compassion, only judgment.

"You have drunk too much, Don Felipe. These are not matters for a young girl's ears."

Don Felipe tried to straighten. "A thousand pardons, Don Estanislao. I have drunk too much because Argentina has elected another soldier. Some day I hope to live long enough to see an Argentine president who isn't a soldier."

Casaverde took his daughter's arm.

"Good evening, Don Felipe. Buenos Aires has survived many things. It will survive being turned into a Federal District. With permission," he bowed, leading Alejandra away.

"English, Don Estanislao! You have to say it in English," Don Felipe called after them.

"Pay no attention. Don Felipe is a bitter man," Casaverde said, guiding Alejandra toward the corridor off the main ballroom.

"But why, Papa?"

"Because he is a Creole and a *porteño,*" Casaverde said, with a faint echo of pride in the very words. "And also because he owes Don Juan Gideon much money. Lack of money makes a man bitter."

"Not more than lack of love, Papa," she said seriously, her voice suddenly that of a woman.

He stopped and took hold of both of her arms.

"More even than lack of God," he said. Then he grimaced impatiently. "But you are too young to understand these things."

"Not so young any more, Papa."

"No," he said thoughtfully. "Perhaps not."

He turned and offered his arm formally to her. They walked together down the hall to the door to the library. One of Roca's personal guards stood at attention beside the door, rifle at his side, barring the way.

"Announce us," Casaverde snapped, looking distastefully at the guard as if seeing in his uniform the emblem of his defeat. "Don Estanislao Casaverde and daughter Alejandra Irena."

The guard looked them over, as if checking them for hidden weapons, then knocked on the door and stepped inside. A moment later, he opened the door for them.

The library was a large room with high latticed windows and floor-to-ceiling shelves filled with leather-bound books. It was done in the English style, panelled in oak that gave it an air of instant dignity, as though it had been there for centuries. Seated on a *chaise-longue* and chairs over port and cigars were the most powerful men in the country: the outgoing president, Avellaneda; Pellegrini, the new Finance Minister; Casaverde's own brother-in-law, Cesar Montoya; John Gideon; and the man of the hour himself, Roca.

Alejandra stared at President Roca. She couldn't help herself. She had heard so much about him that it was hard to believe he was a real person. He looked older than his pictures and oddly enough, kindlier. The famous eyes were indeed blue. One of the other men, big, broad-shouldered and rather handsome, she thought, except for a scar on his forehead, who looked to be in his mid-thirties, moved away from the table he had been leaning against and came toward them, his hand extended in welcome. His eyes were also blue. A darker colder blue than Roca's.

"Don Estanislao. *Encantado*. We are so pleased that you could come," the man said, smiling.

Alejandra felt her father stiffen beside her.

"You wanted to see me, Don Juan. I am here," Casaverde said simply. "Señor *Presidente*," he added, bowing rigidly to Roca.

Gideon's expression froze. For an instant only, then he was smiling again.

"Not to see you, Don Estanislao, but to talk with you," he said, coming closer. "The person I wanted to see was your daughter, Señorita Alejandra." He looked down at her. She felt her face grow hot and glanced away. Something inside her vibrated at impossible speed, like a hummingbird's wing. Gideon went back to the table. He took a long cigar out of a gold case and lit it. "She is acceptable," he announced to the room. "I am agreeable."

Casaverde's face turned red. He held himself upright like a soldier.

"Agreeable to what, if I may inquire?" he said, glaring at Gideon.

"To an engagement between Don Juan Gideon and your lovely daughter," President Roca said, his voice unusually soft and gracious. His voice took Alejandra by surprise. It was a seducer's voice.

"She is only a child," Casaverde sputtered angrily. "I won't hear of it."

"Clearly, one wouldn't presume, Don Estanislao," Gideon said soothingly. "We would wait three years until she is of age. Besides, I have recently acquired a new *estancia*, Ravenwood. It will take that long to turn it into a showcase befitting so fine a jewel," he said, smiling at Alejandra.

Casaverde stared at Gideon as though he suspected him of wanting to pick his pocket. He glanced at his brother-in-law,

Montoya, who made an imperceptible gesture. Casaverde nodded. He went over to the sideboard and poured himself a glass
of port, his movements studied, conscious of their eyes upon
him.

"If your purpose, Don Juan, was to impress me with your
connections, you have, of course, succeeded," Casaverde said,
inclining his head toward the two presidents and Pellegrini.
"I am honored by your interest, as my daughter is, no doubt.
But to what purpose would such an alliance be?"

"Papa!" Alejandra cried out, staring horrified at her father
as though she had never seen him before.

"Be still, *hija*," he snapped, turning back to Gideon. "Truly,
Señor. Let us be candid. What are you after?"

"Wheat."

"Pardon, Señor?"

"Wheat. Also barley and linseed, for the oil. Within the three
years of the *noviazgo*, I can have twenty thousand acres at
Ravenwood under cultivation for export," Gideon said.

"Indeed," Casaverde said politely. "Is that all?"

"No. Beef, also. While we've all been busy killing each other,
the *yanquis* have begun shipping frozen beef in special
frigorifico ships with cakes of ice to England. We can do the
same—with better quality beef and at a better price. I'm going
to make you a very rich man, Don Estanislao," Gideon grinned.

Casaverde frowned, dislike and disbelief plain on his face.
"And from where would the money come for such a ven-
ture?"

"From the British themselves," Pellegrini said smoothly,
speaking for the first time. "Our land *cedulas* are most popular
on the London Exchange."

"With the *Ingleses* themselves putting up the money to build
the railroads," Avellaneda said.

"And for every mile of track, the value of the land increases
tenfold," Gideon added.

"And who decides where the railroads should be built?"
Casaverde demanded belligerently.

"I do," Roca said.

The library went utterly still. They could hear the noise of
the party and the orchestra from outside the room. Alejandra
began to back away from the men in the room, like a cat
sensing danger.

"Papa," she whispered, her eyes fastened desperately on her
father.

Casaverde put down his drink. He tapped his lip thoughtfully with his finger.

"I understand, Señores," he said. "Money for me. Money for everyone. Development for Argentina. But what specifically for you, Don Juan? Why this connection?"

Gideon glanced at Roca and Montoya, then at Casaverde.

"I'll need someone I can trust to act as broker for the grain. Only family can be trusted. Also, Señor, you are a true Creole, of a family *distinguido* and established. I am neither. Finally, your brother-in-law is my dearest and oldest friend, Cesar," Gideon said, gesturing graciously at Montoya. "It would please me if there were a blood tie between us."

"And I," Montoya echoed him.

A ghostly smile played over Casaverde's features.

"Wasn't there an incident between you two during the War of the Triple Alliance?" Casaverde asked.

"A misunderstanding," Montoya shrugged. "Nothing. Less than nothing."

Gideon came over and put his arm around Montoya's shoulders.

"When I learned how Cesar's forces had been under attack by the Indians and that he had never received my message, we were once more as brothers."

"How did you survive?" Alejandra asked.

"The *pampero* came. Those Indians believed that the wind and I were related somehow. They were utter savages. We understood each other perfectly," Gideon said, smiling strangely.

"It was the hand of God that preserved you," Montoya said, his voice clotted with emotion. The two men embraced in a warm *abrazo*.

"*Olé! Eso es!*" exclaimed Pellegrini.

As the embrace ended, the two men clung to each other's arms. Gideon turned back to Casaverde.

"But our new President wishes to be certain that his followers are as one," Gideon nodded toward Roca. "What better way to seal the bond between our families than with a marriage?"

"I appreciate Don Cesar's and Don Juan's generosity of spirit," Roca smiled. "This marriage, especially to the daughter of a prominent *porteño*, will help ease any doubts of my most conciliatory intentions. Buenos Aires has nothing to fear from

Julio Roca. But what of the girl?" he smiled at Alejandra. "How do you feel about all this, *mi niña?*"

Alejandra dropped her eyes. Her face felt like it was on fire.

"I do not wish to marry yet, Señor *Presidente.* I don't know this man," she declared, her eyes flashing at Gideon.

"What is it you need to know, *pues?*" Gideon asked, coming closer. He was much taller than she was and she had to crane her neck to look at him.

"How did you know to buy land north of the *centro?*" she demanded suddenly.

The room exploded into laughter.

"Her father's daughter," Avellaneda said, wiping his eyes and there was more laughter. Only Gideon smiled but did not laugh.

"During the last cholera outbreak, the *gente fina* of Florida Street began to build residences beyond the Plaza San Martin to escape the epidemic. Where *hidalgos* go, tradesmen are sure to follow. So I bought in the north," Gideon said.

"Are you satisfied, little one?" Pellegrini asked her, smiling broadly.

Alejandra looked at Gideon. She looked at his shoulders in his elegant black dinner jacket, his long legs casually crossed at the ankles as he leaned against the sideboard, his strong hands and icy blue eyes, and something trembled inside her. Something that had nothing to do with being a little girl.

"The Crash of '72. Someone said you made a lot of money in it. How did you know it was coming?"

"Yes, how?" Avellaneda asked, turning toward Gideon. "I've often wondered."

Gideon put down his cigar. His eyes narrowed with both amusement and intense interest. He smiled at the girl and it was like a present, meant for her alone.

"When I was your age, I was a soldier, in the Crimea," he began. "The French Emperor, Napoleon III, ordered the fleet to sail without anyone knowing where they were going, or what they were supposed to do when they got there. There wasn't even a map of the Crimea in the whole fleet, French or British! Meanwhile, back in Paris, this Napoleon was consulting his *ouija* board for guidance from the ghost of his uncle, Bonaparte, on where to land the army for the invasion. In short, he was an idiot.

"Many years later, when the Franco–Prussian War broke

out in Europe, everyone assumed the French, with their *élan* and their great emperor named Napoleon, were sure to win. I thought otherwise. The French had the name, but the Germans had the army. The French owed the British bankers an enormous amount of money, which if they lost, they would not be able to pay. A crash," he shrugged, "was inevitable. I instructed my broker in London, Edgerton, to buy gold."

The two of them, Gideon and Alejandra, leaned toward each other. They might have been alone. The men in the room watched them silently.

"You lived with the *gauchos?*" she asked.

"Yes."

"Is it truly as one reads in *Martín Fierro?*"

Gideon smiled.

"Not so interesting. And dirtier. But they are a rare breed."

"And they like to kill?" she asked, scarcely breathing.

Gideon thought for a moment.

"Not 'like,' " he said, "For them, killing is like eating, or breathing, or being with a woman. It is what a man does."

"And you? You've killed men?" she said softly.

"Yes."

The girl looked into Gideon's eyes. She took her time doing it, as if whatever was written there could be read like a page. She turned to her father.

"If you wish this thing, Papa, I will do it." All at once, she whirled around. A little girl again. "Why do you have a horse in the ballroom?" she asked Gideon. "I think it very strange."

Gideon looked at her with great seriousness.

"That is much horse. *Mucho caballo.* The best perhaps, in Argentina. That horse is your horse, *niña.* I put him there as a present for you."

"Were you so sure of us, *pues?*" Casaverde said, putting his arm protectively around Alejandra's shoulders.

"Sure? Yes," Gideon nodded slowly. "But of the value of what you had to offer, that I didn't know," he said, still looking at the girl.

Later that night, a shadowy bearded figure made his way through the narrow muddy streets of the Barracas, a notorious district of *pulperías* and brothels for the lowest classes of men, criminals, seamen of every race and the Italian field workers, *golondrinas,* swallows, they were called, imported by the shipload for the harvests. The streets were unlighted, except for lanterns in some of the windows where young girls sat, breasts bared for passers-by. The darker-skinned ones were *chinas*, from the countryside, but most were white slaves, brought over from Europe.

The night was cool and smelled of rain. From the *pulperías* came the sounds of noise and laughter. There was a muffled curse as the figure stumbled over a body in the street, snoring and smelling of vomit. The figure stepped over the body and turned towards the darkened doorway of a two-story corrugated metal house; one of those thrown up in a day, as many of the brothels down here were. The figure knocked loudly and when the door was opened, went inside.

"Where is he?" the figure said, untying his cape. He was a big man, heavily bearded, smelling of expensive tobacco and cologne.

"Upstairs," the woman said, taking his cape and hat. Her face was pasty yellow despite heavy rouge, and her Spanish heavily French-accented. Her low-cut dress was worn and strained at the seams under her arms. She looked like the madam of a brothel. In this district, there was never any surprises about what people were.

"Is he dead?" the bearded man asked.

"Bien sûr," the woman nodded vigorously. The way her curly hair shook, it was easy to see it was a wig.

"Good," the man smiled, showing white even teeth. "Who did it?"

"Two Corsicans," the woman said. "They leave on the morning tide for Marseilles."

"You have done well, *chéri,*" the man said, chucking her under the chin.

"Save your charm, Monsieur," she said, pulling her chin away and holding out her hand. Her eyes were hard, greedy. A whore's eyes. "First the money, then you can do as you please."

"As soon as I see," the man said, jingling a small heavy sack in his palm so she could hear the coins. "What about the girl?"

"Downstairs, locked in the *sótano,*" she said, jerking her head toward the dark stairway to the cellar. The man grabbed her arm, twisting it.

"What does she know?"

"Nothing! She knows nothing," the woman said. "We arranged it so she woke up next to the body. She's down there, crying, convinced we've sent for the police."

"Are you sure she knows nothing?"

The woman shrugged.

"Who knows what she thinks? She speaks little French, less Spanish. An *Inglesa*. Of what value is an *Inglesa*? Pretty though," she said, grimacing. "If she weren't so pretty, the men would ask for their money back. Why you wanted her, I cannot imagine."

"I'm glad to hear of it," the man said softly, holding her face between his hands. "If a harmless whore were to understand why I do things, she might not be so harmless."

The woman wrenched herself away. Her wig had fallen sideways and she straightened it with trembling fingers.

"I know nothing of such things, Monsieur. I wish only to be paid and then to leave, as was agreed."

"*Bien*. Where are the Corsicans?" the man asked.

"This way," the woman said, taking a candle from the table and leading him up the stairway. The stairs creaked and groaned as they climbed, the candle dancing in the draughts of air. The upstairs was a long corridor filled with cubicles, each covered by a shabby curtain. The woman led him to one of the cubicles and pulled aside the curtain.

The two Corsicans jumped up as they entered. They had been sitting on the bed next to the body and the bearded man caught the glint of metal in someone's hand as they stood aside. The dead man was naked. He had been young, handsome, and his hands were curled in a way that made him seem oddly defenseless. The bearded man touched the body. It was still warm.

"How did he die?" the bearded man demanded.

"Strangled," one of the Corsicans said. He was a short man, olive-skinned, with a milk-white cataract in one eye that gave him a disjointed, evil look.

"How?"

"With this," the one-eyed Corsican said, holding up a knotted cord.

"No other marks? Nothing?"

"*Nada*, Señor," the Corsican smiled. He held the cord up, stretched taut between his hands, as if for show. "Not a mark, nor blemish, except on the neck. It was most easy, *bien facile*."

"*Très bien, mes amis*," the bearded man said. He took the

sack of coins out of his pocket and counted it out for each of
them. The rest he gave to the woman. The Corsicans grabbed
their hats and started to leave, but the bearded man stopped
them.

"A moment, Señores. We're not finished yet," the man said
in a silky voice that froze them in their tracks. He turned to
the woman.

"If you please, Señora. Where is the dress I requested? The
red ball gown?"

"Downstairs, Señor," she said, her face paling.

"Bring it up. Also the rope and the other things," he ordered.

"Yes, Señor," she said and left.

The bearded man turned back to the Corsicans. He motioned them closer.

"Now, you two," he said.

"Señor?"

"I want him castrated. Now."

"Señor?" the one-eyed Corsican said, his eyes blinking rapidly.

"I want it off," the bearded man said, pointing at the body.
"All of it."

"But Señor," the other Corsican said. "The man is dead."

"Cut it off!" the bearded man said, his voice echoing in the
corridor.

The one-eyed Corsican licked his lips. He revealed the knife
in his hand as he leaned over the body. He looked back at the
bearded man, his face twisted as if trying to keep from being
sick.

"Are you sure, señor? Is there a reason for this?" he whispered.

"A vendetta," the bearded man replied. "You understand
vendetta?"

"Of course, Señor," the Corsican said, exhaling with relief.
He looked at the dead man with renewed interest. "With permission, what did he do, this one?"

The bearded man smiled. The Corsican had never seen such
a smile. It made him shiver.

"Nothing," the bearded man said. "To me, nothing."

"What then?"

"The worst sin in the world. The thing for which there is no
cure. He picked the wrong parents."

"*Dios*," the Corsican breathed, crossing himself.

The bearded man reached into his pocket and tossed a coin onto the body. It gleamed golden in the candlelight and the Corsican snatched it up. He reached down and sawed with his knife, holding up the bloody flesh for the man to see.

"What should I do with this, Señor?" the Corsican asked.

"Leave it in the bidet," the bearded man said. There was a rustle of petticoats in the corridor.

"Here it is, Monsieur," the woman said, holding up the dress. Her eyes went wide at the sight of the castration.

"Put it on him," the bearded man told her. "Also rouge on his face and lips, *comme une femme*, understand?"

"Of course," the woman said, recovering slightly. "You two, help me," she told the Corsicans. "And pay attention. I don't want any blood on me." She turned back to the bearded man. "And when we're finished, what?"

"Hang him from the rafter. Make it look like a suicide."

The woman and the Corsicans struggled to put the body into the dress. Suddenly, the one-eyed Corsican straightened. He looked with interest at the bearded man.

"I understand," the Corsican said brightly. "You want him to be for a *maricon, entonces*. For this then, he kills himself, yes?"

"For this," the bearded man said, lighting a long thin cigar, "and for the *escandalo* for his poor Papa, who thinks he deceives me with *abrazos* and dares to call me 'brother.'"

The Corsicans looked at him and nodded slowly.

"One thing more," the bearded man murmured. "When you finish here, go back to your ship. Never speak of this again. If you do, you will die as he did," pointing at the corpse. "Exactly as he did."

"Señor," the one-eyed Corsican said, breathing hard. "This," he gestured at the body, "this is a vengeance of greatness, *un vendetta grande*."

"No," the bearded man said softly. "It has barely begun."

She was a young woman, seventeen or eighteen, perhaps. She wore a thin white nightgown and when the bearded man unlocked the cellar door, she was hugging herself, as if to keep warm. The *sotano* was dark and narrow. It was lit by a single candle and smelled of earth, like a grave. She looked up as he came in.

"Are you the *policia*, Señor?" she asked in an awkward Spanish.

The man stood over her, saying nothing.

"Señor?" she said finally, making an odd futile gesture with her hands.

"How are you called?" he asked her.

"Luz, Señor," she answered in a low despairing voice. "Here, they call me Luz."

"Why did you kill him? The man upstairs?"

"I did not. I swear, Señor!"

"But you were with him?"

She fell to her knees, clutching desperately at his trouser legs.

"Please, Señor. I know nothing. When I wake, he is already dead."

The bearded man pulled her roughly to her feet.

"What are you?" he demanded. "French? English? *Una Inglesa?*"

"*Si Señor. Soy Inglesa,*" she nodded.

"Speak English, then," he said in English.

She looked incredulously at him. Her fingers clutched spasmodically at his jacket, as though she were afraid he might disappear into thin air.

"Oh please, sir. Do you speak English? Can you help me? Oh please!"

"Why should I? A common whore?"

"Oh sir," she said, her eyes filling. "If only you knew. I was not born to this," she said, covering her face with her hands. "I'm not bad. I'm not," she said, crying.

He watched her cry. As she sobbed, he could see the movement of her breasts under her nightgown. She was young and very pretty.

"How did you come to be here?" he asked. "The truth, mind."

She looked at him, her eyes shining.

"I will, sir. I swear it."

"Swearing's dirt easy, girl. It's truth that's rare as virtue," he growled, pulling up a wooden box and sitting. He relit his cigar and crossed his legs expectantly. "Where do you come from?" he asked, blowing out the match.

"From Prestwich, sir. In Manchester, if you know it," she said, in a Lancashire twang that sent a pang through him.

He shook his head no.

"What's your real name?" he asked.

"Davenport," she said. "Elizabeth Davenport. My father was a mill owner."

"Oh my," he grinned. "Why not a duchess, while you're at it?" he said, getting up.

"Oh please," she begged, clutching at his feet. "It's true. I swear it's true."

"Well, if you swear," he said nastily. "The word of a whore, no less." He sat down again. "This is fascinating. Tell me more, Miss Davenport."

A tear edged its way down her cheek.

"What's the good?" she said, dully. "You'll never believe it. No one will believe it."

"Convince me," he said, watching her. "Maybe you won't have to hang."

She nodded as she wiped her eyes with the back of her hand. Her bones were very fine, he thought. She was born to a better class. A blind man could see it.

"My father was Nigel Davenport," she began. "He owned a mill. Davenport and Sons. We lived in a big house, near St. Ann's."

"What happened?"

She clasped her hands in her lap. It deepened the valley between her breasts. Overhead, he could hear muffled sounds. The Corsicans leaving, he thought.

"Father began to come home more often. He was very irritable. No one could talk to him. He walked about the house wild-eyed, muttering about depentures and cotton futures and Argentine bonds and someone he called 'That accursed Edgerton.' "

"What was that name?" the bearded man said, leaning forward.

"Edgerton. Why? Do you know him?"

"No, no. Just go on," the man said, gesturing with his hand.

"It was as if a curse had been put on us," the girl said, the crescent of her face illuminated by the candlelight. "There was a fire at the mill. Flames shot into the sky. They say it spread all the way to the Bolton Road. Oh, it was terrible. You could see smoke all over the city. But Father was almost relieved. He talked about insurance. But then it came out it was arson. One of Father's employees, a man named Quayle, was said to have started it on Father's orders. Quayle himself couldn't testify. His body was found in the ruins."

"And your father?"

"When the bailiffs came, Father retired to his study to get some papers. There was the sound of a shot. They found him sprawled across his desk, the pistol still in his hand."

"What about the rest of the family?"

"My brother came down from Cambridge. He spoke in a loud voice about solicitors and papers, but it was as if he wasn't there. No one paid attention to him and after a bit, he began to spend all his time in the pubs.

"Then one night my brother's body was found in the blackened ruins of the mill. Someone had crammed his body into a space they used to call 'the Wading Hole.' It was a narrow space under the jennies where scraps of cotton cloth would collect. It was too small for a grown person; children were used down there."

"Were they?" the bearded man said.

Something in his voice made her stop. In the silence, they could hear each other's breath.

"Yes," she said, faltering. "They were. It was a tiny space. The constabulary couldn't determine how whoever had done it had managed to cram his body into such a place."

"Did they ever find who did it?"

"No. He was seen leaving the pub with a big bearded man, but they never . . ." she stopped, her face ghost white.

"And your mother?"

"Please . . ." she whimpered.

"And your mother?" he demanded harshly.

"He was her favorite," she said. "She wouldn't believe he was gone. They had to take her to Bedlam. I never saw her again."

The bearded man leaned forward.

"This man Quayle. The one who set the fire. Did he leave anyone?"

She shook her head.

"He had no family. There was a woman, a harlot, they said. They hanged her for murder. She killed an old witch everyone called 'Deathwatch Mary.' Over tuppence, an old debt or something . . ."

"You mean like this," he said, holding out his hand. In his palm were two English pennies.

She stared at him, her eyes perfect round mirrors reflecting the candle flame.

"Who are you?" she whispered. Her hand, as if it had a life of its own, reached out for his beard and pulled it off.

"But why? For the love of God, why?"

He grabbed her hair, twisting her head back. He pulled out a revolver and put it to her throat.

"Please," she pleaded, her eyes rolling white in the darkness. "I'll do anything you say."

"Imagine," he chuckled softly. "Davenport's daughter." He rubbed his hand over her breasts.

"Oh yes, please," she said, moving desperately against him. "Anything. Anything."

"You are 'Luz.' You will be 'Luz' forever. You will live on my *estancia*. My property. *Mine*," he said, easing her onto her back. He ripped away her nightgown. Her body was soft and white in the flickering light. He looked down at her, at her long naked legs, uptilted young breasts, creamy thighs opening for him. He got on top of her. She gasped as he began the slow inevitable slide. All at once, he stopped. "You may never have a child. Never. Understand?" The muzzle of the revolver was still against her throat.

She nodded once, not saying anything.

"It isn't finished. Not yet. As for you, your line is tainted, understand?" Gideon murmured, thrusting violently inside her. "It ends with you."

17

December 9, 1939
The Graf Spee

AFTERWARD, SCHENCK sat in the wardroom over a cup of coffee and thought about what had happened. He should have seen it coming, he told himself. He had known almost from the beginning that Heiss had it in for the kid. Although he hadn't known why until last night on the poop deck, in the shadows of the depth-charge racks, when one of the ratings told him about it.

Schenck stretched his feet onto another chair and leaned back so he could see through the porthole. The wardroom was surprisingly large, almost twenty meters long on the starboard side of the fo'c'sle deck, and from here he could see the blue sky and the deeper blue, almost purple, of mid-ocean. The wind was hot and steady from the northeast and the sea was moderate. Good hunting weather, Schenck thought. The spotter plane was due back in forty-five minutes and they would know for sure.

Leutnant Reinhardt came into the wardroom and sat down.

"So, Schenck. What do you think?"

"What's to think?" Schenck shrugged. "It's curtains for him."

"I know," Reinhardt said, uncorking a metal flask and offering it to Schenck. When Schenck shook his head, Reinhardt took a quick swallow himself and put it back in his pocket. "It's too bad. He was a nice kid. Everybody liked him."

"What time's the court-martial?"

Reinhardt checked his watch.

"In an hour, unless the spotter plane turns up something. I don't know why the *Alte* is so nervous. I think he sees the Englanders in his sleep," he grinned.

"Maybe he does. He was at Jutland," Schenck said, looking out at the sea. The sun sparkled on the water as if there wasn't another ship for miles.

"Maybe it was the heat," Reinhardt said, and Schenck knew he was talking about the kid again. Herrmann, that was his name. Herrmann. "It's hot as hell down there," indicating the deck.

Schenck shook his head. He motioned Reinhardt closer.

"I heard it's because Heiss thinks the kid's a Jew. Heiss says he can smell even a one-eighth Jew a mile away," Schenck whispered, looking around to make sure they weren't overheard.

Reinhardt looked curiously at him.

"Where did you hear that?"

"From one of the ratings."

"That's crazy!" Reinhardt said. "How could a Jew get on this ship? Besides, it's got nothing to do with it. Heiss was just looking for an excuse. He's a swine."

"Sure he's a swine. What are we going to do about it?"

"We find the kid guilty," Reinhardt shrugged, lighting a cigarette. "What else can we do? Heiss was after the kid. It was only a matter of time."

Schenck nodded. Reinhardt was right about that. It was always only a matter of time. Heiss had been riding the kid almost from the day they had left Wilhelm shaven. Little things. Snap inspections. Extra duties that made him miss meals. Extra watches. Sending him up to man the A.A. tower for eight hours straight in heavy seas that rocked the ship like a metronome during the treacherous passage between Iceland and the Faroes when they had to sneak past the British fleet. Things that on land you'd mutter a curse about and shrug off, but which in the deadly confines of a ship would have you staring at the back of a man's neck in the darkness of a midnight watch.

Then, the day before yesterday, in a bright sunny calm, with only a few puffs of cloud, like ack-ack bursts in the sky, it happened. They had spotted the distant smoke of a big freighter, the British steamship *Streonshalh* it turned out. She had seen the warship and was moving west very fast. It was going to be a race to catch her. The *Alte*, in a masterstroke, had them break out the French ensign. With the tattered tricolor flying from the last, the freighter slowed and they were able to get her in range. It wasn't until they were within a few thousand yards that they broke out the swastika flag and ordered the *Streonshalh* to stop for boarding. That's when it happened.

Reinhardt, over the loudspeaker hailer, had ordered them not to use their wireless. Then a messenger came to the bridge. He handed the flimsy to Schenck, who took it to the *Alte*.

"Wireless signals are being transmitted from the ship, *Herr Kapitän*," Schenck said.

Captain Landsgorff nodded, his pale eyes distant.

"Open fire," he ordered.

Schenck jumped to the intercom and gave the order. Almost instantly, the battle ship trembled with the sounds of the guns firing. It was practically point-blank range for the big 11-inchers and they almost blew the *Streonshalh* out of the water with a single salvo. There were fires all over the freighter. Her back was broken and men were jumping into the water. As was reported later, at that moment *Leutnant* Heiss ordered Herrmann to open up with the machine gun on the men swimming in the water.

The freighter was sinking in a spectacular blaze of fire. Oil on the water was burning and they could hear the British seamen screaming over the roar of the guns. The kid hesitated.

"Fire, you idiot!" Heiss screamed at him.

The kid looked fearfully at Heiss, then at the men in the sea. He fired a brief burst at them, then stopped. He turned back to the *Leutnant*, a sick look on his boyish face.

"They will die anyway, *Herr Leutnant*," he whispered.

"Shoot, you piece of shit! This is war! That is the enemy!" Heiss shouted, pointing, thrusting his face next to the boy's, his eyes bulging out.

The boy's lips worked. He wanted to say something but it wasn't coming out.

"They can't shoot back, *Herr Leutnant*," he said, swallowing.

"You shit! You piece of Jewish shit!" Heiss spat full into the boy's face. "I will have you court-martialed! I will have you shot, you Jew bastard!"

All at once, the kid broke. He let go of the machine gun and swung at Heiss, catching him in the shoulder and knocking him to the deck. He jumped on Heiss, pummeling him and howling, "I am not a Jew! I am not a Jew!"

It took three seamen to pull him off Heiss. Heiss got up and, brushing off his uniform, told them to place the kid under arrest. As they led the boy away, Heiss turned to one of the others, a look of grim satisfaction on his face, and ordered him to open fire. The sound of the machine gun echoed over the water till long after the freighter had sunk and there wasn't a moving figure to be seen in the water.

They heard the sound of the spotter plane now. Schenck checked his watch. It was back early and the engine was sputtering. He and Reinhardt looked at each other. There was something up, all right. Just then Heiss came into the wardroom.

Heiss went over to the counter and poured himself a glass of ice water. There was a picture of the Führer mounted over the counter and Heiss gazed respectfully at it for a moment. That was Heiss all over, Schenck thought. No one else ever gave the picture so much as a second glance. Heiss came over and sat down.

"So. It is hot enough for you?" Heiss grinned. His face was

red and sweaty and he was beaming as if he was enjoying himself hugely. In a way, you could understand why, Schenck thought. He had the whole ship under his thumb. Everyone was scared of him now, even the *Alte*.

"Plenty hot," Schenck nodded.

"This is nothing. You should go down to the for'ard engine room. Down there, you couldn't hear an 11-incher go off if it was next to your ear and the heat, *Gott in Himmel*, like a Jewish cunt in Hell," Heiss grinned.

Schenck grinned back, glancing at his watch and wondering how soon he could decently leave. Heiss was guzzling his water, looking as if he was settling in.

"What were you doing down in the engine room?" Reinhardt asked, stubbing out his cigarette.

"I wanted to check on that Herrmann. They had him locked up in a holding cell down there, those idiots!" Heiss said, looking completely disgusted.

"What's the matter?"

"What's the matter? There's not going to be a court-martial. That's what's the matter."

"What happened?"

"He's dead. Killed himself, the little Jew bastard."

"How?" Reinhardt asked, glancing over at Schenck.

"Hung himself. They forgot to take his shoelaces away from him, those idiots! His feet were only ten centimeters from the floor. Ten centimeters!" Heiss said.

"That's too bad," Reinhardt said carefully.

"I know," Heiss said. "I wanted to make an example of him. Do you know what the little bastard did?" The two officers shook their heads. "Banged his head on the bars till he drew blood, then wrote, 'I am not a Jew,' in blood on the wall."

"Maybe he wasn't a Jew," Schenck said.

"Sure he was a Jew. I can smell them," Heiss said, tapping his nose.

"Maybe it's yourself you smell," Schenck said.

Heiss didn't say anything. He looked at Schenck as though he hadn't heard him correctly. Reinhardt put his hand on Schenck's arm, but Schenck shook him off.

Heiss shrugged. "What difference? He was a coward. This is war. The Fatherland needs men who know their duty."

"We know our duty, *Herr Leutnant*. We don't need you to tell us our duty," Schenck snapped, standing up.

"No?" Heiss said, his eyes narrowed. "Maybe you do."

Suddenly Reinhardt jumped to his feet.

"*Achtung!*" he bellowed, and they all snapped to attention as Captain Langsdorff entered the wardroom. He stood in the middle of the room, sunlight grazing his face.

"Stand easy," he told them. He looked at Reinhardt. "The spotter plane has engine trouble, *Leutnant.* I want it back up as soon as possible. The British navy is in these waters. I can almost feel them."

"*Zu Befehl, Herr Kapitän,*" Reinhardt said, clicking his heels. He started for the door, then stopped. "We have had no indication of the Englanders, *Herr Kapitän.* What makes you so sure they're coming?"

Langsdorff smiled ironically.

"You don't know the Englanders, Reinhardt," he said, gazing toward the porthole as if he could see the smoke from their stacks. "*Sie kommen.* They're coming." He turned back toward them. "We have orders," he told them. "We need to be outside Buenos Aires by the seventeenth. Set a course for the River Plate, Schenck."

"*Zu Befehl!*" Schenck said, snapping to attention again.

"I want everyone to keep their eyes open," the captain frowned. "We have no more time for discipline problems," this to Heiss. "I want lookouts twenty-four hours, fore, aft and top."

"*Jawohl, Herr Kapitän!*" Reinhardt said.

The captain had already left the wardroom. The three officers looked at each other. Reinhardt went out. Heiss turned to Schenck. He was smiling broadly.

"So, Schenck, what do you think? Argentina, eh?"

"Sounds like shallow water," Schenck frowned, his tone worried.

"Yes, and plenty of British freighters. You are too nervous. Like the *Alte,*" Heiss grinned. "Just wait till you see Buenos Aires. Such a city!"

"Do you know it?" Schenck asked.

"Don't worry," Heiss said, clapping his arm familiarly around Schenck's shoulders. "You will like it, Schenck! Spanish pussy!"

18

THEY SCRAMBLED into position. Julia was on the floor, naked, near the far wall, her back to the door. She sat straddling the stuffed trousers and shoes, moving her hips as though she were making love. Stewart leaped for the overhead hooks he had positioned over the door. He grabbed onto one of the hooks with both hands and swung himself up, catching the other hook with one of his legs, behind the knee. He hung from the two hooks like a monkey, by a hand and a leg. In his good hand he held the piano wire by the lipstick handle, the wire turned into a noose.

It was an impossible position. The hook dug into the back of his knee and the pain shot up his arm from his injured hand. He gritted his teeth. He couldn't hold this position for more than a few seconds. But he had to. Hang on, he told himself. Hang on!

The sounds of the bar sliding open reverberated through the tank. He could hear someone talking in German, but couldn't make out the words. Down below, Julia began to moan, moving her buttocks around and out and squeezing them tight. She really looked like she was having sex. It was impossible to look at her and not get excited, he realized, as with a loud metallic clang, the door swung open.

The conversation stopped. Julia groaned, arching her back, her hips thrusting back and forth, faster and faster.

"Was zum teufel?" one of the Germans muttered.

Stewart hung on desperately, praying they wouldn't look up. Look at her! he silently ordered. The pain in his hand was unbelievable. They were still outside the refrigeration tank.

Just then Schmidt stepped inside. He was holding a Luger pistol.

"Blick, Hans. Wie zwei Hunden," Schmidt said to someone behind him, still outside the tank.

Don't look up! For God's sake, don't look up! Sweat dripped from Stewart, and a drop hit Schmidt's forehead. He started to look up.

Stewart dropped the noose over Schmidt's head. Before Schmidt realized it was there, Stewart was pulling up on the wire, looping it over the tip of the hook that he was holding onto with his injured hand. Schmidt gasped, his eyes wide with horror, as Stewart kicked his leg free of the other hook. He dropped like a stone. As he fell, hand tight on the lipstick handle, his weight pulled Schmidt up like a pulley. The piano wire bit deep into Schmidt's neck. He hung in the air, less than a foot from the ground, kicking madly.

Stewart grabbed for the Luger. It fired once, twice, the shots deafening in the narrow confines of the tank. One of the bullets just missed Stewart. It drilled a hole through the far metal wall. The other bullet richocheted around the tank like a deadly metal insect.

Schmidt was dancing in air, his face tomato red, his eyes popping out. He tried to turn the Luger toward Stewart, the fingers of his other hand clawing at the wire around his neck. Stewart fought him for the gun, still hanging onto the lipstick handle with his other hand, but slowly Schmidt managed to turn the muzzle toward Stewart straight at his chest.

Schmidt's finger tightened on the trigger.

Stewart closed his eyes.

Julia screamed.

Suddenly, Schmidt's body jerked sharply, spasmodically, fragments of flesh erupting bloodily out of his chest.

The other German had shot him by mistake.

Stewart ripped the Luger from Schmidt. The other German was standing in the doorway, his eyes wide, his pistol aimed at Stewart. The German fired again as Stewart let go of the lipstick and dropped to the floor.

Schmidt's body fell almost on top of him. For an instant, as Stewart switched the Luger to his good hand, Schmidt's falling body screened him from the other German. A shot pinged beside Stewart's ear. Stewart fired the Luger, rolling toward the side wall. He fired again and the other German staggered. The German shot again, but it was wild. Prone on his belly, Stewart aimed with both hands and fired. The German threw out his hands and went down.

Stewart staggered to his feet. Schmidt was still alive. He

was on the floor, his face red and terrible. Stewart swayed on his feet, his chest heaving. The Luger felt as though it weighed a ton. Schmidt stared up at him, his eyes black with hate. Stewart aimed down and fired.

The other German lay sprawled on his face just outside the tank. He lay in a dim yellow pool of light from a single electric bulb surrounded by shadow. It had become night outside. Stewart leaned heavily against the side of the doorway to steady his hand. He aimed at the other German's head and fired again. The other German never moved. He was probably already dead, Stewart thought, turning back to Julia.

She was sitting huddled on the floor of the tank, her eyes wild and strange and unbelieving. He went over to her and fell on his knees. Their arms went around each other. They rocked like children, holding tightly to one another.

"I thought . . . I thought he was going to kill you," she whispered.

"So did I."

They sat there for what seemed like a long time, though it might have been seconds. Numb, like soldiers after a battle.

"We have to go," she said, finally. She held his injured hand and kissed it. "Poor hand," she said. "It needs looking after."

"A lot of things need looking after," he said, grabbing his clothes. They stumbled outside the tank without even checking what was out there. It was as if neither of them could stand to be inside any more for even another second. Outside, the *frigorifico* was deserted and dark, except for the one electric light. There was no light coming from the office. Stewart walked around, peering into the shadows, but the space felt empty. There was nothing except for the rows of hooks hanging from the ceiling tracks and the occasional cry of a gull coming from the river.

He went back and, still keeping the Luger in his hand, began to pull on his clothes. Julia was already dressed. In her tennis whites in the cavernous emptiness of the *frigorifico*, she looked wildly out of place, like a character on a stage. Somehow, they were separate again. It was a little like dressing after lovemaking, Stewart thought, as he straightened his tie and retrieved his hat. There was a feeling of emptiness, of leaving something behind.

Julia went over to the dead German and picked up his pistol. She held it for a moment, cradling it almost. Stewart came over and took it from her, as he knelt and began to go through the dead German's pockets.

There wasn't much. Spectacles, some money, cigarettes, matches, a streetcar ticket. Stewart lit one of the cigarettes, the match flaring in the darkness. Julia jumped at the sound of the match.

"Did you mean what you said before?" she asked suddenly.

"About what?"

"About loving me?"

He didn't answer. From outside came the sound of a barge making its way down the river.

"You don't have to, you know. Now that we're not going to die," she said, not looking at him.

His heart stopped when she said that. He had heard the expression before and had never believed it, but it was true. He grabbed her.

"Yes," he said, holding her so tightly she winced. "I meant it."

She looked at him, unbelieving, wildly happy.

"Oh God, *yanqui*," she cried, throwing herself into his arms. "What are we going to do?"

"Get the hell out of here." He motioned for her to get hold of one of the dead German's feet, as he took the other. Together, they dragged him into the tank, the head banging sickeningly on the metal step as they pulled him in.

The tank was hot and still; it smelled of blood. Schmidt lay there, staring at the ceiling. His face was swollen and the piano wire was still tight around his neck, like the string on a balloon. Stewart and Julia went through his pockets. There were only the usual things. Money. A German passport identifying Schmidt as one Rolf Meissen, an engineer from Hamburg. The key to the tank. A box of matches from the Atlantis Club. There was an address scribbled on the box. Someplace on Caminetta. A chill went through Stewart. He knew that address.

Ceci Braga.

He could tell by Julia's face that she had seen it too.

"You know Ceci Braga," he said. It wasn't a question.

"Yes, of course."

"I saw her. She told me not to tell you."

Julia closed her eyes just once, like a camera shutter. There was a vein beating in her neck. He watched it beating.

"Sometimes I think love is like water. Too little and you wither. Too much and you drown." She smiled bitterly. "With Ceci, I drowned."

"You think she's connected to the Nazis?"

She shook her head.

"She could be in danger," she said softly.

"She could," he agreed. "What do you think Schmidt was doing with her address?"

"I don't know," she shrugged. "Ask von Hulse."

"I may," Stewart smiled grimly. "The next time I see him."

He pocketed the matches, along with the key and the money, and looked around the tank. The place was like a slaughter house with the two dead Germans and Hartman, still hanging from the hook, and Stewart started to break out into a sweat again. The tank was hot and sticky and he knew it would be in his dreams for a long time.

They went outside the tank, closed and barred the doors and padlocked them. They tiptoed to the side door where von Hulse had first brought them in and waited, listening in the darkness. Outside, the street was deserted. After a moment he took her hand and they began to walk hurriedly toward the intersection, their footsteps echoing in the night.

"SEÑOR SANCHEZ, *por favor. Señor Portsmouth al habla,*" Fowler's voice came through the telephone in labored Spanish.

"Cornwall. The Gran Rex cinema on Corrientes. The WC. Take the streetcar," Stewart said rapidly in English.

"Where were you? I went—"

"You're being followed. A man in a trilby. Get rid of him," Stewart said and hung up. He looked around the noisy, smoke-filled *boliche.* Everyone was busy eating and talking. No one appeared to have overheard.

Stewart dropped a bill on the table and went outside. He walked to the nearby Plaza Italia, hailed a taxi and had it take him to the Farmacia Nelson, across the street from the cinema. After the taxi pulled away, he crossed the street to the cinema and went inside. As he sat in the last row, he checked his watch. Using a streetcar and doubling back, it would take Fowler at least another fifteen to twenty minutes. Plenty of time, he thought, looking around.

The theater was dark and crowded. On the screen they were showing an American film. Bette Davis was going blind. She was trying to convince George Brent she could see, so he wouldn't have to watch her die, and a woman in the audience began to sob.

After a minute, Stewart got up and went to the men's *lavabo*. There was a trough for a urinal and a single Spanish-style stall, just a hole, with a water tank above. He stepped inside the stall, took out the Luger and checked the clip. There were three bullets left. He put it back into his belt and took out the automatic, the one he had taken from the second German. It was a Beretta and it still had five rounds in the clip. It was smaller than the Luger and would make less noise. He checked to make sure the safety was off and cocked it.

He latched the stall door, leaning against the partition to wait, breathing through his mouth to minimize the stench. He could see the *lavabo* door through the doorjamb crack of the stall. The partitions were decorated with the usual badly drawn sexual organs and obscene Spanish invitations. An elderly man came in and Stewart listened to him at the trough, waiting, his finger on the trigger, till he was gone. Twenty minutes later, Fowler showed up.

Stewart emerged from the stall, positioning himself against the wall behind the *lavabo* door, in case someone followed Fowler in. Fowler stared at the Beretta.

"Why this place? It's positively filthy!" Fowler said, his face contorted with disgust.

"I know. It's a dirty war. It's getting dirtier all the time," Stewart whispered, holding a finger to his lips as a caution. "What about the tail? Did you get rid of him?"

Fowler looked uneasy.

"I think so."

"You think so!"

"It wasn't easy," Fowler said defensively. "There was a front tail too. In a leather jacket, heat and all. One of the Gestapo's pimply-faced legions, no doubt. Never mind all that. What's happened?"

"Hartman's dead."

"Dear God!" Fowler said, swallowing hard.

"Don't waste any crocodile tears on him. He was working for the Nazis. They almost got me too."

"Then perhaps they found out about the Raven from—" Fowler stopped suddenly as the *lavabo* door opened.

The man in the trilby came in. He took a step toward Fowler. Stewart put the Beretta to his head.

"Don't move! *Nicht bewegen!*" Stewart ordered.

The man in the trilby froze. Stewart grabbed his jacket by the back of the neck and pressed the muzzle hard against the side of the man's head.

"*Gehen Sie!* Into the *toilette!*" Stewart said, nudging him toward the stall.

The man resisted.

"I think no," the man said in German-accented Spanish. He smiled nastily. "You don't shoot. Too many people around. Too much noise," he said, starting to turn.

Stewart fired.

The man collapsed on the floor. Fowler stared at Stewart, horrified.

"My God! He's dead!" he gasped.

"I told you to lose him, dammit! At least help me get him into the stall," Stewart said, grabbing one of the dead man's arms.

Fowler still hesitated.

"But he's dead!" he whispered.

"Of course he's dead." Stewart glared at him. "What the hell do you think we're playing at here?"

Fowler took a deep breath.

"Of course," he said, grabbing the other arm. Together they dragged him into the stall, leaving him face down over the hole. Stewart placed the Beretta into the dead man's hand.

"With any luck they'll think it's a suicide," he explained, closing the stall door and bending the dead man's legs so they weren't sticking out from under the door. Then he and Fowler walked out of the *lavabo*.

The lobby was still empty, though they could hear a buzzing from the darkened theater. A man in a *taquillero*'s tunic came rushing up to them from the ticket office.

"What happened? I thought I heard a shot?" he asked them.

"So did we. It came from in there," Stewart said, jerking his thumb at the *lavabo*. "You check there. We'll call the *policía*."

"Of accord," the *taquillero* nodded and ran to the *lavabo*.

Stewart and Fowler went out into the street. They walked down the Avenida Corrientes. Behind them, there was a commotion by the cinema entrance and a traffic *guardia* wearing big white gloves ran past them. At the corner, a wildly colored *colectivo* stopped to let several people out, and Stewart and Fowler piled in. They took the *colectivo* up toward the Obelisk. They got off and walked along the Ninth of July to the nearest sidewalk café and sat down.

The waiter came over and Stewart ordered a Breeder's Choice, one of the local whiskies. Fowler, still shaken, just nodded. Neither of them said anything until after the waiter brought the drinks, Fowler taking out a handkerchief and wiping his glass with it before he drank.

"Bloody awful stuff," Fowler muttered.

"Kills the germs," Stewart said, motioning him closer. "It's a coup all right. The Nazis plan to kill Ortiz at the Vargas *estancia* on the seventeenth. The *Graf Spee* will be anchored offshore, just in case anyone in the Argentine military wants to go against Castillo. They're doing it just like Austria and Czechoslovakia. Attack from within while threatening force from without. That's the pattern."

Fowler gripped the table with both hands.

"The *Graf Spee*? Here in the River Plate? Despite Argentine neutrality?" His eyes bored into Stewart. "This is vital, old boy. Are you quite, quite certain?"

Stewart nodded.

"She'll be here. I hope that gives your Navy enough time. I imagine you've got a few ships out there looking for her."

"I dare say," Fowler said, patting his lips with the handkerchief. His eyes darted around excitedly. "This is a tremendous coup!" He sat back for a moment. "So there is a spy, after all. Your so-called 'Raven.' No wonder the Jerries are buzzing all over us. In the short time you've been here, you seemed to have poked quite a stick into the hive, Mister Stewart. Quite a stick, indeed!" He raised his eyebrows speculatively. "Are you going to let us in on it?"

Stewart shook his head.

"I'm giving you the *Graf Spee*. And try to get to President

Ortiz. Warn him away from the Vargas *estancia*. I'll work the Raven."

"What will you do now?" Fowler asked, gazing out over the boulevard. The Argentines advertised Ninth of July as the widest street in the world and sitting there at that late hour, watching the cars go by with their headlights on through the shadows of the trees along the sidewalk, was like sitting on the bank of a heavily trafficked river.

"Go to ground. Handle some things. Get this taken care of," Stewart said, holding up his injured hand. Fowler winced when he saw it.

"Who did that?"

"Fuentes. Be nice to know which side he was on."

"Indeed," Fowler murmured, looking toward the Obelisk. It was lit up with floodlights and it looked white and mysterious in the night, like a relic from an unknown civilization. "Pity about Hartman," he said, pursing his lips. "Was he a friend of yours?"

"No," Stewart said. "We pretended to be, but we really weren't." He started to get up, then stopped. "Now it's up to you Lim—" he hesitated. "To you English," he corrected himself.

Fowler almost smiled. Then he got serious again.

"No. It's up to the Royal Navy now, poor devils." He looked up at Stewart, a strange concern on his face. "There's something I don't understand," he said tentatively.

"What's that?"

"This is a great triumph. The first break we've had in God knows how long. By rights, you should be ecstatic, but you're not. What is it?"

Stewart nodded grimly.

"I know. There's something going on that I don't understand. It's like there are two wars. The one between us and the Germans and another one, that we don't know anything about. I can't put my finger on it, but the Raven is in it up to his neck. It's crazy," Stewart shrugged. "But then, as somebody told me recently, there are deeper secrets in this world than those sought out by spies." He took out a cigarette and lit it. The smoke drifted towards the lights of the cars streaming by.

"Astonishing city. So beautiful, but at the core. . . ." Fowler shuddered. "God, I hate it here," he said.

Stewart stood up.

"No more meetings, Fowler. It's too dangerous. For both of us," Stewart said.

"Take care, Cornwall. I hope you find your other war, before it finds you," Fowler said, not looking up. When he did, Stewart was gone.

Stewart caught a taxi in the circle around the Obelisk. He needed a place to lie low, to lick his wounds and sort things out. The Plaza was out; the Nazis were sure to have it covered. Then he remembered the place Julia had mentioned back in the *frigorifico*, where she and Ceci. . . . He leaned forward and told the driver to take him to San Telmo. The Hotel Siracusa was a small dilapidated hotel on a narrow street, with empty carts parked on the sidewalk and wheelbarrows left leaning against the sides of buildings. It was the kind of place where you never have to ask whether they have a room available.

Stewart checked in without giving a name to the man behind the desk, a swarthy Sicilian with unshaved jowels, reeking of wine and garlic. The Sicilian didn't ask for his *cédula* and after Stewart paid, led him up the stairs to a small room, steaming hot and smelling of mildew and disinfectant. Stewart gave the Sicilian five pesos and told him to bring him a bottle of whisky and a doctor, in that order. His hand was throbbing badly.

He lay down on the bed, not bothering to get undressed. He tried to rest, but all he could think of was Julia. How sexy she was in that tank, the killings and how she looked afterward, in the *frigorifico* and near the Retiro station when he had left her to call Fowler. He had almost fallen asleep when there was a knock at the door.

"Come in," Stewart called, reaching for the Luger, but it was too late. The door crashed open and four military *guardia* rushed in, guns drawn. Standing in the doorway, also holding a gun, was the curly-haired man. Behind him, grinning broadly, was Colonel Fuentes.

"*Oiyée, gringo!* You are keeping everyone so busy," Fuentes said.

20

HMS Ajax

THE TRANSMISSION came in on the wireless just after 0400
hours. Leading Telegraphist Porter woke Lieutenant Chalmers, who decoded it in the tiny office just behind the After
galley, that Brookings, the ship's gunnery officer and resident
wag, insisted on calling "the WC office," for "Wireless Cod-
ing." "Chalmers is going to the WC for another little packet
from the gods," Brookings would announce happily, as
Chalmers would stalk off, muttering: "Bloody public school
humor." But Chalmers did spend a lot of time in there. It and
the WT office were his private realm, where he kept the secrets, the cypher machine and code-books, as though there
was something holy about them, like the tablets of the Ark.

But this night, Chalmers stumbled reluctantly into the office, blinking sleep out of his eyes. He was annoyed with Porter for waking him up. "Couldn't it have waited?" he said
irritably to Porter's retreating back, as he started setting out
the code-books, but once he got past the "Intro group" he took
a deep breath and began to work fast and very carefully. When
he finished, he whistled silently to himself as he studied the
message. Jesus bloody Christ, he thought. Although he was
certain he hadn't made any mistakes, he crumpled the paper
up and set about doing the decoding again from scratch, just
to make sure. It was likely to be the most important message
he had ever received.

One by one, the letters dropped out of the groups of seven.
There were no mistakes, he thought, his heart pounding. He
turned and using the old Remington, two-finger typed it up on
the flimsy, then burned his scratch pages in the ashtray. When
he was ready, he turned out the overhead lamp and popped

into the WT office. Porter was sitting there, smoking a fag and reading a well-thumbed Dick Tracy. He looked up at Chalmers, who rattled the flimsy in his hand.

"Don't mention this, Billy. Not to anyone, got it?"

Porter put the comic book down for a second.

" 'Ere, what's 'at? Somethin' interestin'?"

"Just keep your lip buttoned," Chalmers warned, unable to keep the excitement out of his voice. There was something about the intimacy of the office in the pre-dawn hours. The lights on the wireless gleamed in the dim light. They made it seem safe and cosy, a haven. But that was an illusion, Chalmers thought. The flimsy in his hand said so.

He climbed up the ladder to the upper deck. It was dark and cool and there were stars everywhere. He headed forward past the smokestack, the midship Oerlikons and pompoms, the forward stack, the foremast and up the ladder to the flag deck. He hesitated for a second, wondering whether he should tell Captain Nichols first, or go directly to the Commodore's quarters. No, he thought. This is for the Commodore, by God. He knocked softly on the door.

There was no answer. He knocked again, louder.

"All right, all right. Come in."

Chalmers went in and saluted. Commodore Harwood was in his dressing gown and slippers and there were dark circles under his eyes. The lamp by his bunk was still on, reading glasses left on an open book. He must have just fallen asleep, Chalmers thought.

"Sorry to disturb you, sir. But this just came in," Chalmers said, handing him the flimsy.

"Stand easy, Lieutenant. You've caught me napping, so let's not stand on ceremony," Harwood said, looking around for his reading glasses. "Where's this from? DNO?"

"No sir. It's from our embassy in Buenos Aires. It's the real thing though."

"Oh? How do you know that?" Harwood asked, finding his glasses and sitting down at his desk.

"It's presumably from a Mister Seabrook of the FO. That's a special War Office code, sir. SIS authenticated. Same code as last week, when we were off the Brazilian coast. They warned us then they might have something, sir."

"I remember," Harwood muttered, studying the flimsy. He looked up at Chalmers. "Listen, Johnny. I want all senior officers to meet me in the wardroom in, um," he checked his watch, "fifteen minutes."

"Yes sir," Chalmers said, starting to leave.

"Oh—and Johnny?"

"Sir?"

"Wake them yourself. And don't rouse the whole bloody ship while you're at it."

"Yes sir."

"They're going to need all the sleep they can get, poor devils," Chalmers heard Harwood mutter, as he closed the door behind him.

Fifteen minutes later, eight of the *Ajax*'s senior officers were seated around the wardroom table. As a precaution, Lieutenant Commander Fielding had stopped off in the charthouse on his way over and had brought in an armful of rolled-up charts, for which he took a bit of early morning ribbing. Only Westlake wasn't there. As Officer of the Watch, he remained up on the bridge.

There wasn't much talking. A few smoked or drummed their fingers on the table. They avoided each other's eyes. Something was up, all right. The smell of it was in the air. When the steward finished making tea, he scuttled out. Chalmers, standing near the door, heard something. He stepped outside for a second and they heard him say, "All present, sir."

As Commodore Harwood entered the wardroom, the officers stood to attention, chairs scraping on the floor. The Commodore's face, normally genial, was set and grim and the officers glanced uneasily at each other.

"Be seated, gentlemen," Harwood said. He sat down and took off his cap, placing it on the table beside him. The others took their seats. Chalmers closed the door. Harwood looked around the table. The flimsy was in his hand.

"As you know, Force G, consisting of the light cruisers *Ajax*, *Achilles* and *Exeter*, which is due to rendezvous with us— when, Harry?" Harwood paused, glancing at Captain Nichols.

"Just over an hour if Bonnie Bell's on time," Nichols said, checking his watch.

"Captain Bell is always on time," Brookings intoned.

"Quite," Harwood murmured. "As I was saying, Force G is one of eight hunting squadrons scouring the Atlantic Ocean for the *Graf Spee*. Half the Royal Navy, gentlemen, for one ship. That's how important the Admiralty deems it." He looked around the table. "Some time within the next forty-eight hours, this ship will do battle with the *Graf Spee*."

There was dead stunned silence in the wardroom. For a moment, Brookings even imagined he could hear the slap of waves against the sides of the ship.

"How sure are we? Has she been spotted?" Nichols asked, turning to Chalmers, who shook his head.

"No sir. Not since the last transmission from the *Streonshalh*. That was five days ago."

"So she could be anywhere-r-r?" McAllister burred, his Scots accent getting thicker, as it always did when he wanted to make a point.

"Except," Harwood said crisply, tapping the flimsy. "We don't need to know where the *Graf Spee* is at this moment."

"Sir?" Fielding asked.

"Because, gentlemen, we know where she is going."

"Bloody hell," McAllister breathed. Then realizing he had spoken out loud, looked around guiltily.

"This," Harwood said, holding up the flimsy, "is a secret communication from our embassy in Buenos Aires. We have good reason to believe that the *Graf Spee* is due to arrive there by the 16th."

Everyone started talking at once. Brookings felt it himself, a sudden need to get up, to move, to do something. He gripped the arms of his chair. A glance from Harwood silenced them.

"How reliable is this information?" Nichols asked into the silence. "All this cloak-and-dagger nonsense."

"It's highly reliable, sir. We've—" Chalmers started.

"I'm inclined to believe it, Harry," Harwood said, cutting him off. "SIS has been making noises for some time about a possible spy in the Argentine. It's one of the reasons I decided to head down this way, even though almost all of the earlier sightings of the *Graf Spee* were off the African coast."

"I was wondering about that, sir," Nichols said, his eyes sparkling. "I thought you just might have something up your sleeve, as the Yanks say."

"Well, we've got something, all right." Harwood drew a line with his finger on the table. "We're going to set up a picket line of all three of our cruisers to patrol the entrance of the River Plate. That, gentlemen," he said, closing his fist like a trap, "is where I mean to catch them." He looked around the table. "Questions?"

No one spoke. Finally, Commander Cooke, Senior Engineering Officer, cleared his throat.

"Just the obvious one, sir. We're just three ships. Light cruisers. *Ajax* and *Achilles* have six-inch guns. *Exeter* eight-inchers. The *Graf Spee* has eleven-inch guns, sir. What's to stop the Jerries from staying well beyond our range and blowing us out of the water, one at a time?"

"Not a bloody thing," McAllister muttered.

Harwood glanced at him for a moment, his eyes suddenly old and distant.

"No, of course. Not a thing," he agreed softly. "Three cruisers, two of them light, against a pocket battleship. Like hounds round a stag. And that's how we're going to do it," Harwood said. "We're faster than she is, more maneuverable. We'll harry her. We'll close from three directions at once, every gun blazing for all it's worth. She won't know which way to turn first. It's our only chance," he muttered, as if it was something he had said to himself many times. "If we stand off and try to fight it out at long-range, we're dead."

The officers nodded. There was a general murmur of agreement.

"With any luck, she might even charge right at us," Captain Nichols said.

"Why on earth would Jerry do that, sir?" Chalmers asked. Cooke and McAllister glanced at him for his temerity, but Chalmers, as the youngest and most junior, enjoyed a sort of midshipman's freedom, and even Harwood smiled.

"Because, if the picket line's stretched out far enough, they might not spot all of us at once," Nichols explained. "If they only saw a single ship, a light cruiser say, on the horizon, it would represent little threat to them. They might chase it in order to prevent it from running away. As well as to make it easier for them to blow it out of the water. But if they got within range of all three of us . . ." Nichols said, raising his eyebrows. "I dare say we might warm things up a bit, even for the *Graf Spee*."

"Which is why," Harwood said, "it is absolutely vital that we spot her before she sees us." He looked at Tunstall, who with his long face and sad eyes looked like an intelligent basset hound. "What's the weather forecast over the next two days, Dickie?"

"Same as yesterday, sir. Clear, hot and sunny. Almost perfect visibility," Tunstall replied.

"Hmmm. That cuts both ways, them and us," Harwood said. "Seas?"

"Dead steady, sir. Winds nor'easterly, light or none. Like being in church."

"All right," Harwood nodded, leaning forward. "From now on, wireless silence must be absolute. Only semaphore and Aldis lamps for ship-to-ship. All noise kept to a minimum."

"We'd better get the spotter plane up," Fielding said.

"No. No spotter plane," Harwood frowned. "We know they're there. No need to tip our hand." He turned to McAllister. "I want double shifts on the Asdic and lookouts posted round-the-clock fore and aft. Also up on the AA tower, and rig something on top of the masts. Both of them. I know it'll be uncomfortable for the men," he grimaced. "But we have to see them first. That's key. Everyone else on stand-by, ready for battle stations at a moment's notice. And tell all lookouts to keep their eyes bloody peeled. There's a commendation in it, and an extra tot of rum, for the man who first spots her." He turned to Nichols. "What do you think, Harry? Can we pull it off?"

Nichols sat back in his chair and crossed his legs. Everyone watched as he took a puff from his cigarette.

"It's quite clever, really," he said thoughtfully. "Brilliant, I dare say. Going to be bloody difficult, though. Most of these lads have never seen battle before."

"Neither-r-r has the *Gr-r-raf Spee*," McAllister said.

"Except against unarmed merchant ships," Cooke murmured, a bitter tone in his voice. He'd had an aunt on the passenger liner *Athenia* torpedoed by a U-boat on the first day of the war.

"Quite," someone said quietly.

"The thing is," Nichols said, "with us charging like mad, the *Graf Spee*'ll have to retreat to stay out of range. She's never had to do that before. Old Jerry's not bloody used to running away, is he?" he smiled grimly.

No one said anything. They all turned to Harwood.

"All right, then," Harwood said briskly. "Anything else, anyone?"

Fielding hesitated, then spoke up.

"The River Plate, sir . . ." he began.

"Yes?"

"It's wide, but there's shallow water there. Very tricky. If we could somehow get the *Graf Spee* into the estuary, it could cut down on her maneuverability."

Harwood smiled.

"If she would prove so accommodating." His expression turned serious. "Charts please, Peter. Let's lay out the picket line." As Fielding got up and started to spread the chart out on the table, there was a knock at the door. It was one of the junior officers, Midshipman Peabody. His face was red and nervous at breaking in on such a senior meeting and it took a second before he could catch his breath.

"Beg pardon, s-sirs. Commander Westlake sent me. We've sighted *Exeter*. She's about four miles off the starboard bow," Peabody managed, sweat dripping from his face.

"Bonnie Bell strikes again," Brookings piped up, and there was quiet laughter around the table.

"Good. Let's have a look," Harwood said, getting up. "Mac," he turned to McAllister. "Lay out the course and picket line. Chalmers, get the Aldis going. Brief Captain Bell on what we're up to." He looked at Nichols and Brookings. "Harry, David, come with me. Let's have a look," he said, the gleam in his eye betraying an old sailor's impatience to get topside and see for himself.

They went out on deck and up the ladder to the bridge. Although it was still dark, the air was warm and still. Westlake glanced briefly at the Commodore, but kept his eyes focused on the sea. Leading Seaman Peary was like a statue at the wheel, holding rock steady on course. Though he hadn't been at the meeting, Westlake somehow gave the impression that he knew what was going on. There are no secrets on a ship, Nichols thought.

Dawn was breaking as a yellow ribbon of light. The silhouette of the *Exeter* was trapped in it, outlined clearly on the horizon. Closer, barely a thousand yards off, was their sister ship, *Achilles*; long, lean, guns bristling, slicing silently through the water. A light from the Aldis began to flicker below them. After a moment, there were answering flashes out of the darkness from the *Exeter*.

"There's Bonnie Bell," someone said.

"Thank God," Nichols murmured, his eyes straying along the line of the horizon where the dawn was brightening quickly. The silhouettes of the *Achilles* and the *Exeter* were sleek as greyhounds in the orange light. They were, in their way, among the most beautiful things ever made by the hand of man, he thought. He looked down at the superstructure of his own ship, *Ajax*, at the for'ard pompom and the "B" and "A" turrets and their big 6-inch guns protected by four inches of solid steel armor plating. It looked sturdy as hell, until you realized that it offered about as much protection against an 11-inch shell as a sheet of tissue paper against a bullet.

As though he had read Nichol's mind, Harwood turned suddenly toward him.

"Light cruisers against a bloody battleship," Harwood said.

"Yes sir," Nichols replied.

Below them, the Aldis lamp flashed its message across the still-dark sea.

PART THREE

Julia

He has asked me about that night. To confess for the sake of my immortal soul. I told him I couldn't remember.

I lied. No Gideon ever forgets anything.

The night of my betrothal, the night my life was frozen in time, like a photograph. That's what destiny is: a moment that lasts forever.

The fiesta de noviazgo *was held at the* estancia, *at Ravenwood. There were flowers everywhere and the* hacienda *was lit so brightly it could be seen for miles. Lanterns and tables had been set out in the gardens, but in the afternoon it had begun to rain and everything had to be moved inside. I remember standing by the open French doors, looking out at the rain. It was still light and I could see the clouds bundled low over the Pampa and in the garden strands of drops hung like pearls along the branches. In the center, dominating everything, was the giant* ombu *tree, where once, long ago, one of my father's* gauchos *had found a raven.*

And then my mother came and took me into her sewing room and told me it would have to be called off.

"You can't marry him," she said.

"Why, can't I?"

"You can't."

"But why?"

"He's a Montoya. The last male Montoya. Don't you understand?" she cried, her tiny hands white on the back of the chair she was holding on to.

"But you're partly Montoya too, Mama!"

"Yes!" she said fiercely. "Do you want a life like mine? He hates them. Don't you know he hates them?"

"No, Mama! No! You're jealous! Because you're old!" She recoiled when I said that. As though she'd been slapped in the face. "You're jealous because I'm young and pretty and Federico and I are going to Paris! You just can't stand it, can you?" I said. I wanted to hurt her. I was my father's daughter.

"You fool!" she cried. "He'll destroy you. You want Paris? Go to Paris. Go now! Tonight! Wait, take my jewels! You'll need money."

She began to ransack her sewing table for her velvet jewelry box. I tried to stop her. The box fell open, spilling the jewelry all over the floor. An incredible array of diamond and emerald necklaces, bracelets, brooches, rings and tiaras, Burmese sapphires and rubies as big as pigeon's eggs. I once heard the servants whisper that the emerald necklace alone had cost over two hundred thousand English pounds. My mother scrambled after the jewels on all fours, plucking madly at them. Suddenly, she stopped and looked at me.

"Where are my diamond earrings?" she said. "Have you seen them?"

"No, Mama. No," I stammered. I was very frightened, though I didn't know why. I hadn't taken anything. She just stared at me. She put the jewelry back into the box and stood up. The box was shaking in her hands.

"Take it, mi hija. Take it and go, now, while you can," she whispered.

"Please, Mamacita," I pleaded, kissing her forehead. "It's too late. The guests will be here in a moment."

Something passed before her eyes. She put the box back in the drawer.

"Yes," she said softly. "It's too late."

Everyone was there that night. The new President, Señor Quintana. Others too. Julio Roca. Alcorta. So many. Everyone glittering in ball gowns and evening clothes and I was the princess in white, all white. I waltzed with my novio, Federico, and later we danced the new dance, 'el ragtime.'

Mother was very animated. Her color was high and she laughed and talked with her friends. I hadn't seen her so happy in a long time. Even when my father danced by with his new mistress—she was a singer, an Australian, very beautiful, very famous, anyone would know her name if I said it—my mother only smiled. But when I saw that smile, it was like a knife. It was my father's smile she was wearing.

The fiesta lasted till late. It was a great success. Everyone teased Federico and me about having many babies and go-

ing to Paris. Everyone was a tour guide. Don't miss Maxim's. The apache *dancers and the* bals musettes *in Montparnasse, so* bien amusants. *The pressed duck at the Tour d'Argent. Monsieur Eiffel's tower, so ugly a monument to our* age moderne. *And after a night on the town (wink, wink), coffee at dawn among the market wagons at Les Halles. I hadn't noticed my mother's disappearance until suddenly, it was late, I got a strange feeling at the back of my throat. Federico wanted to come with me, but I told him to stay with the last remaining guests.*

I looked through the house for my mother. No one had seen her. She wasn't in her bedroom or any of the salons. Then I remembered the sewing room.

She wasn't in the sewing room. I was about to leave when I saw the light coming from the baño.

She was sitting on the floor, slumped against the wall, both hands in the bidet. My father's razor lay open on the rim of the bidet. She had been serious about it, cutting the veins in both wrists vertically, not horizontally, so that they would empty in a hurry. Her jewel box was on the floor, empty. She had put all her jewels in the bidet. They lay there, soaked in blood. Suddenly, the image of my father and the Australian woman dancing flashed into my mind. I could see her laughing, beautiful, the sparkle of light amidst her dark curly hair. She had been wearing my mother's earrings.

Later, after everyone left, after everything, I crept alone up to the old Mirador, *my secret place ever since I was a child. It was still night, still raining. I left the light off. I wanted to cry, but I couldn't. The rain came through the open window, soaking me to the skin, but I didn't close the shutter. I sat on the floor, shivering, unable to move.*

There was a creaking on the stair. A man's shadow filled the doorway.

"Federico?" I whispered. "Go away. Please go away."

And then he was on top of me and it wasn't till then, until the sudden sharp pain as he forced himself inside me, that I finally understood.

That was the night my daughter Julia was conceived.

—From the journal of Lucia de Montoya-Gideon

21

IT WAS a look-out on the *Ajax* who spotted her first, a tiny smudge on the northwest horizon. Dawn had broken clear and warm. The sun was up over the horizon and the sea was flat and golden, the only waves the widening ripples made by the three British cruisers as they ploughed northeast in a straight line, one after another, like ducks on a pond.

Commodore Harwood and Captain Nichols were up on the bridge when the sighting came in and they immediately trained their binoculars to port, though if there was anything there it was too far away to see. But there was no mistaking the excitement in Westlake's voice as he gave the heading.

"If it's her, we'll be coming out of the sun, by God," Nichols muttered under his breath. He turned to Harwood. "Should we make the recce ourselves, sir?"

Harwood shook his head. He had nicked himself shaving, and for some reason Nichols found himself staring at the tiny patch of sticking plaster on Harwood's neck. There were dark circles under Harwood's eyes. He had been practically living on the bridge since yesterday's predawn meeting.

"No, send *Exeter*," Harwood said. "If it is the *Graf Spee*, we'll want *Exeter* in the lead."

"What about the spotting plane, sorr?" McAllister, as Officer of the Watch, asked, going over to the phone.

"Not yet, but get the catapult ready," Harwood said. "And signal Captain Bell. Tell him if it's her, he may break wireless silence."

"Aye, sorr," McAllister said and began to talk into the phone. He turned back for a second. "What about us, sorr?"

"Maintain course," Nichols said crisply. He motioned Petty Officer Sterling over and whispered in his ear. Sterling left the bridge.

"What was that?" Harwood wondered aloud.

"Just ordering Davie Brookings to get his rump over to 'B'

turret gun control, in case. I take it you don't want action stations yet?" Nichols told him.

Harwood shook his head. "We'll wait for *Exeter*'s signal. It could be anything," he said, going to the glass on the port side.

The *Exeter*, some two miles astern, her Aldis winking acknowledgment, made a smooth turn north. As she did so, her superstructure momentarily gleamed like copper in the sunlight. Harwood watched her turn. Through the binoculars, he could now see a barely perceptible smudge that broke the perfect line of the horizon. He turned his head.

"What's the range?" Harwood said to McAllister, who spoke quickly into the mouthpiece.

"Estimate 19,400 yards, sorr," McAllister reported.

Harwood looked over at Nichols.

"Where's her spotter plane, Harry? Surely she's seen us by now," Harwood said.

"At that range, she might not be able to make out much more than the tops of our masts, sir. Perhaps she doesn't take us seriously," Nichols said.

"That plane worries me," Harwood muttered. "If I were her captain, I'd have it over us already."

"Maybe it isn't her. An excited lookout mistaking a cloud for smoke from a stack. They're just young lads, after all," Nichols shrugged.

Lieutenant Chalmers burst onto the bridge, his eyes wild with excitement.

"Signal from the *Exeter*, sir!"

"What is it?"

"I think it is a pocket battleship," Chalmers said breathlessly.

Harwood and Nichols stared at each other.

"Got her, by God," Nichols murmured.

"Action stations!" Harwood called to McAllister. He turned to Chalmers. "Signal *Achilles* to engage."

"Yes sir!"

Nichols glanced over his shoulder at McAllister.

"Break out the battle ensign!"

"Aye, sorr!"

"And get that bloody plane up!"

"Aye, aye, sorr!"

The sound of the alarm horn and McAllister's voice calling

"Action stations!" over the loudspeaker electrified the ship. Nichols could see seamen scurrying like ants across the deck to the gun positions.

"Half-ahead, port 20!" Nichols called.

"Half-ahead, port 20!"

"Midships!"

"Midships!"

"Steady as she goes!" Nichols said, going to the telescope as the *Ajax* swung toward the distant smudge on the horizon.

"Can you see her, Harry?" Harwood asked. "What's she doing?"

Nichols looked up from the telescope for an instant, a grim smile of satisfaction on his face.

"She's coming right at us, sir. Just as you said. Right bloody at us!"

"All guns ready, sorr!" McAllister reported.

"Tell them to commence firing," Nichols snapped, his voice almost drowned by the howl from the catapult as it sent the spotter plane streaking out over the sea. All three British ships sped towards the distant speck that was the German battleship. Harwood's eyes darted everywhere, from the *Graf Spee* to the *Achilles* running parallel to them, to the *Exeter*, racing ahead, the plume of smoke from her stacks trailing far behind her.

A giant waterspout shot up from the sea less than a hundred yards from the *Exeter*'s port bow. The *Exeter* seemed almost to hesitate in her forward thrust as the first salvo thundered almost simultaneously from both of her forward 8-inch gun turrets. Even before the sound of the *Exeter*'s guns could reach them over the water, the *Ajax*'s bridge trembled from the recoil of her own "B" turret's twin 6-inch guns. A second giant waterspout blossomed just off *Exeter*'s starboard side. Harwood dropped his binoculars and stared at Nichols in horror.

"My God, Harry! She's bracketed already!"

"I know, sir. That's unbelievable accuracy," Nichols said, looking very worried.

"How is it possible? Unless—" Harwood's mouth tightened. He looked angrily at Nichols. "She's got radar. Her guns are radar-controlled."

"But the Admiralty assured us the Jerries don't have—"

Nichols's voice was lost in the booming of "A" turret's guns, followed like an echo by a salvo from the *Achilles*'s forward turrets. A powerful explosion came from the *Exeter*. They could see flames shooting up from the boat deck. *Exeter*'s forward turrets were wreathed in smoke as they fired again. There was a staccato hammering of blast after blast as the three British ships fired their big guns almost non-stop.

"Range down to 18,000, sorr!" McAllister announced.

A towering waterspout sprouted up from the sea barely fifty yards ahead of the *Ajax*.

"Now it's our turn," Nichols said.

Harwood nodded grimly. For more than a year, Admiralty Intelligence had been assuring them that the German radar was a crude device still in the lab. Well, here was proof positive that the Jerries had it, and it wasn't the least bit crude or in any bloody lab, either.

"What's happening with that plane?" Harwood barked at McAllister.

McAllister put the receiver down for a second, a bleak wintry look in his eyes.

"Spotter plane reports several hits on the *Graf Spee*, sorr. Only—"

"Yes, what is it?"

"Our shells, sorr. They're just bouncing off her sides!"

Nichols touched the binnacle for a moment, as though it were a kind of talisman.

"Light cruisers against a battleship," he muttered bitterly.

"Your orders, sorr?" McAllister asked, standing by.

Suddenly, they heard the clap of a tremendous explosion. All eyes turned toward the *Exeter*. An orange fireball glowed red on the glass around the bridge. A moment later, the glass rattled with the sound. The *Exeter*'s foredeck was completely obscured by fire and smoke. All at once, the smoke partially cleared and they could see, only they could hardly believe their eyes.

The armor shield on *Exeter*'s "A" turret was blackened and badly dented. But "B" turret was gone. There was nothing left of it but a black smoking hole in the deck. Even worse, her bridge was a complete shambles. It had been shredded like confetti by a hail of shell fragments. No one on the bridge could have possibly survived. All from a single murderous 11-inch shell.

"Oh my God! Bonnie Bell!" Nichols gasped.

The sea was filled with waterspouts from exploding shells.

The guns pounded one after another. It was impossible to tell where shells were landing because there was no way to distinguish between who had fired what.

"Signal *Exeter*. Who's in command?" Harwood demanded.

Incredibly, *Exeter*'s "A" turret fired back at the German battleship as *Exeter* began a hard turn to port. *Ajax*'s deck trembled underfoot as "B" turret fired another salvo, the smoke swirling up from the gun deck. Good old Brookings, Harwood thought.

"WT—Bridge! WT—Bridge!" Chalmers exclaimed excitedly. "Captain Bell's alive! He's made his way aft to the emergency steering position!" Chalmers's voice dropped to a whisper. "Everyone else on the bridge was killed."

"Torpedoes, sorr! From the *Exeter*!" McAllister shouted, pointing.

"Damn all this smoke!" Harwood coughed. "What's the *Graf Spee* doing?"

"She's turning away to avoid *Exeter*'s torpedoes. Estimate the enemy's bearing at 330, sir," Nichols replied.

"Signal from *Achilles*, sir. She's been hit! Her aft mast is down!" Chalmers said.

Nichols ignored him; his binoculars were riveted on the *Graf Spee*.

"What the devil?" Nichols said suddenly in a puzzled tone and everyone looked. A distant fuzz of greyish-white smoke smeared on the horizon. "She's laying down a smokescreen! She's running! Old Jerry doesn't like torpedoes!"

"Hot pursuit!" Harwood ordered. "Signal all ships!"

Nichols glanced at him, worried.

"It might be a ruse, sir."

"Doesn't matter," Harwood said. "The closer the range the better. Besides we don't want her to get away."

"Yes sir," Nichols nodded. He turned to Peary at the wheel. "Heading Two-seven-five!"

"Two-seven-five!"

"Full ahead!"

"Full ahead!"

The bell rang as McAllister marked the full-ahead.

"Tell Cooke I want everything she's got," Nichols said to McAllister.

"Aye, sorr-r-r," McAllister burred and spoke rapidly into the tube, as another near miss sprayed water against the bridge's windows. The Jerries hadn't missed by much that time, Harwood thought. If Nichols hadn't started the turn just when he did, they'd have put it right down the stack, he thought, as the *Ajax*, her battle ensign streaming red, white and blue behind her, turned in fast pursuit of the retreating German battleship.

"Thirty-eight knots and gaining," McAllister called. A mile to port and slightly astern, the *Achilles*, her guns booming, raced on a nearly parallel course to the *Ajax*, directly towards the *Graf Spee*. The *Exeter* had turned to the east again, apposite the *Graf Spee*'s course. As they passed across from each other, only eight or so miles apart, the *Exeter* fired a broadside at the German with all remaining turrets. From the *Ajax*'s bridge, they could see flashes amid the smoke, but there was no way to tell where the shells were landing.

There was the terrible whine of an incoming shell. The officers on the *Ajax*'s bridge didn't have time to duck. The deck heaved under them, knocking them off their feet. A blinding flash of fire soared up toward the bridge.

"A" turret was gone. In its place was a flattened twisted mass of smoldering metal. A stunned AB, his face blackened with oil, staggered alongside the capstan, just staring at what was left of the turret.

"Jesus!" Chalmers murmured.

"Hard to starboard!" Nichols shouted.

"Hard to starboard!"

A second shell whistled in and everyone hit the deck. The explosion splashed water in sheets all over the glass. It had missed them by at most a yard or two.

"Hard to port!" Nichols called.

"Hard to port!"

Another waterspout sprouted just off the starboard bow. The *Ajax* and *Achilles* plunged forward, weaving between the waterspouts like skiers in a slalom, their forward turrets blazing.

Suddenly, there was a muffled boom from the direction of the *Exeter*. She had been hit again. They saw her begin to turn, smoke pouring from her mangled superstructure. Only one turret aft, "Y" turret, was still firing. Harwood could only stare at her and wonder what on earth was still keeping her afloat.

"Look!" Nichols cried, pointing.

"I see it," Harwood said.

White tracks in the water. In desperation, *Exeter* was firing her aft torpedoes. Harwood and Nichols glanced briefly at each other, then back at the tracks. Two of the torpedoes were running straight and true, right at the *Graf Spee*. The *Exeter* and the German battleship were less than 14,000 yards apart. The *Graf Spee* turned and began to speed away. Black smoke poured from her stacks. It was going to be very close.

"Come on, come on, you bloody bastard," Nichols prayed audibly, his fists tightly clenched. "Come on."

The torpedo trails disappeared in the battleship's wake. One of them had missed by less than ten yards. The *Graf Spee's* big guns boomed again across the open water.

"We've got to save *Exeter*," Harwood said, a tremor in his voice. "We must make Jerry pay attention to us. No more weaving! Straight at him with everything we've got!"

Nichols just stared at him. Harwood didn't say anything. After a second, he turned back and raised his binoculars again. Nichols stood there, an instant longer. Then his face changed.

"Full ahead, midships!" Nichols shouted.

"Full ahead, midships!"

Nichols whirled to face McAllister.

"Fire everything!" he shouted.

"Every gun, sorr?"

"Even machine guns. Pistols. Everything!"

"Aye, sorr," McAllister said and shouted into the phone.

The *Ajax* and *Achilles* plunged straight at the German battleship. There was a savage crackle and hammering, as every gun on both ships opened up. Pompoms, Oerlikons, turret guns, everything. They were answered by a roar like a freight train. A massive explosion in front of them shattered the glass on the bridge, tossing them like toys against the bulkheads.

Harwood and Nichols were up before the smoke cleared. The smell of cordite was everywhere. "B" turret was shattered. It was burning badly. They watched a gunner jump out of the wreckage, a human torch, screaming and beating futilely at the flames all over him before collapsing to the deck, charred and twisted like a burned matchstick figure.

"David," Harwood whispered to himself.

" 'B' Boiler room," McAllister called. "She's taking water, sorr!"

"Get Cooke. Tell him to close it off!" Nichols ordered.

"There are two ABS still in there, sorr."

"Close it off!"

McAllister stared at Nichols, blinking rapidly.

"Aye, sorr."

"WT—Bridge. Signal from *Exeter*, sir. Captain Bell reports all turrets out of action and taking water. He believes the *Graf Spee* has been hit," Chalmers said, then his voice dropped sharply. "He requests permission to withdraw, sir."

Harwood stared bleakly at the battered hulk of the *Exeter*. She was smoking badly, a fire amidships obviously still out of control. One of the aft turrets hung askew, like a child's toy twisted off. Seamen swarmed like ants with hoses and buckets to fight the blaze.

"Permission granted," Harwood nodded. "Tell Bonnie—" he croaked wearily. "Tell Captain Bell to make for the Falklands. We'll cover him. Oh, and let's have a damage and casualty report," he added, his mouth a grim line. Bell wouldn't have asked, he knew, if the situation wasn't desperate.

The *Ajax* shuddered, as another shell landed aft, taking out the after pompom and setting fire to the Auxiliary Tower. Of the three British ships, only the *Achilles* was still firing from her forward turrets. They couldn't take much more, Harwood thought.

He squinted through his binoculars at the *Graf Spee*, a black shape in the smoke, only 11,000 yards away, close enough to see the flash, followed a second or two later by the boom of her big guns. So close, he thought. If they'd only had one working turret left on the *Exeter*, he thought, raking the *Graf Spee* with his binoculars. Apart from some battering to her superstructure, she looked virtually undamaged, invincible almost. The deck canted as the *Ajax* swerved again to avoid an incoming salvo. Two giant waterspouts cascaded over her bow.

"Break off!" Harwood announced suddenly. Nichols and McAllister stared at him. "Signal *Achilles*. Fire torpedoes and send up smokescreens."

"Thank God," Chalmers murmured under his breath.

"Half-ahead, Starboard 20!" Nichols ordered.

"Half-ahead, Starboard 20!"

"Fire port torpedoes! Smoke!" McAllister shouted into the phone.

One after another, three torpedoes shot out of the port tubes and splashed into the water. One of them veered off, but two of them sped right towards the path of the *Graf Spee*.

"She's seen them! She's turning," Nichols announced in a disappointed voice. They watched as the battleship turned south, a distant gray shape swirled about with smoke. The torpedo trails sped futilely across where she would have been if she hadn't turned away.

Despite the brightening morning, it became increasingly difficult to see as all four ships began to lay down smoke. They lost sight of the German battleship.

"What's she doing? Check the spotter plane," Harwood snapped.

"Spotter's hit. He's coming in." McAllister announced.

"Well? Did he see anything?"

"Near as he can make out, sorr, the *Graf Spee*'s weaving west. Looks like she's making for the bloody Plate. An' there's one more thing sorr! It looks like she's got a hole in her side, about six foot he figures, only a yard or two above the water-line," McAllister said, grinning broadly.

"Why?" Nichols said, looking puzzled, his hands on his hips. "Why'd they run? They had us dead to rights!"

"No," Harwood shook his head. "Their captain's got a six-foot hole in his side and he doesn't want to chance the North Atlantic in winter. Not with the whole Royal Navy looking for him. He'll either lie low, or head to a neutral port for repairs."

"Buenos Aires?" Nichols asked.

"From a naval point of view, Montevideo would be better," Westlake said, coming onto the bridge. His face was grimy and there was blood on his shirt. "Closer. Less shallow water. Less chance of sabotage. Closer to the open sea."

"Signal from *Exeter*, sir," Chalmers said in a hushed voice. "Sixty-four dead. Men and officers. No word yet on wounded."

Harwood looked at Westlake.

"The forward turrets?" he asked.

"Seven dead, sir."

"Brookings?"

Westlake shook his head.

Harwood blinked once. No more silly jokes in the ward-room. "I think you're right," he said to Westlake. "Montevideo."

"Orders, sorr?" McAllister asked.

"Fall back out of range. Signal *Achilles*. We'll sit on her tail till she's in the River Plate," Harwood said. He turned to Chalmers. "Signal DNO, Johnny. Tell them to send us every-thing they've got." He looked around at all of them. "The

Renown and the *Ark Royal* are around the South Atlantic somewhere. With any luck, we'll nail her yet." He checked his watch. "Ninety minutes. That's all it took."

"Yes sir. Light cruisers against a battleship," Nichols murmured, gazing out over the fires and twisted wreckage of his ship. Smoke and flames were coming from the *Achilles* and they could see *Exeter* in the distance, burning badly. She was low in the water and her deck was tilted at an angle, like a grand piano top. She'd need dead calm seas and a lot of luck to make it to Port Stanley. "It's crazy! She had us! She beat the bloody hell out of us!" Nichols declared suddenly.

"She had us, all right," Harwood agreed, leaning wearily against the binnacle. "She just didn't know it."

22

"I SURPRISED you, *gringo*. Admit it," Fuentes grinned.

"It's true," Stewart said, looking out the car window. They were in the back seat of Fuentes's official car. The curly-haired man, Navarro, Stewart had learned his name was, was driving. They drove through San Isidro, a suburb of old colonial homes and gardens near the river. It was midmorning; the sky was blue and warm and servant women in aprons were shopping from colorfully painted horse-drawn wagons parked in front of the big houses. "How did you find me?"

"The desk clerk, of course," Fuentes told him. "He has been on our payroll for many years. Also we alerted all our informants to watch out for a *gringo* with an injured hand. As soon as he called, we came."

Not Julia, the concierge, Stewart thought, feeling something ease inside him, as though he had been holding his breath for a very long time.

He lit a cigarette, holding it with his bad hand. A doctor had come to the prison. He had put sulphur on the open wounds and sewed up his little finger and it was feeling much better. The doctor had given him something and he had slept through most of yesterday. That had helped too.

Getting his clothes back, being secretly moved into the Alvear Palace hotel and getting cleaned up had helped even more. That and the headline in the newspaper Fuentes had stopped to pick up from a corner kiosk shortly after they had started out this morning:

GRAF SPEE IN MONTEVIDEO. WAR IN THE RIVER PLATE?

"Is that why you're being so accommodating, *Coronel?* Afraid the Germans might not win?" Stewart asked, rattling the newspaper in his hand.

Fuentes stopped smiling. For a moment, Stewart wondered if he hadn't gone too far. But it was only a moment and Fuentes was all friendliness again.

"Why not, Señor Stewart? I told you once before, I think, that it pays to be on the winning side. In this country," he grinned, "the winning side is the only side."

"Do you know what's happening?" Stewart asked, indicating the newspaper.

"They are going crazy," Fuentes said. "Everyone is in Montevideo. Buenos Aires is emptied the way a housewife empties a bucket of dirty water. The Germans are over there arguing that the Uruguayans should allow the *Graf Spee* to stay in port for seventy-two hours, instead of the twenty-four hours allowed by international law."

"What do the English say?"

Fuentes leaned back in the seat, tapping the ash from his Havana cigar out the window.

"Curiously enough, the same thing. The Señor Fowler of the British embassy here—the one who always looks like the world is something he would like to flush down the drain because he doesn't like the way it smells—has gone over to request the very same thing. Interesting, no?"

"What will the Uruguayans do?"

"What the Uruguayans have always done," Fuentes laughed. "Bend over and hand the *grasa* to whoever pays them the most!" He used the phrase, *untar las manos*, to grease the palms, a play on the two uses of the word "grease." Stewart smiled to show he got the joke. "Ha! Ha! Ha!" Fuentes's laugh boomed and he delightedly slapped Stewart's knee. Up front, Navarro was also laughing. Stewart could see his teeth in the rear-view mirror.

"*Ay, caramba,*" Fuentes sighed, wiping his eyes. "But I wonder how the *Ingleses* knew that the *Graf Spee* would be at the mouth of the Rio de la Plata. I do not imagine you would know any such thing of this, Señor?" Fuentes asked, still smiling.

"I? What would I know?"

"No," Fuentes said, judiciously studying his cigar. "I did not think so. And the letter case? From the safe in Cardenas's office? What was in that? The *Graf Spee* perhaps? The newspapers speculate that the *Ingleses* set a trap for the *Graf Spee*. That they had secret information," Fuentes said, tapping the newspaper with his finger.

"The press has never let a lack of facts get in the way of its conclusions, *Coronel,*" Stewart replied.

"There is speculation that the *Graf Spee* was on her way to Buenos Aires, only she was too badly damaged to make it. That would make it our affair," Fuentes said, studying his cigar.

Stewart didn't answer. They rode the quiet tree-lined streets in silence. On the lawn of one of the houses, two maids were mounting a life-sized Christmas crèche, complete with papier-mâché shepherds, animals and wise men with camels. It seemed very strange amid the garden flowers and palm trees and warm summery breeze coming through the open car windows, and somewhere, to make the feeling of foreignness even stranger, a radio playing the Andrews Sisters singing the "Beer Barrel Polka." Fuentes turned slowly to Stewart.

"How many more dead bodies have you left lying around my city, *gringo?*"

"Where are you taking me, *Coronel?*"

"You will see soon enough."

"You also."

Fuentes tapped his cigar ash into the ashtray on the back of the front seat. He blew on the cigar tip, so it glowed red, before putting the cigar back into his mouth. His flat face was utterly expressionless, more like a cat than ever. All at once, he smiled.

"*Ay, gringo, gringo,*" Fuentes said. "You speak our language, but like all *yanquis*, you make things very difficult for us." He gazed out the window. "Tell me. How goes it with the Señora Vargas?"

"She's an interesting woman," Stewart said carefully.

"And so beautiful, too."

"That too."

"Of course," Fuentes nodded understandingly. "Who could blame you? A woman like that. With a husband who feels he must always prove himself. The manhood, the *machismo*, is a thing not to be taken lightly here, you know."

"What does Arturo Vargas have to prove?"

"His father's business failed in the *Quiebra* in '29. They say he drank himself to death. And on his mother's side. . . ." Fuentes shrugged.

"What about his mother's side?"

"*Ay*, Don Carlos, all the Montoya males have ended badly. Arturo Vargas is the last of that line. Except for his children, of course."

A chill went down Stewart's spine when he said that.

"Tell me, *Coronel*, how is Arturo Vargas related to the Montoyas?" he asked.

Fuentes looked surprised.

"His mother, Angelica, was Cesar Montoya's only daughter. Why else would Julia have married him? His father, Claudio Vargas, was of good family, yes. But for a Gideon? Pah!" Fuentes snorted. "The old one, the *viejo*, Gideon, would come out of his tomb at such a match, otherwise!"

Stewart stared out the window at the houses and the sunlight glimmering through the branches of the trees.

"Gideon. Always Gideon," he murmured. "No matter how one turns in this affair, one always comes to him."

"Why have you always to keep harping on this?" Fuentes said, crushing out his cigar in the ashtray with sharp angry gestures. "It is absurd. The *viejo*, Gideon, died, what? Thirteen, fourteen years ago? And he was a very old man then. In a wheelchair, *pues*. Raoul de Almayo was murdered only two months ago!"

"Raoul again? Are we back to him?"

"Oh yes, *gringo*," Fuentes said seriously. "We never left him."

"But I thought we agreed that the Nazis killed him."

"We agreed nothing. *You* said the Germans did it. We did

not. But now we have identified the other man. The other
body in the hotel room where Raoul and the *puta* were killed.
He was a German. What was his name, Luis?" Fuentes said to
the curly-haired man.

"Genscher. Heinz Genscher, *mi Coronel.*"

"Ah yes," Fuentes smiled. "From one of those Nazi organi-
zations. What was it?"

"The Federation of German Benevolent and Cultural Soci-
eties," Navarro answered.

"Always a mouthful from the Germans," Fuentes grimaced.
"It operates out of the Number 145 Calle Veinticinco de Mayo,
just above the offices of the Banco Germanico and, of course,
the German embassy."

"So you think he was from the Gestapo?"

Fuentes smiled.

"Or from the Abwehr. That thought had occurred to us, yes.
But," Fuentes continued, "if this Genscher was a Nazi, why
did they kill him too?"

"Perhaps Raoul did, defending himself. He had a gun,"
Stewart said. "Maybe they killed each other?"

"No, Señor Stewart," Fuentes shook his head. "Not from
the position of the bodies. Also there is another fact. Something I omitted telling you when we first met."

"Deliberately?"

"Of course," Fuentes grinned broadly. He was enjoying himself. "You see, we found two pistols in the room. A .25 caliber,
which we know Raoul got from Señora de Castro that night.
And a Luger, which we assume belonged to the German."

"So?"

"Raoul and the whore were both killed with the .25. It is the
German who is of interest."

"In what way?"

"Because, Señor Stewart," Fuentes said, "the German was
killed by another gun. One we have not found. The bullets
taken from his body were of .38 caliber."

Stewart stared at him.

"Why didn't you tell me this before?"

"And why did you not tell us about the *Graf Spee* information in the letter case?" Fuentes retorted sharply. Then his
expression suddenly changed. "But we are here," he said, as
the car pulled up to the gate of an old-style cream-colored
Spanish house.

A plainclothesman in a tight jacket that didn't conceal the gun he was carrying stood at the gate. Navarro stopped and the plainclothesman peered suspiciously into the car. Although he couldn't see them, Stewart sensed that there were other eyes watching. On the other side of the fence, two big German Shepherd dogs were barking furiously. The house looked ordinary, but he wouldn't want to try to break into it, Stewart thought.

Fuentes and Navarro handed their military *cedulas* to the plainclothesman, who, compared their pictures on the *cedulas* with their faces. Then, while they waited, he went to a small guardhouse concealed behind a hedge and telephoned. After a moment, he was back. He returned the *cedulas*, then pressed a button to electronically open the gate. Navarro drove slowly through the gate onto the landscaped grounds. Stewart turned to Fuentes.

"What is all this, *Coronel?* What are you up to?"

"Prepare yourself, Señor Stewart. You are about to meet the President of the Republic."

"Have they given you your things back?" President Ortiz asked Stewart.

"Yes, Señor *Presidente*. Everything except my gun."

"I will see that it is returned to you," President Ortiz nodded pleasantly. "But please, you will help yourself to the tea. And please try the *dulce de leche*. I cannot have it myself, but I am told it is very good. Doctors," he sighed, raising a limp hand, then letting it fall back into his lap. "If there is any pleasure left in life, doctors will find a way to ruin it for you. Stay away from them."

"I'll try," Stewart smiled.

"Do that," President Ortiz said, holding up a cautionary finger. "The only person who profits from an association with a doctor is a pharmacist," he smiled. "But first you must try the *dulce* and let me know how it is."

"It's very good," Stewart said, smearing the jam on the crêpe and taking a small polite bite, the kind that would have made his mother proud.

They were in President Ortiz's upstairs sitting room. It was a large room, with tall French windows that looked out over a meticulously laid-out garden and lawn that led down to the River Plate. The sun was sparkling on the water and in the

distance, two sailboats slanted toward each other like sea-
birds. President Ortiz was seated in a leather armchair facing
the windows, his feet up on an ottoman. He wore a silk dressing robe, despite the heat, and dark glasses. Before sending
him in, Fuentes had warned Stewart that President Ortiz was
virtually blind. Everything about the Argentine president was
clean and elegant. His white hair was trimmed and his hands
beautifully manicured, but he smelled of sickness. The whole
room smelled of sickness.

"I am pleased," President Ortiz said. "I can still remember
what they tasted like. Better not tell the doctors, though, or
they will forbid me even to remember," he smiled. He turned
to Stewart. "So. What does the United States government
think the Uruguayans should do about the *Graf Spee?*"

"Officially, I suppose, the American position is one of strict
neutrality," Stewart said.

"And unofficially?"

"I don't know, Señor *Presidente*. I am not—"

"I am aware of that," President Ortiz said. "Also that you've
made our German friends very unhappy. Of course, they have
other things to worry about now. Have you heard the BBC
Overseas Service today?"

"Not yet."

"The BBC says the British fleet patrolling the mouth of the
Rio de la Plata has been reinforced with a battle cruiser and
an aircraft carrier. That the *Graf Spee* is trapped. Do you think
it's true?"

"I don't know, Señor *Presidente*. But if I were the British, I'd
either have the ships there, or I'd have them burning every
last drop of oil they had to get there."

"Of course," President Ortiz nodded. "They want to come
here, you know. The *Graf Spee*. I've been approached for permission."

"You can't let them," Stewart said.

"No, of course not. But Castillo and his Fascist friends will
howl."

"Let them."

"I can't," President Ortiz said, his mouth trembling. Stewart couldn't tell whether it was because of the diabetes, or his
age. "You see, I'm dying, Señor Stewart. Castillo will be President soon. Then the Fascists will have Argentina. Whether
with Castillo, or someone from the Army."

"Don't let them."

"I can't stop them. Except," President Ortiz turned his dark glasses toward Stewart the way a blind man does, partially, aiming his ears as much as his eyes, "by staying alive. That is the one hope we have. That I can stay alive until your United States enters the war. It is no longer a question of Argentina's beef, but of the survival of civilization itself," he said.

"Then you must not go to the Vargas *estancia*, Señor *Presidente*. There is an assassination coup against you planned for the 17th."

President Ortiz looked blindly toward an oil painting of a woman on the wall, groping toward it like a memory.

"They chose well," he said. "That is one event I must attend. There is no choice."

"*Qué va?* A dead man's birthday? I don't understand."

"Everyone will be there, Señor Stewart. From the *Concordancia*, you understand? It has become a tradition, a gathering of the most powerful men in the country—to see the polo match and, informally, to decide policy. If I am not there, the Party will say I am too feeble and support Castillo's bid to take over the Presidency. *Entonces*, they would not need a coup to get rid of me."

"If you go, they'll kill you," Stewart said.

"Yes. I had also a warning of this from the English. A Señor Fowler. But what can one do? I must be there," President Ortiz shrugged helplessly.

"There is one thing," Stewart said. He explained it to the Argentine president. When he had finished, President Ortiz smiled.

"Perhaps you should have gone into politics, Señor Stewart. Such deviousness would find a natural outlet there."

"I'm having enough trouble staying alive as it is, Señor *Presidente*."

For a moment, neither of them spoke. Stewart sat there, sipping his tea. In the silence, he could hear the ticking of a clock on the mantel.

"It is reading that I miss the most," President Ortiz announced suddenly. "That is the worst part of losing my sight. I have my niece come in to read to me, but it is not the same." He felt for his tea cup on the little table and drank, the cup rattling on the saucer. "Ahhh," he smacked his lips. "If people knew about my niece they would whisper about me the way they used to do about Yrigoyen. That he interfered with young girls, understand."

"Did he?"

"Not in that way," President Ortiz frowned. "He was senile at the end. He refused to see anyone from the Senate, so they would send young girls, as a way to get him to sign things. He would drop things and ask them to pick them up so he could see their underpants when they bent over. It was more pathetic than evil," he shook his head. "The great Revolution of 1930, General Uriburu and all that followed, was all so that we could get goods moving again through the port, because that old man insisted on signing every single shipping permit himself. *Qué estupidez!* And now comes another fool, Castillo," President Ortiz said disgustedly. "He calls himself a Creole of pure stock, *un criollo de pura cepa*, and makes a big show of drinking *yerba mate* through a silver straw like a *gaucho*. But in the end, soldiers will replace him too, the way we did Yrigoyen. And for the same reason, *pues.*"

"What is that, Señor *Presidente?*"

"The same mistake I made," President Ortiz grimaced. "The worst mistake a politician can make: to begin to believe what you say about yourself."

"Is that bad?"

"In my case, it was worse," President Ortiz said. "I tried to keep my campaign promise to hold honest elections!"

"No wonder the Conservatives want to kill you," Stewart grinned.

"The final delusion of outgoing Presidents and dying men," President Ortiz agreed, smiling sadly. "That one is finally free to act. Gestures, Señor Stewart, are better saved for the theater stage, than real life." President Ortiz gazed toward Stewart with his blind eyes. "And the Vargases, Señor? This plot? Are they also linked to the Nazis?"

Stewart stopped smiling. If Arturo Vargas was the Raven, he had to be protected at all costs.

"Yes and no, Señor *Presidente.* It is not entirely clear. But Minister Casaverde and Castillo and also Vargas are all connected. They are not to be trusted, any of them."

"No," President Ortiz agreed. He pushed a button on the table. Stewart assumed the interview was over and started to get up. "Wait," President Ortiz said, gesturing with his hand for him to stay. Although the hand was shaking, it was an oddly graceful, old-fashioned gesture. "I am told that you and the Señora Vargas. . . ." he stopped. "Do you love her, young man?"

Stewart hesitated.

"Yes, but there are complications."

"Of course. There are always complications."

"If love were all that mattered. . . ."

"But it isn't, is it?"

"No, Señor *Presidente*. It isn't."

"Actually, it is. There are only two reasons to do something. Love or fear. And love is better. But that's easy to say when you are dying and you don't have to do anything about it," President Ortiz smiled.

A butler came in. President Ortiz heard him and gestured for him to take away the tea.

"Do you see her soon?" President Ortiz asked.

"Soon. But first I have something else to do."

"For this *business*?" President Ortiz used the English word.

"Yes," Stewart said, fingering the packet of matches in his pocket. The one with Ceci Braga's address on it that he had taken from the dead German. "It has to do with the murder of Raoul de Almayo."

President Ortiz looked at him curiously.

"The poet? His death is involved in all this?"

"I don't know, Señor *Presidente*. I think so."

President Ortiz nodded slowly and began quoting:

> " 'Farewell, Argentina. All these sad-eyed tango dancers.
> Ravens of a dead god who never heard of Gardel,
> Hearts imprisoned like flower-pots behind window railings,
> The only way to leave Argentina is to die.' "

The word "Raven" embedded itself into Stewart's mind like an arrow. What the hell was going on?

"Did Almayo write that?" he asked.

"Oh yes," President Ortiz nodded. "He enjoyed quite a vogue at one time." He turned to Stewart with his blind man's eyes. "Do you know who killed him?"

That question again, Stewart thought. Only it was the wrong question.

"Yes, I think so, Señor *Presidente*."

"But you are not prepared to tell Colonel Fuentes?"

"No, Señor *Presidente*. Because what matters in this case isn't who killed Raoul, but why. Besides, officially Colonel Fuentes is no longer on the case."

"Of course," President Ortiz smiled grimly. "I keep forgetting. Another of Castillo's little games. And the Señora Vargas? What will you do?"

"I don't know."

President Ortiz nodded. He kept on nodding for so long, Stewart thought the interview was over.

"I envy you. I envy the passion, no matter how it ends," President Ortiz said. "She's an unusual woman. It's an unusual family."

Stewart looked curiously at the old man.

"Did you ever meet the grandfather?"

"You mean Gideon? The *viejo* himself? Only once," President Ortiz nodded. "Long ago. Back in '23, it was. Marcelo de Alvear was there. He was President then. That was during the time when he broke with Yrigoyen. The government was falling apart. The Conservatives met secretly with Alvear at Gideon's boathouse in Tigre. Gideon was an old man then. In his eighties, I think. Nothing came of the meeting as I remember. Alvear couldn't be convinced to renounce his pledge to end corruption and the patronage system. Another politician destroyed because he believed his own propaganda," President Ortiz mused. "How can I face the people?" I remember him saying and Gideon responding: "Economic nationalism. Give them foreigners to hate. Wrap a steer's ass in the flag and you can get the whole nation to kiss it!" He was a hard one, that Gideon. *Un hombre duro.* They were all hard men from the time he came from. But even among these, he was exceptional. And such eyes he had. Dark blue, they were. You never saw such eyes."

"Why? What was different about them?"

"They were very different. There was something hypnotic about them. Old as he was, you could feel the force of his will coming from them like heat from a lamp. Only one other time in my life have I ever seen eyes like that."

"When was that, Señor *Presidente?*"

President Ortiz stared blindly at the sunlight on the window.

"Adolf Hitler has such eyes, Señor Stewart."

BY THE time Stewart found Tino the Dwarf it was late afternoon, after the siesta hour. He found him in a *whiskería* on Pedro de Mendoza, not far from the tango palace, the fourth place he had tried.

The little man was sitting at a small dark table, stacking sugar cubes from a bowl, one on top of the other. He had erected a shaky tower of cubes, and when Stewart sat down the dwarf looked up at him belligerently, as if he expected Stewart to knock it down. When he recognized Stewart, his expression changed.

"Hey, pal. How's it going?" the dwarf said in English. His eyes were swimming and there was an almost empty bottle of *caña* at his elbow. He was drunk, but Stewart couldn't tell how much.

The waiter came over and Stewart ordered a bottle of Kentucky bourbon and fresh glasses.

"Hello, Tino. Where's Ceci?"

The dwarf squinted intently at his sugar cube tower. His tongue peeked out of the corner of his mouth as he concentrated on putting another cube on the top of his Tower of Pisa without toppling it.

"They used to have me doing this shit in the hospital. Therapy for my hands," Tino said, dropping the cube into place. The cube balanced precariously for an instant, then the whole tower collapsed on the table. The little man stared at the rubble as though it were a metaphor for his life.

The waiter brought glasses and a bottle and Stewart put some money on the table. The waiter made change and poured the drinks, leaving the bottle on the table. Tino picked up one of the glasses.

"Mud in your eye," he said and drank. "Hey, you know

where that expression came from? From the World War. I guess we gotta call it the First One now, huh? Anyways, the Doughboys used to say it 'cause if you heard an incoming shell in time to hit the dirt, then you were okay. You'd still be alive, get it?"

"Where is she, Tino?"

The little man looked down at the table top. He started arranging the sugar cubes in a pattern.

"I don't know nuthin'," he said sullenly. "Ain't nobody seen her. She didn't show at all last night. And she was supposed to stop by this morning to do the books. And to pay me."

"I went to her place, Tino. The door was locked and there was no answer. The tango palace was closed up too, so I came looking for you. Where is she?"

"I don't know, I tell ya," the little man said in an aggrieved tone. "She ain't showed. We're all closed down. Jeez," he looked blearily up at Stewart. "What the hell are we gonna do?"

Stewart didn't answer. Tino licked his lips as if it had been weeks instead of seconds since he'd had a drink.

"She's in trouble, ain't she?" Tino said.

"I'm worried about her, yes," Stewart said. "The Germans know about her. They're interested."

"Why? On account of Raoul? That crazy faggot?"

Stewart looked curiously at him.

"What do you mean 'crazy'?"

"Aw, he was nuts. One time at the Del Rio he got locked in the men's john. Just for a minute, mind you. Jeez, you coulda' heard him screaming down in Mar del Plata. Nuts, I tell ya. Why? You think he was up to something with them Nazis?"

"I don't know. But Ceci knew something. Something that may have gotten her into a whole bunch of trouble. Any ideas?"

"I don't know nuthin'," Tino shook his head. He went back to the sugar cubes. "I don't want to know nuthin'. All knowing stuff does is get you in trouble. Even when you don't know stuff, it gets you into trouble."

"When was the last time you saw her?"

"When the hell was it? Night before last, I think. Yeah! That was it!" he said, awkwardly snapping his misshapen fingers. "At the Del Rio. Must have been around four in the morning. Closing time. She was going home. That was the last time I seen her."

"Did she act different in any way? Nervous, or frightened maybe?"

Tino's eyes brightened.

"Yeah. Now that you mention it, she did seem kind of nervous. Her hands kept fluttering around like birds. You know how dames get."

"Was she scared?"

"Who knows? Maybe," he shrugged. "No, more nervous-like, I'd say. Why?"

"Just fishing," Stewart said. "Listen. I don't suppose you'd have a key to Ceci's place?"

The little man didn't say anything. He was arranging the sugar cubes in straight lines. Stewart took out a hundred pesos and laid it on the table.

"If Ceci hasn't paid you, you must be running short," Stewart said.

The little man didn't look up. He poured himself another drink and downed it.

"You had the key all along," Stewart said quietly. "If you didn't go, it was because you were afraid of what you might find. You didn't want to know, did you? That's why you're sitting here now. Looking for your *cojones* in the bottom of a bottle." He held out his hand. "No more bullshit, *amigo*. Give me the key."

The dwarf squinted up at him.

"Tough guy, huh? You guys all think you're so goddamned tough. What do you know, anyway?"

"The key, Tino. Give it over," Stewart said, his eyes narrowing.

The dwarf's eyes were red-rimmed, lost.

"I don't know nuthin', understand? Nuthin!" Tino insisted, reaching into his pocket. He dropped the key into Stewart's hand, snatching the money from the table with his other hand. Stewart stood up. The dwarf went back to his sugar cubes.

"Hey, *amigo!* Whaddya think? Think she's dead?" Tino asked suddenly, not looking up.

"I don't know. I think part of her's been dying for a long time," Stewart said. From this angle, he could see that what the dwarf was constructing was a cemetery, the sugar cubes arranged in neat precise rows like tiny white tombstones.

"Everybody's dying," the little man nodded. "It just takes some of us longer than others."

*   *   *

Stewart walked over to the Camineta. It was nearing dusk as he crossed the little square, the tin houses gleaming like bronze in the setting sun. It was hot and humid; a golden heat haze hovered over the streets. It was going to be a hot sticky night.

He turned the corner to Ceci's house. There was no one outside. He could hear people talking Italian in one of the apartments. Later they would bring their chairs outside and sit, but now was still too early, he thought, going inside and up the stairs to her apartment. He knocked, and when there was no answer, pressed his ear against the door.

There were no sounds of movement inside. Nothing. Not even house noises. If there was anyone inside the apartment, they weren't alive. Stewart pulled the Colt .45 from his shoulder holster and flicked off the safety. He put the key he'd got from Tino into the lock, turned it and stepped inside.

The apartment was a shambles. Someone had turned it upside-down looking for something. The *chinoiserie* lay smashed to pieces on the floor, the sideboard and brass-topped table had been knocked over, the Persian rugs ripped up. Whoever had done it had taken a knife to the divan and torn big gaping holes in it. The stuffing lay scattered around it like cotton entrails and Stewart began to get that prickly feeling at the back of his neck.

He searched the apartment, going from room to room, gun first. At every moment, he expected to turn a corner, or to open a closet and find Ceci dead. Every room had been torn apart, just like the living room.

The apartment was empty.

Stewart sat down on one of the ruined chairs, feeling a strange mixture of relief at not finding Ceci's body and chagrin, because he had been so sure she was dead. He looked out at the window across the street where the shoemaker had lived. The window gleamed like a sheet of gold in the setting sun. Now what? he asked himself. No Ceci. And if there had been anything worth finding in the apartment, whoever had torn it apart would have already got it. Once again, the Germans were ahead of him.

He lit a cigarette, looking on the floor for the ashtray he remembered had been on the brass-topped table. It was lying on the floor, next to Ceci's address book. He picked the book up and shook it out, hoping for a slip of paper the searcher might have missed, but nothing fluttered out. Aimlessly, he turned to "A" to see if she had Raoul's address written down. It was there, printed in a neat schoolgirlish hand, but that wasn't what interested him. At the bottom, hastily scrawled in pencil, was the address of a Señora de Almayo on the Calle Balcarce in San Telmo.

Stewart stared at the entry. It had to have been recent. It was the last entry on the page and Ceci had been in a hurry when she wrote it, because it was scrawled, not printed, and in pencil. She had grabbed the first thing she could get her hands on.

But it made no sense. Raoul was a homosexual. Everybody knew it. He wasn't married. There was no Señora de Almayo. There couldn't be. Unless, something whispered to him, it was a sister. Or his mother.

Raoul had left something behind, Stewart thought. Whoever had torn Ceci's place apart had been looking for it, figuring Raoul had given it to her, because Ceci was the last one to see Raoul alive.

Stewart memorized the address, then closed the book and placed it back on the floor, exactly where he had found it. The apartment was getting dark; it was almost night. Stewart tiptoed out of the apartment, locking it behind him with the key. In the street, the lights had come on and the cafés were starting to fill. He began to walk faster.

The address was in an older *barrio*, not far from the San Telmo church. Stewart had the taxi leave him off at the corner, waiting till the driver pulled away to make sure he hadn't been followed. He stood in the shadows, out of the glare of the streetlamp, where a group of laborers played *bochas* in a vacant lot. A match flared and there was a murmur of conversation and the soft click of the balls. Now and again, a ship's horn sounded from the direction of the river. Stewart studied the street. It was a block of old houses, most of them broken up into working-class apartments, or replaced by tenements that became instant slums. The air hung hot and close over the gabled roofs, the kind of night that makes a sickroom of the whole city. When Stewart was sure no one was following him, he made his way to the address on the Calle Balcarce.

It was a very old house, surrounded by a high hedge and a heavy iron gate. The house came from another time; no one

made houses like that any more. From the street, it looked
abandoned. The windows were boarded up and the garden
choked with weeds. Whoever had lived here had left a long
time ago.

Not wife, not sister, Stewart thought, looking at the house.
Mother.

He wondered what it must have been like for a small boy to
grow up alone in that house and shuddered. *Farewell, Argentina*, he thought. *Ravens of a dead god.* He pushed the creaking
gate open, rust from the handle coming off on his hand, and
walked up the gravel path to the house.

The air was thick with the smell of magnolia. There was a
cistern in the courtyard with a wrought-iron trellis overgrown
with vines and abandoned flowerpots on the stone lip. Weeds
sprouted out of the cracks in the wooden steps. An old-
fashioned balcony sagged over the front door. It was covered
with creepers and spider-webs, and somewhere in the darkness Stewart could hear the faint sound of insects buzzing. He
looked around for a bell or door-knocker and, seeing none,
tried the front door. It was open.

He hesitated on the threshold, listening, his hand still on
the doorknob. Everything was still. He was sweating badly.
He pulled out the .45, cocked it and went inside.

The house was dark, silent. Stewart lit a match. He was in
a small entry hall with a flight of stairs on one side. There was
a candle in a holder on a sideboard in the hall that looked as
though it had been used recently. Stewart lit it and went on.
The air was stale and moldy and curiously, even though he
was inside, he could still hear the insects buzzing. He went
from room to room, almost soundless on thick Oriental rugs.

The furniture was old, Victorian, a museum almost. Everything was coated with dust. In the salon, there were books on
the shelves, but they looked as if they hadn't been touched in
ages. Stewart went back to the hall and up the stairs. The
steps creaked under his feet and at the sound, he froze, listening intently. The sound of the insects was louder.

There were a number of bedrooms on the second floor. The
first two were empty. He found Ceci Braga in the third.

She was lying on her back on a big canopied bed. She was
stark naked, her arms and legs spread wide, white as marble
except for the small muff of dark hair on her mons. Her eyes
were open; flies were buzzing on them. A long quaint dagger,

Venetian in design, perhaps used as a letter opener and obviously from this house, had been rammed upward into her throat and through the back of her neck, pinning her to the bed like a butterfly in a display.

Stewart brushed the flies away from her eyes. He tried to close them, but rigor had set in and the lids wouldn't move. They felt squashy and immobile and he jerked his hand away in disgust. The flies returned immediately. Stewart wiped his hand with a handkerchief, then held it over his nose.

The smell in the room was very bad. It smelled of death and unopened windows and the sickly sweetness of the magnolias seeping in from outside. It was a rotten shame, he thought, shuddering. He had liked her, but at that moment, all he wanted to do was to get out of there. Instead, he sat down and lit a cigarette.

Why had Ceci come here? he wondered, looking at her naked body. Without the mannish clothes she always wore, she looked very much a woman. Her clothes were bunched at the foot of the bed. He went through them quickly without finding anything. She had come here because of Raoul, he thought, looking around. Raoul had left something behind. That's why Ceci's place had been ransacked. But Ceci didn't have it. She had come here looking for it. To Raoul's mother's house. Only this house hadn't been ransacked.

Why not?

Because Ceci had it with her and the murderer took it from her when he killed her?

Or maybe there was nothing from Raoul. Maybe the Germans were just closing down the network and Ceci had been the last one to see Raoul alive.

Or else, Ceci never had it. Whatever Raoul had left behind was still here. And the murderer either didn't realize that, or hadn't had time to look.

Stewart began to pace up and down. If it was here, where would Raoul have hidden it? It might be anywhere. This was a huge house and he had no idea what the hell he was looking for.

Jesus, Raoul, he said to himself, what the hell were you up to? What did you find that the Germans want so badly? And if you did find something, why'd you come here, to your mother's house to hide it? Momma's boy? Was that it? Did she have something to do with you being Queen of the May? Was that why you came back to this mausoleum? He flicked the ash from his cigarette onto the carpet and rubbed it in with his shoe. So where'd you hide it, kiddo?

If it was hidden here, it was Raoul himself who had hidden it, he thought. What did he know about Raoul? That he was a homosexual. A society type. A poet. Books! Stewart snapped his fingers. But the books downstairs looked like they hadn't been touched in years. There was something else, though. Something the dwarf had said. About how Raoul had "gone crazy" when they had accidentally locked him in the john. Did he have a thing about bathrooms? Stewart stopped pacing. Roaul was claustrophobic.

Where would a claustrophobe hide something? he wondered. Someplace enclosed. Because if it was the one place he most feared, he might think others would be reluctant to look there. So if he had hidden something, it would be in a bathroom, or a small room, or a closet, or a hidden panel, or something. Come on, Raoul. Where'd you put it? Someplace safe. Someplace you'd think somebody else wouldn't be likely to look.

A bathroom most likely, he thought, starting for the door, before he realized that he was looking at the closet.

The closet in Raoul's mother's bedroom. Mommy's room, Raoul. Is that where you used to hide when you were a kid? Did you want to be like Mommy? That's where the power was, huh Raoul? Mommy! The room Ceci had been killed in. Stewart stared at the closet. It was a huge mahogany thing, a monstrosity of Victorian excess, the panels carved to look like birds perched on a branch and in the middle, an ornate flowering crucifix. *Ravens of a dead god.*

The hairs began to stand up on the back of his neck. God, Raoul! You were telling us all the time. We were all just too stupid to understand you. He went over to the closet and opened it. Inside were faded dresses smelling of mold and on a shelf above the door, hatboxes. Stewart searched along the floor and shelf, then began pulling the hatboxes down and opening them.

Inside were women's hats, very old, the lace flowers on them crumbling to dust in his hand like yellowed paper. In the last box, concealed under the hat, was a Catholic missal. Stewart opened it. According to the bookplate, it belonged to a Father Stefano Damiano, S.J., of the Iglesia Del Socorro, Church of the Assistance. Stewart sat back for a second. He thought he knew where that was, on the Calle Juncal. Written in a shaky hand under the priest's name, the words: "Come Thursday, after late mass." Scrawled in the margin, in another hand and with another pen, was the sentence: "A Daniel come to judgment," and a number: 222.

Shakespeare, Stewart thought. *The Merchant of Venice. Toujours la poésie*, huh Raoul? And 222, a page number, maybe. He slipped the missal into his jacket pocket and put the hatboxes back on the shelf. Just before he left, he looked back at Ceci. He hated leaving her like that. He picked up the candle and walked out of the bedroom.

He went down the stairs to the salon, scanning the shelves for a Shakespeare. Curiously, it was still dusty. That didn't make sense, he thought, turning to page 222.

He was barking up the wrong tree. *Titus Andronicus* was on page 222, not *The Merchant of Venice*. And the book exhaled dust as he turned the pages. It hadn't been touched in years, decades even. He put it back. What the hell else could it be? he wondered, scanning the shelves again. "A Daniel come to judgment."

His eyes stopped at a small black Catholic Bible. Even by the candlelight, he could see fingerprints on the binding. He pulled it out and turned to page 222. Joshua reading the law to the people. That wasn't it either. He tried Daniel, Chapter 2, verse 22:

> "He revealeth the deep and secret things: he knoweth what is in the darkness, and the light dwelleth with him."

He stared at the page. Jesus, Raoul, he said to himself. What the hell were you up to? What "deep and secret thing" did you uncover?

He snapped the Bible shut and put it back on the shelf. Raoul had found something all right, he thought, going back to the entry hall and blowing out the candle. And whatever it was, the Germans were on to it too. Because someone had killed Raoul, Cardenas, and now Ceci. And the Germans had killed Hartman. And finding Ceci's name on that matchbox was no coincidence. They were all links in a chain that led to Julia and Arturo Vargas.

Julia.

She was next.

Stewart stepped outside and closed the front door behind him. Smelling the magnolia and seeing the streetlights was like stepping back into time. It wasn't until he was halfway down the block that he realized he was still holding the gun in his hand. He turned toward the nearest building and put it back into the shoulder holster and buttoned his jacket over it. He was sweating heavily and it wasn't just the heat. Something was happening that no one knew about. It was as if they were fighting a battle with surface ships, while all the while the real danger, a U-boat, prowled under the water, unseen and deadly.

He walked quickly toward the Plaza Constitución. Something was urging him on, telling him to hurry, and he had to force himself to keep from running.

Julia.

The night he had spoken with Ceci Braga, she had quoted something Julia had said once: "There are all kinds of war; love is only one."

When he reached the Plaze Constitución, he hailed a taxi in front of the Great Southern Railway station and told the driver to take him to the Church of the Assistance.

24

Montevideo

THE TWO German officers, awkward in civilian clothes, crouched behind the depth-charge racks on the stern deck, waiting for the diversion. *Leutnant* Heiss kept aiming his Naval Luger at the dockworkers below them on the quay, making a soft popping sound with his mouth for each imaginary hit. He turned to Schenck, his eyes burning with excitement.

"So Schenck, what do you think? There will be an aeroplane there, yes?"

"There'd better be," Schenck said, raising his voice to be heard over the hammering of the working crews, still laboring feverishly to repair the *Graf Spee*'s damaged hull and super-structure. Along the docks, a quartet of stevedores were load-ing crates onto a crane pallet, while others stood around, talking and joking.

"Look! This isn't a country, it is a cabaret! What we would load in an hour in Wilhelmshaven, they take three days to do!" Heiss said disgustedly. "Uruguayan shits! We never should have come here."

"What was the alternative? Taking on the whole British navy and the North Atlantic in winter with a hole in our side?" Schenck snapped. He refrained from mentioning that it was Heiss's error in identifying the masts on the horizon as destroyers, instead of cruisers, when they had first spotted the enemy, that had led the *Alte* into the ghastly miscalculation of charging into the range of the enemy's guns in the first place.

"If only we'd had the spotter plane," Heiss sighed. "That was rotten luck, having the engine trouble just when we needed it. But I still say we should have pursued. You know what is the trouble? Jutland."

Schenck looked at him curiously.

"What are you saying?"

"The Battle of Jutland, in the World War. The *Alte* was there," Heiss said wisely. He motioned Schenck closer. "Per-sonally, I think the Englanders have him spooked," he whis-pered.

"That's stupid," Schenck said, but privately he wondered if it might not be true, glancing sideways at Heiss, who grinned wolfishly back at him. Heiss was a bastard, all right, Schenck thought. But he was uncanny at sniffing out weakness in peo-ple. Schenck looked back at the dock, toward the far end where von Hulse was supposed to be waiting with a car be-hind a stack of crates. "It's almost time," Schenck said.

"Good," Heiss said grimly. "I have no intention of spending the remainder of the war interned in this ridiculous banana-land."

Schenck nodded, checking his pistol one last time. He un-derstood Heiss's bitterness, at least. At last night's secret meeting, the wardroom echoed with unvoiced recriminations.

"You have to leave by 1800 hours, tomorrow. There will be no further extensions," Gehrmann, the man from the German embassy in Montevideo, had said. "President Baldomir is adamant. If you have not left, you will be interned."

"This is absurd!" von Hulse snapped irritably, getting up. "Doesn't this Baldomir understand who we are? That this is an insult to our *Führer?*"

"He understands perfectly. Unfortunately, the Uruguayan Red Party doesn't take their instructions from Berlin. It is Roosevelt's backside that they have learned to lick," Gehrmann said.

"That Jew!" Heiss snorted.

"Nevertheless," Gehrmann said, "the English and Americans are strong here. In Montevideo we don't have *Bunds* as in Buenos Aires. Only support from a few Whites. And everyone can read," he added, indicating the newspaper on the table. The headline in the local *El Día* read:

"BRITISH SHIPS 'ARK ROYAL,' 'RENOWN,' ARRIVE IN RIVER PLATE. BATTLE IMMINENT!"

"I know," Captain Langsdorff said wearily, his voice down to a whisper. He seemed to have aged years in the past four days. "I have telegraphed Admiral Raeder for instructions."

"With respect, *Herr Kapitän*. This could be a plant," Schenck said, tapping the newspaper. "I don't believe it."

"Why not?" Captain Langsdorff said, looking at him with interest.

"Why have the British been so anxious to delay our sailing? And since when are their war plans suddenly so public? If one wishes to know what the British Admiralty is planning, it seems one need only pick up a Uruguayan newspaper."

"Or to turn on the BBC," Reinhardt added.

"What are you saying, *Herr Leutnant?*" von Hulse asked.

Schenck leaned forward, his forearms on the table.

"This ship fought well, *meine Herren*. I am certain the big cruiser we put out of action. When we last saw her, she was burning and listing badly and every one of her turrets had been hit. So for all we know," he looked around the table, "the only thing that stands between us and the open sea are two crippled light cruisers."

"If only we had an airplane. Just one," Captain Langsdorff

muttered. "What about the Uruguayan airline? Could we charter, or buy something?"

"Or just take it?" Heiss grinned.

"This swine, Baldomir, has sent troops to guard the airport. It is also thick with English agents," von Hulse said. "But there is something." The others all turned to him. "A tiny airstrip on an *estancia* outside Atlantida, perhaps fifty kilometers from here. There are a couple of old private planes there. The owner is a Jew, of all things," he grinned. "We could be there in forty-five minutes."

"Then what have you been waiting for? Get those planes up!" Captain Langsdorff thundered angrily.

"Unfortunately, we have no one on this side of the River Plate who knows how to fly such aircraft. Or who would know what to look for at sea," von Hulse said. "We were hoping one of your officers, perhaps. . . ."

"I can fly, *Herr Oberst*," Schenck said to von Hulse. He turned to Captain Langsdorff. "I wanted to be an aviator, *Herr Kapitän*. But in those days, because of the Versailles limits, there were twenty applicants for every airplane in the Luftwaffe. But I flew," he explained.

"And I have flown gliders. And once, a small private plane. For the sport," Heiss put in.

"Good. Then it's settled. We have only to arrange something so that we can sneak you both off the ship," von Hulse said, putting his hands on the table to stand up.

"One moment, *bitte*. Aren't we forgetting? What if the English aren't bluffing? What if they have their battleships and aircraft carriers waiting for us. Just as they say? What then?" Gehrmann asked.

"Buenos Aires," von Hulse said into the sudden silence. He turned to Captain Langsdorff. "All you have to do, *Herr Kapitän*, is to make your way across the Plate. Once in Argentine waters, with Castillo as the new President, just as we planned, you will be safe. And," he grinned, "Argentina will be ours. And with Buenos Aires as a base, the entire South Atlantic."

There was a knock on the door. A messenger came in and saluted, then handed a flimsy to Captain Langsdorff. After a moment, he looked up.

"Is it from Admiral Raeder, *Herr Kapitän?*" Reinhardt asked.

Captain Langsdorff shook his head.

"It's from the *Führer* himself. 'No internment in Uruguay. Under no circumstances is the *Graf Spee* to be allowed to fall into British hands,' " he read aloud. He stood up, his hands held rigidly at his sides. "*Meine Herren*, we have our orders." He stared at them, his eyes bloodshot and determined. "No matter what, I will never let the Englanders take this ship," he muttered.

Heiss now nudged Schenck's arm. On the dock, two of the stevedores started shouting and pushing each other. Other workmen started to gather around. One of the stevedores punched the other in the face, drawing blood. The onlookers shouted as the two men began to grapple with each other, pounding away with roundhouse swings. Other laborers and onlookers ran over. But Schenck's eyes were riveted not on the fight, but on the squad of Uruguayan soldiers stationed at the foot of the gangplank. Except for one, who steadfastly kept his eyes on the gangplank, the others were all watching the fight.

"Come on," Heiss said, dropping a rope ladder over the side. He swung over the railing and climbed down. He jumped the last few feet and walked quickly along the wharf toward the crowd. Schenck followed. As soon as his feet touched the dock, a seaman pulled the rope ladder back up.

Schenck walked toward the stack of crates near the warehouse. He felt funny in civilian clothes and very conspicuous. He carried his Luger in a straw basket, as though it were his lunch. He and Heiss made their way around the edge of the crowd. The workmen were all talking and shouting the combatants on. As the two Germans approached the stack of crates, one of the new bullet-shaped Fords pulled out, the rear door open, and the two Germans jumped inside. Von Hulse was in the front seat. He turned around grinning.

"This is Strauss," he said, introducing the driver, who pulled away from the dock area. Strauss stopped at a barrier, handing a pass and a folded banknote to a Uruguayan soldier, who waved them on without even bothering to glance at the pass. Strauss waved back and drove out of the port area, turning onto the Rambla, the broad boulevard that ran along the riverfront. He drove moderately and carefully down the Rambla, past Ramirez Beach, crowded with bathers and vendors, and on the left, across from the beach, the Ferris wheel and merry-go-round and palm-lined greens of Rodo Park.

"It is best not to hurry," Strauss explained, slowing to let a car pull in ahead of him."

"Just get us there," Heiss said, snapping the mechanism on his Luger.

The traffic on the Rambla was mostly Twenties-vintage cars and mule-drawn wagons. Men in straw hats strolled the promenade, eating ice-cream and eyeing the girls in their summer dresses. Low apartment buildings and shops lined the side of the street facing the beaches. Many of the shops were decorated with cardboard Santa Clauses and fake snow. Outside one of the shops, a man with an accordian played "Silent Night," that most German of Christmas carols, plucking at Schenck with a sudden pang of homesickness. Strauss glanced at them in the rear-view mirror and speeded up, not saying anything.

Near Carrasco, the Rambla was bordered by elegant old houses shaded by plane trees and the beach side was empty, with high sand dunes running parallel to the river.

"A pretty country," Schenck commented.

"*Ja*. A pity to waste it on such a shit people," Heiss said.

"First Argentina," von Hulse smiled. "Then Uruguay becomes a mere *Nachspeise*, for the dessert."

After Carrasco, the road turned inland, rising and falling over low rounded hills, brown from the summer sun. The traffic thinned out and they were alone on the road, except for an occasional farm wagon. After half an hour, there were no more villages. It was cattle and sheep country. Cattle lay in shade under the trees, and every now and then they would pass a lonely *hacienda*, white and red-tiled in the sun. Ahead, they could see the outskirts of woodlands and white patches that were sheep grazing in the open fields.

Strauss slowed and turned off onto a bumpy side road that led between tall stands of pine and eucalyptus trees, the eucalyptus bark hanging down in long curling shreds. The car raised a cloud of dust behind it. Everyone began to tense up.

"Where is everybody?" Schenck asked. "I thought this was a working *rancho*."

"Work and Uruguayans!" Strauss snorted. "That is a contradiction in terms."

"It is siesta time. We planned it so, to make it easy. Look! There is the airstrip," von Hulse said, pointing to an opening in the trees. Through the gap they could see a rusty tractor

and an old Model-T Ford resting on the grass. Two small
planes, one a Moth biplane, the other a battered Avro Avian,
sat by a cleared dusty space next to a wooden hut. A drooping
wind sock hung from a pole near the hut. There was no one in
sight. Strauss started to turn off the track.

"Stop the car!" Schenck said.

"What are you talking about, Schenck?" von Hulse said,
turning around.

"I don't like it. Even if they're sleeping, they have to be
somewhere."

"It's good," Strauss insisted. "What do you think? That we
called ahead to let them know we were coming? Don't worry
so much!"

"Stop the car!" von Hulse commanded, anxiously scanning
the tree line. "He could be right."

Strauss slowed to a stop. Schenck got out, crouching and
using the car for cover. He ran doubled over toward the tree
line. When he got there, he signalled to them and disappeared
into the foliage. Strauss drove on to the hut.

The three Germans got out of the car and surrounded the
hut. Von Hulse nodded to Strauss, who crashed the door open
and jumped inside, waving his gun. The hut was empty.
Strauss stepped back out. The three Germans started toward
the airplanes. They had just passed the Model-T when the
sound of a gun being cocked froze them in their tracks.

"Don't move! Drop the guns!" a voice ordered in English.

Heiss whirled and fired, just missing.

"Drop it, old boy! Or Señor Levy here will blow you apart!
Come on! Hands in the air!" the Englishman said, coming
foward. Next to him was a scowling heavy-set man in farm
clothes, leveling a double-barreled shotgun at them. The three
Germans dropped their guns and raised their hands high. Von
Hulse's eyes narrowed.

"Herr Fowler. What are you doing on this side of the River
Plate?"

"Might ask you the same thing, old bean," Fowler said,
motioning them to step back away from their guns. "Careful
now. Don't try anything silly."

Fowler knelt and picked up their guns.

"It was *ein Falle*, the set-up," von Hulse said.

" 'Fraid so," Fowler allowed himself a small smile. "We
knew you'd be desperate to get an airplane up. Stood to rea-

son. But while we tried to cover virtually every aircraft in Uruguay, of which, fortunately, there aren't that many, we knew you'd be bound to try something. So we leaked the information about Señor Levy's aircraft. We knew it would get to Señor Strauss. I'm afraid our people here have had you under surveillance for some time, Señor Strauss. Oh, I'd appreciate it if you chaps would move away from the aircraft."

"You are going to shoot us, *nicht wahr?*" Heiss said.

"Just step away from the airplanes, please," Fowler said, motioning with his gun. The three Germans glanced at each other. Behind Fowler and Levy, they could see Schenck creeping slowly through the grass. They tried to avoid looking at him. "Come on. We don't want to damage anything," Fowler said sharply.

Suddenly, Heiss dropped his hands. He took a step toward Fowler.

"If you are going to shoot me, do it now. Only don't expect me to make it easier for you. You and your pet Jew," Heiss said, spitting a large gob of spit on the ground.

Fowler's face contorted.

"My God, that's disgusting," he shuddered. "It's teeming with germs," he said, aiming the gun at Heiss's face.

"Drop it, *Englander!*" Schenck shouted from behind.

Fowler whirled and fired, but it was too late as Schenck's bullet smashed into his shoulder, spoiling his aim and staggering him. Von Hulse hit the dirt. Heiss dived headfirst for his Luger. Strauss started to run toward the hut till the blast from both barrels of Levy's shotgun almost cut him in half. Fowler fired at Heiss, the shot going wild as a bullet from Schenck ripped through his throat. Fowler was dead before he hit the ground. Levy struggled to reload the shotgun. Schenck fired again, the bullet hitting Levy's thigh, knocking him off his feet, the shotgun clattering, breech still open, to the ground.

Heiss grabbed his Luger and stood over Levy, who held his hands up, trembling, in front of him, as though they could ward off a bullet.

"No, don't!" Schenck cried. "Don't!"

Heiss looked contemptuously at Schenck.

"Jutland," he sneered. "Just like the *Alte.*"

"Heiss, wait!" Schenck shouted.

Heiss looked down at Levy. He wrinkled his nose in disgust as the Jew lay there, whimpering.

"Filthy Jew," Heiss muttered and fired. The bullet ripped through Levy's hand and into his head.

Schenck came toward Heiss, his face grim and set. Von Hulse, getting up, started to say something, then stopped. The two German officers glared at each other as the distance between them lessened. Heiss opened his mouth to say something, but Schenck brushed past him, knocking him aside as if he weren't there. Schenck stalked over to the Moth. He raised the engine cowling, put his hand in, feeling for something. Then he turned in disgust, went over to the Avian and did the same thing. He came back toward Heiss, his face furious, his hand black with engine grime.

"You imbecile! You *Dummkopf!*" Schenck shouted, spittle spraying from his lips as he came toward Heiss. "The distributor rotors are gone. On both of them. They hid it! We could have questioned the Jew, you *Scheissekopf!*"

Heiss turned pale; he lowered his Luger.

"I didn't know," he stammered. "I thought . . . but he was a Jew!"

"Imbecile!" Schenck shouted, backhanding Heiss savagely across the face. Heiss staggered back, a smear of black like a tire track across his face.

"Don't you touch me! Don't you dare!" Heiss screamed wildly, waving the Luger.

"I wouldn't dirty my hands on you, black as they are. I'll leave it to the *Kapitän* to deal with you," Schenck said, walking past him and toward the Ford. He had only gone a couple of steps when Heiss fired twice. The first bullet hit Schenck in the back. The second took off most of his jaw as he whirled around, the light dying in his eyes as his knees buckled beneath him.

Heiss and von Hulse faced each other. Heiss's chest was heaving, as though he couldn't catch his breath. But the Luger was rock-steady in his hand.

"So! And what about you? Or are you also a Jew-lover?" Heiss demanded harshly.

Von Hulse stared at Heiss for a moment. Suddenly, a slow smile began to break across his face.

"Actually, *Herr Leutnant,* I am thinking of contacting Admiral Canaris himself about you," von Hulse said. "I believe you have a talent for this kind of work."

THE DOORS of the church were wide open, the interior brightly lit like a department store, as though they were having a sale on God. Stewart took off his hat as he stepped inside. Despite the heat, hundreds of candles were burning before a Virgin near the entrance. The church was empty, except for a few older women bent in prayer and an altar boy doing something near the pulpit. Above the altar, a realistic, almost life-sized Christ writhed in agony on his cross. Spanish Catholicism, the real McCoy, Stewart thought, going up to the boy, who led him to the sacristy, then went to find the priest.

"You wished to see me, Señor?" the priest said, coming in. He was younger than Stewart had expected, with dark wavy hair and an energetic manner.

"Father Damiano?" Stewart asked.

The priest frowned for a split-second, then his face smoothed out again.

"I'm Father Martin. Could I help you instead, perhaps?"

"Why? Is there a problem in seeing Father Damiano?"

"No. Clearly no," Father Martin said soothingly, a shade too quickly, Stewart thought. "It's only that Father Damiano isn't," he hesitated, searching for a word, "active." Father Martin smiled. A professional consoler's smile.

"I need to see him, Father. It's urgent."

"I see," Father Martin nodded. "A personal matter." He studied Stewart for a moment, a curious appeal in his eyes. "Is this something of the first urgency, *premioso*, Señor?"

"There's been a death, Father. A murder. There may be others."

"I see," Father Martin said again. "A matter involving the *guardia, pues?*"

Stewart nodded, hoping the priest would take him for a plainsclothes cop.

"Is Father Damiano here?"

Father Martin shook his head.

"He has a small room not far from here. Just off the Calle Arroyo." He told Stewart the address.

"Thank you, Father. Your cooperation is appreciated," Stewart said in an official voice. He went to the door.

"He's a good man," Father Martin called after him.

Stewart stopped at the door and turned around. It was a curious thing to say.

"Aren't most priests?"

"He spent many years in the provinces," Father Martin offered, as though that was an explanation of sorts.

"What happened to him in the provinces?"

Father Martin raised his eyes to a crucifix on the wall.

"Every man carries a cross, Señor. Not only Our Lord."

"Then what's different about Father Damiano, Father?"

"Not every man drives in the nails himself, Señor."

Stewart glanced up at the crucifix.

"No," he agreed, opening the door. "Only the good ones. . . ."

"Go with God," Father Martin said after him, his professional smile back on his face once more.

Stewart left the church. He walked through the steamy tropical night down Juncal towards Esmeralda, then over to the Calle Arroyo. The address was on a street of small apartment buildings and rooming houses; the kind of neighborhood where businessmen keep a room for trysts with their secretaries and people with nowhere else to go finally come to rest.

The house was a two-story building with imitation Colonial railings on the windows and a "Room To Let" sign tacked onto the front door. Stewart checked the names on the mailboxes in the dark hallway. Father Damiano's room was on the ground floor in the back and Stewart had to strike a match to see the name, "Stefano Damiano"—not "Father," not "S.J.," he mused—handwritten on a scrap of paper pasted on the door. Stewart knocked.

"Come in," a voice said.

Stewart opened the door and went inside. It was a dreary room with a bed and a sink and a wooden table with a couple of chairs under a light bulb dangling from a wire. Father Damiano was seated at the table in his undershirt, an open bottle of Orfila in front of him.

"Father Damiano?"

The priest didn't say anything. He was a thin-faced man, who appeared to be in his late sixties. He hadn't shaved and there was a gray stubble on his face. Stewart sat down at the table and Father Damiano poured him a glass of wine and pushed it toward Stewart as though he'd been waiting for him all along. Stewart took the missal out of his pocket and handed it to the priest, who glanced at it without interest.

Father Damiano tossed back his wine, wiping his lips with the back of his hand.

"You are not the man I gave this to. His name was Raoul. Raoul de something," Father Damiano said.

"Raoul de Almayo."

"That's it, de Almayo," the priest nodded. "Where is he?"

"He's dead. Murdered."

The priest nodded again, as if he had expected no less.

"You don't seem surprised, Father?"

"I gave it to him months ago. When he never returned, I. . . ." Father Damiano looked up at Stewart for the first time. His eyes were utterly bleak, a trace of wine on his lips like lipstick. "I thought I had been given a reprieve," he said, lowering his head.

"Reprieve from what, Father?"

"From hell. Dante was right, you know."

"In what way?"

"We make our own," he said, staring at Stewart from under his brows in a way that if he wasn't a priest would have had Stewart reaching for the .45. "You don't fool me, Señor, *tampoco!* I always knew you would come."

"How could you know that, Father?" Stewart said carefully, unbuttoning his jacket in case he had to get at the holster.

The priest drew back, his face twitching as though he had the DTs. The way he stared at the wall behind Stewart almost made Stewart turn around to look.

"I knew someone would come," Father Damiano said. "What difference does it make who?"

"Come for what?"

"I can tell you nothing. Nothing!" he whispered. "That's what I was going to tell the other Señor. The Señor de Almayo."

"Why not?"

Father Damiano smiled, almost triumphantly.

"I can tell you nothing. It is under the seal, understand?"

"The seal of confession?"

"Yes, that."

"And you, Father? Are you also under the seal?"

Father Damiano jumped up, knocking his chair over as he did so. He stared wild-eyed at Stewart.

"Demon! Satan! Get thee behind me!" he cried, holding the missal in front of him like a shield.

"Father Damiano, please!" Stewart shouted, wondering how to break through to him. "You have to help me!"

"Help you? Help you?"

"Yes, Father. Listen. Someone is killing people. I have to stop him before he kills again."

"The seal, Señor! The seal is a sacrament!"

"Hitler doesn't believe in sacraments, Father," Stewart said. "To help stop him, God will forgive much, I think."

Father Damiano stared at Stewart, his brow furrowed.

"Why tell me this, Señor? Why come to me?"

"Because I don't know where else to go."

Father Damiano righted his chair and sat back down. He refilled their glasses and they both drank.

"Salud!"

"Salud."

When Father Damiano looked up at Stewart, his eyes were very old and sad.

"Do you know why this Raoul came, Señor. . . ?"

"Stewart. Charles Stewart. In Spanish, Carlos."

Father Damiano nodded.

"I remember your Señor de Almayo. He was a nervous man. A sinful man, I think. I did not like him. Are you a sinful man, Señor Stewart?"

Stewart looked into the priest's eyes.

"Yes. I am."

Father Damiano smiled faintly.

"There is no other kind. Do you know why he came, this Raoul de Almayo?"

Stewart started to shake his head no, then stopped. He had an incredible idea. It was as if all the pieces in this bizarre affair were beginning to implode into a single shape.

"Gideon? Does this all have something to do with John Gideon?"

Father Damiano stared at him, horror-struck.

"You know!" he cried. "After all these years, you know!"

"Not enough!"

"Now it begins," Father Damiano whispered. "First comes one, this Raoul. Now you. And if not you, another. No matter how deep you bury the truth, sooner or later, like Lazarus it comes crawling out of its grave."

"Whose grave, Father?"

"Ours, Señor Stewart. There is only one grave," the priest said.

The two men sat quietly over the wine in the stifling hot room. From an apartment upstairs came the smell of steak frying in a pan and the faint echo of a record, something from the Twenties, "The Sheik of Araby," being played over and over on a victrola.

"This all happened long ago. More than thirty years now," Father Damiano began. "I was a young man then, fresh out of seminary. My superiors had posted me to Lujan. Do you know Lujan, Señor?"

Stewart shook his head.

"It's a colonial town. Very pretty. Once, long ago, when the Spanish first came, a *burro* pulling a wagon carrying a statue of the Virgin stopped and could not be made to move from the spot, no matter what anyone tried. It was taken for a miracle. People still come.

"But for me, back then," he sighed, "to be sent to the provinces was like a prison sentence. I was certain Our Lord had big things, important things in store for me. Back then, Señor, I was certain of many things."

"You sound like an old man, Father."

"I am fifty-five years old, Señor."

Stewart stared at him, shocked. The priest looked at least ten years older than that.

"About Lujan, Father?"

"Lujan," the priest nodded. "I was the priest there, at the Compania, the old Jesuit church. Also, I was assigned as the chaplain of the *Misericordia* of the Sisters of Santa Catarina, which was outside the village, on the Pampa."

"A hospital?"

"No, Señor Stewart. A *casa de orates*. An insane asylum," the priest said, reaching for the wine. "You must understand,

Señor. I knew nothing of such things. But I consoled myself
with the thought that it was only for a brief time and would
not matter. For me, the provinces were a way station. Once I
got back to Buenos Aires, then my real career would begin.
How could I know what a precarious thing a man's soul is,
pues? That it can be shattered in an instant like Venetian
glass. I, who was so certain of everything. How could I know?"

"You met Gideon?"

"Not ever."

"And it shattered your life?"

"You cannot imagine the manner of man he was, Señor."

"I am beginning to," Stewart said.

"His whole life was a war. I think he believed life *is* war. He
may have been the ultimate Darwinian."

"War against whom, Father?"

"Against God," Father Damiano said, leaning forward, the
shadows sliding along the creases in his face.

"What happened?" Stewart prompted. "At the *casa de
orates?*"

"A night. Just one. A winter night," Father Damiano remembered. "I was doing accounts in the church. Bitter cold,
it was. The wind blew through the cracks in the walls and I
remember I had to keep stopping to warm my fingers with my
breath. I had just decided to go to bed early, when there was
a knock on the outside door.

"Someone's died, I remember thinking. Why else send for a
priest on such a night? Why couldn't he have picked some
other night, I grumbled to myself as I went to get my breviary
and stole, just in case. But it was Sister Maria Jose from the
Misericordia. I will never forget the way she looked standing
in the doorway, her cloak billowing in the night wind.

" 'You have to come, Father. At once,' she told me.

" 'What is it?' I asked, pulling on my coat.

" 'You will see,' she said, turning on her heel and walking
quickly. Although she was a small woman, tiny, really, I had
to hurry to keep up with her.

"The village streets were deserted, and I remember the
moon reflected in an icy puddle. The wind howled around the
corners of the houses and the only other sound was a dog,
barking in the darkness.

" 'Is it a death?' I asked her, as we hurried down the road,
the ruts under our feet frozen hard as iron.

" 'Neither death, nor birth. An aftermath, more like,' she muttered. I could see her breath in the cold.

" 'A baptism, *pues?*' I asked.

" 'There'll be no baptisms, Father.' She motioned me closer. Her eyes sparkled. Whether with religious fervor, or malice, or pleasure in another's misfortune, I couldn't say. But I could see she wanted to tell me. 'It's the mother,' she whispered. 'She was big with child when she came to us. And of a family of much importance,' she said, rolling her eyes. She had a trace of Indian blood in her cheekbones, Sister Maria Jose, and I could see that the family's wealth had impressed her. 'It happens sometimes,' she told me. 'Women of good family who fall from grace and are brought to us to have the baby in secret. Then, they are taken away and an adoption arranged and that is the end of it. But not with this one.'

" 'What was different in this case?' I asked.

"She motioned me yet closer. I had to bend over as we walked, so small she was.

" 'They say she tried to destroy the child before it was born. Or failing that, herself. We have to watch her night and day. She has a devil, that one,' she whispered.

"A chill went through me when she said that, that had nothing to do with the wind or the night. These country people were all superstitious. Normally, I paid no attention to such talk. But this time, I couldn't help myself.

" 'What happened?' I asked her. She just shrugged.

" 'A child was born four nights ago. A girl. That same night, a man came by horse from Buenos Aires. A big man, dressed in black.'

" 'Who was he?'

" 'No one saw him except Mother Superior. But everyone heard him cursing when he learned the child was a female.'

" 'He wanted a boy?'

" 'Of course. It is the natural thing.'

" 'And then?'

" 'He said, "She'll have to do," or words to that effect. The baby, he took away that same night. Out into the cold, that poor little thing. But the woman was to remain with us.'

" 'Why?' I asked. 'Is she mad?'

"Sister Maria Jose's eyes darted about, like dark birds in a cage. I smiled to reassure her.

" 'At first, we thought not,' she said. 'But when the woman

learned he had taken the child, she went wild. She was screaming and throwing things and ripping apart the fine clothes she had brought with her bare fingernails. Like an animal she was, Father. We had to remove everything from her room and keep her locked in, the way we do for only the most dangerous patients. Even so, two nights later, she tried to commit suicide.'

" 'But how? I thought you removed everything.'

"A grim knowing look came to Sister Maria Jose's eyes.

" 'You don't know this one, Father. She bit open the veins in her wrists with her teeth. We almost lost her.'

" 'And now?'

" 'She wants a priest. To make confession,' Sister Maria Jose said.

"We came to the outskirts of the village and walked the road to the Misericordia. The light from the windows of the asylum was the only light in the vast darkness, except for the icy glitter of the moon and stars. Winter on our Pampa, Señor, shows us the unbearable loneliness of eternity. The emptiness!" Father Damiano whispered, his eyes wide with horror. "That's why God made the world," he nodded desperately. "An emptiness so profound, even *He* couldn't stand it!"

"What happened at the *casa de orates?*" Stewart prompted.

"Another nun, Sister Marco, let us in. Sister Maria Jose took me to a separate wing, locked off from the rest of the building. She led me down a long corridor, cold and utterly silent, to a heavy wooden door at the end of the passage. The door was locked and barred. It was like the entrance to a tomb.

" 'Why is she being kept locked up like this?' I asked, unable to suppress a shudder. It was awful there.

" 'Orders,' Sister Maria Jose said.

" 'Whose orders?'

"She smiled shrewdly. In her smile I could see the peasant girl she had been, a daughter of *colonos* tenant farmers. 'This man in black, Father. He was an *hidalgo*, a man of importance,' she said.

" 'I understand.'

" 'Clearly. I come from the Catamarca, Father. There we say, "The *Comisario*'s horse always wins." '

" 'In Buenos Aires, we say the same,' I told her. 'But all this,' I gestured at the barred door. 'I don't understand.'

" 'You will,' she said, raising the iron bar and turning a

large iron key in the lock. I went inside, very conscious as I did so of the door being closed and locked behind me. And then I saw the woman, her face lit by a single candle, and I understood what the Sister was trying to tell me.

"She looked up and straight at me, the way a deer does, and I had to breathe through my mouth to get enough air. She was very beautiful. Not merely beautiful, you understand? She was beyond that. She was the kind of beauty you might glimpse once in a lifetime on a street somewhere and not forget till the day you die. Her hair was black and very long and her face was oval, like a Renaissance madonna's. She was very young, in her early twenties at most. The same age as I was then. She wore a white lace dress and priest and all, I couldn't take my eyes off her. That such a creature should be in such a place was beyond believing. If it weren't for the bandages that were still on her wrists, I wouldn't have believed any of it.

" 'I have come to hear. . . .' I started to say.

" 'I know why you have come,' she said. The sound of her voice made me tremble. It was low and silky soft. When she spoke, it was as if she touched you."

"I know," Stewart murmured, barely breathing. Father Damiano stared at him for a moment, as though they were accomplices in some terrible crime. He took a sip of wine and went on.

"There was a wooden screen in the room, with a velvet kneeling stool on one side and a chair on the other. I went behind the screen and sat down. There was a rustle of silk from the other side of the screen as she knelt. It sent shivers up my spine to hear it.

" 'Begin, my child,' I said. I was barely able to talk. God had sent me into this room. I could feel it.

" 'Bless me, Father, for we have sinned,' she said in that extraordinary voice.

" 'We? Sin is personal, not collective,' I said, thinking I couldn't have heard her right. It was blasphemy.

" 'We is you and I, Father. What we do. What we are about to do,' she said and there was more rustling of silk.

"Do you understand? Do you understand, Señor?" Father Damiano demanded, staring at Stewart. "I could hardly breathe. She was a vision, beyond imagining. My vision! My priest's vision that my whole life had been built on denying, turned into flesh and blood. It was as if the Devil himself had peered into the innermost crevice of my heart and found her image hidden there, looking exactly what I most loved and desired: the Virgin Bride of God Himself! I tried to get control. I tried!

" 'Remember yourself, daughter. How . . . how long has it been since your last confession?' I said, nearly strangling on the words.

" 'Too long,' she answered, coming around the screen, and I knew I was lost forever. She was utterly naked. Her eyes were deepest blue and brilliant. She devoured me with her eyes.

" 'Stay away!' I cried, getting up and backing away. 'I want you to. . . .'

" 'I know what you want,' she said, kneeling at my feet. 'I know what you all want,' leaning forward, her breasts swinging free, her breath warm on my trousers.

" 'It's a sin!' I said. 'A terrible sin!'

"She looked up at me.

" 'That's the best part,' she said, touching me. I had never felt anything like that touch. It burned and cooled at the same time. Her breast grazed my hand, the nipple just barely touching, and I couldn't resist. I plucked it like a flower. And then we were at each other like savages. I was on top of her on the cold stone floor, the two of us scorching each other, and as I entered her, the word she screamed was 'God!' and when I erupted inside her, it was like a sacrament of sin."

Father Damiano slumped heavily in his chair.

"That was all," he added, in a parched dead voice. "Except for the knowing expression on Sister Maria Jose's face when I left, though how she knew I don't know. That, and the sure and certain knowledge that I was damned to everlasting hell for all eternity."

"Because of a single sin?" Stewart objected. "Surely. . . ."

"No!" Father Damiano said. "You don't understand. It wasn't just the one time. We were lovers," he rasped. "For a quarter of a century we were lovers. Every time I was there. It's why I stayed all those years in the provinces. Because I loved her!"

"But surely God in his infinite mercy . . ."

"No! Because it wasn't God I loved, but Satan! Because I loved her more than God! I loved the *sin* of loving her more than I loved God! And this, Señor," Father Damiano shook a warning finger in the air, "God will not forgive!"

The two men sat there in silence. In the apartment upstairs, the record came to an end. Stewart reached for his glass and drained it.

"The woman? She was Gideon's daughter?" he asked finally.

"Lucia, yes," Father Damiano nodded. "Lucia de Montoya-Gideon. His daughter."

"And the baby? The one he took away?"

"Julia. He named her Julia. He told the Mother Superior he was naming her after another who had died. Judith, I think."

Stewart put his glass down and wiped his face with a handkerchief. The room was hot as a steambath.

"I still don't get it, Father. Raoul came to see you only a couple of months ago. People are getting killed over this now and somehow the Nazis are involved. Why? Everyone is dead. Gideon is dead. This poor woman, this Lucia, is dead. . . ."

Father Damiano looked curiously at Stewart.

"You are mistaken, Señor. Gideon's daughter, Lucia de Montoya-Gideon, is still very much alive."

26

THE ROAD to Lujan was straight as a line on a map. On either side of the road lay the Pampa, flat and endlessly green. There were no towns, no trees, no roadside *tiendas*. Only blue-tipped grass and barbed wire fences strung taut and straight as a bricklayer's line and at intervals as regular as kilometer markers, iron windmills, the only things to break the line of the horizon.

As Stewart drove, all he could think about was his conversation over the telephone with Julia. At first, she was fine.

How goes it?

Everything is well. We'll be leaving for the estancia *shortly to get ready for the fiesta. Dido's here. Also Athena. She's been singing "We're Going to Hang out the Washing on the Siegfried Line," all day. It's driving Arturo crazy.*

What about the children? Are they well?

They're here. We've brought them down from school. God, they're so bonito *in their school jackets. One moment, I'm coming,* she called to someone.

Her voice changed suddenly.

I have to see you. What happened?

I was arrested again.

Oh, no!

It's all right. I'm out. You heard about the Graf Spee?

Yes, everyone's talking. Her voice dropped to a whisper. *Whatever they are planning is still on. Hurry,* yanqui!

Julia? Ceci is dead.

The line went silent. He could hear the faint chirps of music from a radio through the receiver.

Julia? Julia?

I'm here, she said finally.

Take care. Keep the children close.

Oh God, yanqui! *What are we going to do? I can't stand him. I cringe when he comes near me and afterwards, I want to wash where he's touched me till the skin comes off. All I think about is you. I'd rather be back in that filthy* frigorifico. . . .

Julia? Would you leave him?

Silence.

Julia?

Ceci loved to play the man, yanqui. *I think she liked the power of it. She liked me to swing my hips and make a Cupid's Bow mouth and bat my eyelashes like a* puta, *a caricature of a woman. Like Arturo and his* machismo *is a caricature of a man. And how is it with you,* yanqui? *What kind of fantasy am I for you?*

I love you.

You don't have to say it, yanqui. *I'll sleep with you anyway.*

I know.

Who invented love anyway? Christ? No wonder they crucified him.

Julia . . . he started to tell her about her mother, but something stopped him. *I have to do something. I'll need a car.*

Do you want the Dusenberg?

Too conspicuous. Is there something else?

I have a little Morris-Oxford I keep for running around town. I'll leave it outside the gate with the key on the floorboard.

Hasta mañana, pues. *Til tomorrow,* he whispered.

Yanqui?

Yes?

Come soon.

Now more than ever, he felt conversation not as what was said, but what wasn't said. It existed not in words, but in the spaces between the words. He felt her slipping through the spaces.

Julia?

I'm here.

Would you leave Argentina?

He could hear her breathing over the line.

What about the war?

There wasn't any answer to that so he didn't say anything. After a moment, she replaced the receiver on the hook.

Stewart slowed as he came up behind a horse and wagon. He pulled around it and sped on. The road ahead was flat and empty for as far as could be seen.

Julia's point was both simple and stunning. Her or the Raven. He couldn't have both. She was the link. And the *Graf Spee* was proof of just how important it was. If he didn't mind sharing, he could screw her all he wanted and still fight the Nazis. But if he wanted her to himself, to love her, to save her—Go on, admit it, he told himself. Sir Galahad, Defender of the Faith and Adulterous Wives and never mind that you're getting your own *cojones* off on it—then he had to walk away from what was turning into the biggest break of the war.

Which war?

The one against the Germans, or the one he was driving to? The Raven's other war. The one that had already killed Raoul and Cardenas and Ceci Braga. And maybe even Hartman, too. And time running out on all of them. The coup against Ortiz was set for tomorrow.

Would you leave Argentina? he had asked her.

The only way to leave Argentina is to die, Raoul had written. Stewart stepped down on the accelerator. Ahead, he could see the buildings on the outskirts of Lujan.

Stewart crossed the bridge over the muddy Rio Lujan and into the town. Lujan was an attractive colonial village, with cobbled streets and red-tiled houses and shady trees along the river bank. He drove down the Calle Constitución past the cathedral and stopped for lunch at the café not far from the old Cabildo. He ordered a sandwich and a beer and read the papers till the waiter came with the food.

It looked as though the Finns were putting up a hell of a fight at Suomussalmi. *This is no time for small countries,* Julia had said in the Dusenberg that night on the way to Tigre. In Buenos Aires, three bodies had been pulled out of the Riachuelo. Hartman and the two krauts, Stewart thought. Rival *compadritos,* the paper said, playing up the gangster side of it with lurid descriptions of bullet-riddled bodies. Nothing about Germans. That was Fuentes's fine hand, Stewart thought, finishing a cigarette.

When the waiter came for the bill, Stewart asked directions to the Misericordia. The waiter told him, giving him a funny look as he did so. You had to expect that, asking about a *casa de orates,* Stewart told himself. He left the café and drove to the outskirts of the town.

The Misericordia didn't look as Father Damiano had described it. Stewart had expected to find it isolated on a vast empty plain. Instead, there were streets and houses all around the walls. Over the years, the town had encroached upon the Misericordia grounds. Stewart parked the car and went to the front gate. It was locked, and he pulled a bellrope that clanged softly on the other side of the wall.

A nun in a black habit admitted him and led him through a well tended garden courtyard to a large white building. Three women were sitting under the trees. One was young, pregnant. She was staring at a dry fountain with a look of unutterable boredom, her hands resting on her bulging abdomen in the complacent way pregnant women have. Her companion, an older woman in black, was chattering and knitting non-stop. She seemed perfectly normal, except that there was no wool on the needles. The third woman lay on the grass. She was olive-skinned and pretty, voluptuous even. As Stewart walked by, she said: "I hate you, you bitch!" to the nun.

"I'm sure you don't mean that, Antonia. You're only saying that because there's a visitor," the nun said, glancing back at Stewart to see how he was taking it. She led him into the building and disappeared into an office. A moment later, she was back and gestured for him to go in.

An elderly nun, he assumed it was the Mother Superior, was

seated behind a desk. She was a small woman, so small he wondered if her feet behind the desk touched the floor. She had sharp eyes and dark skin of the kind Argentines call "Negrita." Stewart had a sudden intuition she might be the Sister Maria Jose that Father Damiano had told him about.

"Why do you wish to see the Señora de Montoya-Gideon, Señor?"

"People are being killed, Mother Superior. She may know something. I spoke with Father Damiano," Stewart offered, by way of explanation.

"We have orders to keep her isolated."

"The man who gave those orders died a long time ago, Mother Superior. Why is she still here?"

"It was the family's wish, Señor."

Stewart looked sharply at her. What family? There was only Julia and Arturo.

"Truly?"

"Truly, Señor. And also," the Mother Superior hesitated, "she has been here almost all of her adult life. For her, the world stopped in 1908. Think of this modern world, with its telephones and radios and wars, Señor. How could she. . . ." she pursed her lips. "In any case, this is her home, Señor."

"Is she mad?"

The Mother Superior picked up a rosary, her fingers counting off the beads quickly and automatically, like a pea-sheller in a factory.

"I do not know, Señor. In this place, questions like that are not so clear. She is not like you or me, though. Tell me, Señor. Do you believe in God? Truly?"

Stewart hesitated. It was a test of some kind. Only by giving the right answer was she going to let him see her.

"No, Mother Superior. Not after Spain."

Her face tightened.

"God triumphed in Spain, Señor," she said sternly. "Franco brought back the Church."

"Perhaps He did triumph, Mother Maria Jose. Maybe I just don't like His methods."

The Mother Superior smiled strangely, her eyebrows raised, as if his knowing her name was a surprise, but not an exceptional one.

"Less bad, though you are mistaken. If you believed in God, you would understand things here differently."

"I know the daughter, Julia. Also, Father Damiano," Stew-

art said. "Lives are at stake. Maybe more than lives. Besides,"
he smiled. "Don't you want to know how it turns out, *pues?*"

Her face cracked into a smile and a network of wrinkles.
"They say the Devil is a charmer. I see it is true," she said,
getting up. "Come. Perhaps even a fool of an atheist can shed
some light." She came around the desk, jangling a set of keys
on a large ring. She was very short; in her dark habit and
bustling manner, she was like an ancient child.

She led him down a long dim corridor to a door, which she
unlocked. Beyond it, at right angles, was another corridor.
Silence lay over the corridor like dust. Just before they came
to another door, the Mother Superior motioned Stewart into
an alcove with a plaster madonna set below a wooden shutter
that opened to the outside. They stood in bars of dusty sunlight coming through the slats, and when she spoke, Stewart
could see her words swirling the dust in the light.

"She is unused to outsiders, Señor. Do you understand?"

"I understand, Mother Superior."

"No," she shook her head. "I don't think you do. She has
been waiting for something—I don't know what—all these
years. You must be very careful, Señor." She went to a heavy
wooden door across the corridor, unlocked it and let him in.

The room was cool and dim, despite the heat outside. It
contained a few pieces of furniture, a commode, a bed; the
walls were white and bare, except for an ornate silver crucifix.
A woman was seated near the window, a book in her lap.

"Lucia," the Mother Superior said. "You have a visitor."

The woman looked up. The sight of her struck Stewart almost like a physical blow. He had been expecting an old
woman, a mad ancient crone out of *Macbeth*. Instead, she was
slim, beautiful in a middle-aged way, and he could see fragments of Julia in her face, like a partially completed mosaic.
Her face was curious, without lines. It looked unused, almost.
She appeared to be about fifty years old and her hair was too
young for her face. She wore it very long and curled in a way
that women hadn't done since before the Twenties. She had
strange blue eyes; they were striking, but they weren't Julia's.

"I'll leave you two. Call if you need me," the Mother Superior said, closing the door behind her as she left.

Lucia looked at Stewart across a ray of sunlight embedded
in the stone floor like a spear.

"You are neither Gideon nor Montoya," she said. Her voice

sent shudders through him. It was Julia's voice. She's divided the world into two, Stewart thought. Gideons and Montoyas. The third part, everyone else, didn't matter.

"No, Señora. But I know your daughter, Julia."

She ignored that.

"Did *he* send you?"

He wasn't sure who she meant. The priest, maybe.

"No one sent me, Señora. I learned of you from Father Damiano."

A curious cat-ate-the-cream smile came over her face, something between recognition and complicity.

"God, he had such a lovely penis for a priest. When he put it inside me, I would close my eyes so I could imagine it better, moving in and out of me. This book of Señor Hardy's," her tone changed suddenly. She indicated the book in her lap. "This Tess. Do you think she should have killed D'Urberville?"

"I never understood why she loved such a man in the first place," Stewart said, coming forward.

"You have no idea, Señor," she smiled, "of the capacity of women to lie to themselves when it comes to men. I like the way it ends, though, at Stonehenge. A place of human sacrifice. That's what the world is about, no? Children sacrificed to their fathers' gods? Abraham and Isaac. God and Jesus. Always the innocent child who must die! But what of the Father? Isn't He ever wrong? Ever? Go tell my father, Señor! I am also a Gideon! I do not forgive!" she declared imperiously, clutching the book in her hand like a weapon. "I will never forgive!"

"Forgive what, Señora?"

She looked at him, surprised.

"He destroyed them all, you know. One by one. Even my husband. Poor Federico," she shook her head sadly. "*Tu sabes*, after the wedding, we could not consummate the marriage. I was already with child and my father sent him to Paris. 'On business,' he said, but there was no business there. He wrote me. Twice. 'Paris is *maravilloso*,'" she quoted, closing her eyes and reciting it verbatim in the way of something read over and over again so often that remembering takes no effort. "'The tango is the rage of *tout* Paris and we have so much money compared to here, the French have a new expression, *riche comme un Argentin*. Everyone is *bien amusant* and is

looking forward to your coming here after the baby comes.'
Then nothing for five years, until finally, a postcard: 'Things
have turned against me, *querida*. They are taking me for a
poilu, though I am not French. I embrace you.' Someone told
me he died in a war there. He went there in a taxi. It seems
there was a war in Europe long ago."

"There's a war there now, Señora."

"Ah," she nodded. "A long war, *pues*."

"No, Señora. A different war."

"Did my father start it?"

He looked curiously at her, but apparently she was quite
serious.

"No, Señora."

"Don't be so certain. He got them all, you know. Even old
Cesar Montoya himself," she assured him. "He never recovered from the death of his son. An *escándalo*," she whispered.
"The son killed himself in a bordello. He was wearing a woman's dress. My father took over Cesar's business. Ruined him.
They say he died mad," she nodded, looking around as if
afraid to be overheard. "From the syphilis. Others said it was
the cocaine. They say he took too much of it. The only one who
survived was the daughter, Angelica. She married someone of
no importance. They had a son, but I don't know what happened to them," she shrugged. "His name was Vargas, I
think."

Stewart knew that. The son was Arturo. So why did hearing
her say it make his flesh crawl?

"Your daughter, Señora. Julia. She married Vargas. The
son."

Lucia stared at the bare white wall. Suddenly, she began to
shake. It was frightening to watch, and Stewart started to go
over to her, until he realized that she was laughing silently,
terrible violently suppressed laughter.

"Of course," she gasped, still shaking. Tears slid down her
cheeks. "What better way to destroy someone than to marry
him?" She turned to Stewart. "I still have the two pennies,"
she said. "That's why he can't destroy me!"

"What pennies, Señora?"

Her face hardened. She looked suspiciously at him.

"You have an accent in Spanish. Are you from Hell? My
father told me once it was near Russia, or Turkey, *pues*. He
comes to me at night to try and get them back. As a raven,
black as death. Why do you think he called it 'Ravenwood'?"

"Who comes to you, Señora?"

She smiled strangely at him.

"That's the secret! That God and the Devil are one and the same. That's why there's good and evil. The raven tells me things. My father sends him."

"Señora," Stewart bit his lip. "John Gideon is dead. He died a long time ago."

She made an impatient face.

"Yes. They told me that. Mother Superior told me. But what does she know? She still believes that there are invisible angels watching everything we do and if you touch yourself where only a husband is permitted to touch you, you will go blind. Besides," she said. "They didn't know him. He couldn't die."

"It's true," Stewart said. "If he were alive, he'd be a hundred years old."

"*Qué va?* What of it? You don't know him either," she said, contemptuously. "You don't know anything! Why do you think he took her away from me? That tiny white creature? Don't you know why? Even Mother Maria Jose doesn't know," she said craftily.

"Why did he take Julia away, Señora?"

"Even God doesn't know," she said, getting up from the chair. "That's why He comes every night with His black wings beating. But I won't tell Him. I won't tell you, either. Who are you, Señor? What are you doing here?" She came forward, stepping into the ray of sunlight that lit her head like a medieval religious painting. "I know who you are," she said suddenly. "You're a soldier, like my husband. It's the war, that's why you're here!"

"Yes, Señora. Also for your daughter."

"Do you love her?"

That question again.

"I'm not sure."

"That's a lie," she smiled. It was uncanny. She didn't look like Julia, but it was Julia's smile. "You love her, *verdad?* More fool you. This war you're fighting?"

"Señora?"

"You're going to die in this war," she said, her face serene in the light.

He felt a ripple of fear go through him when she said that. He tried to shake it off.

"About your daughter, Señora?"

Instead of answering, she went and sat down and opened her book again. She looked up at him just once.

"He has you in his claws, you know. My father," she said. "You just don't know it."

December 17, 1939
Ravenwood

STEWART WAS cantering figure-eights and getting his pony used to the mallet when Vargas walked into the paddock area. With him was a tall Argentine, tanned, very handsome, with the kind of thick wavy hair that women like to run their fingers through.

"*Hola*, Don Carlos! What do you think?" Vargas asked. He was talking about the pony.

"He's a little big. What is he? Fifteen and a half hands?"

Vargas smiled; the tight smile of someone who has anticipated a question he doesn't think is fair.

"Fifteen and three-fourths. Is he too much horse?"

Stewart brought the pony to a halt. It hurt a little, using the double reins with his injured fingers, but he liked the way the horse stopped and started, not fighting the bit, and that he showed no fear of the mallet.

"He's all right. I've put a martingale on him and I can reach down."

"You know Giancarlo Paretti, of course," Vargas said, and the tall Argentine smiled.

"Ten-handicap players are hard to miss. How are you, Don Giancarlo?"

"Charlie Stewart! It's been a long time since Meadowbrook," Paretti said, shaking his hand. "Where have you been hiding yourself?"

"I was in Europe until a few weeks ago."

"Truly," Paretti said politely. "Are they still playing polo in Europe?"

"No. Nobody's playing anything there any more." Stewart squinted at Vargas. The sun was high overhead and Stewart could feel his skin burning even under his shirt and riding breeches. "Where's President Ortiz? Couldn't he come?"

A dangerous look came into Vargas's eyes.

"He's coming. He has to, or he's through with the *Concordancia*. But he'll be here, I'm sure. He sent word with Colonel Fuentes, whom I believe you know. But Castillo is here. Everyone is," he said, gesturing jerkily to the side of the field where private viewing stands had been set up. The stands were decorated for Christmas, with grape ivy and poinsettias substituting for holly, and striped awnings had been set over them for shade. Beyond the stands, Stewart could see the gardens and tennis courts and the *hacienda*. Although he had been among wealthy people before, he had never seen anything like Ravenwood.

The grounds were immense and carefully landscaped with trees and shrubs from all over the world. In addition to the tennis courts and polo field and stables, there were three swimming pools, a private lake stocked with trout, dorado and an incredible fighting bass called *"tararira,"* and a private golf course, all separated by avenues of trees from the rest of the ranch. Dominating everything was the immense white house, built on three sides around a courtyard with an enormous towering *ombu* tree in the center.

The house itself was decorated like a French château, except for the paintings on the walls, which were mostly Impressionists, Van Gogh, Cézanne, Monet, Sisley, Renoir. There was a giant Christmas tree in the entry hall and another in the ballroom. Buffet tables had been set up by the polo field. Two whole roasted cows were turned on giants spits over open pits, and the tables were set with Porthault linen, Waterford crystal, Wedgwood china, Puiforcat silver and dozens of servants scurrying around in traditional *gaucho* costume. A tango orchestra played a *milonga* on the sidelines.

Stewart spotted Vice-President Castillo, looking like a plump country judge in a white suit and hat. With him were Casaverde and the other leaders of the *Concordancia*—Pineda, Cantilo, Ruiz Guinazu, Patron Costas, Javier Chavez, publisher of the nationalist rag, *El Pampero*, from the *Radicalista* wing of the Party, Alvear, and the rest of Julia's crowd, the cream of Argentine society, the Puerresons, the Anchorellas, the Montinis, Luis Algazas and his bride, Aurelia, the recent Miss Argentina, Carlos Casalles, whose wealth rivaled the Gideons's, the Martinez de Cerros, the Señora Hosch, Señor Zuberberg and his red-headed mistress, La Miranda, the Herrera-Blancas, Dido in a flowery pink dress, the de Castros, Athena with her blonde hair and tight dress cut to her navel, the Marchesa Baramboli, the German ambassador, von Thermann. For the Army, Generals Marquez and Ramirez in uniform and medals, and Fuentes and his men.

Everyone.

Julia was sitting next to Castillo, her children beside her. Everyone was sipping champagne and talking. The boys, they looked to be about five and eight years old, were dressed in identical Eton-type jackets. They both had dark hair and solemn, handsome faces, like their father. Casaverde was sitting on Castillo's other side. With him was one of the young actresses from the Alvear Palace. The pretty one. Eva something.

"Where's von Hulse? Couldn't he make it?" Stewart asked.

Vargas stopped smiling.

"Baron von Hulse is occupied with other matters," he said coldly. "Unfortunately, the war does not take time off for holiday. Are you ready for our little match, *yanqui?*"

"Why not?" Stewart shrugged. "Though I would have preferred more practice. It's been a long time."

"Nonsense!" Paretti smiled, showing his teeth. "A nine-handicap player! Señor Galeano from the Club was delighted to learn you would be his Number Two."

"And you, Don Giancarlo? Will you be playing at the Number One or Two?"

"Also Two," Paretti grinned. "Don Arturo here will play 'Pivot.'"

It was a set-up, Stewart thought. Vargas wanted to beat him in front of his wife and the world and he had brought Paretti in as a ringer.

"You and I against each other, *pues*," Stewart said to Vargas, watching a *muchacha* serve champagne to Julia and the others.

"It's arranged, *entonces*. I shall go inform Señor Galeano," Paretti said. As he left, Vargas stepped closer.

"I was told you'd been arrested again. And what is this stupidity about the children? I don't like this business of taking them out of school," Vargas whispered.

"Talk to your German friends."

"The Germans wouldn't dare. This is Argentina," he said. "Good luck in the match!" he added loudly, smiling for the benefit of anyone else around. He stared at Stewart in a way that showed he understood what was going on between Stewart and his wife. "You need to be taught a lesson, *yanqui.*"

Stewart leaned forward in the saddle.

"Who elected you teacher?"

"I elected myself."

"An Argentinian election, *pues.*"

"We finish today, *yanqui.* Everything is finished today," Vargas said, turning on his heel and walking stiffly back toward the stables.

Stewart watched him go, wondering what kind of a game he was playing. Had Vargas fallen into the classic dilemma of the double-agent? Not knowing which side he was on any more? Or had he switched sides? If he was acting, he was giving one hell of a performance. One thing was certain, Stewart thought. The coup was on, all right.

The grounds were an armed camp. Castillo had brought his Vice-Presidential bodyguards, even two Grenadiers of San Martin in full uniform. Vargas had men there, in *gaucho* costume like the servants, but with guns. Fuentes had brought Navarro and about a dozen of his soldiers. The German ambassador, von Thermann, had brought some of his black-suited Gestapo thugs, looking as out of place here as a Brooklyn mafioso at a Newport tea party. Everyone waiting for Ortiz. Extras waiting for the star.

And news of the *Graf Spee.*

Was that what the war was coming down to? Stewart wondered. Whether one sick old man showed up at a party? And why, thirty years ago, Gideon had taken a baby away from his daughter, Lucia?

It all seemed so unsubstantial, a cotton candy mission, spun of trivialities and air. Everything connected by the sheerest of invisible threads.

The Raven. Ravenwood. The two wars converging. *God and the Devil, one and the same.*

In a lunatic way, everything that poor half-mad woman had said was true. What was there in all of this that would make

somebody want to murder people three decades later? he wondered, watching Julia talking to someone. He couldn't see her
face. All at once, she turned and looked across at him as
though she knew he had been watching her all along. She
smiled, but it was a public smile; it didn't mean anything.
After a moment, he turned his horse and trotted onto the
playing field.

As they lined up for the bowl-in, Stewart could see Julia and
Castillo and the others watching from the off (right) side, near
the center of the field. Everyone was drinking and talking as
they settled down to watch the match. Julia raised her binoculars and he had the feeling she was watching him. He
started to smile, but something made him turn toward the
other team instead, in time to catch Vargas staring at him
with a look of pure hatred.

The umpire bowled the ball in from the center line. Santelli, playing the Number One position on Stewart's team, got
there first as Stewart used spurs and a tiny flick of the whip to
get his horse moving from a standing start into a fast canter.
Santelli hit an off-side forearm, but it was short as Stewart
galloped hard toward the goal posts. Santelli was after the
ball, looking to pass, as Paretti moved diagonally at him to
ride him off the ball. Out of the corner of his eye, Stewart
could see Vargas cantering toward him, readying to make the
turn.

Just as Paretti's pony slammed against Santelli's, there was
a crack as Santelli shot a hard under-the-neck pass ahead of
Stewart's pony. Stewart moved his pony fast toward the ball.
He bent low, feeling the horse move strongly under him. God,
he'd missed this! There was nothing in the world like it, he
thought, standing in the stirrups, readying his mallet for the
off-side stroke and a clear shot at the goal. For an instant it
was all there: the pounding of hoofs on the green turf, the
horse moving under him, the white ball, the striped posts
against the blue sky, and then Vargas riding directly across
his front, toward the line of the ball.

It was a clear-cut foul. Stewart waited a split-second for the
umpire to call it, but nothing happened. Cursing to himself,
he reined his horse in to avoid the collision, as Vargas knocked
the ball back toward Stewart's goal. Vargas came on after the
ball. He'll want to use an off-side forearm, Stewart thought,
anticipating where the ball was going to be hit. He wheeled

his pony around in a left-about 180-degree turn and began racing back toward his own goal. He was turning in his saddle to look back, when he heard the smack of the ball as Vargas hit it.

For a single instant, he had the whole field in sight: Vargas chasing the ball after his hit, Paretti cutting diagonally to try and head Stewart off, and Stewart's own Number One, Santelli, hanging back to cover Vargas's team's Number Four and to receive a pass in case his team could turn it around. Paretti had got slightly ahead of Stewart. Damn, he was good! Stewart thought. And his pony was very quick. He was going to ride Stewart off. Paretti's pony slammed hard against Stewart's pony's shoulder, knocking him aside. Paretti hit his mallet against Stewart's, but they had overridden the ball. As he pulled his pony away, Stewart leaned far out over his off side, giving his horse plenty of rein so as not to pull him up short, and swung.

There was that wonderful satisfying thwack that is like nothing else when a ball is hit well. It was a difficult shot, a backhand, under the tail of his own pony. It took plenty of wrist and it shot back down to the other end of the field towards Santelli, who got it on the roll and hit it in for the goal.

Paretti came up, grinning and sweaty.

"Out of practice, you said, *yanqui?*"

"He crossed the line of the ball," Stewart said, glancing toward Vargas.

"You *yanquis* expect too much from life," Paretti smiled. "You want more than winning; you want justice, too," he said, shaking his head as he trotted back to his position.

By the end of the third chukker, Stewart's team was down by two goals, eleven to nine. Their pivot man, Fontana, was weak and Paretti could get past him. Then, one on one, Stewart's team's Number Four, Alcazar, was no match for Paretti. They were on the sidelines, getting ready for the last chukker. Stewart took a mouthful of water, swallowed half of it and spat the rest out.

"That Paretti," Alcazar shook his head. "He's riding around us like we were *burros.*"

"We need to do something," Santelli said.

Stewart motioned them closer.

"Next time you hit it in from the back line," he told Alcazar, "don't hit it to me on the side board."

"But you're our best chance, Don Carlos."

"Yes. And they know it. Instead, hit it short, straight ahead."

"Paretti will come in and kill it."

"He'll come in. That's what we want. When you hit it short, instead of going back and defending the goal, follow the ball. Hit it hard and straight to Don Javier here," he said, looking at Santelli. "Only don't shoot, dribble, understand?" he said to Santelli. Santelli smiled. He had brown intelligent eyes.

"Has your pony got that much left, Don Carlos?"

"I've been cantering him more than galloping. He's got lots of *gasolina* left," Stewart said, patting his horse's neck. He climbed up into the saddle, glancing over at Julia as he did so. Her face was flushed and she was holding out her glass for refilling. She looked as if she had been drinking non-stop. Stewart trotted over to the center line and as soon as the line-up formed, the umpire bowled in.

There was a mêlée for the ball, everyone banging against each other and swinging their mallets. Suddenly, the ball squirted out and Vargas was after it. He hit it long and it went out of bounds.

As Alcazar got ready to hit it in from behind the back line, Stewart, at his position along the side board, nodded. He pretended to get ready to receive the ball. Paretti, looking down the field at Alcazar, watched Stewart out of the corner of his eye.

Alcazar hit the ball in short. The ball was only thirty yards in front of the undefended goal. Paretti charged straight at it. He was like a sculpture, his pony galloping flat-out, leaning forward over his horse's neck, his mallet held high like a torch for the near (left) side swing. Alcazar was coming toward it too. Stewart moved toward the middle of the field at a slow canter. Suddenly, Paretti understood. He brought his pony to a complete standstill, all four legs jarring stiffly. But it was too late.

Alcazar smacked the ball hard, straight down the middle of the field. Santelli rode toward the ball. Vargas galloped after him. But now, Stewart came galloping hard at a diagonal. He overtook Vargas and moved slightly ahead of him, extending his arm so his pony's head could go completely forward. His pony's shoulder slammed into and ahead of Vargas's pony's shoulder. At the same time, Stewart turned in his saddle and jerked his shoulder back against Vargas, riding him off and almost knocking him out of the saddle. There was a good feeling of soreness in Stewart's shoulder at the hit. He could just imagine how Vargas's chest felt. Now Santelli had only the Back between him and the goal. He raised his mallet for the shot, but instead of aiming for the goal, he dribbled it short.

The lure was irresistible. The Back charged madly at the ball. Just before he could get there, Santelli hit a short pass sideways to Stewart, coming up. With the Back out of position, the goal posts were undefended. Stewart tapped it in for an easy goal.

Stewart and Santelli rode up to each other laughing. Vargas and Paretti also came up, their faces flushed and sweaty.

"That was good, Don Carlos. But I won't let you do that twice," Paretti smiled, raising a cautionary finger.

"We've got lots more of those," Stewart grinned at Santelli.

"It must be nice, *yanqui*. Having things come so easily to you," Vargas said. He was smiling, but the hate was in his eyes. "You don't even have to ask, do you?"

"Not even," Stewart said, reining his pony to a stop.

"You *gringos!*" Vargas hissed. "You think you can come down here and fuck our women and tell us all what to do."

Paretti and Santelli looked back and forth between the two men, their faces suddenly embarrassed and serious.

"You better stop there," Stewart said quietly.

"You see! You see how they order us!" Vargas said, looking around wildly.

"If you don't stop, we'll be saying stupid things about each other's mother and then we'll have to do something about it," Stewart said and rode off. The others watched him for a moment, then one by one trotted back to their positions. Vargas was the last, his face dark and flushed.

By the time the thirty-second horn sounded, the score was tied. Paretti dribbled the ball toward Stewart's team's goal. Fontana was chasing him, swinging wildly, trying to hook Paretti's mallet. Alcazar was coming forward and Stewart realized that if Paretti passed the ball to anyone, their goal was undefended. Stewart galloped desperately along the side boards. Suddenly, Paretti leaned out over the near side till his head was almost parallel with his pony's muzzle and stroked a backhand right at Vargas, coming from nowhere down toward the goal. It was a stupendous pass and there was nothing between Vargas and the goal.

Stewart slanted across the field, chasing Vargas, coming up

behind him on his off side. Vargas, concentrating on the goal, didn't see him. Both ponies were galloping hard toward the goal. Vargas raised his mallet for the hit. Stewart reached his mallet forward. His pony was fresher than Vargas's and he was within easy hooking range. He was about to hook Vargas's mallet with his, when a cry reached him from the crowd. It was Julia's voice and unable to help himself, he glanced for an instant toward the crowd. Julia was standing, her hand to her mouth. Next to her, the two boys, Vargas's sons, were jumping up and down with excitement. Vargas swung. Stewart whipped his mallet forward to hook and missed. The ball sailed cleanly between the goal posts.

A wild cheer went up from the crowd. Stewart slowed his pony to a walk. He leaned down and patted him on the neck. *"Tu eres mucho caballo."* You are much horse, he whispered, trotting him toward the side boards. Vargas cantered over.

"Even *yanquis* don't always win," Vargas sneered.

"Congratulations! In a good hour," Stewart said. Vargas looked at him, confused. He started to say something, then stopped. Stewart watched him jump his pony over the side boards and dismount. Everyone gathered around to clap him on the back. Stewart watched Julia, standing to one side, drinking. What he had just done, Stewart thought to himself, was as close to a true declaration of love as he had ever made. Paretti came over as Stewart dismounted and handed the reins of his pony to a groom.

"I thought maybe you were a coward, Charlie Stewart," Paretti shook his head. "But now I think maybe it is something else," he added, looking meaningfully at Julia and the children.

"I don't know what you mean," Stewart said.

"That wasn't an easy hook to miss, Charlie," Paretti grinned. "A Zero-player could have made that hook."

"I just missed it," Stewart said, pulling off his knee-pads and cap. "It happens."

"Of course."

They walked over to the buffet tables where Vargas and the others were. Someone handed Stewart a glass of champagne and a towel. Vargas looked sweaty and happy. He had his hands on his sons' shoulders. Only Casaverde was red-faced and grim.

"What's the matter, Don Enrique? Surely you didn't bet against Don Arturo here?" Stewart asked.

Casaverde only glowered at him.

"Don Enrique is upset because of the *Graf Spee*. Baldomir is insisting that the Germans leave Montevideo," Athena de Castro said.

"The Reds Party are dogs!" Herrera-Blanca grumbled. "Roosevelt is behind this, mark my words!"

"The North Americans still say they support a Neutrality Zone in this hemisphere," Pineda put in.

"Which the British navy makes a mockery of," Vargas said.

"Neutrality!" Casaverde exclaimed hoarsely. "Roosevelt talks 'neutrality' with one fork of his tongue and pushes the 'Cash and Carry' through the *Congreso* with the other."

"I have spoken to Secretary Hull. He says 'Cash and Carry' is to apply to both sides," Pineda said.

"*Mierde!* 'Cash and Carry' is for the *Ingleses*, with their warships violating the neutrality of the Rio de la Plata at this very moment. All this *yanqui* scheming!" Vice-President Castillo said angrily. He looked shrewdly at Stewart. "You're the North American. The one who met with our esteemed President the day before yesterday, no?"

Everyone looked at Stewart.

Jesus, he thought, his eyes searching the crowd for Fuentes. He was standing between General Ramirez and his man, Navarro, a smiling bemedaled tabby cat. You bastard, Stewart thought. Playing both ends against the middle.

"I saw the President Ortiz, yes, Señor Vice-President."

"And his health," Castillo inquired delicately. "How did it seem to you?"

"He seemed in good spirits, Señor Vice-President."

"Then why isn't he here?" thundered Casaverde. His face was red and his monocle dropped from his eye and dangled on its ribbon. "It is an insult to our host, Don Arturo," inclining his head toward Vargas, "and to the members of this government, who expect that if a President cannot perform the duties of his office, then for the good of the nation he should resign."

"*Olé! Olé!*" several voices murmured.

"I have already told him that with a world crisis, we can no longer continue in this way. He must turn over the Presidency to me," Castillo announced smoothly. He turned back to Stewart. "Did you and Señor Ortiz discuss whether your Roosevelt plans to lead America into this war? We in Argentina have to know this."

"I have no idea what President Roosevelt plans," Stewart shrugged. "According to the radio, he says no."

"So does the Señor Wilkie," Pineda said.

"Ah, but Wilkie means it," someone said.

"Yes, but he is not President!"

"He's a devil, that Dutchman, Roosevelt. He's up there, sitting on America's guns and money, waiting for countries to come to him, one by one, and sell him their souls," Castillo said. "The trouble with the North Americans is they talk morality, but worship money. One never knows what they're going to do."

"How can one know what they'll do, when they don't know themselves?" Vargas said irritably, lighting a cigar. He glanced coldly at Stewart. "But if you and President Ortiz didn't talk about *yanqui* war plans, perhaps you would care to tell us what you did discuss?"

"The *Graf Spee*, among other things," Stewart said.

Vice-President Castillo turned to Stewart, a gleam in his eye.

"Truly? And did you know, Señor Stewart, that I have assured Ambassador von Thermann that the *Graf Spee* is welcome to the safety of Argentine waters?"

"First they have to get across the Rio de la Plata," Pineda put in.

"They will," Vargas said, calmly puffing on his cigar.

"The English might have something to say about that," Stewart said.

Vice-President Castillo's expression froze. He tucked his chin into his neck like a boxer, swelling his jowls.

"Argentine neutrality will be respected, Señor, I assure you. No matter what that sick old man who should get out of the Pink House* says!"

"He should be here!" Señor Guinazu grumbled. "It's an outrage!"

"If he's too sick to be here, he should get out!" Vargas said loudly.

There were murmurs of agreement. On the fringes of the

---

* *Casa Rosada*, the Presidential Palace.

crowd, there was a restlessness. Guards checked their holsters. There was a smell of blood in the air. Now or never, Stewart thought, checking his watch. He nodded at Fuentes. Now let's see which side the bastard's on today, Stewart thought.

"Ah, but he is here, Excellency," Stewart said.

"What are you talking about, *gringo?*" Vargas snapped.

"In a manner of speaking. Turn on the radio."

"*Qué va!* What is this?"

"That is quite correct, Señors," Fuentes said smoothly, bowing and smiling as he approached. "The President of the Republic is performing his duty. He is making a speech to the nation even now."

In the hubbub of noise that followed this announcement, one of the servants carried a Philco radio out to the buffet, while another paid out a long electric cord. Everyone was talking at the same time.

"This is outrageous!"

"Why weren't we informed?"

"The *Radicalistas* are behind it!"

"He's too sick. It's a sham."

As everyone gathered around the radio, Ortiz's voice came crackling through the static. Someone cried "*Silencio!*" and the tango orchestra fell silent.

" . . . this day informing representatives of the German Reich and the British Crown, that in view of the world situation and in the interests of Pan-Americanism and Argentina's own well-known policy of the strictest neutrality, no warships of any belligerent nation will be permitted in Argentine waters. Any warship of either side which violates this prohibition will be interned, as prescribed by international law."

"That *imbécil!*" Casaverde muttered.

The German ambassador, von Thermann, came rushing over, followed by his thick-necked guards swiveling their heads belligerently from side to side, as if looking for a fight.

"You hear! You hear these lies!"

Vice-President Castillo raised his hand, stopping the German's rush.

"This time he's gone too far. I will not permit it!" Castillo glared at everyone around him. "This is insane."

"But it must be admitted, he has acted," Pineda said, smiling.

"And after Germany destroys England, what then?" Vargas snapped. "What do we do then?"

"*Silencio!*" someone hissed. "Listen!"

" . . . Argentine hospitality, we invite the crews of any ships sunk, regardless of affiliation. . . ."

There was an interruption and a crackling of static. Vice-President Castillo turned to Cantilo and Casaverde.

"We must return to the Pink House at once!" He looked around for Julia to say his goodbyes, when there was more crackling and an announcer's voice came on.

"An urgent war bulletin!" the announcer said.

Everyone around the radio looked at each other. There was absolute silence. Stewart felt a tightening in the pit of his stomach. He looked around the perimeter at the guards. Here it comes, he thought. If the Germans broke out of the British trap, he couldn't see any way he'd live out the hour.

"Late this afternoon," the announcer said, "in international waters, just beyond the three-mile-limit outside Montevideo, the German battleship *Graf Spee* was shattered by a series of explosions. Although British warships were in sight on the Rio de la Plata, no shots were reported fired. It is believed that the Germans scuttled the battleship to prevent it from falling into British hands. Sailors were seen being transferred to a waiting German freighter just prior to the explosions, and no lives are presumed lost. To repeat, the German battleship *Graf Spee* is presently on fire and sinking in shallow water just outside Montevideo harbor. We now return to the President of the Republic."

The radio was silent, but for a faint hissing of the ether. There was a brief burst of tango music, which was immediately cut off. Then President Ortiz's voice came back.

"We extend the hospitality of our shores to *Capitano* Langsdorff and the crew of the *Graf Spee*. Argentina's neutrality remains inviolable. I believe the outcome of events justifies the soundness of our policies. I leave immediately for the Pink House to deal with the situation," President Ortiz said. Tango music resumed on the radio. After a moment, someone shut it off.

"My God!" Castillo said, sagging back against the table. There was a slight commotion and a sound of overturned chairs as Ambassador von Thermann and his entourage headed grim-faced for their cars. Everyone stood around, waiting. After a minute, the tango orchestra started up again, but a few seconds later someone shushed them and they stopped. It was as though there had been a death.

"It's a disaster, a *catástrofe!*" someone muttered.

Castillo grabbed Julia's hand and shook it, distracted, as though she were a man, then realizing what he had done, raised it formally to his lips. "A thousand pardons, Dona Julia. I have to go," he muttered in a strangled voice and was gone, followed by Cantilo, Guinazu, General Ramirez and their guards and aides.

"That Churchill must practice witchcraft. He's probably poking pins in a little wax model of the *Graf Spee* right now," Athena de Castro said suddenly, and someone laughed.

"For God!" Herrera-Blanca said, looking around as though he was just waking up. "You don't suppose it's possible the English could win, do you?"

"Don't be silly!" Vargas said crisply. "It's only one ship. This war's barely begun. Germany is still the wave of the future."

"Whose future?" Ricardo de Castro said, taking out a pack of Players. He offered it around and Stewart lit one up.

"Argentina's," Vargas replied. "The *Concordancia* is behind Castillo. That's what he'll tell Ortiz at the Pink House. We have to support him."

"I must also leave," Pineda said, clicking his heels and bowing to Julia. "It has been most interesting, Dona Julia. When I saw all these armed men, I thought," he hesitated, "well, it is of no importance. *No importa.* An Argentine solution, *pues.* Nothing gets resolved. As always, a pleasure, my dear Julia. Such lovely *chicos,*" he said, patting the boys on the head and leaving.

"I also, *entonces.* Come, my dear," Casaverde said, offering his arm to the girl, Eva.

"That's it, Don Enrique! Go to the Pink House!" Julia said, her eyes sparkling dangerously, as they had that night at the Alvear Palace. Stewart wasn't sure if it was the champagne, or something else. "Everybody's at the Pink House. We should go to the Pink House, too. Come on! Let's go to the Pink House, too!" she cried.

"Julia, behave yourself!" Vargas frowned.

Julia colored, swaying slightly as though she had been slapped. She grabbed onto Stewart's arm for a second as if to balance herself. Vargas's face tightened when he saw that.

"Come with me," Vargas said, grabbing her arm. She pulled away angrily.

"Don't touch me! Don't!" she spat out the words. She looked around like a bull in the arena, not knowing who to charge first. "Do you know what today is? My grandfather's one hundredth birthday. Imagine? If John Gideon had lived, he would be one hundred today! I salute my grandfather, *abuelo mio!*" she declared, raising her glass. Suddenly, her face contorted. She stared at Vargas. "Now why don't you get out of my house, you son-of-a bitch?"

There were startled gasps from some of the guests. Vargas tried to smile, but it didn't work.

"I'm sure Julia didn't mean that. Did you, Julia?" he said intently, a strained look on his tanned handsome face.

"God, you make me sick," she whispered loudly. "How can you look at yourself in the mirror and not throw up?"

"I'm leaving," Casaverde announced, marching off with Eva, who looked back over her shoulder at Julia as she left.

Vargas stared at Stewart and his wife, like a man with an incurable disease.

"I have to go to the Pink House," he muttered. "We'll settle this when I get back."

"Yes. Go to the Pink House. *Vaya.* My grandfather always said it was a place for whores. You and Don Enrique will be right at home there," Julia said, draining her champagne and holding out her glass for another refill.

"You've had enough!" Vargas said sharply.

"The hell I have!"

"That's enough, Julia!" Vargas shouted. He tried to take the glass from her and she threw it in his face. The glass shattered on his forehead. Blood welled from a cut above his eye. Vargas stood there, champagne and blood dripping down the side of his face. The two boys stood between their parents, hands at their sides, looking miserable. The younger one's lower lip trembled, a prelude to crying. Julia grabbed the champagne bottle and a fresh glass from the *muchacha* and poured herself another drink, slopping it over the rim. She looked around at all of them, then raised her glass.

"*Viva Argentina!*" she toasted. "If we're lucky, we won't get what we ask for. That's the best any country can hope for, isn't it?"

No one said anything. Athena went over and put her arm around Julia's shoulders.

"Don't disquiet yourself, *guapa*. It's all right. Everything is all right," Athena said.

"Of course, it's all right," Julia said, shaking her off. "We're having a wonderful time. Aren't we having a wonderful time?"

Vargas looked at his watch.

"I have to go. To repair the damage," he said hoarsely. He stared at Stewart for a moment. "Don't be here when I get back, *gringo*. Don't be in Argentina."

They watched him walk away, a solitary figure, oddly elegant in his riding breeches. Julia knelt down and grabbed the two boys and held them close to her. They suffered her to do it the way children do, their arms stiffly at their sides, miniature versions of their father.

"It's all right, *chicos*. Mama is sorry. Your Papa is right. Mama gets silly when she drinks. Papa's learned how to forgive Mama. You will too," she said, wiping her eyes with the back of her hand. "Now go. Go with Gabriela. I'll come later. Truly."

She handed the boys over to the governess, who led them away. She watched them go across the green lawn toward the *hacienda*, little soldiers in their school jackets and short trousers, on either side of the woman. Everyone began to drift away, as though Arturo's embarrassment had become contagious. Athena lingered, watched her and Stewart, then she too went toward the bar. The band started another tango, one of the violinists putting down his bow and singing:

> "Is it my fault if you've played life by the rules,
> And so, like a dope, you have to eat air,
> And haven't a bed to lie in?
> 'What'll I do?' Honor just died today,
> And Christ's worth no more than the thief!"

Julia leaned wearily back against Stewart, her eyes half-closed.

"You see how it is, *yanqui*. You begin by playing a part and in the end, you become the part. He's sick with jealousy over you." She made a face. "For God's sake, get me a drink, *yanqui*. A real drink. I can't stomach any more of this champagne swill."

Stewart went over to the bar and got two glasses of Scotch. Athena looked at him, but neither of them spoke. He went back and handed one to Julia and she shuddered as she drank.

"What was all that?" he asked. "All this *dramática*?"

"You have to go," she whispered, watching over the rim of

her glass. "He's trying to make you go. It's not just the Germans. It's Castillo too, now. If Ortiz had come, they would have killed you also. Ortiz can't protect you. By tomorrow, every *marrano* with a gun in Buenos Aires will be looking for you. The part about the jealousy is true, though."

"Why? It was his idea. It's not as if," Stewart hesitated awkwardly, "as if it never happened before."

"No," she said softly.

"Then why is he so upset?"

"The others loved me. This is the first time I ever really loved someone back."

Stewart nodded, looking around at the guests on the broad lawns, the scurrying servants, the orchestra playing and Athena and Ricardo doing the tango under the trees. They danced well together, he thought. Another lie.

"Are you leaving?" she asked finally, not looking at him.

"We both are," he said, putting down his drink.

"No, I'm not. I can't," she said, looking toward the *hacienda* in the direction the governess had taken the children.

"Yes, you are," Stewart said. "It's about your mother."

THEY MADE good time on the way to Lujan. Night had fallen and it reminded Stewart of the drive to Tigre: the moon looming over the Pampa, the Dusenberg's headlights carving a tunnel of light in the darkness, Julia fiddling with the radio. The news came on, but it was just commercials and a rehash about the *Graf Spee*. The Finns were still holding off the Russians on the Karelian Isthmus. In Argentina, the big news was that in *futbol*, La Boca had trounced San Cristobal Sud. She turned the dial, trying to find some music, but it was mostly static and after a moment she shut it off.

"I thought she was dead," she said finally.

Stewart didn't say anything. He reached for the dashboard lighter and lit a cigarette, glancing at her as he did so. She had changed her clothes. She wore black slacks, a white silk blouse and pearls, the wind lifting the edges of her silky hair like a raven's wing feathers. She had never seemed so beautiful and so unattainable to him as she did at that moment.

"Did you?"

"Of course! She was buried next to my grandfather, in the Recoleta."

"No," Stewart shook his head. "No."

"But I thought. . . ." she started, then stopped when she saw the way he was looking at her.

"The thing is," Stewart said, picking a shred of tobacco from his tongue, "I'm not a cop, *un agente de policía*. I'm a kind of soldier. Only in an army where there aren't any rules."

"I know that," she said.

"Clearly," he nodded. "You know a lot of things, don't you?"

She fitted a cigarette into an ivory holder and lit it, not looking at him.

"*Qué va?* I don't know what you mean," she said.

"Yes, you do."

She turned toward him, her eyes reflecting the dashboard lights.

"Please, *yanqui*. . . ." she whispered.

"It's no good, Julia. We both know you killed Raoul and the others," he said, his hands tightening on the wheel.

"The Germans. . . ." she started to say.

"It wasn't the Germans," he said bitterly. "They were just trying to keep up, like the rest of us."

"Why are you saying this? I don't understand," she said helplessly. "There's no proof."

"I don't need proof. I'm not a cop, I told you. Besides, we both know it's true, don't we?"

She didn't answer. She stared ahead at the windshield as though into a fire.

"Equally," Stewart went on, "it's like I told President Ortiz. Argentine justice isn't my affair; winning the war is. What mattered in all this was never who, but why."

Julia bit her lip to keep it from trembling.

"Why are you doing this?" she said in a small voice. "Why?"

"*Bueno*," Stewart sighed heavily. "We'll take it one at a time. First, Cardenas. That one's easy, because I never really believed you in the first place. Cardenas was tough, suspicious. A man with a gun would have had a tough time getting to him. But a woman? A beautiful woman, *querida?*" Stewart said, his eyes narrowing. "Someone gave him an overdose of heroin, then bashed his head in with the statue to finish him. He was on his knees throwing up when he was killed. And I found a residue of powder on the desk. So the overdose was given to him by someone who knew he was an addict, someone he trusted. Like one of his partners. Or maybe his partner's wife," he smiled bitterly. "Tell me, did you sleep with him too?"

Her eyes flashed.

"I won't talk to you if you speak to me in this way."

"You people," he said, shaking his head. "You commit murder left and right, but you get indignant about an indelicate question."

"This is *ridículo*. You're just making a guess."

"No," he said. "The club was covered. Fuentes's man, Navarro, in front and krauts all over the place. I had to kill one just to get in."

"You see! You are a murderer too!" she said hotly.

"*Seguro*," he nodded. "Only we know what my motives were, don't we, *querida?*" He waited for her to answer and when she didn't, he went on. "All right, let's go back to Cardenas. With all those agents around the club, you couldn't just tango in there. So either you were working with the krauts, or you killed Cardenas and hadn't left the club when I showed up. At the time I remember wondering why I hadn't heard you come in. It was because you were already there, wasn't it? Besides, *querida*," he shrugged, "you were the one who wanted to make sure I showed up at the Atlantis Club in the first place. You were going to set me up. I recognized your perfume from my hotel room. We even laughed about it the night we went to Tigre, remember?"

"I remember, *yanqui*," she said, turning wistfully toward him. "I remember everything about that night."

"So do I," he said fiercely. "Only that's not what I'm talking about. Not with a war hanging in the balance. Because that's what it's about, isn't it?"

"No," she said, her lips trembling. "It's not like that."

"But it is like that, Julia. You killed Cardenas, all right," he nodded. "Not that it matters. He was scum and no loss to anybody. Besides, it's like I said. It didn't matter. You could have killed fifty Cardenas for all I care!"

"Yes, it's true!" she said. "He was blackmailing me and I. . . ."

"Don't!" he said, holding up his hand to stop her. "There's no point in more lies."

"But it's true!"

"No," he shook his head. "You killed him because he was connected to Raoul and you were afraid of what Raoul might've found out. That's why you had to get into that safe. That's why," he said softly, "you had to kill Ceci."

"No! You don't understand!" she cried, whipping her head from side to side.

"But that's the trouble, Julia. I do understand. It just took me too long to save her," he said bitterly.

"Carlos," she whispered.

"Ceci was Raoul's friend," he said. "The last person to see him alive. She gave him Athena's gun. Raoul was desperate. He might have told her something. He had met with the priest. He knew something about your mother. After Raoul was killed, all those weeks how you must have waited and worried and she didn't tell anyone. If she ever knew anything," he said. "You know why, don't you?" He glared at her. "Because she loved you, didn't she, *querida?*" he said viciously.

"No, no!" she cried, burying her face in her hands. "It wasn't like that!"

"But you still couldn't risk it. So you gave Ceci's name to the Germans. I found her address on the matchbox I took from the dead German. They couldn't get rid of her, because I killed them in the *frigorifico*. And you saw me find the matchbox. So you had to do it yourself. You had to. I was getting too close.

"Equally, it was better if you did it anyway," he went on. "Ceci was wary, scared. She knew the Germans were watching her. She told me so herself. She would never have gone alone to Raoul's mother's house at four in the morning to meet anyone. But she'd have gone for you, *querida*," he said.

Julia looked up at him, her eyes blurred with tears.

"The Dwarf said she was all excited. She loved you," he said softly. "She would have gone and taken her clothes off gladly and then you killed her. I was sorry about that," he said, flicking his cigarette angrily out into the night. "I liked her. I liked her a lot."

"I didn't want to," Julia whispered in a tiny voice. "I liked her too. I couldn't be what she wanted me to be. I can't be what any of you want me to be. I hated having to do it. I hated it!" she said, the tears rolling down her face.

"I believe you," he said. "Only it still doesn't matter. I'm not an *agente de policía*. If Ceci had to be killed to protect the Raven, so be it. Only that wasn't it, either. Which brings us to Raoul," he said, his eyes narrowing.

"It was the Germans!" she cried. "You know it was!"

"No, *querida*," he shook his head. "It was you. Oh clearly, maybe the German pulled the trigger after you fingered Raoul, and you only showed up later to shoot the German," he shrugged. "Or maybe it was the other way around, with you killing the German and then shooting Raoul and the *puta* with Athena's gun, but it was you. Either way, it was you."

She stared at him with horrified fascination, the way a trapped mouse stares at a snake.

"See," he said, rubbing the side of his jaw as though he needed a shave, "the German couldn't have been killed unless it was by someone he trusted. Not in an operational situation like that hotel room. Unless it was, maybe, the person who had helped set Raoul up in the first place. It doesn't really matter how. Probably by somehow getting Arturo to think that Raoul was a double. Then Arturo told von Hulse. Only you had to make sure Raoul died before he could talk and that no one ever connected his death to you. No witnesses. That's why you killed the German in the hotel room. Not that anybody cared," Stewart shrugged. "Another dead Nazi, more or less. Only they weren't *all* Nazis, were they?" he asked quietly. "Except for Hartman, maybe. You sold him to the krauts. Why? Because he was Raoul's contact to us and you had to be sure?"

"No," she whispered, closing her eyes. "You've got it all wrong. It wasn't like that."

"It was, though," he insisted. "Raoul needed money to cover his gambling debts. So he thought of blackmailing you. Something like that. He found out about your mother. That she was alive. For some reason, that meant you had to get rid of him. So you used the Nazis to do it. That's what confused me," he said, glancing at her. "If it wasn't for the message about the *Graf Spee* and you helping me escape both times from the Germans, I'd have thought you were working for them all along."

Julia's face was utterly astonished.

"How could you ever think that?" she gasped.

"Oh don't look so surprised," Stewart growled. "I was beginning to think that it was more than just coincidence that every time the two of us got together, I always got picked up, either by the krauts, or Colonel Fuentes and his *muchachos*, starting with that night at the Alvear Palace. And then, when the Germans put us together in the *frigorifico*, they were using you to pump me, to find out what I really knew. If you hadn't helped me . . . we almost didn't get out of that *frigorifico*," his eyes narrowed, "and when we did, no sooner did we split apart, than Fuentes nabbed me at that hotel. I wanted to believe it was the desk clerk who turned me in, but it was too much of a coincidence. It was you, *querida*. Just you."

"I had to," she said, looking at him from under her lashes.

"Why? Because I was getting too close? Because you didn't want me to find out what Raoul found out. About your mother?"

"I didn't want you to get hurt. I love you," she whispered in a low sorrowing voice. "I thought you loved me too."

"Yes, well like they say in Brooklyn, 'That and a nickel will get you on a subway.' Because loving you turns out to be an awfully dangerous thing to do, *querida*. Or is it just that chance has put us both on the same side in this war?"

"But we are on the same side," she said fiercely. "And we do love each other. Nothing else matters. Not any more!"

He shook his head slowly.

"I wish it were that simple," he said hoarsely. "I wish we could go away on a beach somewhere, with palm trees and silly fruit drinks with umbrellas in them and nobody knows us, or speaks a word of Spanish or English, and they don't even have radios, so we can't hear the war news."

She touched his arm with her hand, resting it there as lightly as a butterfly on a branch.

"Take me there, *yanqui*," she said softly. "I'll go. I swear it. I'll do anything you want. I have money in banks in New York, everywhere. More than you can imagine. I'll go anywhere you want." She closed her eyes. "I mean it."

Stewart pulled his arm roughly away.

"And when do I turn my back on you? Besides, there isn't anywhere," he said. "Before this war is over, there won't be any place it won't get to."

"I know," she said, opening her eyes.

"We're forgetting the most important thing. The 'why.' What this thing was all about. Why John Gideon took you away from your mother and kept her away from the world all these years." *It was the family's wishes,* Mother Maria Jose had said. "And why was it so important to keep it hidden that you had to kill anyone who even came near it?"

She shrank back in the car seat, her face a pale mask in the moonlight.

"I can't tell you," she said, shuddering. "It's . . . personal."

"It was Gideon, wasn't it? It always came back to him," Stewart said. Ahead, he could see the lights of Lujan. She nodded slowly.

"Always," she murmured.

"He must have been something rare, *muy raro.*"

"There was a demon in him," she said. "He saw everyone as an enemy. 'Life is war,' he used to say. The war of the raven," she whispered. "For him, it was, I think. He despised everyone. 'Everyone steals,' he told me. 'The only difference between the rich and the poor is that the rich don't have to go to jail for it.' I asked him once if that meant he believed in 'original sin' and he said the only real reason he didn't believe in it was that people were rarely that original. I remember once he gave a large donation to the Church. After the archbishop had been shown out, I said, 'He must be a very holy man, *abuelo mio.*' And he replied, 'Aye, he's like his god, something between a dirty joke and an imbecile.' He hated everyone. Even God. Especially God."

"Except you," Stewart said. "He loved you. He left you everything."

She closed her eyes for a moment, as though she were praying.

"Not even," she said. "He named me Julia, after her. His first daughter, Judith, her name was. I was to have everything because she had nothing. 'Not even two pennies for her eyes that might have saved her!' he told me once, the night of the locusts.

"They blackened the sky over the *estancia,*" she remembered. "We had dug trenches with overhanging metal plates and when they fell in, we'd pour in kerosene and burn them. It was like hell with all the fires burning, and after fighting them all day like that, Gideon pulled out his revolver and emptied it at the sky in an attempt to kill God before he'd surrender even one inch of land. And then, later that night, when he told me about that other child, it was as if the words were wrung out of his very soul, even after all those years.

"Don't you see? He didn't love me!" she burst out. "He loved her! A little girl long gone. It was his love for her he was giving me. He didn't love me at all! He hated everyone. Even me. Even himself." She looked desperately at Stewart. "You all want me to be someone else. I can't do it anymore. *No puedo.* I can't."

The Dusenberg crossed over the bridge and onto the Calle Constitución. The streets were lit and the sidewalks crowded with people taking the evening promenade.

"Why did you kill Raoul, Julia? What were you afraid he was going to find out?" he asked.

She turned anguished eyes to him.

"I can't tell you. I can't."

"Then you'll have to tell her," Stewart said grimly, pulling up outside the Misericordia. "Your mother."

"It is good you are here," Mother Maria Jose said as she led them down the dark corridor lit by only a few yellowed bulbs. "She's been acting strangely all day. Almost as if she knew you were coming," she said, looking intently at Julia, who was shaking so badly she could barely walk. "This is the daughter?" she asked. "The one he took away?"

Stewart nodded. Mother Maria Jose put her hand on Julia's shoulder.

"I held you in my arms, you know. The night you were born."

"No," Julia said, white-faced, falling to her knees. "Please, *yanqui*," she pleaded. "I can't. Not after all these years."

"Come on," he said furiously, dragging her along the stone floor. "Someone kept her here all these years. It was either you or Arturo. Besides," he said, letting go of her, "don't you want to see your mother?"

Mother Maria Jose stared at the two of them, as if not knowing which of them to believe. Julia grabbed at Stewart's legs, clinging desperately to him as though she was drowning.

"I'm afraid," she whimpered. "Please don't make me."

"It has to end," he told her. "Get up. Get up!"

Trembling, she got to her feet. Mother Maria Jose led them to the door, the sound of the key turning the lock very loud in the silence. Mother Maria Jose opened the door.

"You first," Stewart said, shoving her inside and closing the door behind her. He and the Mother Superior were alone in the corridor. They looked at each other, waiting.

It was only a few seconds. Suddenly, a terrible piercing scream echoed in the corridor. Stewart tore the door open. Julia was standing in the middle of the room, screaming and staring at something in front of her. He had to step around her to see.

Lucia was lying naked on the floor with her legs apart, her head tilted crookedly against the wall. Her eyes were open, a strange doll-like grin on her face. There was a lake of blood around her and protruding from between her legs, a glint of silver. The crucifix. She was dead.

All at once, Stewart was aware of Julia, hand to her mouth, rushing past him, the sound of her heels fading down the long stone corridor. It doesn't matter, he thought mechanically. I've got the car keys. She can't leave. He looked at Mother Maria Jose.

"I don't understand," he said. "How could she have known?"

Mother Maria Jose didn't answer. Stewart started to look around the pitifully bare room. He knelt by an overturned wooden box, then turned back to the Mother Superior. "Why? She talked about her father. About Gideon and Father Damiano and ravens and pennies. Does any of this make any sense, *pues?*"

From outside, he heard the unmistakable rumble of the Dusenberg engine. Stewart raced over to the window, throwing open the shutter just in time to see the back of the Dusenberg as it pulled away. She had another key. She'd had it all along, you fool, he told himself. He walked back towards the body, a white island in a red lake, where the Mother Superior stood staring.

"Is there anything, Mother Maria Jose? Please? Anything missing? Anything?"

The Mother Superior looked at him strangely.

"Only her journal. She kept one for years," she said. "One day, she gave it to Father Damiano. 'An act of penance,' she said." She came closer. "There were two coins, also. For some reason they were important to her. She kept them in the box."

Stewart turned the box over, spilling the contents onto the floor. Books, scarves, sachets, a rosary, loose buttons, a broken strand of pearls. The odds and ends of a woman's life. There were no coins. He stood up.

"I have to get back to Buenos Aires," he told her. "To warn Father Damiano. Do you have a car? A truck? Anything?"

Mother Maria Jose stared absently at him for a moment. She shook her head slowly. Stewart started toward the door.

"Wait!" she cried. "There's the train. It comes every night. It should be here in twenty-five minutes, *pues*. You can be in Buenos Aires in two, three hours."

Stewart nodded as he sprinted out the door. He ran out the front gate and down the street, oblivious of the stares of passers-by. He turned the corner toward the river and followed alongside it, stopping only once to ask directions, down to the train station. He had to bang on the window for nearly a minute before a sleepy-eyed *taquillero* finally opened it and sold him a ticket.

Stewart stepped out onto the platform, his breath coming in great heaving gasps. What a fool, he thought angrily. What a stupid fool! Feeling the tick of every precious second spent waiting and unable to slow the pounding of his heart, until at last he saw the powerful beam of the locomotive's headlight cutting through the night.

29

THE TRAIN pulled into Buenos Aires just after eleven. Stewart caught a taxi at a stand outside the station and gave the driver the priest's address. Back in town, the night was warm and sticky. A Buenos Aires night. Traffic and crowded sidewalks and in the cafés on the Calle Juncal, men in straw hats whispering *piropos* to young women and the inevitable tango on the taxi radio. Being careful to keep it out of the driver's line of sight in the rear-view mirror, Stewart took the Colt automatic out of his shoulder holster and checked it.

The taxi stopped outside the house. Stewart told the driver to douse his lights and wait. He went inside, feeling his way along the dark hallway, the Colt in his hand. He knocked on the priest's door, standing to one side in case of shots. There was no answer. From upstairs, he could hear the phonograph playing. "The Sheik of Araby" again, as though it had never stopped. He tried the door, but it was locked. He stood there in the darkness, with a knot in the pit of his stomach and "The Sheik of Araby" and a terrible feeling that time was running out.

He smashed the door open with his shoulder, the wood splintering, and dived headfirst into the room. It was too dark to see; he pointed the gun all around. The only sound was a monotonous drip-drip-drip from the sink. After a moment, he stood up and turned on the light. The room was empty. Except for a spilled bottle of wine on its side on the table, there was no sign of Father Damiano. Something's wrong, Stewart thought. Something's very wrong.

Stewart went back outside and told the driver to take him to the church. It was the only place left. He paid the driver and walked up the steps to the church. The doors were closed. He tried them, one by one. The middle was open and he went inside.

Except for candles and a dim light by the altar, the church was dark and deserted. The silence had a shape to it, in a way unique to churches and empty theaters. Stewart walked down the long aisle, his gun out. The air was still; the flames of the candles trembled at his approach, as though in the presence of ghosts. He went past the altar and through the door to the sacristy and the priest's darkened office. There was no one.

Stewart leaned wearily against the wall. He has to be here, he thought. An alcoholic priest whose world was his room and the church and his own private hell, where else could he go? Just the local wineshop. Closed at this hour. Nowhere else.

He had just started back towards the altar when he heard a faint sound. It came from behind a closed door down the hall from the sacristy. He opened the door. It led to a wooden staircase descending to the darkness of the basement.

He stood at the top of the stairs, listening in the dark. Slowly, one step at a time, he went down the stairs. One of them creaked under his feet and he froze, his heart beating wildly. Nothing. He continued down. At the bottom was a pool of light from an overhead lamp and in the middle of it, a slumped figure tied to a chair.

Father Damiano was dead. Even in the shadowy light, Stewart could see by the burns and bruises on his naked torso that he had been tortured. Stewart lifted the sagging head. The priest's eyes were still open, wide with horror. As he did so, there was the sound of a hammer cocking. He started to move, but it was too late. He felt the muzzle of a pistol pressed hard against the side of his head.

"*Nicht bewegen*, Herr Stewart. Do not even to make the eyes blink," von Hulse said, coming into the light, a Luger in his hand. "The man with the gun at your head is *Leutnant zur See Heiss*, late of the *Graf Spee*. He knows that you are in some manner responsible for what happened to his ship. I believe it would give him great pleasure to kill you. I suggest you not give him the excuse. Now, if you would be so good, *bitte*, as to turn your *Pistole* around in your hand. Slowly!" von Hulse's voice cracked like a whip. "And to hand me the *Pistole*, with two fingers only, by the muzzle."

Stewart complied. There were three of them, coming out of the shadows; von Hulse, Casaverde, still in his white suit, and a blond young German, who looked like Mussolini, all nose, jaw and arrogance, hulking in civilian clothes. They each had guns, aimed at him.

"Now, up with the hands, *Du Schweinhund*. Higher!" Heiss ordered.

Stewart raised his hands high over his head.

"This, I believe, is what you were looking for, yes?" von Hulse said, holding up a leather-bound notebook. He was smiling, clearly enjoying himself.

"This is *dumm!*" Heiss snarled. "Let me shoot him and get it over with."

"One moment, *bitte*," von Hulse said. "I want to enjoy the moment. You see, Herr Stewart, this," riffling the notebook's pages, "is all we need to completely control the Vargas man and woman. And with their money and influence to finance our operations, all of Argentina. We had to persuade the priest to tell us where he hid it. A stubborn man," von Hulse conceded. "But in the end, he gives us what we wanted. The *Herr Leutnant* is most persuasive."

"Everyone talks. Everyone," Heiss sneered.

"You have been a big inconvenience for us, *gringo*. Fortunately, the time has come to put an end to your meddling," Casaverde said.

"Indeed. We all of us have reasons to want you dead. Now,

if you will please step aside, there," von Hulse pointed with the Colt. "I want to align the bodies. I will use this," indicating the Colt. "You will be blamed for the priest's death. Then, in a fit of remorse, you committed suicide."

"No one will believe it. Colonel Fuentes will know. President Ortiz, also," Stewart said, glancing around desperately. It was pointless. They had him. There was nothing he could do.

"It makes no difference," von Hulse shrugged. "Ortiz is a sick old man. With Herr Minister of Justice Casaverde here in charge of the investigation, I think both America and England will be greatly embarrassed by the outcome. *Amerikanischer* spy kills priest. For shame," he tsked-tsked.

"Herr Oberst, I want to be the one to shoot him," Heiss said, the tip of his tongue peeking out between his teeth.

"Why not?" von Hulse shrugged. He handed the Colt to Heiss, being careful to still cover Stewart with the Luger. "Now step over, *bitte.*"

Stewart took a step, his hands high. His legs felt like they were weighted with lead. Heiss came closer, raising the pistol. Stewart tried to talk. His mouth was very dry.

"The journal," he said. "What was in it?"

Von Hulse shrugged indifferently.

"Why tell a dead man anything?" he said and nodded to Heiss, who aimed the Colt between Stewart's eyes. Heiss smiled.

The sound of the shot was unbelievably loud in the confines of the basement room. For a moment, Heiss stood there, still smiling, as a bright red flower sprouted in the middle of his chest. Stewart saw his eyes go dead as his legs caved under him. Von Hulse was already whirling toward Casaverde, but he was too late, as a second bullet ripped through his head, spraying blood and bits of skull across the room.

Stewart stared stupefied at Casaverde, whose gun was still smoking in his hand.

"Well, don't just stand there, *gringo*. Get your *pistola*. And here, don't forget this," Casaverde muttered, bending down and grabbing the journal out of von Hulse's hand.

"You!" Stewart breathed. "It was you all the time! You're the Raven!" Suddenly, the image of all of them as they were that night in the Alvear Palace, when Arturo saved the Jew, flashed into his mind. They had all been around him and Julia on the dance floor. Vargas, Herrera-Blanca, Casaverde. He had assumed it was Julia because she had said so. Because he wanted it to be so. And because he didn't like Casaverde.

Her hand! he remembered suddenly. In his pocket. She hadn't been putting something in. She'd been trying to take it out! She'd seen something, but not who. Casaverde had fooled them all, even. . . .

Julia.

And the Nazis.

And why every time he came near her, Fuentes or the Germans were able to pick him up. He looked at Casaverde.

"She warned you all? About the priest? And that I would be coming?"

"Of course," Casaverde said. He handed the journal to Stewart. "Here. I've marked the relevant page. Only don't take too long. We have to be out of here. Someone may have heard the shots."

Stewart carried the journal over to the light. He stood next to the dead priest, reading the page; the ink faded, but the neat feminine handwriting still clearly legible, even after thirty years.

I have missed my time for the second month. Now I know. I am with child. The night in the Mirador.

On the floor. In cold and rain and death conceived. What kind of child will this be? What can it be?

I wanted to destroy it. Or if not it, myself. Better for it never to be born.

I went back to the Mirador. *The day was cold and gray and I tried to think how to do it. To seal up the womb like a crypt. To heal the female wound. And then he came.*

He stood by the window gazing out over the Pampa. The land his for as far as could be seen and for fifty leagues beyond that. Patches of gray mist hovered over the land, making everything watery and insubstantial. Nothing seemed real, not even sky or earth itself, as if the waters of the firmament had never been divided, and anything is plausible.

And then he told me. About England and being sentenced to life imprisonment. And how it feels to have your heart stop, just stop, when you learn your child is dead. He named me, Lucia, for the lost wife, Lucinda. But the child, my child, he will name Julio, after the child that died. Judith. And if a girl, Julia. And for his pledge, he gave me the only thing he said he valued in this life: two English pennies.

They came from her eyes.

Her soul still wandered; she had not the pennies to pay the Ferryman. But he would make them pay, he vowed, the pennies clenched in his fist. They would pay and pay.

Only time was running out. He was getting old. That's why he did it. To make another self! *To utterly destroy them. And then he threw me down and entered me again, enemies using love as hate to destroy each other. The penis is the only seal for the female wound.*

I cannot let this child be born. Not to him!

Father. Lover. And the terrible truth: I wanted him!

Stewart stared at Casaverde, dazed.

"Gideon was Julia's father? He did it deliberately? But why? Why?"

"It's as she wrote, 'To make another self.' Think a minute. By impregnating his own daughter, three-fourths of the chromosomes would be his. Don't you see, *gringo?*" Casaverde said, waving his hand impatiently. "It was as close as he could get. But he didn't stop there. Indeed, Gideon stop?" he snorted sardonically. "He had to take the child away from Lucia, keep her isolated."

"But why?"

"So he could be everything to her. Grandfather, father, mother, teacher, everything. You cannot imagine what it must have been like for Julia as a child, living alone except for him. Never seeing other children. Never seeing any other human being, except servants, who were forbidden to touch her, get close to her, except as absolutely necessary. Like ghosts. For the first seventeen years of her life, she lived in a world of ghosts. She had everything and nothing. Like a princess in a fairy tale on that vast *estancia* with that brooding old man, who systematically molded her, day after day after day. Like God, he created her in his own ferocious image. Oh, he was a rare one, that Gideon. *Un hombre muy raro.*"

Stewart nodded slowly. *You can't imagine what it was like,* Julia had told him that night in the Dusenberg.

"But why? What was he after?"

Casaverde laughed harshly.

"He had a reason, *gringo.* A single purpose that burned in

his soul like a forge from hell: To destroy the nation that had given him birth; the corrupt system that had taken his child. Gideon wanted that distant island drenched in blood. He was the ultimate anarchist. Not till its monarchy and aristocracy were rooted out, not till every last Englishman was dead and buried, would he ever know an instant's peace."

Stewart stared at the Argentine, dumbfounded.

"But that's crazy! It's impossible! You can't just destroy a whole people, a whole race!"

Casaverde looked at him curiously.

"Of course you can," he snapped irritably. "What do you suppose Hitler is all about? Now, come on. We've got to get out of here."

"What about him?" Stewart asked, indicating the priest.

"Leave him alone! He's past help. Let's go." Casaverde started up the stairs. Stewart followed. They paused in the hallway.

"Why?" Stewart asked, putting his hand on Casaverde's shoulder. "Why are you helping the English?"

Casaverde frowned.

"I'm a businessman. I have many interests. Also a large *estancia*. Not Ravenwood, but large enough. When Hitler came to power, I made it my business to read that turgid mass of self-justification, *Mein Kampf*. It doesn't take a genius to figure out that Hitler means to use eastern Europe for his granary. The most Argentina could hope for from Germany would be status as a colony." He made a disgusted face. "We're better off selling our beef to the British, though if you *yanquis* ever repealed your stupid Hawley-Smoot tariffs, we'd be your best ally and none of this Nazi business could have ever happened in the first place. *Venga*, come," he said, plucking at Stewart's sleeve, heading towards the altar. They started down the aisle, looking from side to side. When they reached the end of the nave, near the entrance, Casaverde stopped, his face illuminated by the candles set before the statue of the Virgin.

"I can give you twenty-four hours head start, *gringo*. Not more," he said. "After that you must be out of Argentina. Everyone will be after you. The Germans, Castillo, Colonel Fuentes, even me. But I'll see you get twenty-four hours. The Germans will howl, but in the end, will no doubt blame it on Argentine inefficiency." He smiled coldly. "Have your superiors send someone else. Arrange a 'dead drop.' Oh," he stopped. "A final gift. Two, actually. He doesn't know it yet, but General Marquez will have to go as Minister of War. The *Concordancia* will no longer support him. Castillo and Vargas win that one."

"And the second?"

"Norway."

"What?"

"From von Hulse," Casaverde grinned. "Norway. That is where Hitler means to strike next. Though why, I can't imagine."

"Swedish iron," Stewart mumbled mechanically. He was thinking of something else. "That's where the Germans get their ore for steel. Also, if the English could get a base in Norway, they'd control both sides of the North Sea. They could bottle up the German navy in the Baltic."

"Yes, well, I'll leave it to you military types to sort it out," Casaverde said impatiently. "Tell me, how did you leave Julia?"

Stewart told him.

Casaverde stood stock-still. He stared past Stewart at the Virgin, her hands held out in compassion, and when he finally spoke, his voice was strained with shock.

"My God, you are *estupido*, even for an American," he said bitterly. "What passes here? What have you done?"

Stewart blanched under his contempt.

"But what's wrong?" he asked. "I stopped her. We got the *Graf Spee* and saved Ortiz. For the moment, England is saved. Argentina also. What's the problem?"

Casaverde shook his head slowly.

"You understand nothing. Nothing!" he said, his voice rich with contempt. "All this time you have been hearing about Gideon and you still don't understand."

"Understand what?" Stewart shouted angrily, grabbing Casaverde by his lapels, his voice echoing in the nave.

"He was *implacable!*" Casaverde shouted, glaring back at him. "He forged her in the cauldron of his hate like a weapon. Only you stopped her from it, *from the purpose for which she was created!* She doesn't know anything else!"

"What will she do?" Stewart demanded hoarsely.

"God knows," Casaverde whispered, his shoulders slumping. "Something terrible."

"Have you a car? I'll need a car!" Stewart shouted, shaking him.

"I have a Nash outside. Here," Casaverde said, handing Stewart the keys. "Hurry! I'll get a taxi."

Stewart tore open the door and ran from the church. Behind him, he heard Casaverde call, "Go with God." But as he raced down the street, heart pounding, something inside him told him that it was already too late.

STEWART DROVE through the night like a madman. Once past the Avenida General Paz and the *villas miserias* on the outskirts of the city, he kept the accelerator flat on the floorboard. It was late and he drove for long stretches without seeing any other cars or trucks. When one did come from the other direction, he would see the headlights from a long way off, like two distant stars. He would steer for it, not having to think, until the headlights were close enough to be blinding and he would look toward the side of the road to keep his night vision, as the cars roared past each other in the night.

All around was the Pampa, flat and invisible in the darkness. The backyard of Buenos Aires. Argentina had got it all backwards, he thought. The whole country was an appendage to its port, not the other way around. It was the richest soil in the world. Twelve feet and more of topsoil and not a stone or hill or tree root in it anywhere for a thousand miles. You could grow anything in it and never once need to fertilize. And it was lethal.

He tried to think about Julia and Gideon. An exquisite little girl and that insane old man, *her father*, alone in that huge mansion on the vast empty plain. Thinking about them like that made them unreal to him. The princess and the ogre, characters in a fairy tale. *You can't imagine what it was like*, she had said.

And he had loved her. Still loved her. A Nazi. A murderer.
How do you love someone like that? How do you love anybody? Isn't love always a blind leap? Only with Gideon, hate
was a kind of love.

A hate that knew how to wait. And so they came to the war.
Then it all came out, all that festering hate, like crawling
things that come out of the dirt after a rain. This was their
hour. Her hour.

Jesus, Donegan, he thought. You should've picked somebody else for this. Somebody who wouldn't have cared, so
long as we beat the goddamn Nazis. Somebody who wouldn't
have loved her.

The moon had risen and in the distance he saw Ravenwood
looming on the horizon, a massive rectangular shadow outlined by the silvery light.

He turned into the private road down a miles-long avenue
of trees. The tires threw up gravel that rattled loudly on the
fenders. At the end of the avenue, the giant *ombu* tree and the
stark presence of the *hacienda* brooding over the Pampa, like
a fortress on the plain. He screeched to a stop in a shower of
pebbles and ran up to the front door. He rang the bell and
without waiting for an answer, opened the door and rushed
into the entry hall, almost knocking down a terrified *muchacha*, who stared nervously at him, her eyes repeatedly straying to his chest until he suddenly realized that his jacket was
open and she was looking at the Colt in his shoulder holster.

"The Señor Vargas. Where is he?"

"The Señor is in the *biblioteca*, in the east wing," she answered, not taking her eyes off the gun.

"And the Señora?"

The *muchacha* didn't answer.

"Where is she?" Stewart demanded, grabbing her.

"The Señora Julia is upstairs, with the children," she
gasped, gesturing toward the broad curving staircase, which
he was already running toward. He bounded up the stairs as
fast as he could, taking two or three of them at a time. He
raced along the gallery in the direction the *muchacha* had
indicated, then stopped suddenly, unable to go another step.

Julia was standing in the doorway. She was still in slacks
and the white silk blouse, only they were splashed all over
with blood. Her face was bone white, like a skull. Her hands
hung lifeless at her sides, and in one of them she held a large
butcher's knife, dripping blood.

Stewart shook his head, unable to breathe.

"No," he whispered. "Please, no."

"I had to," she said, her voice quavering. She swayed on her feet, barely able to stand upright. "I didn't want to," she said. "I didn't! Only there was nothing else I could do. Nothing!" She whispered, a tiny tear, like a seed pearl, sliding out of the corner of her eye. "But it was hard, *yanqui*. It was the hardest thing I've ever had to do. Here," she said, holding out her hand. In it were two old copper coins. "I don't need these any more." She held her hand out for a moment and when he didn't take them, she let them drop on the carpet, where they rolled an inch or two and stopped.

"The children," he choked. "Julia."

"Why didn't you go away with me, *yanqui*? I would have gone. We could have got drunk and pretended. Isn't that what most people do? They said it hurt. The big one went fast. He just kept telling me it hurt. But the little one, Abelardo, cried, 'Don't, Mama! I'll be good! I'll be good, *Mamacita!*' " she said, shaking badly, the knife in her hand dripping blood onto the carpet.

"But why? Why?"

Her face contorted oddly.

"They were Montoyas," she said, and walked past him down the gallery to tell her husband what she had done.

Postscripts

My dear Stewart,

I am sending this to you by way of *our mutual friend* in the hope it somehow reaches you. It is difficult to imagine the Germans in Paris. *Bratwurst* in the bistros, ugh! They have Norway also. That one I warned you about, remember? The *Ingleses* still seem to be hanging on, despite the Blitz. But then, as Jaime Herrera-Blanca said at a party just recently, only the *Ingleses* could consider a *birria* like Dunkirk a victory. Do you think the RAF can hold off the *Luftwaffe?* They'd better. They owe us money.

As you have perhaps already heard, last month the diabetes finally forced Ortiz to make Castillo acting President, *hacer de Presidente*. The *Concordancia* is falling to pieces. Marquez is out, of course. Also Pineda. And Alem and the *Radicalistas*. And every day the oil shortage becomes more desperate. As if imbecility had not already reached its highest form of expression, Castillo is now talking about invading Brazil! Can you picture him? A pot-bellied actor with a papier-mâché sword who begins to imagine he really is Caesar? Without our friend Vargas to support him, Castillo is lost. No doubt it will all end with some moronic Army general taking over.

Arturo Vargas is dead. A hunting accident. But he wanted to die, I think. After what happened to his sons, he was never the same. He drank heavily, his features became bloated; you would not have recognized him. Of all of us, he was, in his own way, Gideon's truest disciple. He and Julia were locked in a dance of hate. There's more, of course; there always is, but—*de mortuis nil nisi bonum*.

Our little Eva, on the other hand, is flourishing. She has a lead on one of those radio soap operas, *Chispazos de Tradición* (crescendo of music that tears at the heart). Though, as an actress, the Señorita Bette Davis need not retire just yet. Of course, what she really wants is a *caballero blanco*, what you

North Americans so interestingly call a "Sugar Daddy." Love among us *porteños* always takes on the aspects of a business proposition. Our great talent, of course, is to pretend it is anything but. She's bleached her hair blonde, as Julia once suggested she should. It suits her. Do you remember how she used to study Julia, aping her every gesture? But perhaps you never noticed Eva. She's quite common, really. But, of course, that was her charm. Nothing at all like Julia.

Which brings me to the real purpose of this letter. I am enclosing a photograph of Julia from the newspaper. It was taken at her hearing. I thought you might want to have it. I was able to prevent her from going to trial, on grounds of insanity. Subsequently, we were able to have her transferred from the government facility to the Misericordia, the *casa de orates*. A return of sorts. It was there that she was born. One final irony: for security reasons, and to prevent suicide (especially given the family history), she is being kept in the same room in which her mother was confined for all those years.

The end of the Gideons, *pues*. Like the first Gideon, the one in the Bible, his children all came to a bad end. With Arturo Vargas dead and only Julia, legally incompetent, left, I myself have claimed the entire Gideon estate. As you might recall, Gideon's late wife, Alejandra (Julia's grandmother), was my older sister. As a boy, I adored her. When she died, I hated Gideon. Another reason, *pues*, for the Raven to have opposed Julia. You see, *yanqui*, John Gideon was not the only Argentine who understood something about revenge.

Ravenwood is now mine. No doubt, the sound of Gideon's corpse spinning in his tomb is driving all the other ghosts out of the Recoleta. But perhaps not. No one understood better than Gideon that life is a war in which nothing is given, only taken. Nothing, perhaps, except what really matters.

There is an autumnal quality in the air these days, particularly among those of us in countries which have not yet entered the war. The world we knew is dying. We are witnessing its death-throes. Fortunately, some things never change. Athena de Castro has a new lover. A waiter at Richmond's, *pues*. He's in his twenties. Athena seems to feel that being with an older man is a sign of newfound maturity on her part.

I hope you survive your war, *yanqui*. Perhaps one day you will return to Buenos Aires. I have always thought it to be the most passionate city in the world. But then, the heart is such a liar.

My most distinguished sentiments,
Enrique Casaverde

November 11, 1942
Stalingrad

The gully road was icy and deserted and over towards the Barrikady and the tractor works, the slag heaps were hidden under a heavy layer of snow. There were no buildings left standing in this part of the city, only brick walls with vacant window openings and nothing behind them, like a movie set. Poking through the snow were scorched girders, gun barrels at odd angles and everywhere, frozen bodies. Now and again they would come upon a hand thrusting out of the snow, and once Stewart slipped and fell and found himself looking into a woman's face, staring up at him from under the ice.

They made their way from one rubble heap to the next. The firing had slackened for the moment, but there were German snipers all around. They stopped to rest near the top of Krutoy Gully. A machine gun opened up and then the sound of German .75s and heavy firing. From where they were, they could see tracers crisscrossing each other in intricate patterns over by Mamaev Hill. Senior Lieutenant Medvedev turned to Stewart, a split-toothed grin cracking his face. His breath was white in the bitter cold.

"So *Amerikanets*, what you think?"

"*Nye khorasho*. Doesn't look so good," Stewart said.

Medvedev's grin widened.

"This? This is nothing! You should be here before one month. They take ferry landing, part of shore. Forty thousand dead in one day only!"

"You were here?"

Medvedev's expression changed. He pointed at a small cairn made of rubble and twisted metal near the river.

"You see there? There was a pontoon bridge across the river. Workers were running, whole families, trying to reach the bridge. There was one family running and I see the machine gun kill them one after another, first the father, then the son, then the mother. Like that. One-two-three. Only the little girl is left. She sits down beside her mother and begins to touch her, smoothing the mother's clothes, trying to make her better. She is so pretty child and we were only maybe meters away. 'Run!' We are all shouting to her, even standing up and waving for her to come, though it was suicide to do this. You could see the bullets coming back towards her. She look right at me and I can see she is not knowing what to do. She is just a kid, understand? They can see she is only baby. 'Come! Run!' I scream, the bullets coming closer, kicking up pieces of pavement around her. She is pulling at her mother's arm and then the bullet knocks her over and is finished. We go a little crazy then. That place, where she die, is as far as Nazis get in Soviet Union, so we make marker." Medvedev jerked his head toward the cairn. He got up. "Come. We go."

Stewart nodded, looking back over his shoulder at the Volga. Ice floes cluttered the thinly frozen surface like rubble. It was going to be murder trying to cross back to the other side. Ahead, Medvedev was already moving in a crouch, his eyes scanning anxiously from side to side. Stewart and the others followed, single file.

Suddenly, a geyser of snow and rubble erupted behind them. Stewart dived face-first into the snow. Men were screaming behind him. Shells exploded along the side of the gully; one after another, methodically marching along toward them. All Stewart could do was watch it coming and press his body as deep into the snow as he could. There was no way he wasn't going to die, he thought. Oh God! Oh God! Here it comes!

He felt the ground lift up under him. For an instant he was flying and there was a roar all around him. He looked up and saw Medvedev get up and sprint toward a timbered opening in the side of the gully. Stewart scrambled after him. As he ducked inside the opening, he looked back. No one was following him. Of the eight of them who had come together from the ferry landing, only he and Medvedev had made it to the bunker.

A narrow tunnel led down from the opening. It was very low and Stewart had to crawl part of the way on all fours. When he finally got inside, he could see Medvedev standing there, an angry expression on his face. There were at least forty soldiers inside the bunker. In the middle, a man in an overcoat and a fur hat sat behind a table, and near the wall two soldiers were covered by a third with a rifle. The man in the fur hat wasn't an army officer. He had high Tartar cheekbones and behind wire-rimmed spectacles, flat fanatic's eyes. A *politrook*, a political officer, Stewart thought, swallowing. He had come in the middle of something.

"*Shto eto?*" What is it? he asked Medvedev.

"He's waiting for the barrage to lift so he can shoot these two," Medvedev said, glancing at the *politrook*.

"Why? What for?"

"He says they're *Hiwis*," Medvedev frowned, not looking at the two young soldiers. *Hiwis* were Russian defectors to the Germans.

"It's not true!" one of the soldiers burst out. "We ran out of ammunition and were captured. Then a shell exploded and we escaped into the *balka*. We couldn't have been in their hands even an hour!"

"Enough!" the *politrook* shouted, banging on the table with the butt of his pistol. "You are German spies and will be shot!" He looked curiously at Stewart. "Who is this?" he asked Medvedev.

"An *Amerikanets*," Medvedev said. "He's here to see General Chuikov."

"By whose orders?" the *politrook* demanded, curtly motioning Stewart over and holding out his hands for papers. The whole bunker rattled as, outside, shells exploded one after another, like a string of Chinese firecrackers. Stewart took his papers out of his pocket and handed them over.

"These are from the STAVKA," Stewart explained. "And they've been countersigned by Commissar Khrushchev."

"They could be forgeries," the *politrook* shrugged, tossing them aside. "Do you know Comrade Khrushchev?"

"We've met."

"Describe him."

"He looks like a kulak," Stewart snapped. "The kind of peasant who tells dirty jokes and after you shake hands with him you want to count your fingers."

A number of the soldiers in the bunker guffawed. Medvedev was grinning openly, though his eyes were still angry. After a moment, the *politrook* smiled sourly and handed Stewart back his papers.

"In any case, Vassili Ivanovich isn't here. He's established a new HQ on Sovietskaya Street. You can go when the barrage lifts. Tell me," the *politrook* said, lighting a *paprossy* cigarette. "What is an *Amerikanets* doing here?"

"Intelligence matters. For the general's ears," Stewart said. Over by the wall, the two prisoners were looking around wide-eyed at their comrades, as though they couldn't believe what was happening to them. One minute they had been sur-

rounded by their comrades, congratulating them on their escape, and the next they were about to be shot, and when they
looked at them, the other soldiers avoided their eyes. "Also,
my superiors want to know firsthand if Stalingrad is going to
stand."

"Stalingrad will stand," the *politrook* snapped. "When are
you going to open a Second Front?"

"I wouldn't know," Stewart shrugged. "In our army, the
generals don't ask our opinions. They just tell us."

"Here also," one of the Russians called out. "Only no one
listens."

Just then, a curtain opened and a soldier stepped out, buttoning up his trousers. Behind him, Stewart could see a
woman, naked below the waist, on a cot. Her lipstick was
smeared, so that she looked as if she had a rash on the bottom
part of her face. She reached over, wound up a phonograph
and put on the needle. Stewart paled, dumbfounded at the
unexpected sound of Carlos Gardel's voice amidst the bombardment.

> *"And I became what I am through tangos*
> *Because the tango is tough and strong,*
> *And smells of life*
> *And tastes of death."*

The *politrook* looked curiously at Stewart.

"You know this music, *Amerikanets!*"

"From long ago," Stewart said, shaken, remembering something Ceci Braga had said once. Something about the past
lying hidden all around us in bits and pieces, like snares in the
forest. And then, you step on one and it's got you. He turned
away from the *politrook*. Senior Lieutenant Medvedev was
talking to the two prisoners. They were very young, dark-
haired, and for some reason they reminded Stewart of Julia's
two boys. He stuck his hand in his pocket and felt for the two
coins. He had picked them up from the carpet where Julia had
dropped them that night at Ravenwood and had carried them
with him ever since. Medvedev said something to the two
prisoners and came over.

"I know these two," he told the *politrook*. "These are not
spies."

The *politrook*'s expression hardened.

"Nye nado! That is nothing! They surrendered to the enemy. That is enough!"

"They ran out of ammunition," Medvedev said disgustedly. "If just once we had decent supplies. . . ."

"Are you criticizing our effort, Comrade Senior Lieutenant? Maybe you are a defeatist yourself."

"I say only. . . ."

"No one must be allowed to believe surrender is an option," the *politrook* hissed. "If one soldier surrenders, others may be tempted. In the Red Army, no one surrenders and lives. No one!"

"I won't let you do this, Alexei Grigorievich," Medvedev said, clenching his fists. "These are my men."

The *politrook* looked over at the soldier guarding the prisoners.

"As soon as the barrage lifts, take them out and shoot them," he ordered.

"No!" Medvedev said, clenching and unclenching his fists. "These are mine! I command these men!"

The *politrook* sucked in his cheeks.

"You dare contradict an order of the Party, Anatoly Victorevich? Maybe you want to join them."

"Don't be a fool!" Medvedev said suddenly. "Not in front of the foreigner."

The two men looked at Stewart as if they had just remembered he was there. He felt them watching him, and suddenly, it all came together for him, like a puff of cold wind that clears away the fog. The tango, the bombardment, the two soldiers reminding him of Julia's boys, and Russia, where it had somehow begun for Gideon a million years ago.

"Comrades," a soldier near the tunnel called out. "The barrage is lifting." The soldier looked at the *politrook* for orders.

"The order stands," the *politrook* said coldly. "Take them out and shoot them."

"Wait!" Stewart cried, stepping forward. He clenched the two coins he had got from Julia tightly in his fist. "Some might consider shooting them an act of desperation," Stewart said carefully. "The sign of an army about to collapse."

The *politrook* looked furiously at Stewart.

"Sukin sin," the *politrook* growled. "Why are you involving yourself in this, *Amerikanets?* This is nothing of yours."

"A debt," Stewart said, swallowing. He closed his eyes for a second and when he did, he could see Julia as she was in the Dusenberg that night on the way to Lujan. The white silk blouse, the cigarette in the ivory holder, her dark hair stirring in the breeze. He opened his eyes. "I cost two innocent lives once. My fault."

"Why? Why did you do this?" the *politrook* demanded, looking at Stewart strangely.

"To fight the Nazis," Stewart said, the coins tight in his hand.

The *politrook* looked from Stewart to Medvedev, then back again.

"Let them go," he growled, waving his hand disgustedly. He glared at the two soldiers, who could only stare wide-eyed at him, unable to believe their luck. "Just this once, mind. Take the *Amerikanets* to Sixty-Second Army HQ." He shook his finger at them. "You are very lucky, you two. Very lucky." He turned back to Stewart and Medvedev.

"Better they should kill Germans," he frowned.

"Agreed. And *Spasibo*, Comrade Political Officer," Stewart said, heading toward the tunnel.

"Better we should all kill Germans, *Amerikanets*. On two fronts!" the *politrook* called after him, as Stewart followed the two soldiers back outside.

After the bunker, the gray sky seemed bright, almost white, as they made their way out of the gully and along the Volga. It was hard going, because over towards Ninth of January Square there were no streets any more, only snow that had frozen solid and varying levels of rubble. The two young soldiers were grinning and red-faced from the cold. They all stopped behind the cairn Medvedev had pointed out, to catch their breath and share vodka from a canteen. The two soldiers laughed and pounded Stewart on the back, their eyes shining with their reprieve. Stewart was grinning too as he drank. He felt happier than he had in a long time. Raoul was wrong, he thought. There are other ways to leave Argentina than to die.

Suddenly, without warning, a mortar round exploded behind them.

At first Stewart didn't know where he was. Everything was white and he could hear nothing. Then he realized that he was staring up at the cairn from the ground. It had saved his life.

One of the Russian soldiers didn't get up. Stewart saw at once that he was dead. The other Russian touched his friend's shoulder, then stood, shaking his head as if to clear it from ringing. He was saying something; Stewart could see his lips moving, but he couldn't hear anything. Somehow, it wasn't important. All that seemed to matter was the cairn. The way the snow lay on just the tops and one side of the stones, the glint of metal, the pattern made by the dead Russian's blood. And then he understood what it was. The cairn was an altar.

Deliberately, with great care, Stewart pushed himself up onto his knees. He opened his hand and placed the two coins beside the stones.

". . . go, *Amerikanets!* You don't want to keep a general waiting," the Russian soldier was saying, the sound rushing in like an express train.

Stewart staggered to his feet. The Russian clapped him on the shoulder, then turned and started down the street, loping like a wolf toward the next mound of rubble. After a moment, Stewart followed. Behind him, by the cairn, he left the two pennies, each bearing the profile of the young Queen Victoria, lying face-up in the snow.

Historical
Footnotes
and
Workpoints

- After the sinking of the *Graf Spee*, the surviving crew members were interned in Argentina, where they were treated generally as heroes. Captain Langsdorff committed suicide two days later in a Buenos Aires hotel room. At the time, much was made of the fact that he refused to give the Nazi salute at the funeral of crewmembers killed in the battle and that just before shooting himself, he had wrapped himself in the Imperial Navy Ensign under which he had fought in Jutland, and not in the Nazi flag.

- Mention of "Reds" in Montevideo refers not to Communists, but to the classic Uruguayan distinction between the White (*Blanco*) and Red (*Colorado*), political parties dating from Uruguay's nineteenth-century civil wars.

- In mid-1940, Roberto Ortiz was forced by ill health to make Ramon Castillo Acting President of Argentina. Although Castillo favored the Axis, with Ortiz still opposed to Germany, opinion in both the Argentine military and the ruling *Concordancia* split, pressure from the United States increasing and the outcome of the war still in doubt, Castillo had little choice but to remain neutral. Ortiz died in July 1942. Less than a year later, Castillo was overthrown by a military *junta*. In February 1946, a member of the *junta*, Colonel Juan Peron, was elected President of Argentina.

Workpoints and Improbabilities

On the criticality of the naval war in the Atlantic on the outcome of World War Two, Winston Churchill:

"Battles might be won or lost . . .territories might be gained or quitted, but dominating all . . . was our mastery of the ocean routes."

The Soviet Union ran a spy network in Switzerland. One of their agents, Rudolf Rössler, code-named "Lucy," was able to penetrate the German High Command and provide complete German battle plans to the Russians at Stalingrad, a classic example of a spy single-handedly changing the course of history. Stewart's real mission would have been to validate with Generals Yeremenko and Chuikov the accuracy of the "Lucy" intelligence the Russians were receiving. The Russians probably would not have told Stewart about their planned counter-offensive, which began on November 19, 1942, and led to the complete encirclement and eventual destruction of von Paulus' Sixth Army.

During the battle of Stalingrad, two Russian prostitutes set up shop in a bunker to service the troops. Throughout the months of the battle, they never left the bunker and played the same Argentine tangos over and over on the phonograph, an incident well remembered by many Soviet survivors of the battle.

Lucia is the Greek chorus. Everything she says is strange, but true. For example, her husband going to war in a taxi refers to the famous incident in World War I, when French reservists were rushed from Paris to the Battle of the Marne in taxis.

Although the office of Coordinator of Information (the precursor of the wartime Office of Strategic Services, which subsequently became the CIA) wasn't officially formed until mid-1941, its founder, William "Wild Bill" Donovan, had begun to undertake intelligence missions for both the War Department (reporting to General Mac-Arthur) and President Roosevelt as early as 1935. By 1939, Donovan had already established a working relationship with British Intelligence. This book is based on the (not entirely improbable) fictional premise that during this pre-war period, Donovan had already begun to recruit agents, like Stewart, for the coming conflict.

This is a work of fiction, but one based on history. To the best of my knowledge, all of the real persons depicted here, hopefully in a manner consistent with historical reality, are now dead and beyond any discomfort that could be caused by any inaccuracy on my part. Of the Battle of the River Plate, only Commodore Henry Harwood, Captain Bell and Kapitän Langsdorff were real persons. The battle happened pretty much as portrayed here. However, the real reason the British Force G was patrolling the mouth of the River Plate was because of an inspired hunch on Harwood's part and not secret intelligence. Similarly, the reason the *Graf Spee* was in that vicinity was to try and sink the freighter *Highland Princess* (whose scheduled sailing from Buenos Aires had been mentioned in a newspaper taken from the *Graf Spee*'s final victim, the *Streonshalh*, before they sank her). Although consistent with Nazi activities at the time and Castillo's pro-Axis stance, the coup described in this novel is fiction.

To assist the reader in distinguishing fact from fiction, a good rule of thumb is that what seems most improbable (such as the French and British fleets sailing off to invade the Crimea without any idea where they were going to land; Napoleon III consulting a *ouija* board to try and figure it out; the Paraguayan dictator, Lopez, appointing an English whore, Madame Lynch, to execute virtually every male who hadn't already been killed by famine or the Argentines and Brazilians; Argentine tangos during the battle of Stalingrad; the Argentines seriously considering invading Brazil during World War II, etc.) is likely to be true.

As some ornithologists may note, the raven (genus *Corvus*) is not native to Argentina. I choose not to explain how it got there any more than Hemingway explained what that leopard was doing on Kilimanjaro. Indeed, the foreignness of its being there is very much the point and the story itself is the explanation.